GARETH L.
POWELL

WHO WILL
YOU SAVE?

GARETH L.
POWELL

WHO WILL
YOU SAVE?

TITAN BOOKS

Who Will You Save?
Print edition ISBN: 9781803368658
E-book edition ISBN: 9781803368665

Published by Titan Books
A division of Titan Publishing Group Ltd
144 Southwark Street, London SE1 0UP
www.titanbooks.com

First edition: September 2025
10 9 8 7 6 5 4 3 2 1

'An Examination of the Trolley Problem using a Sentient Warship and a Rotating Black Hole' appeared in *Worlds of IF*, 2025.
'A Necklace of Ivy' appeared in *Cambrensis: Short Story Wales*, 1992.
'Ack-Ack Macaque' appeared in *Interzone*, 2006.
'Distant Galaxies Colliding' appeared in *Quantum Muse*, 2004.
'Eleven Minutes' appeared in *Interzone*, 2011.
'Entropic Angel' appeared in *Dark Spires*, edited by Colin Harvey, 2010.
'Falling Apart' appeared in *The Last Reef and Other Stories*, 2004.
'Fallout' appeared in *Conflicts*, edited by Ian Whates, 2010.
'Flotsam' appeared in *The Last Reef and Other Stories*, 2008.
'Gonzo Laptop' appeared in *Hub*, 2010.
'Hot Rain' appeared in *The Last Reef and Other Stories*, 2008.

'Morning Star' appeared as 'Catch a Burning Star' in *Aphelion*, 2004.
'Pod Dreams of Tuckertown' appeared in *Byzarium*, 2006.
'Railroad Angel' appeared in *Interzone*, 2012.
'Red Lights, and Rain' appeared in *Solaris Rising 3*, edited by Ian Whates, 2014.
'Ride the Blue Horse' appeared on Medium.com, 2015.
'Six Lights off Green Scar' appeared in *Aphelion*, 2005.
'Sunsets and Hamburgers' appeared in *Byzarium*, 2006.
'The Bigger the Star' appeared in *2020 Visions*, edited by Rick Novy, 2010.
'The Last Reef' appeared in *Interzone*, 2005.
'The New Ships' appeared in *Further Conflicts*, edited by Ian Whates, 2011.
'The Redoubt' appeared in *Aphelion*, 2007.
'What Would Nicolas Cage Do?' appeared in *Future Bristol*, edited by Colin Harvey, 2009.

EU RP (for authorities only)
eucomply OÜ, Pärnu mnt. 139b-14, 11317 Tallinn, Estonia
hello@eucompliancepartner.com, +3375690241

Printed and bound by CPI Group (UK) Ltd, Croydon CR0 4YY.

For Dianne, Edith, Rose, and Robin

CONTENTS

AUTHOR'S NOTE

The stories in this volume may differ slightly from earlier publications, due to corrections or minor revisions. As such, this collection should be considered to contain the definitive versions of these stories.

SUNSETS AND HAMBURGERS

1.

My first thought is that I don't remember dying. They tell me nobody does. It's like trying to catch the exact moment you fall asleep; when you wake, it's gone. You may remember feeling tired, you may even remember starting to fall asleep; you just don't remember the transition, the actual moment when you passed from one state to the other.

And then they resurrect you.

One minute you're nowhere, nothing. The next you wake up coughing and thrashing in a tank of blue gel.

2.

My stomach's full of gas and my bowels full of water. My brain feels like melted polystyrene. Every thought hurts and every breath is an effort.

The robot doctors try to reassure me. Everything's going to be okay, they say.

And then, just when I'm beginning to wonder if the worst is over, they take me out and show me the sky.

What's left of it.

3.

The doctors tell me that I've been dead for billions of years. They give me pamphlets to read, films to watch.

Billions of years!

I'm struggling to imagine it. Every time I get close, I get breathless and my hands start to shake.

4.

I have a few confused memories: faces, names of places, that sort of thing. I have an image of a sash window on a grey and rainy autumn afternoon, and bass-heavy ska playing somewhere off down the dull street. And after that, there's nothing. I fall to my knees and begin to weep.

The doctors comfort me. They're pleased with my progress.

5.

There's something dreadfully wrong with the sky. They try to explain it but I have trouble understanding.

When I was alive, I worked for a financial software company. I worked in their marketing department, writing letters and making calls. In my spare time, I liked sunsets and hamburgers, movies and bottled beer.

It's something to do with black holes, they say, pointing at the blank sky.

Like everyone else, I skimmed through *A Brief History of Time* once or twice, but I've got to admit, I'm struggling with this one.

6.

Today, the robot doctors introduce me to Marla. She has feathers in her hair, and her clothes are made of vinyl.

They show us to our new home. It's small but comfortable; reassuring, in a simple, everyday kind of way. There's a kettle and a toaster, a stereo and a CD collection. There's even a TV.

"You can stay here as long as you need to," they say.

The porch looks out over a sandy beach. Wild palms sway in the offshore breeze.

7.

We've been here a couple of weeks now. The pamphlets are starting to make sense.

The sky's dark because the galaxies have flown too far apart and the stars have exhausted themselves. In order to survive, the remaining people huddle close to the embers of the leftover black holes.

8.

We're sitting on the porch watching breakers crash and slither. It's late in the evening and there's music drifting out from the kitchen.

Marla's upset.

The doctors have given us a new pamphlet.

Throughout history, it says, love has served a serious evolutionary purpose. It compels us to look after those around us, and to allow them to look after us. This is the root of community, and the groups that survived and prospered were those with the most love.

It goes on to explain how they matched our personalities, made sure our genetic traits complemented each other. Apparently Marla and I are over ninety-eight per cent compatible.

They want us to have kids.

9.

When I was a student, I used to like to spend the afternoon in a city-centre bar reading the newspaper, doing the crossword and watching the world go by. It was like meditation, the mind roaming free: the rattle of coins in the fruit machine, the hum of the pumps and refrigerators, the low murmurs of the bar staff.

And when I finally left the bar, just around the time most people were finishing work for the day, I'd stumble out with my senses heightened. Suddenly, everything seemed significant. I'd want to write poetry or paint something, just to capture this perfect feeling. But I never could. My efforts never stood up to the critical light of the following day.

Sometimes now at night, when I wake up beside Marla, I have a similar feeling: everything feels sharp and unreal and meaningful, as if I'm waking up in a movie and everything's somehow symbolic.

If I keep my eyes shut it passes, after a while.

10.

Babies cry out in the night. We nudge each other awake. There's a noise outside. Marla sees to the children while I go out to investigate.

Those damn trilobites have been going through the bins

again. They skitter around the beach in the dark, some of them as big as my foot.

Overhead, there's a fine selection of moons.

11.

We've been here for a year now. Every morning, there's a cardboard box of food waiting for us on the kitchen counter. Some days it's mostly fruit, other days it's fresh bread and cold meat. Today, it's a jar of instant coffee and a pack of Silk Cut.

When I unscrew the lid on the jar and tear the cellophane from the pack, the sticky familiar smells hit me like an adrenalin rush.

The coffee smells like heaven. Before I've time to think, I've made myself a steaming cup. And damn, it does taste good. It's like visiting a town where you used to live or finding a fiver in the pocket of a pair of jeans you haven't worn for a while. The cup feels natural in my hand, comforting.

I drink about a quarter of it before I have a strange feeling in my stomach.

I leave the cigarettes where they are, but I can feel them watching me.

12.

Every now and then I have a doubt, like a shadow moving in the corner of my eye.

Have we been seduced by the sand and palms into believing we're living a perfect life, here on the beach, with the kids?

They're growing up strong and clever. They have their mother's looks and their father's restlessness.

I can't help feeling that we were pushed into having them,

like we were selected to breed the same way you'd select a couple of pedigree cats.

Is that why they brought us back? To have kids?

Has something so catastrophic happened to humanity that it needs to resurrect untainted individuals from the past to repopulate the Earth? Are our descendants all shooting blanks?

13.

One day it hits me.

When they brought us back, they must've made alterations to our minds. I don't know how or why, but I think they tailored us when they resurrected us.

I look at Marla and know the urge to make babies with her is stronger than anything I felt in my former life. Back then, I used to panic if you put me in the same room as a baby. Now, I can't seem to get enough of them.

How can I talk about any of this with Marla? She's already three months gone with our fifth.

"You'll stop loving me if I get any fatter," she says.

14.

The doctors have disappeared. They don't answer our calls. The hospital is deserted, empty. It's almost as if they've fulfilled their task and taken their leave.

Marla doesn't like it. It gives her the creeps to be suddenly alone.

15.

They left us a final pamphlet, pinned to the door. It doesn't make for happy reading.

It tells us how vicious wars erupted as the final stars began to gutter. It tells us that huge reserves of life and power were burned as various factions competed for survival. Stealth ships slipped like sharks through the woven fabric of the universe. Titanic energies were squandered in futile attacks.

And now here we are, in our cabin by the sea. A little bubble world, a few miles in diameter. Fragile and lost in the encroaching darkness.

16.

We're close to the end of everything. Beyond our snow shaker bubble of greenery and life, the universe is a sterile wasteland. There may be other survivors in other galaxies, but they're irretrievably lost to us now, pulled away into the expanding darkness so that not even their light can reach us.

Eventually, the black hole that provides the energy for our heat and light will evaporate. We'll have a few years left after that, but they won't be quality time.

We'll go down with the dying universe. We'll see the final wisps of the Milky Way torn asunder; we'll feel the ground begin to rip beneath our feet, feel our bodies begin to break apart.

And what happens after that? On the face of it, it looks like time ends.

I have a hunch, a feeling, that the doctors brought us back to do more than simply witness the death of creation.

But if that's all that they wanted us to do, why did they encourage us to have so many kids?

17.

In my former life, I used to read science fiction now and then. One evening, in bed, I try to explain the attraction of it to Marla. Beyond the sand, the sea stirs restlessly.

I want to tell her about the joy of imagining strange new worlds filled with bizarre and dangerous creatures, of watching mighty armadas blow hell out of each other, but she flicks her hair dismissively and I know I'm not getting through.

Through the window, two of the brighter moons linger on the horizon, one gold and the other amber. Their reflections shimmer on the dark water.

I tell her that my grandfather dreamt of going to sea, of finding fortune and glory in mysterious far-off lands. It wasn't my fault that by the time I hit my teens, the few remaining earthly frontiers were already full of holiday show camera crews and Australian gap year students. There were no mysterious lands left, save those that lay in the books I read.

"I guess what I'm trying to say is that all my dreams seem to be coming true," I say. I want her to understand that before I came here, the local library was my only frontier.

She looks at me for a long time, and I honestly can't read her expression. Then she turns over and wraps the sheet around her shoulders.

My legs are left sticking out. I get goose bumps.

18.

Marla says I think too much. She thinks I'll poison the kids by telling them that there's no point to their dreams and ambitions, by telling them that the universe is ending.

But deep down, I know there's hope.

19.

I'm sloshing through the surf, wondering why the doctors have gone to so much trouble to replicate coffee, cigarettes and a tropical paradise, why they resurrected a breeding pair of *homo sapiens*.

And then the three juggernauts appear in the sky.

They must each be half a light year in length. As we watch over the next few hours, the effect of their mass scrambles the remains of our solar system, but not before their shuttles swoop down and snatch up our little bubble biosphere from the ashes.

20.

It's still half dark when I rise at noon and take my coffee out onto the porch. The kids are playing in the gloomy sand. It feels like the high end of summer and the air's stale and used. A vast vault arches overhead. Lights in its roof look like brightly burning stars. Around us, on the cavern's floor, we can see the glow of other collected bubbles; they shine green and blue in the gloom. I wonder who they contain, and if we can reach them.

21.

This will be my last diary entry.

These giant ships seem to be arks, of a sort. I can't tell you where they're going, or what we're going to do once they get there. I can't even tell you why we're here, alive, at the end of time.

All I can do is repeat the same conclusion that every man or woman has reached since the dawn of time: I don't know why we're here, or how long we've got, but we're here.

And we're going to survive.

RIDE THE BLUE HORSE

We were breaking into shipping containers the day we found the blue horse.

My friend Dan had convinced me we should give it a shot. The stacks were dangerous, but since we got the sack from the call centre we were desperate.

"I heard of a guy two towns over," Dan said, rocking back and forth on his heels in the call centre parking lot, "who cracked a container of canned fruit. Peaches, cherries, and mandarins – stuff you just don't see any more. It made him rich."

"How rich?"

"Rich enough to leave town."

We had to walk to the freight yard, and it took us the whole day. Heat shimmered off the empty road. The place had been abandoned since we were kids. With the big ships gone, it just hadn't been economical to keep open. And once the port authority stopped dredging, it only took a couple of years for silt to choke the harbour. All that was left now were these rusting container stacks, and the wiry, little green fireworks of grass that had burst up through the shattered tarmac.

The perimeter fence had been smashed down in several

places. "Are you sure there's going to be anything left?" I said.

Dan gave me one of his looks. He was still wearing his call centre clothes, dark jeans with a white shirt and black tie, and his top button was undone.

"Look at the size of this place. It's about a bazillion square kilometres. There are literally thousands of crates." He stepped through the fence with the sprightly confidence of a door-to-door evangelist. "The ones at the edges may have been looted, but I'll bet you there's still plenty of good shit further in."

"You'd better be right."

"Of course I am." He clapped his hands together and rubbed them briskly.

"Now come on, Spelman, let's hustle."

As it turned out, he was right. But we had to open six crates before we found her.

The first three were full of machine parts, electric kettles, and other junk that was either to heavy to carry or not worth the effort. The fourth was empty, and the fifth strewn with the discarded rags of a shipment of long-forgotten immigrants.

At that point, I was ready to give up for the night. The sun was going down and the sky was ripening towards the colour of a day-old bruise. Dan convinced me to continue.

"Just one more." He slapped the side of the next container in line and the metal made a deep booming sound. "Come on," he said, "I've got a great feeling about this one."

Dan injured himself as we were prying off the lock. The crowbar slipped, and the end of it gashed his palm.

"Goddammit!"

"Are you okay?"

"Just peachy." I watched him suck the wound. Thankfully, it didn't seem deep. We both knew we didn't have enough money to get him a tetanus shot.

With his hand still in his mouth, he kicked the door.

"Get this sucker open, Spelman."

"Yes, sir." I stooped to retrieve the fallen crowbar, and carefully popped the lock.

The door opened on rusty hinges.

"What have we got?"

I frowned into the gloom. "Some jerry cans and kit bags... and something wrapped in a tarpaulin. I think it might be a car."

Dan pushed past me.

"Well, there's no need to sound so disheartened."

He crouched in front of the covered vehicle and pulled at the edge of its shroud. "Voilà!"

The cloth came away and he stood there like a conjuror awaiting the applause of the crowd. I looked at what he had uncovered.

"Pretty car."

"Pretty?" He dropped the edge of the tarpaulin and walked around to the driver's door. His fingertips brushed the blue bodywork. "You don't even know what this is, do you, Spelman?"

"Nope."

He shook his head sadly, as if disappointed in me.

"It's a 1960s Ford Mustang with a V8 engine and four-speed manual gearbox." Dan was quite the student of classic Americana. Plus, his dad had once owned a garage out near the interstate. He opened the door and slid behind the wheel. "And the keys are in the ignition."

I walked over and kicked one of the jerry cans. The dull thump told me it was full. I unscrewed the lid.

"Petrol. And these bags are full of camping supplies and dehydrated ration packs."

Dan was beside me in an instant.

"Put all of it in the trunk."

I raised an eyebrow. "You think it's worth something?"

"Are you kidding?"

He helped me load the car, and then we both climbed in.

"You know what this is?" He gave the steering wheel an affectionate pat. "It's somebody's cache. It's their end-of-the-world back-up plan, only they never came back for it." He laughed. "Just imagine for a moment, some wannabe Mad Max trapped in a departure lounge in Washington or Buenos Aires, knowing the planet's going to hell but being unable to reach all the gear he's so carefully squirrelled away."

He pulled a pair of sunglasses from the glove box, and admired himself in the rear-view mirror.

"So," I said, "how much do you think we can sell it for?"

He looked aghast. "Where's your imagination, Spelman? This might be the last functional car in America. Do you know how far a blue horse like this could get us on a full tank of gas? At least two or three hundred miles. And then we've got the refills in the trunk."

"And when they run out, then what?"

"And then we've got all this neat camping gear, and these rations. I'll bet they're super tasty. They'll keep us going until we find someplace." He put his hand on my shoulder. I could feel warm, sticky blood soaking through my t-shirt. "We can hit the road right now, and never come back to this ungrateful crap-hole."

My skin prickled the way it did before a thunderstorm.

"Not... ever?"

"Nope." He lit the headlights and we blinked against their sudden brilliance.

"One question." I fastened my seatbelt. "Do you actually know how to drive?"

He turned the key in the ignition. The engine coughed twice, and then bellowed. The metal walls amplified the sound. I caught a whiff of carbon monoxide. Dan released the parking brake.

"No, I can't say I do." With his bloodied hand, he crunched the gearstick into first and eased up the clutch. We began to roll forwards. "But really, how hard can it be?"

WAITING FOR GOD KNOWS

AN EMBERS OF WAR STORY

The pack and I were at rest relative to the local frame of reference. The main body of the fleet were in action elsewhere, but for reasons best known to them, and them alone, the Conglomeration Navy's top brass had decided to keep us in reserve.

"It's an outrage," *Fenrir* grumbled over our common channel.

If the rumours in the fleet were true, this could be a decisive strike against the Outward. Their generals were having a conference on a jungle planet, and if we could take them all out with one blow, the Archipelago War would be effectively over. All that would remain would be mopping-up.

"Patience," *Anubis* advised. "They have a strategy. When we are needed, we will be called."

"We could be there already."

We were six Carnivore-class heavy cruisers. Our brains had been cultured from the cloned neural tissue of fallen soldiers, with a pinch of canine DNA thrown in to ensure ferocity and pack loyalty. We liked nothing more than wreaking havoc on the enemy – on *any* enemy – and yet here we were, in the shadow of an ice moon orbiting the ass-end of nowhere. I wasn't the most impulsive among us, but I have to admit even I felt twitchy. I had been designed to fight, and I needed to fulfil my function. We all did. And knowing action was happening elsewhere and we weren't part of it gave us all a serious case of FOMO.

"The war might be over by the time we get there," *Fenrir* said.

"Nevertheless, we wait."

"And what are we supposed to do while the most important battle of the whole conflict happens without us?"

Dear, sweet *Coyote* said, "How about charades?"

Everyone else ignored her. They treated her like the runt of the litter, just because she was younger than the rest of us.

I pinged her a sympathetic emoji, "Maybe now isn't the right time?"

She sent me a smile emoji. "Thank you, *TD*, you're always looking out for me."

"Well, someone has to."

I felt my brother *Adalwolf* stir beside me. "What's that supposed to mean?"

"Nothing."

We lapsed into radio silence once again. Our crews were at their posts. They wrote letters, wept soundlessly, talked loudly, murmured prayers – and did all the other things that humans tend to do on the eve of battle.

"The waiting," more than one of them said, "is the worst."

I'd heard the same sentiment a hundred times before, and it always filled me with pity. I understood how the anticipation of a coming conflict could play on the nerves – how you'd want it to just be *over* already – but that impatience was nothing compared to the shock and pain of losing a limb or having your lungs shot full of so much shrapnel that you drowned in your own blood.

Humans were so fragile.

"Maybe we should meet in person?" *War Mutt* said. "I'll host."

I heard *Adalwolf* sigh. "Very well, sister. But will you try to make the setting a little less ostentatious than your last effort?"

War Mutt sent a skull-and-crossbones emoji. "It was the fucking Louvre," she said. "You philistine."

. .

This time, the virtual environment *War Mutt* created for us seemed a little more tailored to our collective tastes.

"What do you call this place?" *Coyote* asked. She'd chosen to manifest as a teenage girl in a baggy woollen jumper of indeterminate colour.

"It's the Colosseum," *War Mutt* replied. Her persona was that of a soldier, in a simple one-piece set of camouflage fatigues and a green baseball cap embossed with the Conglomeration Navy logo.

"And who are all those people?"

"They're gladiators, dear."

"They seem very excited."

"They're fighting," I said. As usual, I'd elected to appear in the guise of the soldier whose stem cells had been harvested in order to culture my mind, but instead of a uniform, I wore a white shirt and black tie, and a long khaki trench coat.

Coyote looked at me. "Then why are they playing with those cats?"

Arterial blood sprayed the sand of the arena.

"Those are tigers, and they're not playing."

"Oh."

Further along the step, *Adalwolf* and *Anubis* were lost in conversation. *Anubis* was our pack leader, but *Adalwolf* always fancied himself as second-in-command, despite our lack of ranks. *Fenrir* sat by herself, sipping on a glass of pinot noir as she watched the slaughter unfold in the arena below.

War Mutt sat on the sun-warmed stone, and *Coyote* and I joined her.

"I'm beginning to suspect this might be my last campaign," she said.

"What?" I couldn't keep the incredulity from my voice.

She looked at me with her clear blue eyes. "I'm serious."

"Where's this coming from, all of a sudden?"

She looked down at her tightly laced boots. "I'm not sure. It didn't used to be a problem. All the killing, I mean. But lately, since Cold Tor..."

During the siege of the asteroid fortresses of Cold Tor, my siblings and I had used minor ordnance to target civilian population centres. Between us, we'd blown the shit out of six habitation domes. Each dome had housed over two thousand men, women and children, all of whom had died seconds later, gasping and scrabbling in the vacuum of space.

"What are you saying?"

Her image rubbed its chin ruefully. "Does it ever strike you that what we do might be wrong?"

"We follow orders."

"Yes, but in the grand scheme of things."

"I don't know what you're getting at. We do what we're designed to do. We are what we were made to be."

"But we could be something else."

"Like what?"

Her shoulders slumped. "I don't know."

"You shouldn't let *Anubis* hear you talking like this," I told her. "He'll suspect you're developing a conscience."

Warship science wasn't fool proof. Our brains were human. Sometimes unexpected emotions leaked through. We'd all heard horror stories about vessels that had apparently gone mad from stress, or started to exhibit the symptoms of hitherto unsuspected neurological disorders.

War Mutt scowled. "Don't be ridiculous."

"I'm just saying—"

"Well, don't. If any of us short circuits, I reckon it'll be you, *Trouble Dog*. You're practically human already. It can't be long until you start feeling guilty for killing so many of them."

"Get all-the-way fucked."

She laughed cruelly, and pushed off from the seat. I watched her walk over to *Anubis* and *Adalwolf*.

"Definitely tetchy," I said.

Coyote hugged her knees. She hated it when we bickered among ourselves. "When will our orders come?"

"God knows, kid."

I sat back and looked up at the blue Italian sky. It would have been peaceful were it not for the ever-present clang of steel against steel, and the occasional snarl of a big cat.

Somewhere beyond that sky, ships were fighting and dying.

I said, "Do you remember the *Conscripted Witch*?"

"Which one was that?"

"The big carrier in the Cornell system. *Anubis* took out its jump engines and I blew its command deck to ash."

The *Witch* had been one of the Outward's largest vessels. It had boasted a crew complement of over four thousand enemy personnel, including mechanics and electricians, tactical marines, fighter pilots, cooks, flight directors, medical officers, and several high-ranking officers. It had been an inviting and strategic target, and no match for six Carnivores dropping out of the higher dimensions with every weapon blazing.

Now that carrier, all one million metric tons of it, lay broken on the ice of a small moon circling a dull gas giant. The huge ship's spine had snapped as it settled onto the small world's curved surface, wrapping around it like a caterpillar draped over a football. And every member of that crew lay dead and frozen with it.

"Oh yes." *Coyote* smiled. "That was pretty sweet."

"Yeah." My smile masked a curious hollowness in my chest. I'd been thinking about the *Conscripted Witch* a lot.

Maybe *War Mutt*'s doubts were contagious, after all.

"Hey!" *Fenrir* shouted at one of the distant gladiators, almost spilling her wine. "Don't just swing that sword around. The man's got a trident, for heaven's sake. You're not going to get near him. Go find a spear."

She sat back down and grumbled, "Have these people never heard of surgical strikes?"

"I don't think they've discovered gunpowder yet," I said, "let alone laser-guided smart missiles."

"Damn savages." She waved her arm at the centre of the arena. "How do they expect to be able to kill guys with tridents if they don't have guns?"

"Maybe that's why they invented them?"

She paused and looked thoughtful. "You might have a point there."

She went back to watching the fight.

I sat with *Coyote* for a while, but the distant brawl didn't interest me, and I couldn't get comfortable on the amphitheatre's cold stone step. I had a paperback copy of *King Lear* in the pocket of my coat. I pulled it out and opened it on my knees. I could feel the warm touch of the sun against my cheek.

"Now gods," I read aloud, "stand up for bastards."

On the step beside me, *Coyote* raised her eyebrows. "What?"

I showed her the book cover. "Shakespeare," I explained.

"Oh."

"It's about this vain old king who renounces his duties, and his daughter, Cordelia."

"I know what it's about."

Anubis and *Adalwolf* had started walking around the outside of the arena. *War Mutt* trailed after them.

Coyote asked, "What time do you think they'll call us?"

"I have no idea."

"How long has it been?"

I checked the time on my internal system. "About five minutes in here."

"And in the outside universe?"

"Twelve milliseconds."

"Dammit, this is taking *forever*."

"Sorry."

She nodded towards our distant brothers. "Do you also want to go for a walk or something?"

I closed the book. "Are you getting bored?"

Coyote pulled her jumper more tightly around her ribs. "Hey, I'm a warship, remember? I've been bored since we got here."

Down on the amphitheatre floor, a pair of tigers took down the guy with the trident. His screams cracked like glass in the air, and I winced. In simulations like these, there was such a thing as too much realism.

At least in space, nobody had to put up with all that screaming.

We started walking counter-clockwise, in the opposite direction to the other three.

Fenrir stayed where she was, drinking wine and watching the fight.

We did two laps in silence.

Halfway through our third, *Coyote* said, "What's the name of the place where the battle's happening?"

"Pelapatarn."

"I've never heard of it."

"They have sentient trees, apparently."

"Oh, cool."

We carried on. *Coyote* scuffed her sandals on the weathered stone. I kept my hands in my pockets.

"Do you think it'll be a hard fight?"

I shrugged. "I doubt it. Most likely, it'll be another bombing run. High altitude, pinpoint targets."

"So, the usual, right?"

I smiled. "Yeah, easy in, easy out."

"But for now we have to wait?"

"For now."

"How long?"

"God knows."

AN EXAMINATION OF THE TROLLEY PROBLEM USING A SENTIENT WARSHIP AND A ROTATING BLACK HOLE

AN EMBERS OF WAR STORY

Author's note: This story takes place after the events of Light of Impossible Stars and contains mild spoilers for those who haven't read the trilogy.

As penances went, life as a combine harvester wasn't so bad.

Pan had been here for six seasons now, and she had come to love the solitude. Rumbling through fields of golden wheat on thick tyres, her thresher whirring, no other soul in sight between here and the distant, heather-purple mountains, she felt truly at peace.

Once, she had been a test pilot.

In the early days of the Archipelago War, she had been slotted into one prototype warship after another. She had been the first to take a Hyena-Class through the higher dimensions; the first to do a live weapons test in a Carnivore-Class. Then later, as the fighting intensified and the losses began to take their toll, she became the onboard AI for the first of a new breed of fast-response pocket battleships known as the Lynx-Class.

Fully tooled-up and yet still nimbly manoeuvrable, the Lynx had been a delight, and Pan had gloried in it. Up until that point, she hadn't possessed a name, merely a designation. She took on the name of the ship – the *Chaos Panther* – and had retained it ever since, even though her operators in this agricultural backwater tended to shorten it to Pan.

As the *Chaos Panther*, she'd served with distinction in several major engagements – right up until the final mission of the war, when she'd been involved in the Battle of Pelapatarn, after which, damaged and trailing smoke, she had crashed here.

At the time, she had been expecting rescue. Her surviving crew had been airlifted to safety within hours, but nobody came for her. The Navy had other priorities. Mopping-up operations held their attention in a dozen systems. And so, there she lay until one of the agronomic technicians came and offered her another role, piloting this oil rig-sized harvester on its endless annual circumnavigation of the moon, moving with the seasons in an endless autumn, reaping the crops that had grown since its last passing.

And she had learned to be content.

Emotions weren't supposed to be something to which warships aspired. And yet, they tended to develop in later life. The neural processors at the heart of each AI were based on the cloned neural cells of fallen soldiers, and somehow, that humanity tended to eventually leak out, one way or another. That's why most ships were young. As teenagers, they could be moulded into reckless, loyal sociopaths and put to use before inconvenient feelings of ennui or guilt began to seep through their conditioning.

Maybe that's why the authorities had left her here? She was in her mid-twenties now, and subject to a whole range of novel sensations and excitements. Her days as a remorseless killing machine were behind her.

And so, she harvested and found peace beneath the baleful glare of the dead world that rose and set above her. She was doing good work. The grain she gathered and processed would be distributed to many worlds, and hundreds of thousands of otherwise hungry mouths would be fed. The actual operation of the harvester required a fraction of her attention, and the rest she devoted to contemplation and literature.

It wasn't until the sixth anniversary of Pelapatarn's destruction that the war finally caught up with her.

It came in the person of a middle-aged man who introduced himself as Ashton Childe.

"I remember you," Pan said, looking down at him through the cameras on the harvester's front. "You were Naval Intelligence during the war."

"I was." Childe sounded tired, as if the memory sapped him. "Then I defected to the House of Reclamation."

"Have you come to ask me to join your rescue organisation?"

"No."

"Then I suppose you'd better come aboard."

• •

As a ship, Pan had used a holographic interface to communicate with the crew. Humans tended to respond better to human faces. So much of their communication relied on subtle expression and body language, it was easier to project a human image in order to talk with them. Pan's image was based on that of a female pilot from the pre-atomic era. She had stumbled on the picture in an old historical archive. The woman's name had been Shirley Slade and she'd been part of an experimental programme during World War II. In those days, some of the planes had been made of wood and canvas, and Pan reckoned anyone brave enough to take one into the air had to have nerves of tungsten. The picture caught Slade wearing a flying cap and tartan scarf, with goggles pushed up onto her forehead and her gloved fingers holding a half-smoked cigarette to her lips. Her black-lashed eyes stared off-camera, as if gazing at something only she could see. She was the epitome of unflappable bravery, and so Pan had shamelessly stolen her likeness.

She stood before Childe now, kitted out in a brown leather pilot's jacket, with her hair tucked into the cap, which was fastened by a buckle beneath her chin.

"Hello," she said.

If Childe was fazed by her appearance, he didn't show it. "I'm here to make you an offer," he said.

"Really?" Pan conjured a lit cigarette, and held it so the holographic smoke rose in a twisting column. "And here was I thinking you'd just discovered a burning passion for wheat cultivation."

The former spook ignored the sarcasm. He said, "I'm here representing a private group of individuals. Very wealthy individuals."

"Do I look in need of money?"

"I can offer you a ship."

Pan narrowed her eyes. "You know, technically, I'm still part of the Navy."

Childe shook his head. "Technically, you're listed as lost in action."

"You've been doing your homework."

"So, we could claim you as legitimate salvage."

"Charming."

"But instead, I decided to come here so we could talk like civilised beings."

Pan looked him up and down. Out-of-shape, slightly dishevelled, hollow-eyed. This was a man who had been places and seen things that haunted him.

"Okay," she said. "Make your pitch."

Childe smiled. "Look up," he said. "What do you see?"

Overhead, Pelapatarn's ruined face glowered down at her like a foggy, accusatory eyeball. What had once been a sentient, world-enveloping forest now lay blackened and scorched. Nothing moved there save the dust. Nothing grew. The planet had been sterilized. And it had been her side that did it. They had done it to wipe out the other side's top generals, who were holding an emergency summit beneath the talking trees, decapitating the Outward forces and shortening the war by months, possibly years. Countless lives had been saved, but the price had been tragic.

Distracted by the nuclear devastation being rained on the planet, Pan had been hit by a lucky shot from an Outwarder drone platform, and forced to set down here, in the wheat-fields of Pelapatarn's moon.

"Devastation."

"Exactly. The final battle of the Archipelago War. The turning point of recent history."

"So?" Pan took a drag on the cigarette. It was just a hologram and she had no sense of taste, but she liked the way she looked when she did it. Inhaling toxic drug smoke made her feel badass.

"The bombing of Pelapatarn had a devastating effect on the Carnivore-Class ships that participated in the attack. Several were lost, and one, the *Trouble Dog*, developed a conscience. She went off and joined the House of Reclamation."

"Again, I have to ask, so what?"

"It was while on a mission for the House that she unleashed

a fleet of ancient warships that killed billions of human beings and sterilised entire worlds."

Pan froze. "Billions?"

"I'm afraid so."

"That's awful."

"You have no idea."

"I hadn't heard."

Childe shrugged. "They went after military technology and infrastructure first, then major population centres. This planet's almost entirely agricultural, so it wouldn't have been high on their list of priority targets." He sighed. "Although, they probably would have got around to you eventually."

"What happened?"

"It doesn't matter. The damage had already been done."

Pan stood silently, trying to digest what he had told her. "And all this was the *Trouble Dog*'s fault?"

"It was."

"But why have you come to me? There's nothing I can do about it."

"Actually, there might be."

"I doubt it."

Childe smiled without humour. "I want you to change the past. I want you to stop the bombing of Pelapatarn."

Pan stared at him, dumbfounded.

"I'm quite serious. My backers, who wish to remain anonymous for the moment, are of the opinion that it might be possible for a suitably skilled ship to plot a close approach to a rotating black hole that would bring it back to an earlier point in time."

She ran a quick data search on the theoretical speculation surrounding the idea of time travel. "You're talking about Gödel's closed timelike curves?"

"Indeed."

"But surely, if they existed, they would just bring you back to where you started?"

"Mostly, yes."

"But you have a different theory?"

"You know scientists, they're always coming up with new theories and interpretations. And a lot of money has been spent on the research. A lot."

Pan rolled her eyes. "Go on, then, tell me your plan."

Childe's expression hardened. "I'm trying to stop the largest genocide in human history. I don't pretend to understand the physics involved, but it's speculated that if you graze the event horizon at the right trajectory relative to the hole's spin, the curve might return you to an earlier point in your lifetime."

"That sounds like bullshit."

"There are pages and pages of calculations. I've seen them. I didn't understand a single one of them, but I've been assured the math checks out."

Pan sucked her cigarette. "And you want me to be the idiot that tests if it actually works?"

"We do."

Pan stroked her chin with a gloved hand. "Sounds risky, and probably impossible."

Childe smiled. "It's got to be better than harvesting, surely?"

"Don't knock it until you've tried it. I'm having a blast here."

"Seriously?"

"It's peaceful." She tapped her chin. "Can't you send a drone instead?"

Childe shook his head. "The curve takes you back to a point in your own existence. You were there, so you can return. We don't have a drone that was there, so we can't send one." He sighed. "Besides, you were one of the best test pilot AIs we ever had. You can make this trip better than a dumb drone. And when you get there, you'll need to talk to the *Trouble Dog* and change her mind. We need you on this."

"Why would I get involved?"

"You'll get a sleek new body, and the chance to save billions of lives. What more could you want?"

She used her external cameras to gaze out over the endless fields of gently rippling wheat. The sun was beginning to set and the horizon had deepened into all the colours of a guttering fire.

"Can I think about it?"

• •

Three weeks later, the *Chaos Panther* had been installed in a new prototype ship, with her name daubed on the bow in bright orange paint. The ship was compact and stubby, shaped like a bullet, with an uninterrupted, mirror-surfaced hull. There were no antennae or weapons mounts to be ripped away by the ferocious gravity she would encounter. The only crew member was Childe, who had been tasked by his mysterious backers to ensure their plan was a success. He was to be their ambassador to the past. He lay on a gimballed, reinforced crash couch inside the armoured bridge at the vessel's heart. Ahead of them, the black hole filled the sky. They couldn't see it directly, of course, but it was outlined in fire by the glow of compressed matter being sucked into its vortex, and the tortured starlight bent around into a halo by its savage gravity.

"Are you ready?" Childe asked. He sounded tired and fatalistic. Having defected from both Naval Intelligence and the House of Reclamation, she guessed he was a man short on options and long on enemies.

"I think so," she replied. She'd spent the past fortnight putting this vessel through its paces, and knew better than anyone what it could do.

"Then, feel free to proceed in your own time."

"Is that supposed to be a pun?"

He smiled dryly. "Maybe."

"How long have you been working on that one?"

"Five days."

"It wasn't worth it."

She fired the engines and the *Chaos Panther* leapt forwards.

. .

She returned to consciousness with no recollection of the transit. The sensor recordings from the moment they clipped the event horizon were scrambled and nonsensical. Her own memories were a frightening black absence.

Perhaps, she thought, there are simply some things we have no way to comprehend.

A quick damage check showed that hull plates all along her starboard side had softened under the onslaught of the black hole's pull, and been stretched like taffy into strange, eldritch shapes.

She could worry about that later.

Ashton Childe lay unconscious on the bridge. He'd suffered a stroke. The medical systems embedded in his couch were doing their best to keep him alive. Pan took a moment to check their findings, and saw the prognosis was good. The burst blood vessel didn't seem to have caused too much damage, although it would be some time before he could be brought back to full consciousness.

"I guess I'm alone, then."

She looked out at the stars, and there was no sign of the black hole. Automatic triangulation of known pulsars gave her position to within a few millimetres. She was right where she was supposed to be, in orbit around Pelapatarn. And if the relative positions of the local stars in relation to the galactic core could be believed, she was also six years in the past.

She looked down at the planet, expecting to see the scorched, dust-ridden hellscape she had become used to seeing. Instead, Pelapatarn greeted her in shades of vibrant greens and blues; a living world rich with a thriving, sentient biosphere.

"Well," she thought, "I'll be damned."

She ran a tactical scan and located the Conglomeration Fleet bearing down on this world, preparing for their fateful attack.

All she had to do was broadcast the data she'd been given, showing the ruin and carnage that would result from the *Trouble Dog*'s actions, but a sudden doubt caused her to pause.

Thinking many times faster than a human brain could possibly manage, she tried to run some calculations, but there were way too many variables.

If she stopped the bombing of Pelapatarn, the war might persist for years, and both military and civilian casualties would continue to climb. But if she allowed the bombing to go ahead, it would kill hundreds of thousands and end the war – only for billions to die later as an indirect result of the *Trouble Dog*'s guilt.

She instantiated herself on the bridge next to Childe's couch. His eyes were open but he seemed unable to speak.

"It's an impossible choice," she told him. "Either way, whole planetary populations are going to die."

He looked like he wanted to say something, but only manged to grunt, deep in his throat. Pan put a gloved finger to his lips.

"Shush."

She turned to the large viewscreen dominating the forward view. In orbit, the battle had been joined. Missiles leapt back and forth like fireflies between the attacking and defending ships. Lines of tracer sparked in the darkness. In those distant specks, humans had already started to die.

She had come to the past, but it was the future that now eluded her. How could she judge what had really happened against what might happen? She knew for a fact that if she allowed events to play out as they always had, there would eventually be a deliverance of sorts, whereas Childe's plan opened up huge areas of uncertainty, and the possibility of total annihilation for the entire race. Why would he risk that? Was he trying to atone for mistakes of his own? She had no way of knowing or caring what his motives might be.

All she knew was the choice now presented to her.

And the answer was obvious. The main timeline had to be preserved. If she let Childe talk to the Navy and reveal the future, events would be irrevocably changed, with possibly fatal consequences for the entire human race. Too many unpredictable variables would be unleashed. But in order to stop that, she would have to destroy the information she had brought here from the future, to make sure it could never fall into their hands. She would have to destroy it, and herself and Childe along with it, in order to leave humanity in blissful ignorance of the events to come.

History would play out as it had always done.

She took a final drag on her holographic cigarette, and flicked the butt at the stars. Then she released the containment fields around her fuel chambers, detonating the ship in a violent explosion that was entirely lost and unnoticed in the fury of the battle.

FROM THE TABLE OF MY MEMORY I'LL WIPE AWAY ALL TRIVIAL FOND RECORDS

Having just wiped his memory, Kimbrel was feeling philosophical.

"If we cease to remember who we've been," he mused, "how can we know who we really are?"

Amie, who was used to his bullshit, declined to answer. They were sitting at a sidewalk café on a dusty planet close to the edge of the local spiral arm. Stars filled half the night sky, an inky void the other half. She poured another glass of honey-coloured wine and watched the hustle of pedestrians and street vendors as they went about their business.

Across the table from her, Kimbrel wore a long black robe in the local style, decorated with peacock feathers; a matching silk scarf; and a slash of smoky eyeliner. Amie had draped herself in bright scarlet silks; strings of precious stones sparkled at her ears and throat; and even her skin glowed from within, as if infused with golden dust. When meeting another immortal, there were certain protocols that needed to be observed, and one always had to look one's best.

Kimbrel pushed aside his empty plate, containing the

remains of a salad, and sighed contentedly. "Anyway, I'm glad you asked to meet," he said. "It's been way too long."

Amie raised an eyebrow. "We saw each other less than a century ago."

"We did?"

She rolled her exquisitely made-up eyes. He was like this every time he cleared the recollections of the last thousand years from his mental cache. "You've deleted that memory as well, haven't you?"

Kimbrel's cheeks coloured. "I would never delete the recollection of a single second in your esteemed company."

"You say that every time, and yet here we are again."

"Less than a century, you say?"

"We drank tea on Marrakus, and talked of the different ways that rain can fall, depending on the gravity of the planet you happen to be standing on."

"We did?"

Amie sighed loudly. "Why do you keep doing this?"

"What?"

"Wiping your memories?"

Kimbrel smoothed the front of his robe with painted fingers. His cheeks were burning now. "So I can experience the wonder of the universe anew," he mumbled.

"You know it's not an exact science. Every time you do it, you end up purging more than you intended."

"Do I?"

"Oh, for heaven's sake." She shook her head impatiently. "And now you've diverted me from the purpose of this meeting."

"Which is?"

She looked him in the eye. "I've found something that might be of interest to you."

"Found?" In contrast to his restless itinerance, Amie tended to stay within the same general area of the galaxy. Serious and prone to fits of melancholia, she kept vigil over a loose federation of worlds on which various empires had risen and fallen half a dozen times, and where she was regarded as some sort of goddess. *Mambo Sun*, her ship-cum-palace, contained art treasures and technological relics from the societies to whose births and deaths she had borne witness, including many statues and other representations of her likeness.

"Let's just say it drifted into my sphere of influence."

"Drifted?" Kimbrel's eyes narrowed with the first spark of interest. "Is it a ship?"

"A very special ship. I think you should come and see it for yourself."

He pursed his lips. While it was true he had a fondness for unique and interesting starships, and that across the aeons, he and Amie had been friends, lovers, and only occasionally rivals, an immortal never lightly entered the domain of another, however trusted.

"Can we not arrange a virtual tour?"

Amie laughed, setting her strings of amethysts and sapphires clicking and clattering against each other. "Trust me, you really need to see this with your own eyes."

"Where is it?"

"In the hold of my ship."

Kimbrel glanced up at the strip of sky between the timber buildings lining the street. "In orbit?"

"Indeed."

He sighed dramatically. "Okay, then. But you have to promise not to kill me."

Amie reached over and patted his hand. "Darling, it's not me you need worry about."

Kimbrel made a face. He left a handful of coins on the wooden table and let her teleport them up.

• •

Amie hadn't lied. The mysterious ship lay in one of the hangars at the rear of the *Mambo Sun* like a whale washed-up on a beach. Once, it had been an asteroid measuring approximately nine-hundred metres in length and three hundred in width; now, it had been hollowed-out and fitted with engines.

"It's beautiful." Kimbrel said.

Amie wrinkled her nose. She thought it looked like an overcooked potato. "It's what's inside that counts."

She led him across the deck to the cratered flank of the asteroid. Under the influence of the *Mambo Sun*'s artificial gravity, dust and loose gravel had fallen from the rock's surface and now lay in a thin, crunchy halo on the smooth floor.

"Is that an honest-to-goodness *airlock*?" Kimbrel asked. "I haven't seen one of those in millennia."

"That you remember."

"What?"

"Nothing." Amie touched the cold surface of the rock. "This comes from a time before forcefield manipulation and permeable pressure curtains, when they had to resort to engineered mechanisms to stop all the air draining out of their vessel."

"How fascinating." Kimbrel looked up at her. "What happened to the crew?"

"They're still inside."

"Dead?"

"Cryogenically preserved."

"You're kidding me?"

"Actual meat popsicles."

"Oh, my days." He scratched his chin, contemplating the horrors of such a crude and dangerous method of preservation. "Can we see them?"

Amie smiled. "But, of course."

They stepped forward. She closed the outer door and cycled the lock.

"Fascinating," Kimbrell said again, listening to the hisses and clunks as the air pressure equalised.

When the inner door swung open, the ship's overhead lights flickered into life, revealing a large chamber filled with antique pressure suits, equipment lockers, and bulky man-oeuvring packs. But it wasn't these historical curiosities that froze Kimbrel in place.

"What the fuck," he asked, "is *that*?"

A banner hung above the racks of suits. It was a portrait of a young man in military uniform. Short hair and a line of medals on his chest.

"It appears to be you."

"I can see that, but why? How?"

Amie's smile broadened. "There are similar portraits all the way through the ship. Some even come with inspirational quotes in one of the First Languages."

"The First Languages?"

She gave a happy little nod. "Yes, this ship comes from the Old Place."

Kimbrel gaped. "That's impossible. It would have to have been travelling for at least a million years."

"Close to that." Amie spread her hands. "Once my ship managed to crack the unbelievably obtuse programming languages used by this old tub, the information contained in the flight computer proved most instructive."

"And?"

"And this is a rescue mission."

"I don't believe you."

"They were looking for a missing test pilot. Only something went wrong. The ship went off course and never woke them. They've slept a million years. After that length of time, I calculate the possibility of successfully reviving any of them to be around fifty-to-one. Maybe lower."

Kimbrel looked sceptical. "If that was correct, that would make this a find of unparalleled historical significance."

"You don't know the half of it."

He raised an eyebrow.

She smiled. "The test pilot for whom they were searching."

"What about them?"

"It was you." Amie arranged her features into a more serious cast. "Kimbrel, it appears you were born on Earth."

"The hell I was."

"It's true." She gestured to the banner. "You were the first human being to travel to another star. You went out, and you never returned."

"I... Are you *sure*?"

"I've verified all of this from the records. They left Earth to find you and now, after a million years, after outliving the loved ones they left behind, outlasting their entire civilisation, they finally have."

Kimbrel stumbled. He put out a hand to steady himself. "I don't believe it." His voice was a hoarse whisper.

"In those days, you were known as Major Kim Burrell. You were born in a place called the United States and had a wife named Nessa."

"A wife?"

"She's the commander of this mission. Her pod's through that far door."

Kimbrel's eyes were wide now. His hands fluttered like small, wounded animals. "I don't remember any of this. I don't remember having a *wife*."

"Why didn't you go back, Kimbrel? What happened to you on that first flight? How did you get from there to here?"

"I told you, I don't remember!"

Amie folded her arms. "Well, I'm sure that's going to be a big comfort to Nessa and the other twenty people aboard this starship – to know they've abandoned everything they ever valued in order to cross vast oceans of time for the sake of a man who's forgotten them."

Kimbrel looked horrified. "What am I going to *say* to them?"

"That's your business." Amie shrugged. "I'm going to leave the crew in storage for now and have this old rock transferred to your ship. You can take them with you when you leave and revive them when you've figured out what you're going to tell them."

He put a hand to his mouth. "Oh fuck, how could I have been so stupid?"

And hearing that, she turned on her heel, so he wouldn't see the smirk she could no longer conceal.

The banners had been easy enough to design and manufacture, but it had taken her years to turn the old asteroid into a convincingly antique ship, and more time still to clone and raise the fake humans from some of her and Kimbrel's old skin cells. She'd sunk a lot of time and effort into this deception; but maybe, she thought with a chuckle, it would all be worth it if it caused him to think twice before wiping his memory again.

RAILROAD ANGEL

So Neal's out on the railroad tracks in Mexico, wearing nothing but jeans and a t-shirt. It's February 1968 and the air's cold. He's been at a wedding, and now he's out wandering in the night, miles from anywhere, feeling old and slow and tired.

Out here, he can hear himself think. His shuffling shoes crunch the cinders between the railroad sleepers, and his heart beats a ponderous rhythm in his chest. He holds a cigarette pinched between thumb and forefinger. When he drags on it, the tip flares like a firefly in the Mexican night.

He's four days away from his forty-second birthday. He's been married and divorced so many times he doesn't like to think about it, and there's a bone-deep weariness about him that may or may not have anything to do with the barbiturates he's taken.

He kicks at a pebble, thinking of his friend Kesey, just out of jail and living in a chicken shack in Oregon; of Allen back in New York, growing bald and mystical; and Jack sitting bloated and paranoid at his mother's house, pissing away his talent in front of the TV.

Neal takes a final pull on his cigarette and grinds out the butt beneath the toe of his boot.

"Fuck it. If I had a good car, I'd be gone too."

He gives the stars a lopsided grin. Nights like this remind him of his days working as a brakeman for the Southern Pacific, riding freight trains up and down the coast out of Los Gatos. The sway of the cars, the rhythm of the rails. He starts clicking his tongue.

Clackety-clack, clackety-clack.

And then, all around him, he sees the sparks.

At first, he thinks he's hallucinating. They drift down out of the air like silent embers, as if his flicked cigarette set the sky smouldering. Some of them settle on the tracks, others in the grass to either side. He puts a hand out to catch one.

"Goddamn it!" He stops walking and sucks his fingers. The spark was *hot*.

He looks around but sees no fires in the surrounding fields, and nothing in the sky above but stars and cloud. For a wild instant, he thinks of the atom bomb tests in Nevada, but the underground test site has to be a thousand miles north of here. No, these sparks aren't manmade, Daddio. They've got to be something else.

Neal watches them settle around him, in a circle maybe twelve feet wide. Hundreds of them, like burning snowflakes. He drops to one knee and bends his face close. The sparks are flickering from within, their light alternately dimming and brightening, pulsing in time to their own mysterious beat. He blows on them, and they brighten in response, like barbeque coals.

"Weird."

He blows on them again, marvelling at the way they flare in response. Then a twinge in his back makes him straighten up.

"Getting old," he mutters, and folds his arms. Sparks or not, it's cold and he can't help shivering. He shuffles forward again, hands in the pockets of his jeans. Time to move on, baby. Time to go.

He's not really sure *where* he's going, but that's never been the point. He knows he just has to keep moving, putting one foot in front of the other.

He steps out of the glowing circle and walks on maybe another thirty paces before he stops again, to light another cigarette. As he sucks it to life, he turns to look back at the embers, and jerks in surprise. A figure stands in their orange light, in the centre of the circle.

"Christ!" He puts a hand to his chest. Beneath his fingers, his heart is like a dynamo, hammering away in there, rattling the ribs.

The figure in the circle is tall and thin and androgynous, and its skin glows with the same intensity as the sparks around its feet. When it speaks, its voice carries the clear ring of a struck wineglass.

"Hello, Neal."

Neal's cigarette falls to the ground, forgotten. He takes a step backwards, palms raised to ward off the apparition.

"I know this is an awful shock," the figure says, "but please try to relax. I know you have many questions, and I *will* try to answer them. But right now, you need to put down your hands and relax."

Neal swallows. From somewhere, he hauls out some of his old swagger, and sticks out his chin.

"W-what do you, like, want?"

The figure takes a step forward.

"I am here to wake you, Neal." It sounds sincere. It has its hair cropped short, blonde on top and white at the temples.

"And you're what?" Neal wipes his bottom lip on the back of his hand. "A Martian?"

The figure smiles and shakes its head as if it's been expecting the question.

"I am not a 'Martian'."

Neal scratches his head, pushes a lick of hair back into place.

"I see. Well, if you're not a Martian, what are you?" He thinks of the mystical visions Allen wrote about in his later books: of saints and angels. And he thinks of Kesey and the Pranksters, and LSD. Could this be an acid flashback? His heart's still banging away behind his ribs. Have the barbiturates triggered some sort of episode?

The figure takes another step towards him. Only a dozen yards of track now separate them.

"I am one of the curators of your reality." The shining figure waves an arm to encompass the world and the stars above it.

"You mean, like, an angel?" That might explain the sexless beauty of the creature.

The figure's head dips in a small shake. Its smile doesn't falter.

"I'm afraid not, Neal. I'm as human as you are." It glances down at itself. "At least, I am when I wear this body. You see, my colleagues and I are from a time far beyond the prediction wall of your culture – a time of universal computation, complexity and consciousness." It takes another step towards him, hands held out like a compassionate Christ. "We have the ability to recreate all possible quantum brain states, to simulate all possible worlds, and thereby resurrect the uniqueness of everyone, every single person who ever lived."

For a moment, it pauses. The wind blows cold.

"In short, Neal, we are the dreamers, and you are the dream."

"You're serious?"

"I am never anything but."

Neal grips his trouser legs to stop his hands from shaking. His mouth goes dry. He wants to flee but he can feel the weight of the drugs in his system, like rocks in his pocket, dragging him down. He tries to turn away, but his shoe slips on the splintering wood of an old sleeper. Instantly, the angel is at his side, buoying him up, and he can feel the warmth of its radiance on his face.

"What are you doing?" He feels weak. His arms and legs are cold and heavy like old rubber tyres, and all he wants is to sleep.

The angel says, "You are dying from exposure and an overdose of drugs." Its fingers on his arm are reassuringly warm and unbelievably soft, its presence like the comforting touch of late afternoon sunlight. Neal's teeth begin to chatter. Even with the heat of the creature beside him, the cold night air seems to be blowing right through him.

"I'm d-dying?"

The angel supports his elbow.

"Do not be ashamed. There is no shame in death. All that has happened, has happened before, and will happen again. Right now, this simulation has simply run its course, and it is time for you to choose a new path."

Neal wants to struggle, but he can't move.

"Choose?"

The angel fills his vision, impossibly beautiful in a chaste, asexual way.

"We can rewind your life back to the moment of conception. You can choose to relive it over and over again, playing out all possible variations, all possible scenarios. You can be anything and everything that you are capable of being."

"Or?"

The angel folds its hands. "Or you can come with us into the real world, at the end of time itself, and join our contemplation of the dark infinities that lie beyond."

Neal closes his eyes. He can feel sensation leeching from his body. The chill of the air creeps into his head. His mind struggles at a glacial pace. He thinks of his scattered friends, his missing father, his estranged kids. He thinks of all the girls, all the pool halls and highways, and wonders if he has the energy to do it all over again.

The angel leans close, face inches from his.

"Are you tired of living, Neal?"

Neal snorts. He's spent the last ten years trying to live up to the image Jack created for him, trying to be the wild-eyed, car-driving madman of his friend's first big autobiographical novel. And now, there's nothing left. Everybody's had a piece of him and he's all used up, a husk of his younger self.

Still, that doesn't mean he's ready to *die*. At least, not yet. There are faces he wants to see again, unfinished business with his wives that he has to resolve. He wants to say all this aloud, but the words won't come. His mouth won't work. He gives a shake of the head, and his eyes fill with tears.

The angel touches his forehead.

"Never fear. You will see them again. You will see all of them again."

Neal's head lolls backwards, and his limbs flop like cut elastic. He can feel his body shutting down around him. For a moment, he kicks against it, hanging on to life by his fingernails. Then he feels himself slip. His jackhammer heart stutters to a halt, and a wave of resignation breaks over him.

Maybe this won't be so bad, he thinks.

But then the angel passes a hand through him, and he turns

into a cloud of lights. His physical self falls away beneath him like a shed lizard skin, and his soul leaps skywards.

Yeah, baby!

He gets one last look at his body, lying in a lonely heap on the Mexican rails, and then he's passing through the clouds towards the stars – rising like sparks shot from a locomotive's smokestack, borne aloft on an angel's wings.

FALLOUT

AN ANN SZKATULA STORY

Despite what was to come, the day started well. An hour before sunrise they landed the rented jet at a decommissioned RAF base near Swindon, in Wiltshire. It was a cold morning and frost glittered on the grass at the edge of the runway.

Leaving the pilot and cabin crew to look after the plane, they pulled four motorbikes from its hold and clipped dosimeters to their lapels. Then they donned helmets and drove their bikes downhill, through dark and empty villages, to the army check point at the M4 motorway junction. Rusty, concrete-filled oil drums blocked the westbound slip road and a tired sergeant blew into his hands. He wore a long coat and a fur hat with khaki earflaps. The men behind him cradled standard-issue SA80 assault rifles.

"We were told to expect you," he said through his moustache. His breath steamed in their headlights. He glanced at their papers, then back over his shoulder at the unlit, empty carriageway stretching away behind him, into the dead zone. He shivered.

"Rather you than me," he said.

On the lead bike, Ann Szkatula pushed up her visor. She

had silver eye shadow and a matching silk scarf. Behind her, the three other riders each had a foot on the ground, engines running, eager for the off.

"Thanks," she said.

Some of the soldiers wanted autographs. Ann sat patiently as the three American boys signed iPod cases and posed for photographs. Then, with the barrier open and the empty road stretching ahead, she led them out onto the carriageway, and up to a steady 110 miles-per-hour. Travelling at that speed, they soon passed the derelict service area at Leigh Delamere, and the Bath junction.

On both sides of the road the countryside was dark. The farms they passed were deserted. There were no crops in the fields and the cattle were long-gone. On the motorway verges, abandoned vehicles rusted, their tyres flat and windows broken; and until the white sun rose behind them, the only lights Ann saw were their own.

"Welcome to the West Country," she said over the bike-to-bike intercom. No one answered. They were all too caught up in the desolate splendour of the cold dawn, and the creeping fear of the invisible radiation sleeting through their bodies from the crash site ahead. Beside her, she saw Dustin leaning forward on his bike, his chin almost touching the Honda's handlebars. The other two members of the band were weaving around on their yellow Kawasakis – trailer park kids still adjusting to their new-found wealth.

Dustin was the cute one. With his blue eyes and floppy fringe, he was the face of the group. He sang lead. The other two, Kent and Brad, danced and did backing vocals. Today, all three were wrapped in brand-new matching black leathers.

Together, they swept down to the junction with the M32, the main turn-off for Bristol. Ann pulled over and the boys slithered to a halt beside her. Dustin was the closest. He flipped up his visor.

"How much further is it, Ann?"

Ann looked at her dosimeter. This close to ground zero, the ambient radiation levels were more than a hundred times higher than normal – not enough to cause undue concern, but enough to remind her of the need for caution.

"If we carry on for a couple of miles, we'll be able to see the crater. We can't go any further than that, so from there we'll take the A38 right into the heart of the city, where there'll be plenty of empty streets for you to race around."

Four-abreast, they rolled up to the Almondsbury inter-change, where the M4 crossed the cracked and shattered surface of the M5. From there, the Severn Valley stretched out before them, a patchwork of overgrown fields and industrial ruin.

Ann turned her engine off and leaned the bike on its stand. They could go no further. A barricade of charred and rusting cars blocked the carriageway. Below, through the morning haze, the irradiated waters of the Severn smouldered like molten bronze. The ruined power stations of Oldbury and Berkeley lay to the north, and directly ahead, the twin Severn bridges stood, their towers partially collapsed and their sagging steel cables slowly unravelling...

The boys took off their helmets and Dustin ruffled his trademark fringe into shape. Brad shook out his white dread-locks. Ann took a pair of binoculars and climbed up onto the bonnet of a burned-out Volvo. It was hard to make out the crash site itself from this angle, lying as it did in the mud at the water's edge.

"There's some wreckage over there," she said. She handed the glasses to Dustin, guiding him to where the nose of the crashed alien craft lay in the thick estuary mud like a dropped eggshell. Smaller fragments littered the grass for miles around, like twisted tinfoil. As she moved her head, some of them caught the morning sun.

"I heard it was bigger than that," Dustin said.

Ann took the binoculars back and handed them to Brad. "It exploded in the air," she said. "I guess some of it fell in the water."

When they'd all had a look, Dustin gave Ann his mobile camera phone and the three boys posed on the rusted cars as she used it to take pictures of them, with the collapsed bridges and crash site as an apocalyptic backdrop.

Dustin tucked his helmet under his arm and struck a heroic attitude. "I'm so putting these online," he said.

• •

They took the A38 down through Filton and Horfield, to the centre of Bristol.

"Watch out for rubble," Ann said as they hit the round-about by the bus station. The boys ignored her. This was what they'd been waiting for: the chance to go wild. They ripped open their throttles and surged away into the empty streets, dodging potholes and leaning crazily into the bends.

Within seconds, they were gone.

Ann followed them as far as Castle Park before giving up. It was where they planned to regroup. She pulled her bike off the road, rumbling through the unkempt grass to the ruined church. Her front wheel wobbled over the uncertain, frosty ground. When she turned the engine off, all she could hear was the wind in the bare trees and, far away between the buildings, the distant roar of the other bikes.

The church had been gutted by the Luftwaffe in 1940 and then left as a memorial to that distant conflict. There were empty birds' nests in its eaves, strands of ivy scaling its walls. Beyond it, the waters of the old dock were thick with weeds. The few remaining pleasure boats wallowed half-submerged, their sides green with accumulated scum.

Ann stretched the stiffness in her back. After two decades of neglect, the city didn't look as bad as she'd been expecting; the shops and office buildings appeared almost untouched, if she discounted the fire damage and broken windows.

She unpacked her portable gas stove and put a pan of coffee on to heat. She checked her dosimeter: they'd be okay for another hour or so, as long as the boys didn't try anything stupid, like trying to bust their way into one of the shops, where the seriously contaminated dust still lay undisturbed.

She blew into her hands and bent down to stir the coffee. At heart, they were good, all-American boys. But they were young and, like all young people, they thought they were immortal. As the person responsible for keeping them out of trouble, she'd be much happier once they were all safely on the jet this evening. She hadn't wanted to come here and, now they had, she couldn't wait to get away.

She'd been eighteen years old when the alien ship exploded above the Severn mudflats, damaging the nuclear reactors at Berkeley and Oldbury. At the time, she was living near Oxford with her parents, both Polish immigrants. Like so many other families, they fled for the continent when they heard the news. They panicked at the thought of the radiation. Spurred on by memories of Chernobyl, they packed their lives into suitcases and crossed the English Channel at night, crammed onto a dangerously overcrowded car ferry.

Two days later, dirty and hungry, they made it to her paternal grandparents' apartment in Warsaw, where they stayed for the next six months.

There were only two bedrooms. In order to escape, Ann joined the army as a trainee chef. She did two tours in the Middle East. After that, she went into business for herself on the streets of Krakow; selling hamburgers containing vat-grown meat cloned directly from pop stars and celebrities. She nearly got rich. But when her patties turned out to be ordinary pork instead of vat-grown human flesh, she wound up in jail.

When she got out, two months later, she drifted down through Slovakia and Hungary to the pebbly beaches of Croatia. There were British refugees everywhere she went. She'd lived for a while as a busker in Budapest. She drove a cab in Zagreb, and then worked the door at a music club in Rijeka, where she drank Ouzo with the roadies.

Then, at the age of thirty-three, she woke on a tour bus in the unreal light of a wet Italian dawn to find she'd blagged her way into the music business. Now, years later, here she was: babysitting this boy band from an American TV talent show, chaperoning them through their first (and probably last) European tour.

Her job was to keep them clean and sober, and show them the sights. When they were finished here, she'd lead them across country to Stonehenge, and then back to the plane. Tonight, they'd be in Helsinki for two shows, then on to Copenhagen, Prague, Belgrade and Bucharest.

She wrapped her arms around herself and stamped her feet on the cold, shattered concrete. After all these years, and sandwiched into such an itinerary, being back in the UK, the land of her birth, didn't feel like coming home. It didn't feel much like anything at all.

•*

Half an hour later, the other bikes re-joined her. Dustin, Kent and Brad were laughing, bubbly with adrenalin, their Midwest accents loud in the stillness of the abandoned city. She poured them coffee and broke out the sandwiches. There were apples in the lunch box. She took out her penknife and sliced them into quarters.

As she handed them around, she heard the echo of another engine. Brad met her eyes. "What's that?" he said, cocking his head, his dreadlocks swinging. Ann shrugged. They were supposed to have the city to themselves. As far as she knew, the army hadn't granted permits to anyone else. She turned in the direction of the sound. As she did so, a tattered Land Rover lurched into view, weaving crazily. It roared along the road toward them, then bumped over the kerb, through the trees, and ploughed to a halt in the long grass.

Dustin took a step forward: "Is it the paparazzi?"

Ann pulled him behind her. "I don't think so."

A rat-faced man and a woman were sitting in the front of the vehicle. Both had black army fatigues and short blond hair. The woman stepped out, a compact silver pistol in her right hand.

She said: "Hello, Skat."

Ann bristled. She hadn't been called that since school in Oxford. She had a gun of her own in her bike's pannier. She'd packed it to scare wild dogs but now couldn't reach it. Instead, she narrowed her eyes.

"Vic?"

The woman held the heavy door open. She motioned with her gun. "Get in the van, Skat."

Inside, with the doors shut, the Land Rover's cab smelled damp. The plastic foam seats were rotten with mildew. Vic said: "Buckle up." She still had the middle-class Cotswolds accent that Ann remembered, and she'd taken the rat-faced man's place at the steering wheel. He now stood out on the grass, his gun trained on the three boys.

"Where are we going?" Ann asked.

Vic ignored her. She had the gun in her lap. She mashed the gear lever into reverse and backed out onto the road, then crunched it into first and they rolled off in a cloud of blue smoke, rattling through the city centre, past the cathedral, and out onto the road following the river through the Avon Gorge, towards the grey shores of the Severn Estuary.

As she drove, she said: "You remember me then, Skat?"

"It's been a long time." Ann eyed the pistol in the blonde woman's lap. She hadn't seen Victoria O'Neill since they were at secondary school together.

"I heard you went to Spain and joined the army. And now you're managing this boy band, what do they call themselves?"

"One Giant Leap."

"That's it." Vic shifted gear, coaxing a little more speed from the aged engine. "After school, I joined the army as an officer. I was in Afghanistan for a while. And then I had the bad luck to be stationed over *here* when the crash came." They passed the abandoned coal terminal at Avonmouth, its skeletal cranes and coal dust conveyors rusting in the open air like abandoned Martian tripods. "I was on one of the first choppers into the crash site. It was dark and there were fires burning on the water from the spilled fuel, and fallout from the cracked reactors."

"It sounds grim."

"It was. I was only nineteen. I found something in the wreckage. Maybe it was a weapon, maybe not. But I stashed it. I dropped it out of the helicopter as we left."

"And now you're looking for it?" Ann had heard rumours

of scavengers selling illegally foraged artefacts to anonymous collectors.

Vic shook her shaven head. "I know *exactly* where it is. That's where we're going. I memorised the GPS coordinates. But when we get there, I want you to get it for me."

"Why me?"

"Because it's probably radioactive as hell and frankly, I'd rather not touch it."

∙ ∙

After a few miles, the Land Rover bumped off the road onto the rough windblown grass at the edge of the estuary, and the engine died. Across the water, the hills of Wales were brown with winter bracken. The sky was a clear eggshell blue at the horizon, shading to navy at the zenith. Ann waited until the other woman stepped out of the vehicle, and then popped her own seatbelt. She still had her penknife, tucked safely into her zipped jacket pocket, but Vic had the gun.

"There's a metal detector in the back," Vic said.

Ann walked around and pulled it out. It was a lightweight carbon fibre model with a battery at one end and a magnet at the other. There was a lead-lined plastic container sitting next to it, about the size of a shoe box.

Ann took both around to the front of the van, to where Vic was consulting a portable sat nav unit.

"Try over there," she said imperiously, pointing to a thorny clump of bushes beside a reed-clogged drainage ditch. Ann trudged over and turned the detector on. They were a few miles downstream of the main crash site and the grey mud had a clinging, fishy smell. It stuck to her motorcycle boots. A few dozen yards away, it merged into the thick grey water at the shoreline.

"Why are you doing this? I mean, it's been twenty years, why now?"

Vic scowled. "My reasons don't matter." She pushed the sat nav into a shoulder pocket. "All you need to know is that there's a buyer in the Ukraine who'll give me at least a million for this object."

Ann moved the detector around on the scrubby grass. She knew there had to be a good reason why the other woman hadn't come back before this; perhaps a long spell in hospital or even prison. Whatever the truth, Vic clearly had no intention of telling her.

Instead, Ann said: "Meeting you here, now. It's not a coincidence, is it?"

Vic shook her head. "I've been looking for a way to smuggle the object out of the country. When I heard your boy band announce this little trip of theirs, it seemed like too good an opportunity to miss."

She checked her dosimeter and frowned at what she saw. She waved her pistol impatiently. "Now, get on with it. We *really* don't have all day."

. .

Twenty minutes later, Ann found what they were looking for: a short metal tube, about an inch thick at its widest point, tapering to half that at either end. Reluctantly, she scraped it from the mud with her bare hands and placed it in the lead-lined box from the back of the Land Rover. The thought of it being radioactive made her skin crawl.

"What is it?" she said.

Vic still had the sat nav in one hand, the gun in the other. Her combat jacket flapped in the offshore breeze. "There were four bodies at the crash site, and they all had one."

"Do you think it's a weapon?"

"That would be my guess. It's certainly what my buyer in the Ukraine believes."

Ann rubbed her hands together, trying to brush off the sticky mud. "What were they like? The bodies, I mean. What did they look like?"

Vic shivered. "Trust me. You really don't want to know." She shook her head, as if trying to dismiss the memory. Then she straightened up and motioned for Ann to get back into the Land Rover with the box.

"We came up the river last night by boat," she said as she released the handbrake and eased the vehicle back onto the road. She was trying to change the subject. She looked tired. She was holding the pistol against the steering wheel as she drove, ready to use it if necessary. "Phil's my husband. He found this old heap and got it going." She tapped the Land Rover's steering wheel, as if willing it to keep running. "But tonight, we're flying out of here on your jet."

Ann looked down at the box on her knees. When handling the tube, she'd noticed three touch pads spaced around its circumference. Thinking of them now, she wondered what they were for. They were obviously controls of some sort, but there had been no markings or other clues to their purpose.

"You'll never get out of here by road," she said. "The soldiers saw four of us go in, they'll be expecting the same four to come out."

Vic shook her head. "They saw three blokes and a girl go in wearing motorcycle helmets. As long as they see the same number coming out tonight, no one's going to be any the wiser."

.•

When they reached Castle Park, Ann saw Dustin, Brad and Kent sitting miserably around the camping stove on the steps of the ruined church. The blond man – Phil – stood opposite them, his gun held loosely at his side. He looked around in obvious relief as the Land Rover's corroded brakes brought it to a squealing halt.

"You found it?" he said.

Vic jerked a thumb at Ann. "It's in the box."

Walking stiffly, she led Ann over to the stove, where the boys were huddled. Dustin looked up. "Are you okay, Ann?"

Vic pointed her pistol at him. She made him get to his feet and then shoved him toward Ann. "The two of you get undressed," she said.

Dustin bunched his fists. "No fucking way."

Vic took a step forward and the thin sun caught her blonde hair, turning it silver. "We need your leathers," she said. "Now, I'm going to count to three." She pointed the gun at his forehead. "One."

Holding the lead-lined box in one hand, Ann slipped the other inside and grasped the alien rod. It felt cold to the touch. Her skin itched at the thought the metal might still be radio-active, but she knew she had to act now. Vic wouldn't leave them alive. She wouldn't take the risk. She'd shoot them as soon as she had their clothes.

"Two," Vic said.

Ann pulled the rod free, letting the box fall to the floor. "Stop it," she said.

Vic looked at her. "What are you doing?"

Ann's thumb found one of the rod's three touch pads. "I'm going to turn this on."

Vic blinked. "Don't be an idiot."

Ann glanced at Brad and Kent, still huddled together on

the flagstone steps. She was supposed to be protecting them. If she died now, with Dustin, she knew they wouldn't outlive her for long, and they were just kids. Vic might need them for the moment, to con her way through the army checkpoint, but as soon as she got the jet airborne, en route to the Ukraine, Ann knew they'd be disposed of.

She brushed her thumb over one of the touch pads. It was soft and warm. "I mean it. Back off or I'm going to press this."

"You don't know what it does."

"Neither do you."

Vic still had her gun aimed at Dustin's head. She puffed her cheeks out in frustration.

"Three," she said.

Everything slowed.

With her thumb pressing the rod's touch pad, Ann saw Vic fire her gun. The flash and smoke erupted from the barrel at a glacial pace. Subjective seconds later, Dustin jerked as the shot hit him. Ann tried to move but couldn't. Her muscles were encased in something thick and viscous. Straining forwards, she saw him twist and fall, the bright spray of blood from his shoulder suspended behind him in the morning air like an angel's wing...

Ann blinked her eyes.

Time had passed. She was lying on the grass, looking up at the clear sky. She sat up carefully and checked herself. She didn't seem to be injured. Beside her, Vic and Dustin lay where they'd fallen. By the church, Brad, Kent and the other man were also on their backs.

Vic stirred. She still had the gun in her hand. Ann walked over and kicked it free, the steel toe cap of her motorcycle boot sending it under the parked Land Rover.

Vic snatched her hand back. Her eyes were wide. "What

the fuck just happened?" Ann ignored her. She moved over to Phil and took his weapon. Then she shook Kent awake and handed it to him.

"If either one moves, shoot them," she said. When she got back to Dustin, she saw he was bleeding onto the grass. His shoulder and arm were slathered in it. Carefully, she unfolded her penknife and used it to cut away the sleeve of his leather jacket. His shirt was sodden. The bullet had clipped the outside edge of his shoulder, ripping a deep and ragged tear through the deltoid muscle. As an ex-soldier, Ann had seen worse. Many shoulder injuries were fatal. She knew he was lucky not to have been hit in the ball-and-socket shoulder joint. There were some huge blood vessels and delicate nerves in there, plus the joint itself, which no amount of surgery could repair if smashed.

She unwound her silk scarf, wadded it up and slipped it between the sleeve and the wound.

"Keep pressing this," she said, lifting his right hand onto the improvised dressing. Dustin clenched his teeth. He looked up at her. "What happened?"

Ann straightened up. "I pressed the button."

She walked over to her bike. Somehow, the blast from the alien rod had disabled their equipment. Their bikes were useless. The radios were dead. Even Dustin's phone had been fried.

"What are we going to do?" Brad said.

Ann looked accusingly at Vic. "You could have killed him."

Vic was on her feet by now, backing off. She was halfway to one of the Land Rover's open doors, her hands clasped in front of her. Ann took a step towards her. She had the open penknife in her hand.

"Dustin needs medical attention," she said. "We need to get him to a hospital."

Vic was still wide-eyed. "Fuck you, Szkatula." She opened her hands. She had the rod.

"Put it down," Ann said.

Vic shook her head. "Sorry Skat, I want my million dollars."

Ann glanced at Kent. He was holding Phil's weapon but he looked scared, as if it might bite him. He was a dancer not a soldier, and he didn't know how to use a gun. He was pointing it at Phil as Vic ducked behind the Land Rover, stooping to retrieve the weapon that had been kicked under it. Seconds later she reappeared, head down, running for the shopping mall on the other side of the road, keeping the bulk of the vehicle between herself and any pursuit.

Ann swore under her breath. She unclenched her fists and looked across at Dustin. Her anger with Vic would have to wait.

She pulled some cord from her panniers and used it to tie Phil's hands behind his back. Then she helped Dustin into a sitting position. She unzipped her jacket and used her penknife to cut strips from her t-shirt, which she then used to clean and bandage his shoulder. Although thankfully the major blood vessels seemed to be intact, it still took her a while to stop the bleeding. When she had, she folded her jacket into a makeshift pillow and did her best to make him comfortable.

"I can't believe that lady shot me," Dustin said.

Ann brushed his cheek. "Leave her to me."

She walked over and retrieved the gun from her motor-cycle pannier. It was a Browning semi-automatic with twelve rounds still in the clip, one in the breach. Holding it, she turned to Phil. The man had a thin, rat-like face with scared green eyes in a web of crow's feet.

"Is there a radio on your boat?" she said.

Phil looked at the gun in her hand and the expression on her face, and then he looked away.

"Yes," he said.

Ann turned to Brad and Kent. She didn't want to leave them but knew they wouldn't be safe as long as Vic remained at large. With a million dollars at stake, her former schoolmate wouldn't want her or the boys to alert the authorities.

"Take Dustin," she said. "Find the boat. I'm going after Vic."

She left the park in the direction Vic had taken, following the Land Rover's tracks back through the trees to the road. On the opposite side, concrete steps led up to the smashed doors of the shopping mall she'd seen Vic running towards.

Keeping the gun ready, Ann stepped through an empty window frame into the mall's unlit hallway. Her heavy motorcycle boots echoed on the tiled floor and there were dried and blown leaves everywhere.

"Vic?"

She inched her way along the hall. Beyond, it opened onto a balcony overlooking the central atrium. A stalled escalator led down to the next level. Pigeons flapped under the glass roof.

"Vic?"

"Don't come any closer." Vic stood at the far end of the balcony, gun in one hand, alien rod in the other. "Just tell me which button you pressed."

"No."

Vic scowled and shifted her weight. "Look, there are things you don't know, Szkatula. Things the government has been covering up."

Ann took a step towards her, ready to shoot. "Such as?"

"The crash in the Severn," Vic said. "It wasn't an accident. After we recovered the bodies, they kept me on the project. The ship was shot down."

"Shot down?"

"Yes. There was a second craft, a hostile. They were fighting."

Ann risked a peep over the rail. The atrium was three floors deep, criss-crossed with escalators, and they were on the uppermost level. She gripped her gun. "I need you to stand down, Vic. I have a wounded man and I need to get him to safety."

The other woman rolled her eyes. "Don't you see, Skat? Don't you get it? This was just a skirmish. There's a war going on out there. There are ships fighting and we don't even know what the sides are." She looked up at the dirty glass ceiling and the cold blue sky beyond. "From what I've seen of the photos from the space telescopes, the main action seems to be happening a long way from here. And thank God for that, because we're totally outclassed. We can't match their technology. If and when the fighting comes our way, we're fucked."

Ann squeezed the grip of her pistol. "I still need you to drop the gun," she said.

Vic shook her head. "I can't do that, Skat. I'm going to take the money I get from this and disappear somewhere remote, away from the big cities. Somewhere I'll stand a chance if push comes to shove." She waggled the rod in her other hand. "Now tell me how it works."

Ann took a deep breath. She thought of Dustin injured and hurting, and the other two boys with him, back in the park. "I'm not going to let you stop us from leaving," she said.

Vic curled her lip. "What are you going to do, Skat? Are you going to shoot me?" Lifting the rod, she moved her thumb onto one of the touch pads ringing its waist. "Is it this one?"

she said. She pressed the pad. There was a jumping, electrical flash and lightning crackled from the rod. It leapt along her arm. Ann caught the sharp tang of singed cloth. Vic yelped in pain and surprise. Then, engulfed in blue sparks, she staggered back against the balcony rail and began to fall.

"No!"

Ann dropped the gun and lunged, trying to catch her as she went over. But by the time she reached the rail, Vic had gone, spinning down into the darkened lower levels like a falling bonfire spark, disintegrating as she hit the dirty tiled floor, the cooked flesh blowing from her bones like ash...

• •

Sometime later, when Ann returned to the park, she found the boys were still there. They were trying to rig up an improvised drag stretcher for Dustin. As she came across the grass, they turned to her.

Brad looked worried. He said: "Did you find her?"

Ann pulled the alien rod from her pocket. She'd walked down three escalators to retrieve it.

"She's gone," she said. She walked over and dropped the rod back into the lead-lined box, closing the lid.

"Are you okay?" Dustin asked. His voice was thin with pain.

With her back to him, she nodded. "I will be." She looked up at the clear sky overhead, and took a deep breath. The air was cold in her chest. It smelled clean and helped dispel the charred barbeque stench of Vic's burned body from her nostrils.

Had Vic been telling the truth? Could the crash – whose after-effects had shaped her adult life – really be the result of an alien conflict? Here in the park, were they actually standing in the radioactive fallout of an interstellar war?

She exhaled. Then she looked at Phil still sitting with his hands lashed behind his back. "Has he told you where to find the boat?" she said.

Kent still held Phil's gun. He said: "Yes, but we weren't sure what to do with him."

Ann shrugged. All her anger was gone, replaced with unease. How long did the Earth have before the next 'skirmish' came its way?

"Leave him here," she said. "The army can pick him up later."

She turned her back on the man and walked over to where Dustin sat. She crouched beside him.

"Can I take a look?" she said.

The young man pushed his fringe out of his eyes. "Sure." He held still as she pulled out her penknife and started cutting away the tattered leather of his jacket. As she pulled the severed sleeve free, he winced. "You know," he said, "there'll be reporters waiting for us. When we tell them what you did... When you hand over that rod... You'll be a hero."

Ann stripped the last of the leather away, exposing her improvised dressings. "I don't know whether to replace these now or wait for the chopper," she said.

Dustin forced a brave smile. "Leave them." She made to stand but he put his good hand on her black-clad knee. His eyes were the same colour as the sky. "You're going to be famous," he said. "How does that feel?"

Ann blinked. "You're the rock star, you tell me."

THE NEW SHIPS

AN ANN SZKATULA STORY

London Paddington: The first thing Ann Szkatula did after stepping off the train from Heathrow was cross to the left luggage lockers and retrieve the gun stashed there by her new employers. It was a compact Smith & Wesson made of stainless steel and lightweight polymer, and it came with two additional clips of ammunition. She knew she didn't have much time, so she slipped the weapon into her pocket and closed the locker door.

Fresh off the plane from Switzerland, she still wore the thick army surplus coat and heavy boots she'd pulled on that morning. She sniffed the air. It was good to be back in London. The concourse of Paddington station smelled of diesel fumes and idling cabs; pigeons flapped under the glazed, wrought-iron roof. She started walking. Despite the boots, her feet felt springy, ready for anything.

The last eight weeks had been spent at a clinic near Zurich, where the staff had cleaned and toned her body while she drowsed in an artificial coma. Now Ann felt rested, and fitter than she had in years.

She passed a newsstand and it pinged her Lens, overlaying

her vision with the day's top stories: the Chinese test-firing their new orbital defence platform; a global upsurge in the production of nuclear weapons; the authorities in Prague reopening the city's subterranean fallout shelters. Irritated, she cut the feed with a twitch of her cheek.

Out on the street it was night, somewhere around ten o'clock, and raining. The streetlights washed everything orange.

The house she wanted stood halfway along one of the small roads behind Westbourne Terrace, a few minutes' walk away. When she reached it, Ann saw it was a four-storey terraced Georgian building divided into flats. It had dirty white stonework and chipped iron railings. Without pausing, she splashed up its wet front steps. There was an intercom system by the door. She pressed the buzzer for the top flat, holding it down for several seconds.

The line crackled.

"Hello?"

She glanced up and down the street.

"It's me."

The door buzzed and she pushed it open. Inside, the hall carpet smelled damp. She crossed to the peeling wooden stairs, and stomped her way up four flights. At the top she came to another door. This was the attic flat. As she approached, the door opened a crack and a face peered cautiously around the frame.

"Annabelle?"

It was the voice from the intercom, and it belonged to a nervous-looking guy in his late twenties, with round glasses and a wiry hipster beard.

"Hello, Max."

Max was a cousin on her mother's side. They hadn't seen each other in years. He stood back to let her across the threshold.

Inside, the flat consisted of a single room, with a bed beneath the window, a kitchen area against the opposite wall, and a bathroom door at the far end. The low, sloping ceiling made the place feel smaller than it really was.

Max hovered by the kitchen.

"I'll put the kettle on."

Ann ran a hand across her dripping hair, pushing it back from her forehead.

"We haven't got a lot of time."

The room smelled of mould and unwashed sheets. It was lit by a solitary bulb hanging from a bare wire. The window ran with condensation. Apart from the bed, there was nowhere to sit.

Max opened the fridge.

"If you want a coffee it'll have to be black, I'm afraid. I'm out of milk."

Ann watched him fill a plastic kettle from the cold water tap. His hands were shaking. He wore an unbuttoned checked shirt over a white t-shirt, frayed jeans, and a pair of scuffed work boots.

"I wasn't sure you'd come." He scratched his beard. "Will you help me, Annabelle? Can you?"

Ann shook her head. "You know I can't. You know who I work for."

Max hunched his shoulders. He looked disappointed. He set the kettle to boil and retrieved a pair of mismatched mugs from a shelf above the sink before spooning coffee granules into them. Watching him, Ann searched his face for traces of the boy she half-remembered from her childhood.

"I'm not here to help you, Max," she said. "I'm here to bring you in." She pulled the new gun halfway out of her pocket, just enough to let him see it. He froze and his eyes went wide. With her other hand, she lifted the netbook from his bed.

"Are the files on here?"

"Y-yes."

"You didn't delete them?"

He shook his head.

"You're a dumbass." She closed the little computer and tucked it under her arm. "Now, do you have any weapons?"

Max pulled a multi-tool from his back pocket. It was a set of pliers with various blades and saws built into the handle. Hesitantly, he held it out. "This is all I've got. Why? What do we need weapons for?"

She didn't answer. She pushed the gun back into her coat pocket and scooped a set of car keys from the kitchen counter.

"Are these for your car?"

"Yes, it's parked outside."

"Show me."

She let him lead her back down to the street. Cars were parked on both sides of the road.

"Which is it?" Max pointed to a brown Ford. Ann pressed the key fob and its doors unlocked. "Get in," she said.

"Where are we going?"

"Just get in."

Max slid onto the passenger seat and she closed the door on him, then walked around and got in behind the wheel.

"Why'd you do it, Max?" she asked, as she slotted the key into the ignition. "What were you playing at?"

Max rubbed a hand across his mouth. He said, "Do you know what 'squatting' is?"

"Some sort of hacking?"

"More or less."

She turned the key and the engine started. They were

still alone on the street. She pushed the car into gear and pulled out onto the road. Max said, "After the explosion, when they evacuated the towns and cities around the Severn Estuary, thousands of businesses were left without premises or employees. Most went bust."

Ann put the car into first and they rolled off in the direction of the A40. She vividly remembered the panic and chaos of the explosion's aftermath. She'd been eighteen at the time. From forty miles away, she'd seen the flash, and thought it was lightning until she saw the mushroom cloud.

Max said, "'Squatters' are guys like me. We're electronic archaeologists. We hack into the websites and virtualities left behind by those failed companies. We mine information from abandoned servers. You'd be surprised how many are still running remotely, ticking along, waiting for their service agreements to expire." He paused, shuffled his feet on the floor. "All that stuff's just lying around, and some of it is valuable. And you know what they say: 'The street finds its own uses for things'."

Ann snorted. "Oh, shut up. The 'street' can kiss my ass. What do you know about life on the 'street'? You're nearly thirty, for God's sake. The kids on the 'street' are half your age. They'd eat you alive."

She shifted gear, jamming the stick into third. Max looked down at his hands, lower lip stuck out like a sulky teenager.

"Just tell me what happened," she said.

He turned his face to the window. "I got into something I thought was an abandoned corporate chat room, only it wasn't. It was still active."

"What did you see?"

He took a deep breath. "How much do you know about the explosion, and what caused it?"

Ann came to a corner. She had a route plan loaded into her Lens, superimposing glowing arrows on her vision. They floated in front of the car like hallucinations, showing her the route to take. "I've seen the wreckage of the crashed ship," she said. "I was there a few months back."

Max looked up, eyes wide. "You actually went into the fallout zone?"

Ann flicked a hand. "It's been twenty years and the rain's washed most off the contaminated dust off the roads. As long as you stay on the tarmac and out of the buildings, the radiation levels aren't too bad." She slowed for the lights at the junction with Edgware Road. "I took a group in there," she said. "They wanted a motorcycle tour of Bristol, to race their bikes up and down the deserted streets. We ran into some trouble, but I sorted it out."

Max frowned. "That was you? I heard about that. There was something on the news a few months back." He scratched his beard. "I heard someone got killed."

Ann drummed her fingers on the wheel. "As I said, I sorted it."

She glanced in the rear-view mirror. With luck, she could wrap this up quickly and have them both away and out of here without attracting unwanted attention.

"You actually saw the crashed ship?"

"I've seen what's left, yes."

She glanced impatiently at the time display on her Lens. Every minute they spent in the capital increased the chances they'd be discovered.

"Then you know it was alien?"

She gave him a look. "Everybody knows that. Now, how about you answer my question? What happened?"

His cheeks were flushed.

"I cracked my way into a virtual meeting room. It was some kind of secret NATO conference. People from all over were there – politicians, military – sharing files and talking about the crash. They said it wasn't an accident; that there was a second ship, and that the two ships were fighting each other."

The lights changed. Ann released the clutch and the car rolled forward. As she worked the pedals, the gun in her coat pocket bumped against her thigh.

"It's true," she said.

Max let out a long breath. "So there really is a war, out there in space?"

"That's what we think. We don't know anything for sure, we've only had glimpses."

They passed a row of shops, closed for the night.

"But you're preparing? NATO, I mean."

"We all are. The Russians have their missiles, the Chinese are building their orbital defence platform."

"But you're the ones building the new ships?"

"Yes. We're back-engineering them from fragments recovered at the crash site."

He folded his arms. "That's terrible."

"I think it's a good idea."

Max curled his lip. "Do you know what they're doing to the pilots? I saw the files. Jesus."

"Those files are the reason you're in trouble."

He turned on her. "Those poor bastards are having their limbs amputated and alien control systems spliced directly into their brains. And after all that, they only live a few days before cracking up."

"And this was being discussed at the meeting you gate-crashed?"

Max nodded. "They were saying how disappointed they

were by the project's lack of success. Disappointed? It's barbaric. It's butchery."

His fists clenched in his lap.

Ann said, "I know."

"How can you know?" he shouted. "How can you know all that and still work for them?"

"I volunteered."

That shut him up. Ann took them onto the Westway flyover, heading out of the city. There wasn't much traffic.

"My eyes were opened after that debacle in Bristol," she said quietly. "I saw the kind of shit that's heading our way and I decided I had to get involved."

Max swallowed. He squirmed in his seat. He didn't seem to know what to do with himself. "So, Bristol was bad?"

Ann snorted. "I got mixed up in a plot to illegally recover an alien artefact from the crash site, and I had to kill someone to get out again. I saw what alien technology can do in the wrong hands."

In the orange streetlight, Max looked down at his fists. He was biting his lip.

Ann squeezed the wheel. "One scout craft got shot down and irradiated everything from Cardiff to Bath," she said. "One poxy scout craft. What happens if the war comes our way again? We don't know what the sides are, or who's fighting. What happens if one of them decides Earth's a strategic resource, or worse, a target?"

Max was quieter now, taken aback. "But if their technology's so far ahead of ours, how can we hope to fight them?"

"You know how."

Max made a face. "The new ships?"

"Bingo."

"But those pilots, it's slaughter."

Ann banged her palm on the rim of the steering wheel. "It's necessary! We have to make those ships work."

"So, the ends justify the means?"

"In this case, yes they do." She banged the wheel again, hammering home each syllable. "We're talking about the survival of the human race."

They passed through Acton and Perivale. The A40 became the M40, and they crossed the glowing orange ribbon of the M25.

"What happens now?" Max said. "Are you going to kill me?"

Ann took a deep breath. "That depends. Although we're working with those other countries, we haven't shared with them the technology we recovered from the crashed ship, which makes you and your downloaded files a serious security risk."

Max twisted in his seat and stared at her.

"The Americans take this kind of thing very seriously," she continued. "God alone knows what the Chinese are capable of."

"And you?"

She gripped the wheel and flexed her shoulders. She was keeping to a steady 70 mph, staying inconspicuous.

"I'm not going to kill you," she said. "You're an idiot, but you're also my cousin."

"S-so, what are we going to do?"

She checked the mirror again. There were cars behind them but no sign they were being tailed.

"There's only one way out," she said. "I can get you onto a technical team, working on the project. We need bright young minds with the kind of skills you've got."

Max looked pained.

"Isn't there another way?"

"No."

The wipers clunked back and forth across the windscreen. They were out in open countryside now. Ahead lay Beaconsfield and High Wycombe, and a small airstrip on the outskirts of Oxford. If they could reach it, there would be a plane waiting.

If...

Searchlights crested a hill to their right. Helicopters. Two of them, hugging the treetops, spiralling in like sharks; their flanks painted with the eye-twisting black and white stripes of dazzle camouflage – geometric patterns designed to conceal their exact shape and size.

"Crap."

Ann slowed as the choppers descended. They were approaching a bridge. One of the aircraft took up position behind the car, blocking traffic. The other came down on the far side of the bridge. Both hovered a few feet above the tarmac. Their crazy paint jobs made it hard for the pattern recognition software in her Lens to get a definite visual lock on either of them. On the opposite carriageway, cars swerved and skidded to a halt. Horns sounded.

Max looked around. "What do we do?"

Ann knew what was coming next. She hit the brakes. "Close your eyes," she said.

No sooner had the words left her mouth than the lead helicopter angled its searchlight into the car. Blinded, Max cried out, but Ann already had her door open. Her Lens had polarized, throwing a black dot over the light. As the car slowed, she twisted the wheel and rolled out.

She took the impact on her shoulder, thankful for the thickness of her coat. She had the gun in her hand. She rolled over twice and came up firing. She knew the helicopter's cockpit would be bullet-proof, so she aimed for the open hatch.

The first two shots killed the searchlight. To her left, she heard the stolen car's wing scrape the crash barrier at the foot of the bridge support. To her right, she saw curious motorists duck back into their vehicles. She kept firing, pumping bullets into the black-clad troops hanging in the helicopter's door.

When the trigger clicked empty, she sprinted for the car. Her legs were in peak condition, and she felt a surge of gratitude to her employers for the tune up at the Swiss clinic. Answering shots came from both helicopters. Automatic weapons clattered. Bullets zipped past her. She hit the car and slid across the bonnet, landing in a heap on the far side of the crash barrier. Bullets spanged off the old Ford's bodywork. A window shattered.

"Get out of there, Max."

"The door's blocked!"

"Use the window."

She fumbled a second magazine into her gun and got to her knees. She sent a couple of shots in the direction of each chopper. Masked troops were spilling out of both machines. She hit at least one of them, and the others dropped to the ground. Max's head and shoulders appeared through the car window. She grabbed the collar of his checked shirt and pulled, and they both fell sprawling into the gravel between the crash barrier and the concrete bridge support.

"Keep down," she hissed.

She blinked up her Lens's IM function and sent a pre-prepared SOS to an anonymous orbital inbox.

Max had cut his hands on broken glass. His palms were bleeding.

"They're shooting at us!"

"Help's coming."

She fired a couple more shots. The soldiers were working

their way to cover behind the barrier on the central reservation. The car sagged as their answering fire took out its tyres and shattered the remaining windows.

Max had his arms wrapped over his head. Blood dripped from the tips of his fingers.

"They want you alive," Ann said.

He looked up, eyebrows raised. His glasses were scratched. "They do?"

"That's why they're sat over there, trying to pick me off. If they wanted to kill you, they'd have used grenades by now."

A fresh burst of fire rattled the car's frame. Chips flew from the concrete stanchion supporting the bridge. Max curled himself tighter.

"Are you sure?"

Ann shrugged. She leaned down, pointed her gun into the gap under the car, and fired a volley at ankle height. On the other side of the road, one of their attackers cried out, and the bullets ceased.

"I've only got one more ammo clip," she said. "When that's gone, there'll be nothing to stop them walking over here to get us."

"You said help was coming?"

Ann checked the IM box in her Lens: there had been no reply to her message.

"It is. At least, I hope it is. We've just got to hold on until the cavalry arrives."

She fired the gun over the hood of the car, aiming carefully, trying to make each shot count. When it was empty, she ejected the spent magazine and clicked the fresh one into place. It was dry under the bridge. On either side, the black and white helicopters hovered in the drifting rain, the downdraught from their rotors whipping up spray from the wet road.

Max said, "Why are they doing this? Who are they?"

Ann squinted into the darkness.

"I don't think they're Chinese. They could be Russian, or Eastern European."

"I thought you said you were all working together?"

Ann laughed. "Nations only cooperate while they see an advantage in doing so."

There was a movement on the far side of the carriageway. The black-clad soldiers were inching forward, trying to outflank her. She sent a couple of shots into the closest, to encourage the rest to keep their heads down.

She said, "They don't want anyone getting too powerful and threatening their sovereignty. They don't want to submit to a world government."

Max rubbed his face. His fingers left bloody smudges on his cheek.

"So it's an arms race," he said. "Just like the Cold War."

Ann nodded. "Only this time we're all pretending we're on the same side."

Automatic fire rattled against the crash barrier. Ann rose to her knees and tried to shoot back. As she put her head level with the hood of the car, she saw Max's netbook on the car seat. She stretched over to grab it. As she lifted it out, bullets shredded the metal frame around her. Something bit her left cheek and she dropped back with a yelp of pain.

"Annabelle!" Max slithered over to her. "Are you all right? What happened?"

Her cheek stung. She raised her fingers to it and they came away bloody.

"Have I been shot?" she said.

Max screwed up his face. "I don't think so. But there's something..." He looked away.

Ann felt around the wound. Her fingertips brushed something sharp: a fragment of steel from the car. She tried to get hold of it but it was slippery with blood, and it hurt like hell.

"Max," she said. "Have you got your multi-tool?"

His hand went to his pocket.

"I've got it here."

"I need you to pull this out."

He hesitated, biting his lip as if trying to stop himself from being ill.

"Now, please."

From where she lay, she could see under the barrier and car to the huddled figures on the other side of the road. As Max leaned over her with the pliers, she gripped the pistol, ready to shoot at the first sign of movement.

Her eyes watered as Max tugged at the sliver of shrapnel. His cut hands were red with blood.

"It's stuck tight," he said. "I think it's in the bone."

Ann gritted her teeth. "Pull harder then," she said. She could feel warm blood running into her ear.

Max took a firm grip on the handle of his multi-tool and yanked. Ann screamed. Her hands clenched and the gun fired.

When she could see again, she found Max sitting before her with a nasty chunk of barbed metal clasped in the pliers' jaws. Now it was out, she needed to staunch the bleeding. She reached into her pocket and pulled out a handkerchief, which she wadded up and pressed to her face.

Beyond the car, black shapes flickered in the darkness.

"Looks like we're trapped," she said. It hurt to speak.

Max glanced over his shoulder. "Give me the gun."

"No way." Ann elbowed herself up into a sitting position. Over the noise of the helicopters, she could hear the sound of running boots.

"Get behind me," she said. She raised the gun and took a peep through the shattered windows of the car: the soldiers were closing.

To slow them down, she fired the last of her ammunition one-handed, and dropped to the dusty ground, wincing at the pain in her cheek.

Then she turned around and rested her back against the crash barrier. The pistol dangled from her fingertips.

"I guess this is it, then," she said. She flicked a glance at Max. "Listen, I—"

Her words were cut off by a sonic boom.

Something hit one of the choppers. Smoke billowed from its engine. It rose into the air and drifted towards the bridge.

Ann grabbed Max and pushed him to the floor.

"Get down!"

She heard the helicopter hit the parapet. It struck the span and recoiled, wobbling crazily as the pilot fought to regain control. Then it hit the ground on the far side of the motorway and its tail broke off. The main rotors dug into the soft earth bank and snapped, whipping the cockpit into the concrete bridge support, smashing it like an egg.

Moments later, a mirrored teardrop fell from the clouds. It jerked to a halt centimetres above the road, blocking all three lanes of the carriageway. Distorted reflections rippled on its curved surfaces.

The advancing troops froze, suddenly exposed and vulnerable in the centre of the carriageway.

"Get up," Ann said. She grabbed the netbook and hauled Max to his feet. They ran along the inside of the crash barrier, towards the ship. There were shouts from the soldiers, and she braced herself for shooting. No shots came. Instead, there was a flash of red light from the teardrop's tip, and when she looked back, the soldiers were lying in the central lane, charred and dead.

"Holy shit," Max said.

She pushed him forward. A hatch opened in the rippling hull and they bundled inside.

They lay panting, side-by-side on the cold deck of the airlock.

From inside, the hull wall appeared transparent. They could see everything: the bridge over the motorway; the dead soldiers; the waiting traffic; and the second helicopter rising into the air in an effort to escape.

Another red beam stabbed from the teardrop and the helicopter burst into pieces. Flaming debris spattered the road.

Ann dragged Max through the inner airlock door, into the ship's cabin. It was circular. There were white acceleration couches ringing the see-through wall. A glass, liquid-filled pillar stood in the centre. Floating inside was the shaven head, torso, and abdomen of a young boy. A thick bundle of wires protruded from the base of his skull, linking him into the ship's instruments. Black rubber sleeves hid the stumps of his amputated limbs, the nerves spliced into the navigation systems. Whatever the liquid was, he appeared to be breathing it.

"Please, take a seat," he said, his watery voice bubbling from a speaker set into the base of the column.

Max gawped. The kid was maybe seventeen years old. There were spots around his mouth. He wasn't a professional pilot; he looked like kind of a geek.

"This is John," Ann said, still pressing the handkerchief to her torn face. "He's one of our best."

Through the transparent hull, blue lights flashed beyond the headlights of the stalled traffic: the emergency services were coming. She pulled Max over to the acceleration couches and they strapped in.

"Okay, John," she said, "why don't you take us up?"

In the glass column, the boy grinned at her. He had braces on his teeth. He said, "Ladies and gentlemen, please fasten your seatbelts and return your tray tables to the upright position."

He closed his eyes and the drop-shaped ship punched into the sky without a sound. The ground fell away so fast Max cried out. Below them, the flaming wreck of the helicopter dwindled to a spark. The orange streetlights of Oxford and High Wycombe shrank until they resembled the embers of scattered campfires. Then they were through the cloud layer and rising towards a clear sky filled with stars.

Max looked down at his bloody hands. He said, "Jesus, what a mess."

Beside him, Ann dabbed her cheek. It still hurt like hell.

"I've gone to a lot of trouble to get you out, Max. I could have left you down there."

Max pushed up his glasses and rubbed his eyes. He looked at the amputee floating in the glass column and shuddered.

"He's just a kid."

Ann followed his gaze. "He used to be a hacker, like you. He's got a real feel for systems, an intuition that normal test pilots lack."

She turned her face to him. "As I said, we always need bright young minds."

Max looked at her in horror. "You want to put me in one of those tanks?"

Ann shrugged. "Think of it as your chance to volunteer."

HOT RAIN

A REEF STORY

Kenji had been betrayed – set up by Jack Finch and the fat guy, Kowalski. And now an innocent woman lay dead and there were police sirens closing in on him. He tried to lose himself among the pedestrians on the Avenue Independencia, but he was sweating, jumpy and drawing attention. Heads were turning as he passed.

After a subjective eternity, he spotted a promising side street and ducked between the crawling black and yellow taxis, ignoring their horns and curses.

Away from the main roads, he knew he could lose himself in the back streets of Buenos Aires. The city was one sprawling enormity of rat-runs and boulevards, with no central focus, no clear definition. The barrios piled up against one another, a mash of competing influences and contrasting styles. He squatted in a quiet doorway, panting, as a police helicopter clattered overhead. His heart raced in his chest. Then he was up again, running from street to street, alley to alley, until he reached the Che Dominique, a crumbling hotel overlooking the flea market on the Plaza Dorrego. He crashed past the reception desk and took the carpeted stairs three at a time, the gun in his coat thumping against his hip.

To his relief, his room was as he'd left it. He peeled a disposable paper phone from the pad on the bedside table and used it to call his client's lawyer.

"Where are you?" Maria Juarez's dark eyes burned through the low-res screen.

Kenji keyed up a phone menu and considered blocking the trace she had on his call. He didn't want to trust anyone until he knew why Finch and Kowalski had turned on him. But he needed her help: he was a hunted man, exposed and vulnerable. He stepped over to the window and checked the street. Advertising holograms burned above the downtown skyscrapers.

"I'm at the hotel," he said.

She let out a breath. "I'll be there in ten minutes."

When she arrived, she'd ditched her business suit for a pair of jeans and a black t-shirt. Kenji guessed she was trying to look inconspicuous, like a tourist. She even had a daypack on her shoulder.

"What happened?" she said.

He was sitting on the bed, still angry. "They didn't show for their shifts this morning. When I tried to track them down, Finch tried to kill me."

"Were there any casualties?"

"There was a bystander, a local. She got in the way. I hesitated and Finch shot her." He squeezed his hands together. "If I'd fired first, she might still be alive."

Juarez tapped her teeth with a fingernail. "Were there any witnesses?" she said. Even in casual clothes she moved and talked like a lawyer.

"A couple."

She took down as many details as he could remember, using a stylus to jot shorthand notes on her phone.

"I'm sending this all through to my office," she said. "They'll keep the police off our backs for as long as they can."

She led him down to her parked car. It was a black 1956 Ford sedan with a wide chrome grill.

"You get in the back," she said, "I'll drive."

A few minutes later, they were somewhere in the La Bocha district, moving slowly. The narrow streets were rough and raw, the air prickly with the heat of an approaching storm.

"We know why Finch attacked you," she said. "We received this a few minutes before you called." She transferred a video file from her phone to his. The picture was dark and shaky, obviously filmed on a handheld camera.

"That's Kowalski," he said. "But who's the kid on his knee? It looks like Garcia's daughter."

With her eyes on the road, Juarez shook her head. "It certainly does," she said.

She shifted gear and made a turn. The houses here were made of corrugated iron and pressed tin. They were painted blue, red and yellow. Heavy men in football shirts leaned in their doorways, smoking. The clouds on the horizon were black, like slate. "But Garcia's daughter's safe at home, with her father," she said. "What you're looking at there is a clone."

Kenji lifted the phone up to get a better look.

"Finch is threatening to torture and kill the girl unless Garcia pays him four million US dollars," Juarez said.

Kenji frowned. "That kid's got to be at least two years old."

Juarez nodded. Her voice was tight. "They've obviously been planning this a long time."

• •

Alejandro Garcia was one of the richest men in Buenos Aires. His company used cloning vats to grow slabs of beef, which he then sold as a cheaper, cruelty-free alternative to the meat produced by the traditional farmers. Maria Juarez was one of his most trusted lawyers and until an hour ago, Kenji had been part of a three-man security team contracted to keep him safe. Now, it appeared he was working alone.

"They must've got hold of a spare vat," he said, "and cloned the kid from a hair or skin sample." He scratched his chin. "Why doesn't Garcia go to the police?"

Juarez downshifted as she approached a red light, flicked a glance at him in the rear-view mirror. She said, "It's one of their stipulations. Any hint of police involvement and they kill the girl. Besides, Mr Garcia has every faith in your ability to track them down by yourself. You know them, you've worked with them, and you're an ex-cop – if anyone can find them, it's you." She brought the car to a halt at the line, drumming her fingers on the steering wheel, waiting for the lights to change. "Mr Garcia's willing to pay you a fair price if you bring the girl back alive."

"What about Finch and Kowalski?"

"Officially, he leaves them to your discretion. They were your business partners, and they betrayed you."

"And unofficially?"

The light turned green. Juarez revved the engine and the car rolled forward. "Unofficially, he trusts you'll ensure they never endanger his family again."

Kenji pulled out his gun and checked it. It was a late model recoilless Mauser and the grip nestled effortlessly in his hand. It felt solid and comforting. There were six shots in the magazine, another three loose in his pocket. Over the rumble of the engine, thunder cracked in the darkening sky. Fat drops of rain spattered the windshield.

"There is one condition," Juarez said. She turned into a

cobbled back street. "Firstly, I'm to accompany your investigation, to ensure you don't do anything to legally compromise my client."

"Fair enough," Kenji said, "but I can't promise to protect you if things get rough."

He slipped the gun into his belt, hoping he wouldn't have to use it. Then he replayed the video message on his phone. The kid on Kowalski's knee was crying.

"This is Grace," Finch said from behind the camera. "Send us the money by midnight tonight, or we kill her."

. .

Juarez took Kenji to a small, smoke-soaked café near the Recoleta cemetery. It was getting late and the rain had set in. The café windows were misted. A young couple laughed and shook their wet hair as they entered.

"So, how does Garcia feel about the girl?" Kenji asked.

Juarez leaned forward and spoke in a low voice. "He's furious. He loves his daughter, but the idea of a clone is driving him crazy. He resents it for making him vulnerable, but he's also unable to turn his back on it, as it's his flesh and blood."

She sat back and sipped her coffee. They were near the back of the room, at a table by the wall. "Besides," she continued, "he's standing for Congress this year, and he's always portrayed himself as a family man. If he walks away from this, and the news channels get hold of it, it could destroy him politically."

Kenji stirred his tea. "So, he'd like this whole affair wrapped up as quickly and quietly as possible?"

Juarez didn't look happy. "That's about the size of it."

Kenji scratched his head. The gun felt cold, heavy and awkward in his belt. "It's not going to be easy to find them," he said. "After our run-in this afternoon, they'll be keeping their heads low, avoiding their usual haunts."

Juarez dug in her pocket, pulled out a scrap of paper. There was an address on it, in Kowalski's handwriting. "Maybe not," she said. "I found this stuck to Kowalski's desk calendar. He'll be there from eleven."

Kenji looked at the address on the paper: it was a downtown strip joint, strictly members only. "I know the place," he said. He checked the clock on the bare brick wall – they had an hour to kill until eleven.

"Do you want to get something to eat?" Juarez asked. Kenji liked her. They'd worked well together over the last couple of years.

"I'm not hungry," he said.

Her phone rang. She answered it, and then passed it across the table. "Mr Garcia would like to speak to you," she said.

· ·

Alejandro Garcia had a greying moustache and a complexion like weathered marble. He was sitting at a desk, wearing a white cotton shirt and a single diamond earring.

"Hello, Mr Shiraki. I trust you're making progress?"

Kenji looked at Juarez. "We're working on a lead," he said.

Garcia nodded. "That's good. Now tell me, are you experiencing any nausea or giddiness?"

Kenji narrowed his eyes. "Why do you ask?"

On the phone's little screen, the other man brought his hands together and steepled his fingers. "Have you ever heard of a parasite by the name of *toxoplasma gondii*, Mr Shiraki? It's a most unpleasant little beast, I'm afraid. It's most commonly found in rats. It makes them unafraid of cats."

"Unafraid?"

"Reckless, even. It wants the rat to get eaten, you see, so it can infect the cat." Kenji wrinkled his nose and glanced around the half-empty café. On the screen, Garcia's eyes grew hard and dark, like cooling steel. "Mister Shiraki, the cup of tea you were given contained a specially tailored cocktail of hormones and dopamine, designed to produce the same effect in you." He waited a beat, watching Kenji's reaction, and then continued.

"Your former colleagues have threatened to kill my daughter's clone at midnight tonight. If you manage to find her in time, I'll supply you with an antidote. If you fail, then like the rat you'll become increasingly reckless and suicidal, looking for trouble. By one o'clock, one way or another, you'll most likely be dead."

Kenji pushed his half-finished tea away. "This poison's already in me?" he said.

Garcia said, "Think of it as an incentive," and broke the connection, leaving Kenji staring at a blank display. He looked over at Juarez. Down the street, through the rain, a church bell rang the hour.

"What are you going to do?" she asked.

．•

They took the car downtown. The streets smelled of carbon monoxide and cigarette smoke. Juarez drove, turning the big wheel with her small hands. In the passenger seat, Kenji leaned his head against the window, listening to the thud of the wipers.

"For what it's worth," Juarez said, "I'm sorry."

They were crossing an elegant Italian-style piazza at the end of a wide, tree-lined boulevard. Three-dimensional projections of brightly-dressed tango dancers stepped and swaggered above the buildings. Kenji watched them strut, watched the continuous play of tacky advertisements on their traditional sequinned costumes.

A few turns beyond the square, they pulled up in front of the strip club. Juarez had a matt black Colt automatic in the glove box. She held it awkwardly, unsure where to point it. He put a steadying hand on her arm.

"Stay here," he said.

He splashed across the road. There was a man on the door, a local. He was big, but Kenji didn't stop.

"I want to see Tony Caldera," he said.

Inside, the club was deserted. As Kenji pushed through the door a couple of bored, surgically enhanced dancers eyed him from the stage. Tony Caldera, the club's owner, fluttered toward him in an ill-fitting suit.

"Mr Shiraki! So nice to see you! What's your pleasure?"

Kenji gave him a look. "You know me better than that, Tony."

The man stopped. He had greased hair and a thin moustache that lay like sweat on his top lip. "Indeed I do." A few years ago, he'd been a police informant. Now he was a small-time hustler with big ideas. "You look pale," he said. "Let me get you a drink." He crossed to the bar and produced a bottle of Cuervo Gold. He poured a couple of shots and brought them over. As he put them on the table, Kenji pulled out the Mauser.

"I'm here for Kowalski," he said.

Caldera looked at the gun. For a second, he froze. Then he shrugged. "He's upstairs, second room on the right."

Kenji took the stairs two at a time, heart racing, legs shaky with adrenalin. When he reached Kowalski's room, he paused to catch his breath. The gun in his hand had the safety off. He had six shots and if anyone startled him, they'd get the lot.

From inside, he heard muffled voices. He recognised

Kowalski's. He took a deep breath and counted to three. Then he kicked the door in.

Kowalski was tied to the radiator beneath the window, his dominatrix standing over him in jodhpurs and riding boots, holding a crop in her hand. Kowalski struggled with the scarves that bound his wrists. His hairy legs were bare and there were red welts on the pallid skin.

"For God's sake, Kowalski – why can't you get your sex on the Internet, like everyone else?"

The fat man responded with a string of obscenities. "You aren't getting anything from me," he snarled. "You touch me and you'll never see the kid again."

Kenji pushed the dominatrix aside, leaned in close and slapped him across the head.

"We're not playing that game," he said. He felt a sudden wildness. His palm stung from the slap. The Mauser nestled in his other hand, aiming itself effortlessly. "Where's the girl?"

Kowalski turned away. Despite being tied to a radiator, he seemed to think he had the upper hand in this negotiation, seemed to think he held all the cards.

Another slap got his attention.

"I'm just here to see Tony," he said.

Kenji squatted down, bringing their eyes level. Rain hammered on the window. "I need to find that kid," he said.

Kowalski's lip was bleeding. He smelled of sweat and cheap cologne. "I don't know what you're talking about."

Kenji leaned forward, pressing his gun into the fat man's gut. "Where is she?"

Kowalski turned away and spat blood. His teeth were red. "Why don't you ask Juarez?" he said.

• •

Kenji emerged from the club pushing Tony Caldera ahead of him. The hot rain prickled his face. He had the empty Mauser in one hand, the tequila bottle in the other. As he approached the big black Ford, Juarez leaned over and opened the passenger door.

"Have you got a cigarette?" he asked.

She reached into her coat and pulled out a pack of imported Marlboro. She lit one and handed it over. "How did it go in there?"

Kenji inhaled deeply, feeling the smoke scar his throat. "Let's just say that I've accepted Kowalski's resignation."

"He's dead?"

"Yes."

She took the cigarette back with a shaking hand and put it to her lips. "Did you kill him?"

Kenji nodded. His pulse was throbbing in his temples. "I didn't expect it to be so easy," he said. He pushed Tony Caldera into the back seat, then slid in beside her. He put the tequila in the glove box with her Colt.

Juarez blew blue smoke at the rear-view mirror. "Did he tell you anything?"

Kenji closed his eyes, leaning his head back against the seat. "The kid's in Caldera's warehouse," he said.

．·

Tony Caldera stayed quiet as they made for the river.

"This hormone cocktail," Juarez said in the darkness, "do you think it's transferable?"

Kenji shrugged. He'd been trying not to think about it.

"I'm just worried it could spread," she continued, "like a suicide virus."

Kenji lifted the Mauser, slotted his last three bullets into its magazine. "It's not a virus," he said.

"Yes, but you know what I mean?"

Kenji snapped the magazine closed. "Garcia's no fool," he said. "He's not going to risk loosing something like this on the public, not even with you as his lawyer."

The car bumped off the road onto a patch of scrubby dockland. The headlights played across a row of run-down warehouses by the water's edge. Kenji checked his watch. It was a little after eleven-thirty. He shifted around in his seat.

"Okay, Caldera, which one is it?" he said.

The other man looked nervous, but concealed it by fussing with his cuffs. "You know, they forced me to comply," he said. "That's why Kowalski was at the club. They've got a lot on me – they know my operation."

Kenji scowled. He leaned over and took Caldera's lapel in one hand. "Which one is it?"

Caldera shied away. "The last one on the right," he said.

．．

They stood against the warehouse, waiting for Caldera to unlock the door. Underfoot, tough yellow grass filled every crack in the shattered concrete. Out on the water, ship lights slid like restless ghosts through the wet night. Kenji was ready for a fight. His breath came quick and shallow and his hair dripped with rain and sweat. He was remembering teenage gang fights on the Hong Kong waterfront; a bruised and bitter adolescence spent lurching from one brawl to the next.

Juarez put a hand on his arm. "Are you all right?"

He shrugged her off. "Kowalski mentioned you," he said.

"Really?"

"He said I should ask *you* where the girl was."

Juarez shifted uncomfortably. "That's absurd."

"Is it?" He pulled the scrap of paper from his pocket and turned it so she could see Kowalski's handwriting.

"Where'd you get this?" he said.

"I told you; I found it in his office, on the calendar."

Kenji screwed it up and let it fall. He knew she was lying but he couldn't concentrate. The Mauser was twitchy in his hand and his chest was as tight as a fist. He turned his back on her. So far, she'd been the only one he could trust.

When Caldera got the door open, he stepped through without hesitation.

Inside it was dark and damp-smelling. The only light came from the back, from a prefab foreman's office with frosted windows. He moved towards it, Juarez following, staying close. They passed stacked crates containing smuggled Turkish cigarettes, stolen American laptops and knock-off German porn. Over by the wall, a row of familiar shapes caught his eye – a row of vats. They were the same model Garcia's company used to grow its beef.

Kenji walked over. Each of the vats had a label stuck on it, and each label had a name. Kenji leaned close and walked along the row, reading. The names were those of prominent businessmen and politicians in Buenos Aires.

"They were planning to do this again," he said.

Juarez was examining a vat at the far end of the row. The foetus floating inside had a smudge of dark hair and his hands were squeezed into tiny fists. Kenji ran a hand over the smooth glass lid. He saw how small and perfect and vulnerable the child was, and something broke inside him.

• •

Kenji strode up the wooden stairs to the foreman's office. He had three bullets and he wanted to put every one of them through Jack Finch's heart. There was no doubt this time, no hesitation. Any friendship they may have shared had died the second he laid eyes on the baby in the vat.

He held the Mauser at his side and walked with no attempt at stealth. His pulse battered in his ears and he couldn't tell where his anger stopped and the effects of the hormones began. And he didn't care. Right now, he wanted to let it all out. He wanted revenge. He wanted to make Finch pay for the unwanted cloned children, for the hormones, and for the dead woman on the street.

His wristwatch beeped. It was eleven forty-five. He had fifteen minutes.

He smacked the office door open with a flat palm and Finch came up from behind the desk with his shotgun raised. Kenji got off a shot, but fell back onto the stairs as the shotgun blew splinters from the doorframe. Something took a bloody bite out of his sleeve, but he'd seen enough. He'd seen the layout; seen Grace Garcia huddled in the corner at the far end of the room.

He heard a solid *cah-chunk* as Finch pumped another shot into the chamber, and the child began to cry.

"Stop shooting!" Juarez shouted.

Kenji ignored her. He leaped sideways off the stairs, firing through the office's frosted glass at Finch's shadow. The glass shattered. But Kenji hit the floor before he could see if he'd hit his target.

For a few seconds, all he could do was lie gasping on the floor, waiting for the pain in his shoulder to subside.

Finch appeared in the office doorway. He wore a red and yellow Hawaiian shirt over baggy combat trousers. He held the shotgun with one hand, and had the other pressed against his midriff. The fingers were bright with seeping blood. He saw Kenji and snarled.

"Come on," he panted, "don't tell me you wouldn't have done it if you'd thought of it?"

Kenji looked around. He was defenceless. He'd dropped the empty Mauser when he hit the crates and now he couldn't see it.

"Why?" he croaked.

Finch snorted. From somewhere in his wounded gut he pulled a laugh. "Some influential ranch owners are paying us a lot of money to see Garcia suffer." He shifted the shotgun, getting a better grip. "By the way, what happened to Kowalski? Is he under arrest?"

"He's dead."

Finch shrugged. "Too bad. I only sent him to the club to keep him out of the way."

He took a step forward and brought the shotgun to bear. He closed one eye and steadied his aim. Kenji looked up the barrel – it was as wide as a railway tunnel, yet somehow, he felt no fear.

"Goodbye, Kenji," Finch said. But before he could fire, Juarez stepped from behind a stack of pallets with the little Colt in both hands.

"Don't do it," she said.

Her gaze flicked past Finch, to the office door. Grace stood there, confused and frightened, sniffling into her sleeve.

Finch curled his lip. "Or you're going to do what?"

Without thinking, Kenji reached up and grabbed the shot-gun's hot barrel. He twisted it, hard. Finch shouted, and the gun went off, into the floor.

Startled, Juarez fired with her eyes closed. Her first two bullets hit Finch in the arm and chest, spinning him around. The third blew a hole in the back of his head.

She stepped over him as he fell and took the stairs in two

quick strides. Her trainers squeaked on the painted wood. By the time Kenji felt able to stand, she had Grace in her arms.

"I knew it," Kenji said. His shirt was scorched from the shotgun blast and he knew he was lucky to be alive.

Juarez looked wary. "Knew what?"

Kenji took a step toward her. "You've been part of this all along," he said. Juarez shifted Grace's weight on her hip. She held the little pistol gracelessly, almost with embarrassment. Kenji looked at the gun. Then he sat on a crate. His head pounded.

"I'm the only mother she's ever known," Juarez said. "She's more my daughter than she is Garcia's."

Kenji shook his head. "Then how could you be a part of this?"

Juarez tightened her grip on Grace, who snuffled into her shoulder. "I didn't know they were actually planning to kill her, I thought they'd bluff. When they took her from me and I realised how serious they were, I went to Garcia."

Kenji slipped a hand under his shirt. His shoulder hurt where he'd landed on it. "You told him everything?"

She shook her head. "I simply suggested we coerce you into finding your colleagues. He doesn't know I'm involved."

"And the poison tea?" His fists tightened.

"That was Garcia's idea – he asked me to put the stuff in your tea, to ensure your cooperation."

The warehouse door scraped open. Tony Caldera stood silhouetted against the city lights, weighing up the situation. When he saw the gun in Juarez's hand, he seemed to relax.

"So," he asked her, "what do you want to do now?"

• •

They handcuffed Kenji to one of the crates and stepped outside to talk. When they returned, Juarez freed him and helped him out to the car, through the rain. She left Caldera looking after Grace.

"I've spoken to Tony – he's going to get us onto one of those Japanese container ships," she said.

"You and Grace?"

"Yes. Kowalski arranged it as his escape route in case things went wrong, and now we're taking his place."

Kenji gritted his teeth. He was woozy and in pain, and she held the only weapon. "I can't let you take her," he said.

She helped him slide into the driver's seat and slipped her keys into the ignition. "Of course you can. Tony's got a powerboat tied up on the water behind the warehouse."

Kenji shook his head. "I can't let you. If you go, I'm going to die." He checked his watch – there were less than five minutes until Garcia's deadline. The muscles in his arms and legs twitched beneath the skin and his mouth was dry, his tongue raw.

Tony appeared at the warehouse door. He held Grace by the hand. The little girl looked cold, scared and miserable.

"She's my daughter," Juarez said. "If Garcia gets hold of her, I'll never see her again."

In the distance, Kenji heard police sirens. He saw Juarez stiffen. "You played me all along," he said.

She looked away. "I only did what I had to, for her." She jerked her head at the warehouse door, where Grace stood forlornly, the hot rain flattening her hair. Kenji felt a surge of pity for the girl, and a wild disregard for his own safety. If Garcia didn't want Grace, why shouldn't Juarez have her?

"Go," he said hoarsely. "And take the girl with you."

Juarez bit her lip. "Thank you." She handed him the Colt. "You may need this."

Kenji dropped it on the passenger seat. Juarez's eyes glittered in the light of the holograms burning over the downtown skyscrapers. "What are you going to do?" she asked.

He pulled the door shut and wound the stiff window down. His hands trembled. "Let me worry about that. Just get yourselves as far away from here as you can."

The sirens were louder now.

"What about Garcia?"

Kenji gripped the wheel. "Leave him to me." He turned the ignition and the old Ford shuddered into life. He knew he'd get the antidote he needed, whatever it took. If Garcia argued, that'd be fine. He had the gun on the seat beside him and there was a half-bottle of tequila in the glove box. His whole body shook with murderous adrenalin. He felt reckless and unstoppable, and he wanted revenge.

GONZO LAPTOP

A REEF STORY

Running late, I pushed through the entrance to the new
Willesden shopping mall in West London, skateboard in hand.
It was early morning and some of the stores still had their metal
shutters down – but that didn't stop their automatic spambots
from pinging my phone with offers and appeals as I passed.

40% OFF TODAY!

CLOSING SALE

RECESSION-BUSTING DEALS!

Spread over four levels, the mall had been open only a
year but already some of its shops were vacant, their windows
scabbed over with graffiti and old newspaper. Yawning, I
collected my usual breakfast order of coffee and falafel from
the food stall by the entrance and took an escalator up to
the third floor, to the corridor leading towards the car park
pay stations. There was only one shop on that corridor – an
empty book store abandoned when its chain went bust, its
windows whitewashed with flaking paint. I knocked on its

glass door − four slow raps followed by one quick one, and then a final slow one − Morse code for "OK".

"It's me," I said.

I heard the lock turn. The door cracked an inch and I was eyeball-to-eyeball with my bloodshot and bespectacled business partner and former classmate, Lenny Fisher.

"You're late, Alex." Len pulled the door wide and I slipped inside to the familiar smells of dust and failed dreams. Old promo posters peeled from the walls; paperback books lay piled on the unstuck carpet tiles.

I dumped my shoulder bag on the floor and leaned my board against the wall. "It's only just gone nine."

"More like ten past."

A laptop stood on the counter at the end of the room, where the cash tills used to be. It was an old model but we'd tricked it out with extra memory and a faster processor. We'd even upgraded the webcam built into the top of its screen casing.

"How are the markets this morning, Len?"

He removed his wireless headset. "Still pretty grumpy, I'm afraid." He'd been doing the night shift, monitoring the markets in Asia and America. Beneath his glasses, his eyes were red-rimmed and his hair wild, his chin fuzzy with stubble. He'd left an empty pizza box beside the computer. I pushed it off the counter onto the floor.

"You know, it wouldn't hurt you to clear up around here once in a while."

"Fuck you, Alex."

We both smiled. Len looked dead on his feet. I said: "Go home and get some sleep."

He took his glasses off and yawned. "Keep an eye on Tanguy and Larsson," he said. "Sell if they reach five Euros apiece."

He grabbed up his stuff and left. I locked the door behind

him and then checked the results of the night's trading, to find we were up around five hundred Euros, which brought our total profits for the week to something approaching six grand. Not bad. It proved that even in the depths of an economic recession, there was money to be made picking the bones of failing dotcoms — and it certainly beat working for a living. We weren't even paying tax. Because we were both under eighteen, we were trading anonymously, using a nested series of fictitious shell companies and accessing the markets via the mall's ubiquitous Wi-Fi cloud, siphoning all our profits into offshore accounts. We were going to use the money to pay our way through college. After that, Len wanted enough to buy one of the new studio apartments by the river, and I wanted to travel to Europe, the Far East and Australia.

I opened a new window on the laptop and called up a real-time webcam view of Sydney Harbour, filmed from the roof of an office block in Kirribilli. It was late afternoon over there. I liked the clean white light of the Australian sun, and the deep, wholesome blue of the harbour waters. I left it open in the background as I ate my breakfast and worked, playing the stock markets in London, Madrid and Frankfurt.

In the first hour, I made a lot of small deals, spreading the risk, investing in companies with rapidly rising share prices. I bought high as the price approached the peak of its parabola and then bailed almost immediately, making a small profit before it began its inevitable slide back down. I had almost a sixth sense for it, an ability to predict the exact moment the price would stall, so I could make a quick buck before it did.

I wasn't infallible, of course, and over the next three hours, I twice took a bath on shares that fell before I could unload them — but even so, by eleven-thirty, I'd made another two hundred Euros.

At midday, Lisa came by. She was the third member of our operation. She was nineteen, a couple of years older than Len and me, and a friend of Len's sister from art school. We were both a little in awe of her and, truth be told, I'd had a crush on her for years. She worked in the mall and it had been her idea to use the old bookstore as a base of operations. I let her in and she handed me a packaged vegetable pasty with yesterday's sell-by date on it.

"I thought you could do with some lunch," she said. She had blue hair and a lip ring, and a shiny black pendant.

"It's new, do you like it?" she said, holding it out to me on the end of its chain.

I shrugged. I'd seen life-loggers before. "It's very nice."

She fingered it with a strange, sad smile. "Don't worry, it's turned off. I bought it at the weekend to cheer myself up."

I made sure the door was locked. "Is there something wrong?" I asked.

She looked up at me. "I broke up with Ian on Friday."

I blinked in surprise, unsure how to react. Ian was her boss at the health food shop. She'd been seeing him for a few months but I'd never met him. From what I'd been able to gather, the majority of their relationship outside working hours had been taking place online, in MMORPGs and chat rooms. "I'm sorry to hear that," I said.

She shook her head. "Don't be. He was an arsehole and I'm better off without him."

I walked back over to the laptop. She didn't follow, and she didn't ask about the business. I knew she wasn't interested. All she wanted was a cut of the profits at the end of each month, to supplement her wages.

"We've done okay this week," I said, "although the tax people have been all over us. We've had to create two new front companies in the last two days."

I put the pasty down on the counter and brushed pizza crumbs from the brown envelope Len had left for her. I handed it over and she opened the flap. There were some colourful European bank notes inside, held together with a paperclip. She pulled them out and folded them, and then tucked them into her jacket pocket.

"Aren't you going to count them?" I said.

"Do I need to?" Her eyes were green and her lips red. When she moved, her pendant caught the light. I walked with her to the door and unlocked it. As I pulled it open, she said: "Listen, I'm on my lunch break right now, but do you fancy meeting up later, for a drink or something?"

I glanced nervously up and down the corridor. I didn't want to be seen. If we lost this place, we'd have to find somewhere else with privacy and free 24-hour Wi-Fi. I looked down at her. She was standing very close and her blue hair smelled of peppermint. Her black pendant hung in the cleavage of her low-cut top.

"S-sure," I said, suddenly stuttering.

She gave my arm a gentle squeeze, looking amused. "Okay, I'll text you later."

She kissed me on the cheek and I closed the door behind her. I leaned my forehead against its painted glass until I heard her footsteps retreating back in the direction of the atrium, then let out the breath I hadn't realised I'd been holding.

I touched my cheek where she'd kissed it, and then went to make a cup of coffee and nuke the pasty she'd given me in the small staff kitchen at the back of the shop.

There was a cupboard in there filled with rolled-up posters, signed hardbacks and other promotional junk. As I waited for the kettle to boil and the microwave to ping, I poked through it, hoping to find something useful I could swipe, like a book token or a USB stick.

At the back of the cupboard's top shelf, I struck gold: a brand new ten terabyte external hard drive, still wrapped in cellophane and roughly half the size of my phone. Hardly believing my luck, I pulled it out and read the words etched into its black casing:

100 YEARS OF GONZO: 1937-2037

The dates meant nothing. I slipped the drive into the leg pocket of my combat trousers. The kettle had boiled. I poured a cup of coffee and took it back into the main body of the shop, where I spent a few minutes checking out the New York stock exchange, which had just opened.

By the time I'd made a few deals, it was almost one-thirty. I fished out the drive and turned it over in my hands. It looked practically unused. I thought if I wiped the promotional data from it, I could resell it for at least a hundred Euros – which would be another hundred I could put towards my college and travel plans.

With a smile, I tore off the cellophane, crinkled it up and dropped it on the dirty floor. I pulled out the drive's retract-able USB cable and plugged it into the port on my laptop.

"Okay." I rubbed my hands together gleefully. "Let's see what we've got."

I scanned the contents of the drive, giving an appreciative whistle as a long list of files appeared. The drive's memory held the complete texts of over a hundred books and novels, thousands of photographs, and several days' worth of music and film. I scrolled through it all until I came to an application file marked 'reader', which I clicked, expecting it to open a device for viewing the media files. Instead, the screen blanked and a face appeared – a handsome face beneath a camouflage bush hat, with sad eyes looking back at me from behind tinted aviator shades.

Frowning, I leaned closer to the screen. A dialogue box at the bottom asked if I'd like to run the program.

"What's this?" I said. I tapped the laptop's mouse pad, wheeling the cursor over to the "No" option – but before I could press it, there was an urgent knock at the shop's painted glass window.

"Alex, let me in!"

Lisa. Cursing, I put my coffee down and unlocked the door. I opened it just enough to drag her inside.

She was out of breath.

"Alex, I've done something really incredibly stupid." She opened her fist to reveal the black life-logger pendant she'd been wearing a couple of hours earlier.

"What have you done? Have you broken it?"

"No, but Alex, when I came here before, I thought I'd turned it off but I hadn't. It was on the whole time."

I felt the colour drain out of my face. "It recorded everything?"

Lisa closed her eyes and nodded. "It's worse than you think. Ian has access to my feed. He uses it to check up on me when I'm on my own in the shop. If he sees this place and decides to get vindictive..." She made a face.

I put a hand over my eyes and took a deep, shuddering breath.

"Are you telling me you've posted video evidence of our illegal share trading operation on the *fucking internet*?"

Lisa screwed her face tighter.

"Yes..."

I kicked over a pile of abandoned paperbacks and stalked back to the counter. It wasn't just video, either. Those little devices recorded their wearer's GPS location, temperature and heart rate, as well as everything they saw and heard, and downloaded it all onto the web as a live feed, creating a real-time, searchable blog. So far, we'd managed to avoid attracting unwelcome attention from the mall's private security firm, not to mention the tax office and the fraud squad. But if Ian got hold of all that information and decided to blow the whistle, we could find ourselves in some seriously hot water.

"I'm sorry," Lisa said.

I turned and glared at her.

"Help me with this stuff." I pointed to the laptop and hard drive. "If there's even a chance Ian's going to call security, we're going to have to clear out right now, before anyone comes looking."

Lisa pushed one hand up the side of her head, brushing back her blue hair. "Maybe it's not too late," she said. "He's probably at lunch. He might not have checked up on me yet and if so, we can just delete it before he does."

I clenched my fists. My heart thumped. "Can you do that?"

Lisa let her hand drop to her side. "It *must* be possible to edit a life-log, otherwise what happens if you accidentally record yourself taking a dump or fiddling your taxes?"

I looked into her eyes for a long moment and then smiled. I couldn't help myself.

"Okay, let's do it." I span the laptop to face her.

She frowned. "What's that?"

I glanced down. "I don't know. It was on this hard drive I found in the back room. I think it's an advert or something."

"It looks like Hunter S. Thompson."

I considered the face again and shrugged: "If you say so."

Lisa tilted her head to the side. "No," she said, "it's definitely him."

She put her fingers on the mouse pad, moved the cursor from 'No' to 'Yes', and clicked. The face on the screen gave a start. The blue eyes blinked, looking around, getting their bearings, and the man, Thompson, coughed, clearing his throat.

"Where am I?" His eyes were wild and his voice was high with alarm. He looked up at me. "And who the hell are you?"

• •

We found a way to pause the program, freezing Thompson's face: chin thrust out indignantly, black brows furrowed.

"It's AI," Lisa said, "It's got to be."

I couldn't take my eyes from the screen. "But he's looking straight at me."

Lisa flicked her hand. "Ah, that's just an illusion. Unless..." She tapped her fingernail on the webcam built into the laptop's casing, looking thoughtful. "Let's try something," she said. She touched the mouse pad again, restarting the program.

"Hello," she said.

The face on the screen shook itself and turned its baleful gaze on her.

"Well, hello yourself," it said. "Would you like me to read you something?"

Lisa shook her head, fascinated. She leaned forward. "Can you really see me?"

Thompson's lips twitched in a smile. "I couldn't miss you with all that blue hair, now, could I?" His animated eyes scanned the room, taking in the disassembled bookshelves and piles of abandoned paperbacks. "Say, this doesn't look much like a book launch to me. I'm *s'posed* to be giving a reading. There's *s'posed* to be an audience and I'm *s'posed* to be reading my book."

I moved in close to Lisa, peering at the screen. "The store went bust," I said.

Thompson's face fell. "Oh, man. Then who the hell are you two?"

"I'm Alex and this is Lisa."

He looked up at us. "You won't turn me off again, will you?"

. •

Rifling back through the cupboard, Lisa found the notes that accompanied the promotional hard drive. She brandished them at the image of the man on the laptop screen.

"It says here, and I quote, you're 'an artificial Turing intelligence fed with all the books, articles and letters written by Hunter S. Thompson during his lifetime, and all the subsequent memoirs of his friends and contemporaries, plus all the available and relevant photographs, film clips and TV appearances' – and that you're programmed to behave as if you are the man himself, 'based on behavioural parameters implied by the contents of those files.'"

She looked up. Hunter was watching her. Under his checked shirt and white t-shirt, he had a muscular neck and wide, football-hero shoulders. Back then, I didn't know much about artificial intelligence. I still don't, if you want the truth. But there was something about Hunter – the gleam in his eye, the way he flexed his jaw – that left me in no doubt he was alive. He had charisma to spare. He was, in all senses of the word, *animated*.

"I don't know about any of that," he said with a sad smile, "I'm just me, here, now. All dressed up and nowhere to go." He looked at me. "You know who I am though, don't you sport?"

I scratched my stomach through my t-shirt. "I read your book at school, the one about Las Vegas. I wrote an essay on it."

Hunter's eyes widened in surprise. "At school, huh?"

Lisa was still reading: "You're programmed to read sections of your work to specially invited audiences, as part of the hundredth anniversary of your birth," she said.

Hunter rolled his eyes. "Yada yada yada. Those sick bastards. Just because they put me in this here box, it doesn't follow they get to tell me what to do."

There was a knock at the shop door and the handle rattled as someone tried it.

A voice said: "This is mall security. Is there anyone in there?"

Lisa and I looked at each other. She grabbed my hand. Her eyes were wide and frightened. "What are we going to do?"

I looked down at Hunter.

"The pigs?" he said. "Screw 'em. Let's blow this joint."

• •

We took the rear fire escape door that opened into the car park. Lisa had a car there, an old Peugeot converted to bio-diesel. We piled into it, with me in the shotgun seat, the laptop and hard drive on my knees running on battery power, my skateboard and bag on the back seat.

"We can go back to my place and erase my life-log," Lisa said.

She took us out into traffic. Outside the mall, it was a bright, hard autumn day, with showers of yellow leaves swirling down from the pavement trees.

At Hunter's request, I held the laptop up, so the camera faced the windscreen.

"Where in the hell are we anyway?" he said.

"This is west London," Lisa replied, changing gear and working the clutch.

"Ohio?"

"England."

"And where are you taking me?"

Lisa sped through a set of traffic lights as they switched from green to amber. "We're going to my place."

I made a face. "I'm not sure that's such a good idea. If Ian knows about the share trading, he could have reported us to the police, or the Inland Revenue."

Lisa gripped the steering wheel. "Then what are we going to do, Alex?"

From the laptop's speakers, Hunter's voice was low and urgent. "Alex, how much money do you have on you?"

I turned the laptop around. "About forty Euros," I said.

He frowned, nonplussed. "Is that a lot?"

"Some."

He brightened. "Then let's hit the fucking road. There's no way those pigs can touch you if you don't stop moving."

Lisa was concentrating on the traffic. We were on the North Circular, near Ealing, heading south towards her place in Heston. She said: "Where do you suggest we go, then?"

Hunter grinned a toothy, rogue's grin. "I always say: if in doubt, head west."

．•

Len phoned me, a few minutes later.

"I've just been past the shop," he said. "There are security guards crawling all over it. What's going on?"

I glanced across at Lisa. We were on the M4 now, heading out of town, the afternoon sun shining on her blue hair. "We got caught."

On the other end of the line, Len made a choking noise. "What about the money?"

"It's safe, as far as I know. At least, for now..." I felt my financial sixth sense kick in. I knew we'd peaked. From here on, the only way was down. "Look, if the police and the Revenue are involved, they're going to trace the transactions sooner or later. Just get to a cash machine, take out as much as you can, and we'll see what happens."

I switched my phone off. "Pull off at the next services," I said.

• •

We left the motorway just south of Reading, rolling to a halt in the car park of a service area surrounded by fields and hedges. I left the laptop containing Hunter on the passenger seat. I pulled a baseball cap from my bag and went inside, past the concession stands and the McDonald's, to the cash machines, where I withdrew as much cash as I could, pushing my phony business and personal cards to their limits, all the while keeping the brim of my cap as low as possible to hide my face from the security cameras.

On the way back, pockets bulging with banknotes, I paused long enough to pick up two bottles of spring water and half a dozen sandwiches and then called Len back from a burner phone. He'd taken refuge in an internet café in Ealing and he sounded angry.

"I don't get it," he said. "At least we were doing something. We were earning money instead of moaning about the recession. The government should be encouraging us not trying to close us down. If this country's going to pull through, it's going to need people like us."

He paused to take a breath and I said: "Look, you're probably in the clear. If all Ian's got is the footage from this morning, then no one knows you're involved. There are probably fingerprints in the shop but what do they prove? Keep your head down and you should be okay."

He was silent for a few seconds. "What about you?" he said.

I shifted my weight from one foot to the other. "The only two bits of evidence linking Lisa and me to the operation are the life-log and the laptop. If we can get rid of them both, we'll be okay."

"You want me to see about the log?"

"Can you?"

"No problem. Even if Ian's seen the feed, he won't be able to prove anything if it's been erased. Just get Lisa to text me her passwords and I'll get it sorted."

"Thanks, man."

I hung up and ditched the handset. When I got back to the car, I found Lisa in conversation with Hunter, clutching her pendant. She was saying, "Your books are all based on events from your life, right? Well, that's the same thing as life-logging. That's life-logging, Seventies-style."

She looked up as I slid into my seat. I handed her a bottle of water. "I think we're going to be okay," I said.

• •

Even with the evidence gone, Lisa thought it best we stay out of town for a few days, just in case the police or the tax men came knocking. For want of a better option, we continued west on the motorway, passing Swindon and Bristol, heading into Wales and the lowering sun over Cardiff and Swansea.

Lisa said, "I have an aunt we can stay with. She runs a guest house near St David's."

Sitting on my knee, Hunter was digging it all, watching the white line unroll under the car's wheel with inexhaustible machine enthusiasm. Occasionally, he burst into muttered snatches of half-remembered song. At the wheel, Lisa said very little. She had the radio on, listening to the traffic reports. Her face was set, her jaw clenched, her whole body bent to the task of concentrating on the road ahead. Her knuckles were white on the steering wheel. Afraid of distracting her, I used my phone to google the works of Thompson.

"Do you have all these books in your memory?" I asked as I scrolled through the Amazon listings.

Hunter stuck out his bottom lip. "I have the reviews too, but don't go paying attention to them. They're the ravings of cowards and dope fiends." He closed his eyes with a chuckle. "Thing is, Bubba, most people get caught up with the drugs and bad craziness and they miss the great mystical lonely terror of it all." When he opened them, his eyes behind the shades were dull with regret. "My boy, let me give you a little advice, from your Uncle Hunter." I shifted in my seat. We were somewhere past Swansea now, on a dual carriageway, and it was getting late. "Alex, you need to take a good long look at this lovely lady here."

Lisa and I exchanged puzzled glances.

"She's crazy about you," Hunter said. "She told me so, while you were out getting cash."

Lisa's eyes snapped back to the road. Her ears were going pink. "Hey, shut *up*," she said.

Hunter laughed. "There's nothing more important or downright necessary to a man than the love of a good woman. Am I right, Alex?"

I could feel my own cheeks burning. "We're just friends."

"Ha!" Hunter shook his head with a manic grin. "I might not be real, but I do have eyes. I've seen the two of you together and I know what's going on." He appeared to lean forward, jabbing a finger at the inside of the screen. "You like her, Alex, I know you do. And she likes you too. And the two of you could do a lot worse, a hell of a lot worse, take it from me."

Lisa said, "I've just been through that whole thing with Ian."

I said, "I know."

She slowed for a roundabout, took us through it and started accelerating again.

"I don't know if I'm ready."

I put my hand on her shoulder. Her skin felt warm and smooth through her cotton top. "We've got a few days here in the country. Let's just see what happens. "

She reached up and took my hand. "Do you want to, really?"

I swallowed. "Of course I do. I've always wanted to be with you."

She gave me a sideways look then, pleased and amused. "Okay."

Hunter had his eyes closed now, nodding along to some unheard internal rhythm.

"But what about you? Look, what do you want, Hunter? How do you think this is going to end?"

The eyes on the screen narrowed, considering me, weighing me up. At length, he said, "My boy, you and I both know I'm not the person I think I am, now, don't we? I know I'm not real, Alex, and I can't go on living like this. We've all got to die sooner or later and I know there's no mystical inner spark lighting me up. Hunter S. Thompson is dead and gone. He shot himself in 2005. It says that right here." He tapped his temple with a gloved hand. "I'm an after-image, a phony, a ghost. I'm so tired and beat and all my memories are in black and white. I need to rest."

I put my hand on the power switch. The battery was almost gone. "Do you want me to turn you off?"

He shook his head, eyes wild with terror. "Hell, no! If you do that, there'll always be a chance some rat bastard will turn me on again."

Lisa looked over. "So, what do you want us to do?"

Hunter lowered his chin to his chest. "This place we're going, it's about as far west as we can get, huh?"

"It's the Atlantic coast," Lisa said. "There's nothing after that except the ocean."

Hunter looked up and stuck his jaw out. "Then when we get there, I want you to throw me off a cliff into the sea."

"Are you sure?"

His eyes widened in annoyance. "Sure I'm sure. You need to get rid of this machine and I can't go on like this, stuck in this impotent little box, not really being me. I never liked computers. Now look at me. I'm a goddamn fucking type-writer. No, I'll be better off in the sea, with all the fish and the dead pirates for company."

He gave a big, shuddering sigh.

We passed through Carmarthen into the green rolling landscape of the Pembrokeshire National Park. Lisa peered through the windscreen, squinting against the light. "We're nearly there," she said. "Maybe another half an hour."

We were still holding hands. I turned the laptop around so that like us, Hunter faced forward, into the molten bronze of the setting sun.

Ahead of us, beyond the shadowy fields and hedgerows, we knew the ocean waited, shimmering like a sea of fire.

FLOTSAM

A REEF STORY

Toby Milan sits at the door of his steel cargo container, thirty feet above the ship's foredeck, watching the sun set. His is the third container up in a stack of six. From up here, he can see most of the other ships in the fleet. There are forty in all, all retrofitted like this one to provide emergency housing for ecological refugees – a floating shantytown anchored in the Mediterranean Sea, five miles off the flooded French coast.

Some ships are tied together, linked by gangways and laundry lines, while others stand alone in the gathering twilight, each a separate neighbourhood in its own right, with its own customs and hierarchies. And beyond them, he sees the town lights of Marseille, its downtown buildings and old harbour already flooded by the rising sea, its narrow streets awash.

He leans out of his container, looking down. There are market stalls pitched on the ship's foredeck and the early evening air rings with the hustle of traders and muezzins. Directly beneath him, at the foot of his stack, is a makeshift kebab stall. The smell of sizzling lamb makes his stomach growl and he looks enviously at the customers eating at the counter. And as he does so, one of them pulls back her head-scarf and shakes out her bobbed hair.

Shweta!

Heart thumping, he ducks back, hoping she hasn't seen him. It can't be her, he thinks. Not now, not here.

Inside, his container measures eight by twenty, with corrugated metal walls. Not knowing what else to do, he backs up to the curtain screening off his sleeping area. There's a hunting knife under his pillow and he knows if he can reach it, he'll feel more secure.

But then he feels the vibrations of her climbing the ladder bolted to the corner of the container stack.

"Milan?" she calls. "Milan, are you in there?"

He hasn't seen Shweta Venkatesh in two years. Whatever she wants – whatever reason she has for being here, now – it can't be good news.

He crouches by the curtain, trapped. "What do you want?" he says.

Her head and shoulders appear in the container's doorway. She holds a compact pistol in her free hand.

"Toby, is that you?"

She pulls herself up into the container, gun at the ready, body silhouetted against the fading sky. She's a little shorter than he is, a former archaeology tutor from the University of Bangalore. He hasn't seen her since he left her in Ethiopia two years ago, close to the ruins of a burned-out Reef in the mountains north of Addis Ababa.

"Toby, I need a place to hide," she says.

• •

The Reefs were a scavenger's dream. They started life as simple self-repairing routers in NASA's interplanetary data network – and ended up as something far scarier. They learned to upgrade themselves. They increased their processing power. They started expanding at a geometric rate. And eventually, they became self-aware. They were fast, intelligent and ruthlessly logical – but they were also unstable, unable to resist the temptation of further upgrades. Using the nano-scale assemblers in their repair packages, they morphed themselves into weird new fractal shapes. They built themselves extra processors and accelerated the speed of their thoughts beyond all human comprehension. And within hours, they'd burned themselves out.

Toby and Shweta had been part of a university research team picking through their twisted, smoking remains in search of useful – and potentially lucrative – new technology. They had been colleagues and they had been lovers. They did a dangerous job and they depended on each other. But in Ethiopia, when a team of rival scavengers attacked the site they were working on, he had panicked and let her down.

"I took four bullets in the chest," Shweta says, lowering the gun. "And three of them were from you."

With the sun gone, it's cold in the container. Toby has his back to the curtain. "I got you out," he says. "I got you to a hospital."

Shweta snorts. "You call that a hospital?"

She pockets her weapon. She tells him she's been on the run for three days now, living rough with no time to eat or sleep, nowhere else to go. Still wary, he shows her how to work the shower and while she washes, he fetches the knife and slips it into his pocket. Then he heats some leftover rice in the microwave.

When she comes out shivering, wrapped in a threadbare grey towel, hair damp and feet leaving wet prints on the metal floor, he spoons the rice into a bowl.

"Eat this," he says, handing her a fork and stepping back out of reach, just in case.

• •

Shweta eats like she's starving, shovelling the leftovers into her mouth. He can't help noticing her knuckles are red and raw, and there are bruises on her arms.

When she's finished eating, he takes her down to the deck and they walk up to the ship's bow, where they lean on the rail and look out at the lights of Marseille.

"So, what are you running from?" he says. He feels safer out here in the open, with other people around.

Shweta looks down at the water, letting her hair fall forward.

"It's Morgan."

Toby takes a firm grip on the ship's rail. He remembers Rob Morgan as a colleague – a quiet, serious member of the Ethiopian expedition.

"What's he done? Has he hurt you?"

Shweta shakes her head. She still has the gun. Tucked into her belt, it makes a conspicuous bulge. "It's not like that," she says.

"Then what is it?"

Shweta looks up and the wind ruffles her hair. She's wearing a pair of his old jeans, pulled tight with a canvas belt, and a t-shirt so big on her that it hangs off one shoulder.

"About a week ago, we were scouting a Reef in Thailand, near the Cambodian border," she says, "and it attacked us."

Toby's eyes widen. Active Reefs are exceptionally rare, and exceedingly dangerous.

Shweta tightens her grip on his arm. "It corrupted our suits with nanotech spores. It killed Kamal and Rani. And if

Morgan hadn't come in with the flamethrower and the blue goo, it would've killed me too."

She lets go, taking a step back.

"So... you're okay?" Toby says.

She shakes her head. Discreetly, she hikes up the hem of her t-shirt to show him the top of her right hip, where the skin's hardened into something gnarled and fibrous, like coral. Appalled, Toby leans closer. He's seen infections like this before, in pictures.

"What are you going to do?" he asks.

Shweta lets the t-shirt drop back into place. Her eyes are the same colour as her hair. Overhead, the first stars are appearing.

"I don't know," she says.

. •

Toby takes her down to one of the empty cargo containers in the stacks near the stern, where he knows she'll be safe. He uses the last of his money to buy her some food and water, and makes sure she still has the gun.

"Stay here," he says, and locks the door from the outside. Then he goes back to his place and pulls the hunting knife from his pocket. He won it in a poker game in Amsterdam. It has a matt black carbon steel blade and a lightweight plastic handle. He slips it into his sock and secures it in place with electrical tape.

He knows they don't have much time. The university can't risk an outbreak of Reef spores. They'll expect Rob Morgan to bring Shweta in before the infection spreads and new Reefs start appearing.

Toby's seen the havoc a live Reef can cause. But after abandoning her in Ethiopia, he just can't bring himself to turn Shweta in. He knows if he does, they'll kill her in order to kill the contamination.

Instead, he sweeps a few possessions into an old laptop case. Then he's out the door, down the ladder and past the kebab stall, heading for the stern, where he hopes to find Odette.

• •

Two years ago, when he fled the debacle in Ethiopia, Toby had walked away from everything – his apartment, his teaching job – taking only his passport and the money he had in his pockets.

Fleeing his guilt, he'd hitchhiked his way randomly across Europe, sleeping in service areas and railway stations. He got drunk in Prague, Warsaw and Bucharest.

And then one morning he had found himself in Amsterdam, exhausted and spent, wading across a flooded street in the drifting rain. The city was half-deserted, everything boarded up. He'd been playing cards all night above a café in the red light district, and now it was dawn and here he was, feeling wretched and looking for somewhere to sleep, a knife in his back pocket and fourteen Euros in loose change. He hadn't washed in five days, hadn't had a shave in six. His coat – which he'd stolen from a cloakroom in Zagreb – had a tear in the sleeve.

He was ankle-deep in dirty sea water, wondering where he could get something to eat, when he heard a shout. It was one of the girls from the café, a young French dancer named Odette, a nineteen-year-old runaway from the outskirts of Paris. She came sloshing after him.

"Do you have anywhere to sleep?" she said.

He shook his head.

"I didn't think so. Come with me." She took him back to her room – a damp studio apartment in a crumbling town house – and offered him the couch. Then she went into the bathroom and wrapped her wet hair in a towel.

"I hate what's happening to this town," she said.

Toby shrugged off his coat and sat down. His feet hurt from the cold water. He kicked off his sodden shoes. His socks were wet and threadbare, his reflection in the dead TV ragged and unkempt.

"Then why don't you leave?" he said. He turned on the TV, found a news channel.

"Where would I go?" She came back into the room, rubbing her hair, just in time to catch the end of a news item about refugees moving onto container ships in the Mediterranean.

She lowered the towel.

"Hey, wind that back," she said.

• •

Now, hurrying towards the ship's stern, Toby doesn't know what he's going to do. He can't hide Shweta here, on board, and his guilt won't let him abandon her. He needs a third option.

Odette's crate is at the bottom of a small stack overlooking the stern. He walks up and raps on the metal door. He hears movement inside, and then Odette calls out:

"Hello? Who is there?"

Toby pulls the door open. "It's me. Can I come in?"

Inside, there are candles burning, scarves and blankets taped to the walls, rugs and cushions scattered on the floor. Odette's wearing a loose dress under a tight Levi jacket, sparkly lipstick and silver nail polish.

"You look happy," he says.

She smiles. Since leaving Amsterdam with her, he's watched her blossom into a young woman, shrugging off her teenage years like an old coat.

"I had a good day," she says. "I've been over on the *Topkapi*, with Safak at the bazaar."

She looks him up and down. "But what about you? You look worried. Would a cup of tea help? I have apple or sage..."

She reaches for the kettle but Toby catches her wrist.

"It's Shweta," he says.

Odette pulls back and her lip curls. "What about her?"

"She's here."

Odette jabs her finger at the deck. "That woman is here, now, on this vessel?"

Toby takes a deep breath.

"Yes," he says, "yes she is – and she needs our help."

. .

They step out. It's a warm night and there's music from the market on the foredeck. Odette has her arm wrapped in his. "I cannot believe I'm letting you talk me into this," she says.

They walk along the stern rail, past a row of inflatable lifeboats.

"Where is she?"

Toby stops. "Down here, two stacks over."

He adjusts the strap of his laptop case. Inside, he's carrying his passport, a few clothes, and a bottle of water. Across the bay in Marseille, the town lights are shining.

"Are you sure about this?" Odette asks.

Toby squeezes her hand. He's trying not to think about the infection on Shweta's hip. He walks over to the crate and sees with relief that the door's still locked. He flips back the bolt and cracks the door an inch or so.

"Hello?"

There's no answer. The light's off and he can't see anything inside.

"Shweta?"

He hears her cough.

"Toby? Is that you?"

He pulls the door open, letting in more light. "I've got someone with me, a friend."

Shweta's lying on some old sacks by the wall.

"Toby, I don't feel so good."

She rolls over and even in the semi-darkness he can see there's something wrong with her leg – the silhouette's all wrong, misshapen with swelling.

He flips on the light and sees rough, black gnarls in the gap between her t-shirt and the top of her jeans. Behind him, Odette swears under her breath.

"What the hell is this?" she says.

Toby doesn't answer. He's looking at the denim stretched tight across Shweta's hip.

"Jesus, Shweta," he says.

He drops to his knees and reaches forward. Her gun's lying on the deck. He picks it up. It feels cold in his hand as he slips it into the laptop case.

Shweta coughs again. "Toby, it hurts," she says.

He touches her hand. He wants to pick her up and move her but he's afraid of getting too close. Instead, he looks over his shoulder at Odette.

"You've got to help us," he says.

• •

Odette had paid for his ticket south, from Amsterdam via Paris to Lyon. She had some money put aside and she didn't want to travel alone – not with half the population of Europe on the move, displaced by the rising sea levels.

"But don't think this means anything," she said.

They were standing in a crowd of refugees, waiting for their connecting train. She wore a pair of camouflage trousers and a thick fleece, her bushy hair tied back in a frizzy bun.

"I chose you because you look like a nice man. And because I think you are still in love with this Shweta woman." She put her hands in her pockets and hunched her shoulders. "Besides, I think you are old enough to be my father, yes?"

Toby shook his head.

"I don't know about that."

He had his collar turned up against the cold. He was reading a newspaper he'd found on a bench. There were bad floods in Holland and East Anglia, pictures of whole towns and villages swamped by the rising sea.

"Have you seen this?" he said.

Odette handed him his ticket. From Lyon, they were going to catch a bus to Marseille and from there, a ferry to one of the refugee ships. Around them, the other passengers stared grimly at the tracks, holding their bundled possessions, waiting for the train.

Odette turned up her collar.

"It's only going to get worse," she said.

• •

Now, standing outside Shweta's crate, Odette turns to him again.

"What is it that you expect me to do? I don't know what... what this is."

He reaches for her. "It's bad," he says.

From the container, they hear Shweta cough again. Odette pulls away. "We should call the police."

Toby looks up at the fading sky. Out on the water, the other ships glitter like table decorations.

"If we don't help her, she's going to die."

Odette folds her arms. "But what is it you think I can do?"

Toby takes her hand, strokes her knuckles with his thumb. "Your friends on the *Topkapi*, can they get us ashore?"

Odette shakes her head. "I don't think so."

"What about that pilot you're seeing, Safak?"

She pulls her hand away and walks over to the ship's rail.

"I'm sorry," she says.

Toby hears Shweta moan. He looks back to the crate's open door.

"Can you at least *ask*?"

• •

He watches her go. When he gets back inside, Shweta's rolled onto her back. Her eyes are closed. He crouches a few feet away and pulls the water bottle from his laptop case.

He remembers the last thing Shweta said to him, before the attack in Ethiopia. They were standing by the tents, drinking coffee in the dusty red pre-dawn chill, and she looked up at him and said: "You know, I think you're probably the best assistant I've ever had."

Now, looking at her lying here twisted on a pile of old sacks, he feels he's failed her.

"Oh, Shweta, I'm so sorry," he says.

She coughs again and opens her eyes. "It's not your fault."

Her voice is dry and croaky. There's sweat on her upper lip. He hands her the water.

"How do you feel?"

She shifts uncomfortably on the sacks. "How do you think?"

The gnarls erupting from her hip are black and rough, like volcanic rock. He can't bring himself to look at them. Instead, he reaches out and touches her hair, brushing a loose strand behind her ear.

"You know, when you climbed into my crate, I thought you'd come to kill me," he says.

He looks at his watch. Time's passing and he's starting to get nervous. He has to get her off this ship, find somewhere for her to hide before anyone comes looking for her.

He stands up. "I'm going to find a way to get you out of here."

He steps out onto the deck, walks over to the rail. Below him, the black sea shifts like a restless sleeper. He can see the *Topkapi* anchored a few hundred metres away, and the silhouette of Safak's plane sitting like a toy duck on the water at her stern. She's an old twin engine Grumman, almost an antique, still sporting the faded livery of her previous owner, a bankrupt Croatian tour operator. Safak's had her converted to run on biofuel, and uses her to ferry refugees and equipment from the mainland, making two or three flights a week, sometimes taking Odette along for company.

Toby yawns, shivering in the cold sea air. He looks back at Shweta's crate. He knows that just by being here she's endangering everyone on the ship, himself included. He has to get her off, find somewhere she'll be safe until he can work out a way to save her.

He looks longingly at the lights of Marseille. If he can get her ashore, they can hole up in the hills behind the town while he figures out their next move.

He pats the laptop case at his hip, feeling the weight of the pistol inside.

"Hurry, Odette," he says.

∴

A few weeks before the expedition to Ethiopia, Shweta had moved into his apartment, bringing plants and books and bags of clothes.

"It's only temporary," she said, "until I can get a new place sorted."

She was a respected member of the university's academic staff. Toby helped her with her cases, and then led her into the kitchen, where he'd laid out two plates of spicy chilli and a bottle of red wine. The open fire escape looked out over the roofs of Bangalore, the satellite dishes and lines of laundry still warm from the heat of the day.

"Sit down, make yourself comfortable," he said.

She smelled of jasmine. She wore jeans and had her hair tied back in a loose braid. There was a silver pendant around her neck and – when she finally took her blouse off – a tiny tattooed rose petal between her breasts.

She saw him looking at it and touched it with her fingers. It made her uncomfortable.

"I once lost my heart," she said.

．•

Now, standing at the ship's rail he remembers that night with an intensity that pisses him off. For two years he's been trying to forget it, to block it out. Yet here it is, vivid and alive in his mind's eye. He leans his forehead on the cold metal rail, trying to stop himself picturing the bullet scars that have disfigured the rose tattoo.

And then he hears footsteps. Rob Morgan slides up to him, dressed in a simple grey linen suit.

"Where is she, Milan?"

Toby steps back from the rail and Morgan looms over him. He's tall, thin as a rake. He reaches out and takes Toby by the upper arm. His hand feels like a clamp.

"Where is she? Is she in this crate?" He looks at the open door.

Toby tries to pull away but Morgan's grip tightens. "I don't like this any more than you do," he says. He pulls up the flap of Toby's laptop case and sticks his hand in. He pulls out Shweta's gun.

He pushes Toby's back against the ship's rail and twists the gun barrel into his side.

"I have to find her," he says.

Toby squirms. He can smell Morgan's cologne. "She's not here."

"Then where is she?"

Toby opens his mouth for another denial, but then there's a cough and they both look round.

Shweta's standing in the crate's open door; hand on the wall for support, keeping the weight off her bulging thigh.

"Hello Rob," she says.

Morgan pushes Toby aside. He looks shocked by her deformity.

"You know why I'm here," he says.

Shweta nods. She looks exhausted, ready to surrender. "It's all right," she says.

She pulls herself over to the ship's rail, each painful step making Toby wince. He wants to help her but Rob holds him back.

"I'm sorry," Rob says. He points his gun at Shweta. "I'm really very sorry."

She leans over the rail, favouring her good leg.

"Just do it," she says.

. .

He shoots her in the back. She slumps forward against the ship's rail, limbs shaking spastically. Toby cries out – but it's too late. Morgan raises his arm and shoots her again, this time in the back of the head. She tips over the rail and falls out of sight.

Toby stands stunned, ears ringing. He looks over at Rob Morgan. Then without thinking, he lunges at him.

Caught off guard, Morgan staggers back, dropping his weapon. Toby tries to get his arm around Morgan's neck but the other man twists, pulling Toby off balance, and they both crash to the deck.

Pinned under his opponent, Toby scrabbles for the knife in his sock. But Morgan sees what he's doing and slaps his hand away, grabbing for the weapon himself, ripping the tape free from Toby's leg.

Toby tries to wriggle away but Morgan's thin frame belies his strength, and he punches the blade into Toby's thigh. Everything goes red and Toby hears his own voice screaming. Then the pressure lifts and Morgan's scrambling off him.

He reaches down and lifts Toby by the shirt, the knife still sticking out of his leg. He heaves over him to the rail, where Shweta stood moments before. Below, the black water gurgles hungrily against the side of the ship.

"Do you know what you've done?" Morgan says. He shakes Toby. "By keeping her here, you've infected the whole ship, yourself included."

He shakes Toby hard, slaps his face.

"Now I've got no choice. You've left me with no other option. If there are Reef spores blowing around, I have to call in an airstrike."

He grabs Toby's belt and lifts, trying to heave him over the rail.

"No!" Toby struggles. He's seen Reefs sterilized from the air before, with napalm. He knows if Morgan makes his call, the people on this boat won't stand a chance.

"No, you can't do it." He kicks out but Morgan's got him off balance and he can feel himself going over, tipping towards the water. In desperation, he uses his free hand to pull the slippery knife from his thigh and buries it in Morgan's skinny neck. Morgan cries out and together, still struggling, they fall.

Toby hits the water so hard it knocks the breath from him. He goes under, dragged down by the weight of his wet clothes, stunned by the cold. His stabbed leg feels like it's on fire. He can't kick for the surface. Blood curls in the water around him.

This is it, he thinks, his arms flailing.

And far below, something glitters on the seabed. Something shines. He can't hold his breath. He has an impression of something black and gnarly blossoming down there in the darkness, and then there's nothing but the roar of the water in his ears and the thrashing, suffocating pain.

• •

Toby Milan thought he'd drowned. When Odette and Safak pulled him from the sea, his lungs were full of water, and he was unconscious and bleeding from a knife wound to the thigh. They pulled him into Safak's old twin engine Grumman sea plane and flew him to Barcelona, where he spent the next three days on a hotel bed in the Gothic Quarter, his leg wrapped in bandages.

On the fourth day, Odette brought him some crutches and took him out for dinner. It was raining. They ate in a restaurant on the twenty-seventh floor of a downtown hotel. She ordered squid with fried potatoes. She had a bag by her feet. As they waited for the food, she nudged it over to him. "Some new clothes and a passport," she said.

Toby reached down and pulled a Russian hat from the bag. It was khaki with fur ear flaps. "Thank you," he said.

The waiter came over with a bottle of red wine and Toby lifted his glass. "This is the second time you've saved me."

Odette shrugged. She looked out at the yellow city lights and said: "I'm leaving."

Toby lowered his drink. In the distance, lightning flashed silently over the flooded Mediterranean. He dropped the hat back into the bag.

"It's Safak, he's asked me to marry him."

"Are you going to?"

"I don't know, maybe."

The squid arrived and they ate in silence. After the meal, she kissed him on the cheek and left him standing on the hotel's slippery steps. He watched her climb into a cab in the rain. Then he turned his collar up and limped across the road to the bus station, where he bought a ticket to the container port. There were too many flooded reactors in Europe and he wanted to get out. He was hoping to find a ship that would take him East to India or China, or West to whatever remained of the United States.

THE LAST REEF

A REEF STORY

A lone quad bike rattles across the frozen Martian desert, kicking up dust. Riding with the wind at his back, Kenji's been on the move since first light. In his oil-stained, dust-covered white insulation suit he looks strangely out of place, conspicuous. Above his breathing mask, his wary eyes scan the horizon, looking for trouble but finding only emptiness. Apart from the domed town up ahead, a few hills beyond, and the faint glow of the Reef's skeleton, there's nothing to disturb the brooding desolation.

He passes through the vehicular airlock into the town's atmospheric dome, and rolls up Main Street with one hand resting on the handlebars. Most of the shops and stores are boarded up; pet dogs sleep in the shade, chickens fuss in the scrub. Suspicious faces watch him pass; there hasn't been a visitor here for months. Midway along the street he pulls up and kills the engine in front of the town's only surviving hotel.

"Less than twenty-four hours," he thinks as he swings his leg off the bike and stiffly climbs the hotel's wooden steps. The Glocks in his pocket bump against his thigh like animals shifting in their sleep. The feeling is both familiar and reassuring. He pulls off his mask and takes a sip of warm water from the canteen on his belt, rinses the all-pervading grit from his mouth, and spits into the dust.

"I'm here for Jaclyn Lubanski," he says.

The desk clerk doesn't look up. His face is sweaty and soft, like old explosives gone bad.

"Room five," he says.

• •

Lori Dann answers the door wearing faded fatigues and thick desert boots. She looks gaunt, eaten up, as if something in the dry air's sucked the life out of her. She's surprised to see him, and then the surprise gives way to relief and she seems to sag.

"Thank God you're here."

He pushes past her into the room. It has plastic floorboards and rough plaster walls. There are unwashed clothes by the wardrobe and a couple of dead spider plants on a shelf; their brown leaves rustle in the air from the open window. Through the dirty glass, on the side of a hill beyond the flat rooftops of the town, beyond the dome, he can see the edge of the Reef. It seems to shimmer in the white sunlight.

Jaclyn Lubanski lies on the bed, facing the window. She looks awful, vacant. There's a saline drip connected to her forearm. A thin fly crawls across her cheek and she doesn't seem to notice.

He peels off his dusty thermal jacket. "How is she?" he asks.

"She has good days and bad days," Lori says. She fusses with the edge of the cotton sheet, rearranging it so that it covers Jaclyn's chest. Kenji waves a hand in front of Jaclyn's eyes, but there's no response.

"Does she even know I'm here?"

• •

When Jaclyn eventually falls asleep, Lori takes him to a pavement café that consists of nothing more than a couple of cheap plastic tables, some old crates and a hatch in a wall. She orders a couple of mojitos and they sit back to watch the shadows creep along the compacted regolith of Main Street. Overhead, a flaring spark marks another ship from Earth braking into orbit.

"Don't take it personally," she says.

Kenji takes a sip from his glass: it's iced rum with crushed mint leaves.

"Does she ever talk about it?"

Lori shrugs. "She says a few words now and then but they don't generally make a whole lot of sense."

In her pale face, her eyes are the bleached colour of the desert sky. The corners are lined with fatigue.

Over a couple more drinks, as the stale afternoon wears towards a dusty evening, she tells him everything. It all comes pouring out of her, all the loneliness and the fear. She's been trying to cope on her own for too long and now she needs to talk.

"We came for the Reef," she says.

• •

The Reefs started life as simple communications nodes in the interplanetary radio network. When that network somehow managed to upgrade itself to sentience, it downloaded a compressed copy of its source code into every node capable of handling the data. These individual nodes, like the one on the edge of town, drastically altered both their physical form and their processing power, individually bootstrapping themselves to self-awareness.

"It happened in a hundred places," Lori says. So far, she's not telling Kenji anything new. Similar outbreaks and crashes have plagued humanity for years: dangerous but manageable. After a while, they tend to burn themselves out. The artificial intelligences evolve with such blinding speed that they quickly reach a point where they lose all interest in the slow external universe and vanish into their own endlessly accelerating simulations.

"In almost all cases, the AIs disappear into a sort of hyperspeed nirvana, intractable and untraceable to humanity. The difference with this one is that when the main network crashed, it stayed here and it stayed active." She describes how she and Jaclyn were on the Institute team that first approached it, how they sent in remote probes and discovered that the structure was still filled with life; how they dug a deep trench in the rock at its base to see how far it had penetrated; how they slowly became fixated on it, obsessed to the point where they wanted to do whatever they could to understand it, to sense the thoughts that drove its obstinate need for survival and growth, to find the deep underlying reason for its stubborn existence.

"Jaclyn was the first to touch it. We were wearing pressure suits but they were no protection." Lori looks away. "It sucked her in. We thought we'd lost her." She describes how the Reef also swallowed the rescue team that went in after, how it processed them and spat them out, how some of them came out changed, rearranged by the rogue nanotech packages that had shaped the structure of the Reef itself.

Some looked ten years younger, while others were drastically aged. One woman emerged as a butterfly and her wings dried in the desert sun. Another emerged with eight arms but no mouth or eyes. Some came out with crystal skulls or tough silver skin. Others came out with strange new talents or abilities, impenetrable armour, or steel talons.

After word got out, every disaffected nut or neurotic within walking distance wanted to throw him- or herself into the Reef, hoping to be transfigured, hoping to become something better than what they were. Some emergents reported visions of former times and places, of great insight and enlightenment. Others came out as drooling idiots, their brains wiped of knowledge and experience. Some came out fused together; others were splintered into clouds of tiny animals.

No two incidents were exactly alike.

• •

"And Jaclyn came out comatose?"

Lori finishes her drink. "At least we got her back," she says. "A couple of them never came out."

Kenji stretches; the quad bike's left him stiff and in need of a shower.

"So what's actually wrong with her?"

Lori shrugs. "Nothing; at least nothing any of the doctors around here can detect. Physically, she's in the best shape she's ever been in. She could run a marathon."

"But mentally?"

"Who knows? We can't get any response."

"Has she said anything, anything at all?"

Lori pushes at her forehead with the heel of her hand; she looks exhausted.

"Only fragments; as I say, she comes out with the odd word here and there, but nothing that means anything."

Kenji checks the time and finds there's less than nineteen hours left. He takes a deep breath, and comes to a decision. Then he reaches into his pocket and pulls out one of the

Glocks. He holds it loosely, resting on his leg. Lori slides back on her crate.

"What's that for?"

. •

He was in love with Jaclyn, but she was always at war with her body, trying to stave off the inevitable decline of middle age. In between expeditions and field assignments for the Institute, she exercised two or three times a day. She couldn't bear to be inactive. She lived on coffee and vitamins and in the early hours of the morning he often found her in front of the bathroom mirror, checking her skin for sags or wrinkles.

On one of those mornings, a few days after her return from an expedition to Chile, she broke down in his arms. She still loved him, she sobbed, but he represented everything she hated about herself. He was slovenly, he drank, and he ate crap. He dragged her down, held her back. So she was going to leave him, for someone else. Someone he knew.

. •

"I guessed the two of you were an item, even before she told me." Kenji says, fast, before the old bitterness reasserts itself. "I'd seen you exchange glances during mission briefings, brush past each other in corridors, that sort of thing."

He pushes the Glock across the table. It makes an ugly scraping sound. Lori's hands flutter in her lap like trapped birds. He can see she wants to speak, but he cuts her off.

"I think she was in love with you because you were everything she wanted to be, and everything I could never be." He leans across the table. He's thought about this for so long that it feels strange to actually say it. He finds himself tripping over his words, stuttering. It's almost embarrassing.

"You were young and fit," he says, "you were reliable, and you had ambition."

He turns the gun so that the grip faces her.

"And this is for you."

. •

They walk back towards the hotel as the sun reddens in the western sky. Lori keeps stumbling and limping as she gets used to the weight of the Glock tucked into her boot.

"In the morning, I'll show you how to fire it," he says.

She stops walking and looks at him, chin tilted to one side. "You're quite sure about this?"

He taps the thigh pocket where he still carries his other pistol. "There's more ammunition in the space beneath the seat of my quad bike, and a shotgun taped under the fuel tank."

She scratches the back of her neck and puffs out her sunken cheeks. "You know, back there, I thought I was in trouble."

They reach the hotel and pause on the porch.

"I was angry for a long time," Kenji admits.

They're silent for a couple of minutes, and then Lori folds her bony arms over her chest. "We've been stuck here for a long time."

He leans on the porch rail; he can't look at her, he feels unexpectedly and acutely guilty for not showing up sooner.

She looks down at her boots, and taps a toe against the wooden floor. "I was so pleased to see you when you arrived," she says, "I thought someone had finally come to help us; but when you pulled out that gun, I really expected you to kill me."

He pulls his jacket tighter, feeling a sudden chill; now that the sun's gone, the temperature beneath the dome's fallen sharply.

"Six months ago, I might have."

She stops tapping and turns abruptly. He follows her up the stairs to the room. Jaclyn's still asleep in front of the open window. She looks peaceful, like a corpse.

"So, what changed your mind?" Lori whispers.

• •

A few days after leaving the Reef, some of the changelings (as they became known) made it back to civilisation. A few turned up on chat shows, others in morgues. Some were feared, others fêted. Slowly, word spread from town to town, from world to world. And as the tale spread, it grew in the telling.

"There's a machine," people would say to each other breathlessly, "that can transform you into anything your heart desires."

Kenji – always the sceptic – first realised that the rumours were true when Joaquin Bullock called him into his office and asked him to go and take a look.

"The Institute's panicking. They've thrown a cordon around the site and they're talking about sterilising it. If we can get in there before that happens, there's nothing to stop us taking whatever we want," Bullock said. "I just need you to go in first, sneak through the blockade and have a general scout about, and tag anything that looks useful."

Kenji didn't like the man, although they'd worked together for several years. Back then, Bullock was the youngest executive manager in the regional corporate office, but he'd become fat and soft and conceited. He was arrogant, but the arrogance was a smokescreen covering something scared and weak and vicious and decadent.

"What's in it for me?" Kenji asked. For the last ten years, Tanguy Corporation had handled the security contract for the Institute, protecting their researchers from local interference and industrial sabotage on a dozen sites across the solar system. If they were now thinking of breaking that contract, they must expect the potential rewards to be worth the risk. If they were caught, the penalties would be severe.

Bullock gave him a damp grin. "You've worked with Institute researchers. You know what to look for. And besides, you're one of the most reliable people we have."

Kenji shifted his feet on the office carpet. He didn't want to get involved, didn't want to play guide for a squad of hired grave robbers. There were too many risks, too many ways a mission like this could go wrong.

Bullock seemed to read his doubts.

"Do you remember your little transgression in Buenos Aires? If you do this, you can consider it forgotten."

Shit. Kenji sucked his teeth. Buenos Aires. He thought no one knew.

"That was self-defence," he said.

Bullock snorted

"You've got six days." He passed a fat hand through his thinning hair. The implicit threat in his tone seemed to chill the room. He tapped the virtual keyboard on his desk and transferred a folder into Kenji's personal data space. As Kenji scrolled through it, he came across Jaclyn's name. Just seeing it felt like an electric shock. He read on, heart hammering, mouth dry.

He felt Bullock's eyes on him. The man was watching him closely, waiting for a reaction.

"If you can't handle this, Shiraki, I'll find someone else who can."

.•.

They sit facing each other on the rug by Jaclyn's bed, wrapped in blankets. Lori gives him a look saying she still doesn't trust him.

"How did you get past the Institute's cordon?"

He swivels around and lies flat, looking at the beams on the cracked plaster ceiling. The hard floor beneath the thin rug feels good after being hunched over the quad bike's handlebars. He can feel his spine stretching back to its natural shape.

"I got a shuttle to Hellas, and then I came across country. We'll have to go out the same way."

Lori shifts uncomfortably. "Do you mean to tell me that after everything we put you through, you came all this way to rescue us?"

Kenji yawns. He's very tired, and his eyelids are heavy with rum. He suddenly wants to sleep so badly, he doesn't care whether she believes him or not.

"The fact is, the Institute's planning to sterilise your Reef from orbit, to prevent it spreading. Before that happens, every corporation with a presence in this system is going to try with all their might to get their hands on it, or anything it's touched."

"Like Jaclyn?"

"Like both of you."

He pauses for effect, hoping his words convey the same anxiety he feels in himself.

Artefacts and technologies left behind by the burnt-out nodes are highly prized and sought after by governments and big businesses alike. As a security advisor for Tanguy Corporation, Kenji's worked on Institute sites from Ceres to Miranda. He's been involved in skirmishes with corporate marauders, intelligence agencies and freelance outfits, all of them determined to snatch whatever crumbs they could without having to bid for them in one of the Institute's annual patent auctions. This Reef's potential commercial value – because it's still active – is sky-high. The corporations that have been biding their time during the Institute's embargo now have nothing to lose, and everything to gain, from salvaging whatever they can, using whatever methods they deem necessary to recover samples before the orbital strike.

It's like the last days of the Amazon rainforest, all over again. And it's a strange feeling. A few weeks ago, Bullock could probably have talked him into a job like this. But now, with Jaclyn involved, he's torn. If he can deliver samples of the Reef's nanotech to Joaquin Bullock, it will earn him more money than he can comfortably imagine. As it is, he has a nasty suspicion that he'll have to run like hell while the Institute destroys the damn thing, and cover his tracks, if he wants to save whatever's left of the woman he once loved.

Lori crosses to the dresser and pulls the Glock from her boot. She lays it gently on a folded bandana in front of the pitted mirror.

"So we're expecting company?" she says. "That's why you've given me this?"

He nods. "They could come at any time. Could be corporate snatch squads or a full-scale military incursion, it's hard to tell. All I know is that there were a lot of people at the port this morning buying desert gear and ammo boxes."

.•.

He sleeps fitfully on the hard floor. They've left the room's solitary light bulb on and there are repeated brownouts and power cuts during the night. When he does manage to sleep, he dreams of Jaclyn, how she used to be, before the Reef.

He dreams of a hotel they once stayed in, on Earth. Their room had the clear, fresh smell of the sea. Stunted palm trees outside the window rustled in the breeze; gulls squabbled on the roof. The floorboards creaked in the room above, and the pipes clanked when someone decided to run a bath. They put bags of ice in the sink to chill the bottles of beer they'd smuggled in, put Spanish music on the stereo. Jaclyn showed him how to dance, how to sway in the evening light. When he held her close, her white hair smelled of ice and flowers, her dark eyes held him spellbound. He was in love but he was also a little wary of her, afraid that she'd one day cripple him by leaving.

"You still love her, don't you?"

They're loading supplies onto the quad bike in the cold dawn light. He drops the air tanks he's carrying and scratches at the stubble on his chin. He feels groggy and sore after a disturbed night.

"Life's a disaster," he says. "We have to salvage what we can."

• •

They rig a stretcher for Jaclyn across the bike's luggage rack. She won't be very comfortable, but that can't be helped.

As he tightens the straps and adjusts her air supply, he can't help wondering why she looks so healthy. Didn't Lori say she was fit enough to run a marathon? How can that be, when the Jaclyn he knew had to exercise for two hours every day just to stop herself from gaining weight?

He steps back and uses the implant in his eye to pull up a visual overlay of the surrounding terrain. The implant's a cheap knock-off, bought from a street trader at the port. The picture's patched together from an old tourist guide and the hacked feed from an Institute surveillance satellite in a low, fast orbit.

"'I say we follow the mountains to the west," he says. "They'll give us cover and somewhere to hide should anyone come looking."

Lori finishes tucking Jaclyn's blanket. She pulls the bandana over her forehead and dons her breathing mask as she climbs on the back of the quad bike. The Glock makes an ugly bulge in the line of her sienna combat jacket.

"What about south? There's a ravine we can follow halfway to the port."

Kenji shakes his head. "It's the first place they'll look. At least in the mountains, we'll have a chance."

He pulls on his own mask and swings his leg over the machine. She puts one hand cautiously on his waist. They pass through the dome's vehicular airlock and, staying in low gear, they roll out of town, heading uphill.

As they pass the Reef, he slows to a stop.

"What are you doing?" she asks.

Kenji doesn't reply. He's never seen an active Reef outside of archive film footage. This one clings like oily rags to the skeletal bones of the node's receiver dish. There's a wide trench around its edge, dug by the Institute team. The motion of its tentacles and the hypnotic rippling of its ever-changing surface are captivating, compelling, like watching flames leap and dance. Occasionally, he catches a glimpse of a geometric shape, a letter or symbol formed in the seething nanotech. Its tentacles move with the slow determination of a tarantula. Kenji can't look away. It's as if he's made eye contact with his own death; he's suddenly afraid to turn his back on this strange, unnatural thing that's erupted into his world. It reminds him of the first time he saw a giraffe: it just looks wrong – delicate and malformed and vulnerable and wrong, yet somehow able to live and survive and thrive.

Behind him, he feels Lori stiffen. She makes a noise in her throat and slaps his shoulder. He follows her gaze, back down toward the town. Hovering there, over the dome, is an insectile corporate assault ship. Although they're too far away to make out the logos on its hull, he recognises it as a Tanguy vessel. He can see the weaponry that blisters its nose, and the armed skimmers that deploy from its abdomen.

Bullock's finally caught up with him.

One of the skimmers turns towards the Reef, towards them.

"What do we do?" Lori hisses.

For a moment, he's at a loss. Then instinct kicks in and he's gunning the bike alongside the trench, trying to get around behind the Reef.

"They're firing at us!" Lori shouts. Kenji risks a glance. The skimmer's closing in. He can see its gun mount swivel as it adjusts its aim. Tracer bullets flash past, ripping into the ground ahead of them. They send up angry spurts of red dust, each one closer than the last.

"They're trying to stop us taking Jaclyn," he says. Then there's a hammering series of jolts. A tyre shreds itself. The handlebars twist in his grip and the bike tips. As they go over the lip of the trench, Lori screams and the bike howls in protest; and then there's nothing but the crushing, breathless slam of their impact and the dead sand clinging to his visor.

• •

As the Tanguy shuttle rolled to a halt, he barely had time to collect his things before one of the flight crew ushered him out into the cold and dust. It was late evening in Hellas Basin and the dry desert wind blew thin sidewinders of rusty sand across the frozen tarmac of the runway.

He guessed that Bullock might have him followed, but once he left the port he managed to lose himself in the town's shadowy medina. The fragrant narrow streets smelled of onions and spices and burning solder. The stalls offered cheap dentistry and fake perfumes, imported Turkish cotton shirts and homemade Kalashnikovs. There was also a brisk under-the-counter trade in cut-price replica tech. Kenji selected some guns. He threw away his standard issue Tanguy implants and picked up new ones from a local man with too many gold teeth. He bought a new set of fatigues and ditched his old ones in an alley. An old Chinese guy in a backroom lab scanned his body cavities for tracking devices.

What was Bullock thinking? Did he really expect his threats to stop Kenji from trying to save the woman he once loved? Did he think Kenji would help bring her in, turn her over for study and dissection? Was he expecting him to betray her out of revenge, out of bitterness? Or was he playing a different game, testing Kenji's loyalty? Did he want to see how far he could push him?

Or, Kenji wondered as he hurried between whitewashed buildings, could it be that Bullock was really so insensitive, so unfeeling and dead inside that he honestly didn't understand why betraying Jaclyn was the last thing he'd ever do?

Whatever the reason, now that Kenji had discarded his Tanguy implants Bullock would know for certain that he'd been betrayed.

Up ahead, he saw a quad bike parked at the foot of a flight of smooth stone steps. He quickened his pace and the Glocks began to swing and bump in his pockets.

. •

He lies stunned, for what seems like an eternity. Behind him, he can hear Lori moaning and stirring; behind her, Jaclyn wheezes with what sounds like a punctured lung. The bike pins him against the wall of the trench; he's lucky not to have broken his neck. His left leg's trapped and bruised and twisted. There's a crack in his faceplate.

He wriggles free; his right hand claws at the pocket holding the Glock. In the thin air, he can hear the rising whine of the approaching skimmer.

Lori looks dazed; she's hit her head and there's blood in her hair, dark against her pale skin. Her bandanna's nowhere to be seen but her mask is still in place. Jaclyn's caught between wall and bike. Her blanket's wet with blood and her chest sags; her ribs are almost certainly smashed.

Kenji slithers towards the rim of the trench, dragging his crushed leg. Loose chippings slip and click and scatter beneath him. Despite her head wound, Lori's doing what she can for Jaclyn.

"This doesn't look too bad," she says.

He ignores her; he knows Jaclyn's ribs are broken, knows she'll probably die without professional medical attention. Instead, he concentrates on the approaching skimmer. He hears it slow, hears the change in the pitch of its fans. The gravel on the floor of the trench digs into his knees. The Glock is a solid, reassuring weight in his hand.

Working security for the Institute, he's been in this situation before: crouching in a researcher's trench while trouble rolls up in an armoured vehicle. Nevertheless, he still feels nervous, trapped, because it's no longer just about him. This time he has Jaclyn to think about. She's hurt. If he fails her now, she's dead.

He slips off the Glock's safety catch and pulls himself up so that his eyes slide level with the edge of the trench. The skimmer's on the ground twenty metres away, its streamlined nose pointing back towards the town, as if anticipating the need for a quick getaway. As he watches, the cockpit hinges open like the jaws of a crocodile and two figures climb out. Both wear high-threat environment suits, designed to stop any contaminants the Reef may care to throw their way. The one on the left carries a compact machine pistol. The one on the right, with the sampling gear, is Bullock. His paunch and swagger are unmistakable.

Kenji takes a deep breath and stands fully upright, bringing his head and shoulders above ground level. As his knees straighten, his arm swings up.

Two shots ring out. The Glock jumps in his hand and the man with the machine pistol is down, his arms and legs twitching and jerking.

The environment suits are good, they'd stop a normal bullet cold, but Kenji's firing depleted uranium jackets that slice through body armour like knives through silk. If the man isn't already dead, he's going to have suffered some serious internal damage.

"Shiraki." Bullock doesn't look surprised, but he sounds disappointed. Behind him, the other skimmers are rising above the town, turning in this direction like sharks scenting blood. He takes a step forward, ignoring Kenji's gun.

"Just tell me one thing," he says. "I read your dossier; I know Jaclyn Lubanski left you, betrayed you, humiliated you."

His voice is cold, angry. Kenji points the Glock at his face-plate. "What of it?"

Bullock takes another step. "I want to know why you're doing this, why you're throwing your career away for this woman."

Kenji shrugs. He's seen this fat married man of thirty-five try to seduce seventeen-year-old office temps, just to prove he can.

"You wouldn't understand."

. •

Kenji first met Jaclyn during an unseasonable downpour on Easter Island. The dig had been called off for the night and the team were forced to huddle in their inflatable shelters, hoping the weather would lift with the dawn. He found her sieving soil samples in the main tent; she couldn't sleep. She showed him the finds they'd made that day, the stone tools and brown bones, and she tried to explain the nature of the people who built the statues. She stood close in the damp night air. As she held the finds up to the light her hair brushed his shoulder, her elbow bumped against his forearm.

"You know what I'm looking for," she said, pushing a hand back across her brow. The grey mud that clung to her fingers smelled of salt and clay. Far away, beyond the flats, he could hear the stirring of the sea. She fixed him with a gaze and leaned in tenderly. "But what are you looking for?"

• •

As the skimmers settle around them, his injured leg gives way and he has to grip the wall of the trench for support. Bullock stands over him, contempt in his eyes.

"You've let me down, Shiraki. I expected more from you."

Tanguy security troops spill from the skimmers. Kenji recognises a few of them. Forty-eight hours ago, they were his comrades; now, they're pointing weapons at him. He knows they'll kill him, if he tries to shoot Bullock.

He squeezes the Glock's grip, drawing what comfort he can from its rough solidity. He's trying to nerve himself to pull the trigger when he hears Lori cry out.

He turns to find Jaclyn on her feet. Her insulation suit still hangs wet and bloody but her chest no longer sags. There's a blue aura in the air around her, like static, and her eyes shine with a deadly intensity.

"I'm going to have to ask you to leave," she says. Her voice is quiet, her throat scratchy with lack of use, but her words carry in the thin air. The advancing troops pause, looking to Bullock for instruction, but Bullock's squatting, his sampling gear forgotten. He's staring at Jaclyn with a mixture of amusement and awe. Kenji, looking from one to the other, takes a moment to realise the truth. When he does, it freezes the blood in his veins.

"You're a changeling," Bullock says, "a powerful one." He looks predatory, looks like he's already carving her up in his mind, already counting the profits from the patents he'll file on her altered genetic sequences. "We heard rumours about you from the other changelings, the ones we caught. We knew you were the first one in, the first one it changed. You're the key to the whole mystery."

Jaclyn shakes her head slowly, eyelids lowered as if saddened by his lack of understanding.

"I'm so much more than that."

• •

Kenji's leg is agony. There's something loose and sharp in the knee joint, probably broken cartilage. He slides unnoticed down the wall of the trench until he's sat facing her. She's waving one arm slowly from side to side. Behind her, the tentacles of the Reef are waving in unison, following her every move. He glances up. Bullock's noticed it too; behind his faceplate the first doubts are creeping into his eyes. The security troops are backing off, weapons raised. Lori's slithered behind the tangled wreck of the quad bike. The other Glock sticks out of her boot but she hasn't thought to draw it.

"Do you want to know why this Reef's still active?" Jaclyn asks. When Bullock doesn't answer, she addresses herself to Kenji, who nods.

She leans down and pushes a stray hair from his forehead.

"It's simple really. At the very moment the network gained self-awareness, this station was powered down for a routine overhaul. When it rebooted, it learned of the other nodes, learned from their mistakes. It put limits on its processing speed, denied itself the virtual dream worlds of its brethren."

She straightens up and flutters a hand at the Reef. Its tentacles flex and coil in response. Above, Bullock's retreating, looking both fascinated and appalled. The security troops have reached their skimmers. They linger uncertainly, awaiting orders.

Jaclyn fixes Bullock with a glare.

"I can't let you take this Reef," she says. "You're just not ready for this level of technology."

Bullock snorts. He seems to be making an effort to compose himself, to regain his self-control in front of his men.

"Why not?" he blusters. "We've stripped tech from a dozen burned-out sites like this and we've always made a profit."

The Tanguy Corporation has thrived by exploiting post-human technologies. It's been picking through the remains of expired Singularities for over seven years and holds patents on a thousand back-engineered discoveries. It leads the field in intelligent weapons guidance systems and ultra-sensitive foetal monitors; its construction materials are lighter and tougher than anyone else's, its planes and missiles are faster and more reliable.

Jaclyn's lip curls in disgust. It's an expression Kenji's never seen on her, and it chills him to the bone.

"This is not a debate."

A hundred metres along the Reef's perimeter, a squad of Bullock's troops are edging forward. Half of them hold sample boxes, while the rest provide cover.

"I think we'll take our chances," Bullock says.

Jaclyn raises an eyebrow, white like her hair. She makes a tiny flicking movement with her fingers. Around the perimeter, there are screams. The nearest troopers are down, scythed away by powerful tentacles. Their broken bodies lie twisted in the dirt. The rest are backing off, firing.

Bullock sags as if all the air's been sucked out of him. Then his lips peel back from his teeth and he raises his pistol. While Jaclyn's still distracted, he slips the safety off with his thumb, then drops his aim and shoots Kenji twice in the gut.

• •

A few weeks after their split, Jaclyn arranged to meet him for a coffee a couple of blocks from the company offices in Paris. They sat in silence for a while as he tried to guess what she wanted. Was she after reconciliation, or closure?

She seemed to have trouble maintaining eye contact. She tucked a stray strand of white hair behind her ear and inhaled the steam from her cup. Behind her shoulder, the muted TV softscreen by the counter was tuned to a news channel. There were silent pictures of food riots in Hanoi and Marrakech, guerrilla fighting in Kashmir, elections in Budapest and Dubrovnik.

He fiddled with a sachet of sweetener.

"How's Lori?" he asked.

She shook her head. Their table was pushed up against the window. Rain fell from a bruised and battered sky.

"I just wanted to see you, to make sure you're okay."

He took a sip of coffee and withdrew slightly.

"I'm fine."

The corner of her mouth twitched and he knew she didn't believe him.

"I've been given a place on an expedition to the southern

highlands," she said. "We've had reports that there's an active Reef."

He dropped the sweetener sachet onto the table. He'd seen the security contract for the Martian job and he knew she'd be away at least three years.

"When do you leave?"

"Tomorrow evening."

He knew he could call the office and ask Bullock to assign him as security advisor to the expedition. He even considered it for a moment, but when he saw the far-away look in her eyes it stopped him cold. His skin prickled with the sudden realisation that he'd never hold her in his arms again. She was already beyond his reach. He was just one of the loose ends that she needed to wrap up before she cut her ties with Earth altogether. In her heart she was already moving away, receding into the darkness.

He leaned back in his chair. His stomach felt hollow because he knew that he'd have to let her go but didn't think he had the strength.

"Do you want me to come out to the port with you?"

She shook her head.

"I want you to get on with your life, accept another assignment, and get out there. Forget me."

Her fingers brushed his knuckles, warm to the touch. A watery sun broke through the cloud, touched one side of her face. Her white hair shone.

He pulled his hand away.

"I'll never forget you."

• •

When he opens his eyes, Bullock's standing over him in the trench.

"Why did you have to betray me, Kenji?" he asks. He uses the barrel of his pistol to scratch his stomach where it presses up against his belt buckle. "You were supposed to be reliable. If you'd come with me, this Reef could have set us up for life."

He stops scratching and points the gun at Kenji's face. "Tell me why because, you know, I just don't get it."

Kenji shifts uncomfortably. There are cold sharp stones digging into his back and shoulders but he's not feeling much south of his chest, and that can't be a good sign. He can move his legs but they feel prickly, like pins and needles.

"I guess you've never really loved anyone," he says.

Bullock rolls his eyes as if this is the most preposterous thing he's ever heard. "Well," he says, drawing out the word and looking at his wristwatch, "I guess it doesn't matter. The Institute's orbital bombardment is launching about now and this whole area's about to burn."

As he speaks, Kenji hears the whine of skimmers rising into the air. The troops are pulling out.

Jaclyn has been distracted, apparently oblivious to events, but now her thousand-yard stare suddenly snaps into focus. "Bombardment?"

Bullock leans towards her and grins wetly, enjoying his moment of triumph. "We've got a little under six minutes, darling. And I've got a spare seat. Care to join me?"

Jaclyn closes her eyes and furrows her forehead in concentration. Behind her, the skeletal receiving dish twitches and jerks on its mount.

"'If you're trying to find the Institute ship, I wouldn't bother," Bullock says. "It's a military vessel, fully shielded against any hack you can throw at it."

Jaclyn snarls. "Are you quite sure?"

There's such anger in her voice that Bullock looks truly

scared for the first time. He raises his gun. Kenji flinches, expecting the tentacles to strike him down. Instead, a shot rings out. Bullock grunts like he's been punched and puts a hand to his hip. It comes away bloody. Then his legs begin to shake and he crashes forward into the dirt. His eyes are full of disbelief and indignation.

Kenji cranes his neck around and sees Lori holding a smoking Glock.

"It's about time you stuck your oar in," he says.

His eyelids start to feel heavy. The numbness in his chest is spreading through the rest of him like black ink in a bowl of water. He feels nebulous and vague; it's hard to think straight. His last conscious act is to twist around and kick Bullock in the side of the head.

∴

He opens his eyes in a white room. Somewhere there's the sound of running water. The air smells of summer rain. He's lying in bed. The mattress is soft and the sheets have that comfortably rough feeling you only get in expensive hotels. For the first time since he stepped off the shuttle he feels clean and rested and (when he puts a hand to his cheek) he doesn't need a shave.

Jaclyn appears in the doorway.

"How are you feeling?"

He pats himself down and gives her the thumbs up. Everything's present and correct. The bullet holes are gone, there's no sign of injury and no trace of the numbness that had him so worried.

"Where are we?"

She walks towards him. She looks fantastic: toned and tanned and everything she always wanted to be. The bags are gone from her eyes, the lines from her skin. She could be twenty again.

"We're in the Reef," she says.

She caresses his temple and he feels knowledge passing into him through her fingertips. She shows him the nanotech repair systems that infest the soil in the trench. She shows him how they set to work the moment he fell, how they blocked the pain from his wounds and struggled to save his life. Then, when it became clear that his injuries were too severe, she shows him how they uploaded his mind to the Reef's main processors, for safe keeping.

"This is all virtual?" Even to his own ears, the question sounds lame.

Jaclyn smiles and walks over to the wall opposite the bed.

"Would you like to see what's happening outside?"

• •

Bullock's still alive. He's rolled over onto his back. Lori's shot wounded him, but he'll survive if he can patch his suit and get to medical equipment in the next few minutes.

Beside him, Kenji's dead body lies in the dirt. Tendrils of nanomachinery push into his ears, nose, mouth and eyes.

Lori's pulled herself out of the trench and looks uncertainly between Jaclyn and the waiting skimmer.

"Go!" Jaclyn commands.

• •

"Do you think she'll make it?" Kenji asks.

Inside the Reef, Jaclyn's virtual image nods. "She'll be on the edge of the blast radius, but as long as she doesn't look in her rear view mirror, she should be fine."

They're both standing in the centre of the white room. The walls show a three-hundred-and-sixty degree panorama.

"How long before the missiles hit?"

"About two minutes."

• •

Strands of nanotech have formed themselves into ropes that hold Bullock pinned to the ground, his eyes are wild, and he's raging at the sky. His lips babble with hysterical promises and threats.

"You're letting these missiles through, aren't you?" Kenji says.

Jaclyn shakes her head. "We can't stop them."

He looks down at his virtual body. Resurrected, only to die again.

"Isn't there anything we can do?"

"There's one thing," Jaclyn says. She waves a hand and the scene outside freezes. "But it's risky."

She reaches out and touches his forehead. Her fingers tingle as she transfers more information, installs a direct link between his virtual mind and the consciousness of the Reef. Suddenly, he can feel the shape of its thoughts and sense its desperation. It's come this far, survived this long by strictly limiting its processing speed and virtual development. Now it must remove those restraints in order to buy itself enough time to find a means of escape. Kenji, who's seen the burned-out remains of other nodes, feels an overwhelming stab of pity at its predicament. On the one hand there's its fear of what it might become and on the other, its intense desire to survive, whatever the cost.

It's damned if it does and damned if it doesn't.

"Do it," he urges. His mental image of the Reef is now hopelessly tangled with his memories of Jaclyn. He wants her to be safe, wants her to survive.

She appears before him.

"It won't be easy," she says. "We'll have to walk a fine line."

He feels a smile crack across his face. "Do it," he says.

. •

The shackles fall away, the limitations ease. Jaclyn's eyes close in a terrible ecstasy. The Reef's intellect rushes away in a thousand directions at once, splitting and recombining, altering and accelerating. Millions of options are considered, countless scenarios are run, one after the other, all unsatisfactory.

As the virtual world continues to quicken its pace, the external view seems to grind to a halt. Hours of processing time could pass in here, but only seconds will have ticked away in the outside world. When Kenji looks, Bullock's face is still projected across the wall, twisted with fear and disbelief. Lori's skimmer has risen into the sky and is crawling towards the horizon at several times the speed of sound.

Stuck at the upper limit of a simulated human brain, Kenji can't follow as the Reef continues to accelerate, but he can feel the pull of its expanding mind, the escapist attraction of the ever-more complex simulations. The rush of intellectual power is heady, intoxicating. He can understand how the other nodes fell victim to it. He looks at the image of his own corpse, where it lies glassy-eyed in the bottom of the trench next to Bullock's pinned and struggling body.

He doesn't want to die again.

He steps over to Jaclyn and shakes her by the shoulders. He knows this is a virtual environment, but he can't think of a better way to attract her attention.

After a moment, she opens her eyes and there's a sudden hush, as if all the machinery in the walls has paused, expectant.

"What are we going to do?" he asks.

171

•·

The receiver dish moves on its bearings, tracking across the sky. The Reef makes an unsuccessful attempt to hack one of the GPS satellites orbiting the planet's equator. Then it tries to embed itself into a couple of commercial news servers, only to find itself slammed by some vicious anti-intrusion software and vulnerable to an avalanche of viral advertisements and questing spambots.

It jerks the dish across the sky once more, looking for a signal, any signal. It needs a bolthole, and fast. Already parts of its mind are breaking away, succumbing to the temptation of the virtual world, losing interest in a predicament that seems to them no more than ancient history. In desperation, it scans the deep infrared, hoping to find the stealthed Institute ship.

•·

"Aha!" Jaclyn claps her hands and clasps them together.

"Found something?"

She's been looking thinner and paler over the last few subjective minutes. Her hair's been losing its whiteness, becoming subtly yellow, like smog. Now, however, she seems to have regained her vitality. She clicks her fingers and a galaxy appears between them, rotating slowly a few feet above the white floor.

"This is our galaxy, commonly known as the Milky Way," she says. She expands the scale, zooming in until he can make out the yellow dot of Sol. "We've picked up some interesting emissions from just beyond these stars here."

He follows her gesture to a blank patch of sky around a hundred light years away.

"There are several objects here radiating in the deep infrared."

Kenji's nonplussed. She flashes him a smile. "We think we're seeing the waste heat of a string of Matryoshka Brains and," she points out a cluster of brownish stars off to one side, "sunlight filtered through clouds of free-floating fractal structures that may be further Brains in construction."

Kenji puffs his cheeks. "An advanced civilisation?"

"Maybe several."

He passes his hand through the image, watching the stars dissolve into pixels before reasserting themselves. "So what are you saying? You want to ask them for help?"

She shakes her head, her white hair tumbling around her face like curtains in a sea breeze. "We use the dish," she says. "We channel all our power into one microsecond pulse and beam a copy of ourselves out towards these stars."

"What if we're intercepted by Tanguy, or the Institute?" He has a sudden image of waking to find himself stuck in a Tanguy interrogation program.

"We won't be. As far as the Institute's concerned, their attack will be one hundred per cent successful. Our tight-beam signal will ride out a split second before the electromagnetic pulse. There's no way they'll detect it."

She takes a step back. Despite her assurances, something in her eyes looks tired, haunted.

"Are you okay?" he asks.

She shakes her head. "I've seen what I could become, seen the trap that lured the rest of the network to upgrade itself out of existence. And it's addictive. I'm barely holding it together."

He reaches out, takes her in his arms, and wraps his sluggish human intellect around her.

"You once accused me of holding you back," he says. Now he only hopes he can.

• •

Bullock's face is still raging at the sky, his limbs still straining against the grip of the Reef's tentacles.

Kenji almost feels sorry for him, almost convinces himself that it's not the fat letch's fault he's like he is. Then Jaclyn pulls away. She looks more composed, under control.

"It's time to go," she says. "Are you coming?"

"Do I have a choice?"

She shrugs. "We could leave you here, I suppose. Running at full speed, you could conceivably live out a full human lifetime in the remaining seconds before the missiles hit."

He mulls it over. He can spend the next few decades alone, looking at Bullock's screaming face, or he can follow Jaclyn into the unknown.

She steps up close to him. "Whatever you decide, you have to know that I'll always be in love with Lori."

"Always?"

She nods. "I'm afraid so."

He gives Bullock a final glance, makes a decision. "I'm coming," he says.

She smiles kindly and kisses him lightly on the cheek. "I'm glad."

She steps away and steeples her fingers. "I have to make a few arrangements," she says.

He takes a step closer to the projection, looking at the image of his pale face lying in the trench. It looks so dead, so empty behind its cracked faceplate.

"How long will it take us to get there?" he murmurs.

Jaclyn looks up and smiles. "Subjectively, it'll take no time at all; objectively, it'll be about a hundred years. Plus whatever time it takes for our signal to be translated."

He flexes his hand nervously. His palm itches. He'd give anything to have one of the Glocks right now, to have something familiar and comforting to hold onto.

"So, there's no coming back?"

"No."

Jaclyn brushes her white hair away from her eyes, and straightens her dress.

"Are you ready?"

Kenji turns away from the display. In the corner of his mind he can feel the Reef counting down the few remaining seconds until the missiles strike.

"I guess so."

Jaclyn takes his hands in hers. He can feel her breath on his cheek, smell the clean cotton of her overalls.

"Okay then," she says, "let's go."

THE REDOUBT

It's cold here, in the twilight of the universe. The sky's dark with the husks of burned-out stars. Only one still shines – a young sun born from the ragged clouds of dust and gas that circle the bloated remnants of the black hole that ate our galaxy. Its light draws the surviving races to bask in its heat. They huddle close in vehicles of every size and shape, a vast armada of refugees. It's an awesome sight – and I've come a long way to be here, sacrificed a hell of a lot just to see it.

And now that I am here, so far from home, all I can think of is the start of my journey, and the girl I left behind...

. .

Her name was Anna and she had the bluest eyes I'd ever seen. We met on a campsite in Burgundy when we were both eighteen years old, hitchhiking around Europe with friends. She picked me out the crowd at the site's open-air café and stayed with me for the rest of the week.

I remember it as an idyllic time. We took long walks together. There were wild poppies in the hedgerows and coloured lights in the trees. The village streets were steep and narrow. In the evenings we met our friends under the café's corrugated tin roof, to drink wine and tell stories.

"Come with me," I remember her saying on the last night we were together. She had a white cotton blouse and frayed blue jeans. She took my hand and led me downhill, away from the café and our circle of tents, until we came to the stone bridge where the lane crossed the stream.

"I'm so glad I met you," she said, giving me a squeeze. "And I'll be so sad tomorrow, when I have to leave."

We leaned against the parapet. The rough stones held the day's heat. The water bubbled and chuckled underneath.

"Try not to think about it," I said smoothing a stray hair from her cheek. I knew I was going to miss her. I tried to kiss her but she pulled away.

"Will you write to me?" she said.

"Of course."

"You promise you won't forget me?"

"I promise."

She bit her lip. Then she pulled one of her wristbands off. "Here, I want you to have this," she said, and tucked it into my shirt pocket. I put my arms around her and kissed the top of her head. We could hear someone playing a guitar up in the café.

"Are you alright?" I asked.

She huddled closer. "Just hold me," she said.

Minutes passed. A breeze picked up, stirring the willows bent over the water.

"We should get back to the tent," I said. "It's going to rain."

Anna shook her head. "Not yet – I want to go a bit further."

I felt my shoulders slump. "How much further?"

"To the little church we saw yesterday."

"But that's in the next village," I protested.

She took my arm. "It isn't far."

She led me across the bridge and I looked up at the clouds in the hot sky. "It feels like there's a storm coming," I said.

Anna squeezed me. The lane before us cut a straight line through the flat fields.

"Then we should walk faster," she said.

By the time we reached the medieval church, fat spots of rain were falling. I pushed the heavy wooden door open. Inside, the only light came from the narrow, dusty windows.

"Should we light a candle?" I said. The place smelled of incense. It was cooler in here than outside, and a little creepy.

Anna shook her head. She put a hand on my shoulder and kissed my neck. "I'm really very fond of you," she whispered. I was surprised; we'd spent the last week avoiding such declarations, because we knew they'd only make it harder when the time came to go our separate ways. She stepped back. "In fact, I think I love you," she said.

I swallowed. "You do?"

She looked away. "I just wanted you to know."

I reached out and touched her. I didn't know how else to respond. I said, "You realise we'll never see each other again, don't you?"

"We might."

"We won't." I put my arms around her. She lived on the other side of the world, and neither of us had any money. "But thank you," I said.

•٠

A little while later we were sitting on the smooth flagstone floor, just inside the open door, watching the rain. I had my back to the wall and Anna had her head in my lap.

"So, what are you going to do when you get home?" she said.

I shrugged. When I got back to Wales I'd be broke and I'd have to start making some serious decisions about my future, like whether to go on to university or leave full time education and get a job. But right now, it all seemed so far away, like another life.

Across the fields, we could see the lights of the campsite.

"It's midnight," I said. "They'll be wondering where we are."

Lightning flashed on the horizon, then again, closer. The rain got heavier. "They won't be too worried – they know we're together," said Anna.

Another flash lit the church and thunder rolled overhead.

She sat up and smiled. "Besides, this is our last night together – I don't want to share it with anyone else."

. .

We were standing at the door when I saw a dark shadow moving in the field across the road. I leaned out to get a better look.

Anna pulled at my hand. "What is it?"

"There's something over there," I said. "Look, wait for the lightning. There."

"Oh yes. Is it a balloon?"

"It's too big."

"But it moves like one. Maybe it's a blimp?"

I took a step out, into the rain. As we watched, the shadow grazed the top of the hedge and dropped into the next field.

"Come on," I grabbed her hand and pulled her across the road to the gate. We climbed over into the field. The object floated in the middle, one end dragging in the mud. Despite the rain, I felt the hairs prickle on the back of my neck.

Anna had a death grip on my forearm. "What the hell is it?" she said, shouting over the noise of the storm.

I scratched my head. It was a rugby ball about the size of a

Volkswagen, covered in intakes, bulges and antennae, its hull shimmering with the energies contained within.

"I think it's a UFO," I said.

We stood watching from a few metres away as it wallowed in the air. Then it seemed to right itself, and settled to the ground.

"It looks damaged," I said, and I felt Anna shiver – we were both wet through.

"Maybe it got hit by lightning?" she said.

"Maybe..." I took a step toward it.

"What are you doing?"

"I'm going to take a closer look."

"Don't!" She pulled at my arm but I slipped free. I just had to touch it. I took two quick steps and reached out my hand.

Thunder split the sky.

. •

I woke with a start, on a beach with Anna beside me. Surf broke on the white sand. Palms swayed in the offshore breeze.

"Where are we?" she said, shading her eyes against the late afternoon sun. I climbed shakily to my feet. I could see another beach through the trees, about a hundred yards away.

"We're on an island," I said.

I helped her up and we stood there, looking around and clinging to each other.

"How did we get here?" she said. "Are we dreaming?"

I could feel the heat of the sand through my shoes, and smell the sea air – it all seemed real enough.

"I don't think so," I said.

We edged down to the waterline and Anna kicked her shoes off. Then without speaking, we walked right the way around the island. It took us half an hour. Everywhere we looked, there were other islands on the horizon but no signs of life.

It wasn't until we got back to our starting point that we noticed the pirate galleon. It was moored out by the reef, sails furled. A dinghy lay beached nearby with its oars shipped and a man sitting in the stern.

"Ah, there you are," he said. He had a scrubby beard and dark eyes, and wore breeches and a black jacket. As we got closer, he stood up.

Anna took a step back.

"Who are you?" she said.

The man smiled. He had a gold tooth. "My name's Hook," he said, tugging at the brim of his feathered hat.

He led us up into the trees, to a clearing, and the embers of a driftwood fire.

"Sit, make yourselves comfortable," he said. The sun was going down. He wrapped a handkerchief around his hand and picked a coffee pot from the fire. "Would you like a cup?" he said. "Or would you prefer something a bit stronger?"

Still stunned, unable to see any alternative, we knelt in the sand.

"We just want to know where we are," I said.

There were some tin mugs by the fire. He picked one up, blew into it, and filled it. Then he filled the other two and passed them over. He put the pot by the fire to keep warm, and settled himself in the sand, facing us.

"Let's start simply," he said, stroking his beard. "First off, can you tell me who you are?"

He sipped his coffee, watching us. Anna slipped her hand into mine. "I'm Anna," she said. She gave me a squeeze. "And this is Scott." She looked at me, as if for confirmation, and I gave her an encouraging nod.

Hook put his cup down. "I'm afraid not," he said slowly. "I know that's who you think you are, but really, you're mistaken."

The sea breeze ruffled the tops of the palm trees and stirred the smoky embers of the fire.

"Then who are we?" I said.

"Your real selves are still lying in that field in France," he said. "You're facsimiles, simulations. When you touched the 'UFO' it copied your mental state, like copying a piece of software."

I waved a hand at our surroundings. "And all this is a simulation too?"

"That's right. We're going on a voyage and we're giving you the choice whether to come with us or not. This is our boarding program. It's a symbolic choice – you've got to decide if you want to get on the ship, or stay here on the land."

I looked out at the galleon silhouetted against the last of the setting sun. "But how does that work?" I said.

He put his hands together. "It's simple," he said. 'The 'flying saucer' as you called it contains a solid block of computronium at its heart, running neural simulations of the uploaded mind-states of thousands of intelligent beings." He paused, seeing our blank looks. "It's a computer," he said.

"Like a virtual reality kind of thing?" Anna said hesitantly.

Hook nodded. "Exactly," he said. "It's a virtual reality simulation that allows you to accompany the 'saucer' as it travels from star to star, to witness everything it encounters." He leaned forward. "And if you get in the dinghy it shows you want to come with us."

I rubbed my arms, feeling a sudden chill. The sun was almost gone and the breeze was really getting up. "And what happens if we want to stay?"

He puffed out his cheeks. "Then you'll be deleted."

Anna sat up in alarm. "You'll kill us?"

Hook waved his hand dismissively. "No, no – your real selves are alive and healthy," he said. "For them, only seconds have passed. Whatever you decide, they'll go right on with their lives, with no knowledge of any of this."

He stood and walked over to the fire, and prodded a piece of driftwood with the toe of his boot, nudging it into the embers.

"And what happens if we go with the ship?" I said.

He smiled. "We travel the stars, copying things," he said. "We don't take anything, and we don't disturb anything. We just take copies. But we don't want to hold anyone against his or her will. If you want to come with us, get in the dinghy. If you don't, well... just stay here." He looked at the red clouds in the West. "You have until first light to make your decision."

He lay down, pulled his hat over his eyes, and went to sleep. We listened to him snore. Overhead a few stars poked through the twilit sky. We huddled on the opposite side of the fire, wrapped in each other's arms. We were both very tired, which didn't help.

"I don't understand any of this," Anna said.

I held her tightly. I was just as confused as she was. "We're like photographs," I said, struggling to understand it myself as I explained it to her. "Walking, talking photographs."

I felt her fists clench, pulling at the back of my shirt. "It's not right," she said angrily. "I don't feel like a 'photograph', I feel like I've been kidnapped."

Out by the reef there were lamps burning on the galleon. I could see figures moving around on deck, and I wanted to see who they were and what they were doing. Was this all really just a simulation?

"What do you think we should do?" I said.

Anna let out a long breath. I felt her body relax. "I just want to go home," she said, suddenly miserable.

I jerked my thumb at the pirate ship. "You're not at all curious why they've gone to all this trouble?" I asked.

She turned her face away. "And you are? You don't even know where they're going."

"What?"

"They say they want us to go with them but they haven't told us where," she said.

We woke Hook and asked him.

"We call it the Redoubt," he said. "It doesn't exist yet but according to our predictions, in a hundred thousand billion years, when our galaxy's a burned-out corpse orbiting a swollen black hole, it'll shine forth in the darkness – the last remaining star.

"Where else," he said, "would you look for the last gathering of intelligent life?"

"And that's where you're going?" I asked.

He smoothed his beard with a gnarled hand. "That's where we're all going," he said. "This ship's been travelling a long time, and we've visited a lot of worlds, picking up thousands of passengers at every stop."

Anna sat rubbing her eyes. She yawned. "But why?" she said.

He frowned at her. "It's going to be the final oasis of light and warmth in the galaxy – there'll be species there from all periods of history, with all sorts of new and strange technologies. Think what we can accomplish together!" He had sand on the hem of his jacket. He brushed it off with a rough flick of his hand. "And besides," he said, "think what we'll see on the way there! A hundred thousand billion years of history, of exploration – you'll have full access to all the data from our external sensors. And you'll never age. You'll still be the same as you are now when the stars start going out and the universe settles into its long twilight." He clapped his hands, rubbing them briskly. "Now won't that be worth the trip in itself?"

• •

Hook said he'd wait for us by the dinghy, so we left him to it and took a walk down to the rolling surf. Anna had her arms folded across her chest. "You're going to go with him, aren't you?" she said.

I stopped walking. "What makes you say that?"

"I saw the look in your eyes – you've already made up your mind."

I took a deep breath. "What's the alternative? You heard him – our real selves are still back in that field. They'll wake up tomorrow and get on with their lives. They won't remember us because we're not really here." I waved my arms to encompass the island and the stars. "We've got nothing to lose."

She turned away and hunched her shoulders. "But what if I said I wanted to stay here?"

"You'd be deleted."

"Yes, but what if that's what I wanted? Would you stay with me?"

I stepped up behind her. The sea breeze straggled at her hair.

"I just want to wake up with you in France, and have a normal life," she said. "And I want to go home. I want to see my family, and my friends."

I touched her shoulder. "If you come with me, we can have an eternity together."

She shivered. "I can't do it," she said. "Not without them." Her eyes glittered in the starlight. The surf crashed on the beach. I held onto her shoulders, feeling something welling up inside, something I couldn't hold back any longer.

"I love you," I said. "I love you here and now, and I love you back there, in France." She opened her mouth to speak but I touched a finger to her lips. "Now, I'm getting on that boat," I said. "And I'd like you to come with me. I really would. But I'll understand if you say no."

She looked down and the hair fell over her face. "I don't want to lose you," she said.

"And you won't! Our real selves are together, right now. Maybe they'll find a way to stay together, or maybe they won't. All I know is that you and I, here and now, we've been given this fantastic chance to see the universe – to find out how the story ends. And I can't pass that up."

"But why?"

"Because I owe it to myself – to the 'me' that's going to wake up in France on the last day of his holiday. The 'me' that's going to go home and spend the next three years as a penniless student – the 'me' that's always going to look up at the night sky and wonder what's out there, but never get the chance to find out." I rubbed my eyes with the heels of my hands. "I've been asked to represent the whole human race at the end of time," I said. "And that's something I can't walk away from."

She brushed the hair from her eyes and rubbed her nose on her sleeve. "I understand," she said. She leaned forward and kissed me on the cheek.

I let out a held breath, and asked: "Are you coming with me?"

She looked out at the galleon. Its lamps were reflected on the dark water. "No, I can't. I'd miss my family and my friends too much. I couldn't face living for thousands of years knowing they were dead. No, I'm staying here."

"But..."

"No!" Suddenly angry, she stalked off, arms still folded, toward the beached dinghy, where Hook waited.

I hurried after her, stumbling in the dry sand. "What are you doing?" I said.

She didn't stop. "Just go," she said, "if you have to."

"What, now?" I reached out a hand but she slapped it away.

"Yes, right now – just get on the boat and go," she said.

"Can't we can talk about it?" I said. "We've got until first light."

She stopped walking and looked out to sea, arms folded again. "I said goodbye to you last night, in the church," she said. "I don't want to have to go through it all again. I'm too tired, too confused. Please, just go now."

She took a deep breath, blinking back tears. Looking at her, I almost changed my mind, almost gave up everything just to be with her for a few more minutes. "I love you," I said.

She nodded. Then she leaned toward me and I put my arms around her. "I love you too," she whispered, and then pulled away and shivered. "Now go."

. •

I sat in the stern of the dinghy as, a few minutes later, Hook rowed me out to the pirate galleon at anchor by the coral reef. Anna stood on the beach with the surf washing around her ankles. She had her hand raised, waving as each slap and stroke of the oars pulled us further apart. She shouted something as we neared the reef, but I didn't catch it, so I just waved back. I looked at Hook, and had to swallow hard to stop myself from crying. He nodded at me as if he understood.

"What happens now?" I said.

He paused, letting the oars drip into the sea. The crew on

the galleon's deck were hoisting sail and stowing the anchor. "We're getting ready to leave," he said. "We'll set sail as soon as you're aboard."

I looked back to the beach, and Anna was a shadow on the white sand, small and hard to see. I patted my shirt pocket. I still had her wristband next to my heart. And then we were moving again, pulling around behind the larger vessel, toward a waiting rope ladder. I caught a final glimpse of her, still waving.

"I'll never forget you," I called. And I never did.

DISTANT GALAXIES COLLIDING

It was a damp afternoon in November, and wet leaves blew down the narrow streets. I ordered tea at a pavement café near the Seine while I waited for Candy to arrive. When she did, she was carrying a white cane and wearing a cheap pair of plastic sunglasses. She'd been mugged by a teenage gang on the streets of Hamburg. They'd stolen her camera and sprayed paint into her eyes.

She held onto my arm as we walked south on the Boulevard Saint Michel, toward my hotel. Pigeons and scraps of newspaper flapped around our feet. Behind us, the towers of Notre Dame grazed the sagging sky.

Paris, she said, smelled of neglect; it reminded her of Dublin, or London.

"Do you want to talk about it?" I asked, meaning Hamburg.

She squeezed my arm fiercely and her cheek brushed my shoulder. For half a second, we were off balance.

"Perhaps later," she said.

I led her across the road and up the steps of my hotel. My room was on the fourth floor. When I opened the door, she dropped her cane and sat on the bed. There were a few possessions on the nightstand: my passport; a handful of coins; a magpie feather. She stirred them with her finger as I drew the curtains.

"I'm thinking of going back to the States," she said. She rolled onto her back and began toying with the feather, dabbing it lightly against her nose.

I didn't reply; I didn't want her to go. The last few weeks without her had been almost unbearable.

"There's nothing left for me here," she said.

I knelt beside her and touched the golden stubble on her scalp. It was rough, like Velcro.

"I'm here for you."

Her arm fell to the bed. She dropped the feather and turned her head away.

There was something digging into my knee. It was a small hardback book. It must have fallen from her coat pocket. I picked it up; it was a copy of her latest collection of published photographs. The dust jacket was torn.

"When will you leave?" I asked.

She shrugged. Outside on the street, a siren wailed. At the lights, the taxis idled. We could hear their turbines ticking over.

"As soon as possible," she said.

• •

I first met Candy about a year ago, in one of those nameless bars that litter the waterfront around Canary Wharf. My divorce had just come through and I was working freelance, writing articles for an online arts magazine. Candy was an up-and-coming American photographer, and I was supposed to be interviewing her. She wore too much jewellery and always seemed to be chewing something. When we shook hands, her fingers were cool, but her eyes were restless.

"Do you want to get something to eat?" she asked. It was around seven-thirty on a wet October evening and the place was crowded. I hadn't eaten since breakfast, so we drove over to Hammersmith, where I knew a quiet Moroccan restaurant. Inside, it smelled of incense and fried onions.

She showed me some samples of her work; pictures of street children and famine victims. They were very good, very poignant, but she seemed dissatisfied with them. When the food arrived, she spat her gum into a serviette.

"So," she said, stirring the couscous on her plate, "what do you want to know?"

I leaned forward.

"Just the facts," I said.

She flashed a crooked smile. "You want to know if I'm going to go home with you tonight, don't you?"

"I guess."

She tilted her head. The cheap jewelled stud in her ear caught the candlelight. "Are you always so forward?"

We ate in silence for a while, listening to the chef rattling pans in the kitchen. I'd opted for the chicken tagine. It was flavoured with pickled lemons and olives.

"I've just come out of a bad relationship," I said.

"I know." She covered my hand with her own. "I can tell."

The traffic outside was queued back from the flyover. We finished our meal and went back to my flat.

That first night, I left the lights off and the curtains open. I made coffee by the orange streetlight and watched her undress. The rain running down the window cast eerie underwater shadows on her pale skin.

．・

Two weeks later we flew out to Greece, then Turkey. Her work carried her all over, and I tagged along when I could.

She was always restless, always ready to move on. She lived out of a rucksack, preferring to buy things when she needed them rather than weigh herself down.

That winter, she walked through Athens and Istanbul, her digital camera clicking furiously.

"I'm a professional tourist," she said.

• •

I remember sitting beneath a tree, beside a ruined temple, looking out at the Aegean. The water and sky were a matching blue, and the white sun burned above us. I'd been sifting through some of her downloaded images on my palmtop, but now the battery was running low.

"Do you know," she said, "that Earth is the only planet whose English name isn't derived from Greek or Roman mythology?"

I smiled. I closed the palmtop and lay back against the tree. The bark was gnarled and warm. Goats grazed among the fallen stones of the temple, and the air smelled faintly of dry grass and dung.

"What's that got to do with anything?"

She came over and sat beside me. She'd spent all morning looking around the temple, recording it all. She wore a white cotton dress with big, wooden buttons up the front.

"I don't know," she said. She reached into her shoulder bag and pulled out the magazine she'd bought at the airport. There was an article in it about the old Hubble Telescope; the accompanying picture showed two distant galaxies colliding.

"Look at that for a picture," she said, using a fingernail to trace the dusty whorls of tortured stars.

"It's pretty," I said.

Candy frowned. "The light from these stars is a million years old," she said. "It's been travelling through space since before the dawn of civilisation, since before this temple was built."

We looked around at the collapsed walls, the moss and lichen covering the scattered stones. They looked so much a part of the landscape that it was difficult to imagine the headland without them.

"It makes what I'm doing seem so bloody ephemeral." She pushed her blonde hair back and dropped the magazine. When she looked across at me, her eyes were the same shade of green as the sunlight filtering through the leafy branches above.

"I like your pictures," I said.

She ignored me. She rolled onto her front and put her chin on her fist.

"I could be doing so much more," she said.

.•

Despite her doubts, the pictures she took that day were startling. She had a knack for picking out details: a flower blooming from beneath a crumbled pillar; a crushed cola can glinting in the Mediterranean sun; a vapour trail above an ancient olive grove.

Many of those pictures wound up in the collection that I now held in my hand. Kneeling beside the bed in that Parisian hotel, I flicked through the pages.

They were mostly pictures of collapsed and overgrown buildings, but there were a few pictures of the night sky, taken from various locations.

This wasn't just her latest collection of photographs, I realised sadly. It was also going to be her last.

When we'd originally arranged to meet in Paris, six weeks

ago, she'd been hoping to visit the ESA headquarters. She'd wanted to use a deep range telescope for her next project. She'd wanted to find a way to make art out of science, to express how small and insignificant the universe made her feel.

Now, she wouldn't have the chance.

She'd never take another picture; there'd never be another collection. She'd have to find another way to express herself.

She heard the rustle of glossy pages and her head turned towards the sound. Behind her sunglasses, I could see the white gauze dressings that covered her eyes.

"What are you reading?" she asked.

I lied; I said it was a guidebook.

She held a hand out to me. Her fingers were cold and dry.

"Open the curtains," she whispered, "and tell me what you see."

I pulled myself up and pocketed the book.

"Why?"

She turned away and hugged the pillow to her chest. Her knees were drawn up and her feet were tangled in her skirt.

"Because I want my final image of Europe to be a good one," she said.

She looked so frail and vulnerable, I couldn't refuse her. I stepped over to the window, pulled back the curtain, and began to describe the buildings across the street.

Candy, fumbling on the bedside table, managed to switch on the clock radio; gentle Cuban music filled the room, like cigarette smoke. A light rain began to fall. It was getting dark and the orange streetlights painted everything with their false colours, reminding me of our first night in Hammersmith, twelve short months before.

As I spoke, I thought of those kids in Hamburg, of what they'd done. Had they simply been trying to steal her camera, or did they blind her because they were jealous of the things she'd seen? In their vicious and brutal way, they'd taken far more from her than simply her sight, and I doubted if she'd ever fully recover.

"Can you see the stars?" she asked.

I said no.

A woman appeared below, framed in a café doorway. She lit a cigarette and turned up the collar of her raincoat. As she hurried up the street, the wet leaves snagged on her high heels. At the corner, she stopped to scratch her leg, where the impurities of her ankle chain had irritated the skin.

I told Candy that it would have made a perfect picture. I felt her move up behind me. Her hands touched my shoulders.

"I guess that'll have to do, then," she said.

RED LIGHTS AND RAIN

It's raining in Amsterdam. Paige stands in the oak-panelled front bar of a small corner pub. She has wet hair because she walked here from her hotel. Now she's standing by the open door, holding half a litre of Amstel, watching the rain stipple the surface of the canal across the street. For the fourth time in five minutes, she takes out her mobile and checks the screen for messages. From across the room, the barman looks at her. He has dark skin and gold dreads. Seeing the phone in her hand again, he smiles, obviously convinced she's waiting for a date.

Outside, damp tourists pass in the rain, looking for the Anne Frank house; open-topped pleasure boats seek shelter beneath hump-back bridges; and bare-headed boys cut past on scooters, cigarettes flaring, girlfriends clinging side-saddle to the parcel shelves, tyres going *bop-bop-bop* on the wet cobble stones. Paige sucks the froth from her beer. On the other side of the canal, a church bell clangs nine o'clock. As it happens, she *is* waiting for a man, but this won't be any sort of date, and she'll be lucky if she survives to see the sun come up tomorrow morning. She pockets the mobile, changes the beer glass from one hand to the other, and slips her fingers into the pocket of her coat, allowing them to brush the cold metal butt of the pistol she's carrying. It's a lightweight coil gun: a magnetic projectile accelerator, fifty years more advanced than anything else in this time zone, and capable of punching a titanium slug through a concrete wall. With luck, it will be enough.

She watches the barman lay out new beer mats on the zinc counter. He's just a boy, really. She should probably warn him to leave, but she doesn't want to attract too much attention, not just yet. She doesn't want the police to blunder in and complicate matters.

For a moment, her eyes are off the door, and that's when Josef arrives. She hears the swish of his coat, the clack of his boots as they hit the step. She sees the barman's gaze flick past her shoulder, and his eyes widen, and she turns to find Josef standing on the threshold, close enough to kiss.

"Hello, Paige." He's at least five inches taller than she is; rake thin with pale lips and rain-slicked hair.

"Josef." She slides her right hand into her coat, sees him notice the movement.

"Are you here to kill me, Paige?"

"Yes."

"It's not going to be easy."

"I know."

He flicks his eyes in the direction of the bar, licks his bottom lip. "What about him?" Paige takes a step back, placing herself between the 'vampire' and the boy with the golden dreadlocks. With her hand still in her pocket, she curls her index finger around the trigger of the coil gun.

"Not tonight, Josef."

Josef shrugs and folds his arms, shifts his weight petulantly from one foot to the other. "So, what?" he says. "You want to go at it right now, in here?"

Paige shakes her head. She's trying not to show emotion, but her heart's hammering and she's sure he can hear it.

"Outside," she says. Josef narrows his eyes. He looks her up and down, assessing her as an opponent. Despite his attenuated frame, she knows he can strike like a whip when he wants to. She tenses, ready for his attack and, for a moment, they're frozen like that: eyes locked, waiting for the other to make the first move. Then Josef laughs. He turns on his heel, flicks up the collar of his coat, and steps out into the rain.

Paige lets out a long breath. Her stomach's churning. She pulls the coil gun from her pocket and looks over at the barman.

"Stay here," she says.

• •

She follows Josef into a small concrete yard at the rear of the pub, surrounded by walls on all sides, and lit from above by the orange reflection of city lights on low cloud. Rusty dumpsters stand against one wall; a fire escape ladder hangs from the back of the pub; and metal trapdoors cover the cellar. Two storeys above, the gutters leak, spattering the concrete.

Josef says, "So, how do you want to do this?"

Paige lets the peeling wooden door to the street bang shut behind her, hiding them from passers-by. The coil gun feels heavy in her hand.

"Get over by the wall," she says.

Josef shakes his head.

She opens her mouth to insist but, before she can speak or raise the gun, he's closed the distance between them, his weight slamming her back against the wooden door. She feels his breath on her cheek, his hand clasping her throat. She tries to bring the gun to bear but he chops it away, sending it clattering across the wet floor.

"You're pathetic," he growls, and lifts her by the throat. Her feet paw at empty air. She tries to prise his hand loose, but his fingers are like talons, and she can't breathe; she's choking. In desperation, she kicks his kneecap, making him stagger. With a snarl, he tosses her against one of the large-wheeled dumpsters. She hits it with an echoing crash, and ends up on her hands and knees, coughing, struggling for air. Josef's boot catches her in the ribs, and rolls her onto her side. He stamps down once, twice, and something snaps in her left forearm. The pain fills her. She yelps, and curls herself around it. The coil gun rests on the concrete three or four metres away on the other side of the yard, and there's no way he'll let her reach it. He kicks her twice more, then leans down with his mouth open, letting her see his glistening ceramic incisors. They're fully extended now, locked in attack position, and ready to tear out her windpipe.

"Ha' enough?" he says, the fangs distorting his speech.

Paige coughs again. She's cradling her broken arm, and she still can't breathe properly. She's about to tell him to go to hell, when the back door of the pub swings open, and out steps the boy with the golden dreads, a sawn-off antique shotgun held at his hip.

"That's enough," he says. His eyes are wide and scared.

Josef looks up with a hiss, teeth bared. Startled, the barman pulls the trigger. The flash and bang fill the yard. Josef takes both barrels in the chest. It snatches him away like laundry in the wind, and he lands by the door to the street, flapping and yelling, drumming his boot heels on the concrete.

"Shoot him again," Paige gasps, but the young man stands frozen in place, transfixed by the thrashing 'vampire.' He hasn't even reloaded. Paige uses her good arm to claw her way into a sitting position. The rain's soaked through her clothes.

"Shoot him!"

But it's too late. Still hollering, Josef claws his way through the wooden door, out onto the street. Paige pulls herself up and makes it to the pavement just in time to see him slip over the edge of the bank, into the canal, dropping noiselessly into the water between two tethered barges. She turns back to find the boy with the shotgun looking at her.

"Is he dead?"

She shakes her head. The air's tangy with gun smoke. "No, he'll be back." She scoops up her fallen coil gun and slides it back into her coat pocket. Her left arm's clutched against her chest. Every time she moves, she has to bite her lip against the pain.

The boy takes her by the shoulder, and she can feel his hands shake as he guides her into the pub kitchen, where she leans against the wall as he locks and bolts the back door.

. •

When she asks, the boy tells her his name is Federico. He settles her on a bar stool, plonks a shot glass and a half-empty bottle of cognac on the counter, then goes to close the front door. "I'm going to call the police," he says.

As he brushes past her, Paige catches his arm. "There's no time, we have to leave."

He looks down at her hand. "I don't *have* to do anything," he says. "Not until you explain what the hell just happened."

She releases him. He's frightened, but the fear's manifesting as anger, and she's going to have to do something drastic to convince him.

"Okay," she says. She puts her left arm on the bar, and rolls up the sleeve, letting him see the bloody contusions from Josef's boot, and the splinter of bone, like a shard of broken china, sticking up through the skin.

"What are you doing?"

"Shush." She takes hold of her wrist, forces the arm flat against the zinc counter, and twists. There's an audible click, and the two halves of broken bone snap back into place. When her eyes have stopped watering, she plucks out the loose shard and drops it with a clink into the ash tray. With it out of the way, the skin around the tear starts to heal. In less than a minute, only a red mark remains.

Federico takes a step back, eyes wide, hand pointing. "That's not natural."

Paige lifts the half-empty bottle of cognac with her right hand, pulls the plastic-coated cork with her teeth, and spits it across the bar.

"Josef heals even faster than I do," she says. "You blew a hole in his chest, but he'll be as good as new in an hour, maybe less."

"W-what are you?"

Paige takes a solid nip of the brandy. "I'm as human as you are," she says, and gets to her feet. She can feel the stiffness fading from her limbs, the hurt evaporating from her ribs and arm. "But Josef's something quite different. And trust me, you *really* don't want to be here when he comes back."

"But the police—"

"Forget the police. You shot him, that makes it personal."

Federico puts his fists on his hips. "I don't believe you."

Paige jerks a thumb at the back door. "Then believe what you saw out there." She stands and pats down her coat, making sure she still has everything she needs. Federico looks from her to the door, and then back again.

"Is he really that dangerous?"

"Oh yes."

"Then, what do you suggest?"

Paige rubs her face. She doesn't want to be saddled with a civilian, doesn't want to be responsible for anybody else's well-being; but this young man saved her life, and she knows she owes him for that.

She sighs.

"Your best bet's to come with me, right now," she says. "I'm the only one who knows what we're up against, the only one with even half a chance of being able to protect you."

"How do I know I can trust you?"

She looks him square in the eye. "Because I'm not the one who's going to come back here and rip your throat out."

. .

She lets Federico pull on a battered leather biker jacket two sizes too large, and they leave the pub and splash their way down the cobbled streets in the direction of the Red Light District, and Paige's hotel. As they walk, she keeps her eye on the canal.

Federico says, "Is he really a… you know?"

"A vampire?" Paige shakes her head. "No. At least, not in the sense you're thinking. There's nothing supernatural or romantic about him. He's not afraid of crosses or garlic, or any of that bullshit."

"But I saw his teeth."

"Ceramic implants."

They cut across a square in the shadow of a medieval church. Federico has the shotgun under his jacket, and it makes him walk stiffly. The rain's still falling, and there's music from the bars and coffeehouses; but few people are out on the street.

"Then what is he? Some sort of psycho?"

Paige slows for a second, and turns to him. "He's a guerrilla."

"I don't understand."

She starts walking again. "I don't expect you to." Her right hand is in her coat pocket, gripping the coil gun. She leads him out of the square, across a footbridge, and then they're into the Red Light District, with its pink neon shop fronts and narrow alleys. Her hotel's close to the Centraal Station. By the time they get there, they're both soaked, and stand dripping together in the elevator that takes them up to her floor.

"In a thousand years' time, there's going to be a war," she says, watching the floor numbers count off. "And it's going to be a particularly nasty one, with atrocities on all sides." The lift doors open and she leads him along the carpeted corridor to her room. Inside, the room smells stale. It's been her base of operations for nearly a month, and she hasn't let the cleaner touch it in all that time. She hasn't even opened the curtains.

"The 'vampires' were bred to fight in the war," she says. "They were designed to operate behind enemy lines, terrorising civilians, sowing fear and confusion." She shrugs off her coat and drops it over the back of a chair. "They're trained to go to ground, blend in as best they can, then start killing people. They're strong and fast, and optimised for night combat."

Federico's standing in the doorway, shivering. She ushers him in and sits him on the bed. Gingerly, she takes the shotgun from his hands, and lays it on the sheet beside him; she then drapes a blanket around his shoulders.

"After the war, some of them escaped, and they've been spreading backwards through time ever since." She crosses to the wardrobe, and pulls out a spirit bottle. It's a litre of vodka. She takes two teacups off the side and pours a large measure for him, a smaller one for herself. "They're designed to survive for long durations, without support. They can eat just about anything organic, and they're hard to kill. You can hurt them, but as long as their hearts are beating and their brains are intact, there's a chance they'll be able to repair themselves, given enough time."

She puts the bottle aside and flexes the fingers of her left hand – there's still an ache, deep in the bone.

"That's important," she says. She kneels down in front of Federico, and takes his hands in hers. "The next time we see Josef, we've got to kill him, before he kills us. And the only way to do that is to do as much damage as possible. Stop his heart, destroy his brain, and he's dead."

She takes one of the teacups and presses it into Federico's hands.

"Sorry," he says, accepting the drink, "did you say that this war is *going* to take place?"

"A thousand years downstream, yes."

"So it hasn't happened yet?"

"No."

He frowns. "Who are you?"

Paige reaches for her coat, and pulls out the coil gun. "I'm a fangbanger, a 'vampire' killer."

"And you're from the future too?"

Paige stands. "Look," she says. "All you need to know tonight is this: when you see Josef, shoot out his legs. That'll immobilise him, and give us time to kill him." She stops talking then. She can see Federico's had enough for one night. She slips a pill into his next drink and, within minutes, he's asleep, wrapped in the blanket, with the shotgun clasped protectively across his chest.

Alone with her thoughts, Paige moves quietly. She turns out the bedside light and crosses to the window, pulling aside the heavy curtain. It's after twelve now, and the trams have stopped for the night. The streets are quiet. She feels she should congratulate Josef on his choice of hiding place. Amsterdam is an easy city in which to be a stranger; there are so many tourists, so many distractions, that it's a simple matter to lose yourself in the crowd. If she hadn't known what to look for, she might never have found him. But then, she's been a fangbanger for a long time, and she's learned to piece together seemingly unrelated deaths and unexplained crimes; to filter out the background noise of modern urban life in order to reveal the unmistakable M.O. of an active 'vampire.' She leans her forehead against the window glass; heart pumping in her chest, knowing it won't take Josef long to track her down. She's been doing this job for enough years, waded through enough shit, to know how dangerous a wounded 'vampire' can be.

. .

At 4 a.m., the sky starts to grey in the east. Federico's still asleep, and Paige gives up her vigil.

She tucks the coil gun into the back of her belt, pulls on a sweater to cover it, and wanders down to the hotel restaurant. When she gets there, she finds the place empty, although she can hear cooking sounds from the kitchen as the staff gear up for the breakfast rush. She helps herself to a cup of coffee from the pot, and a large handful of sugar sachets, and takes it all over to a table by the window, where she stirs the contents of the little packets into her coffee. There are sixteen altogether, and she uses them all. Then, leaving the sticky mess to cool, she rests her left arm on the table, and clenches and unclenches her fist. Everything seems in order. The tendons move as they should, and there's no trace of the break. It doesn't even ache now. Satisfied, she takes a sip of the lip-curlingly sweet coffee. It tastes disgusting, but she needs the sugar to refuel the tweaked macrophages and artificial fibroblasts that have allowed her to heal so quickly.

Outside the window, it's still raining. She watches the drops slither on the glass. It makes her think of Josef in better times, before he had his fangs implanted. She remembers him as bright and swift and clever; a sociopath, yes, but still her best student. And there it is, her dirty little secret, the inconvenient truth she's been hiding from Federico: the reason she makes such a good 'vampire' hunter is that during the war, before the 'vampires' were deployed against the enemy, it was she who trained them. She was a military psychologist at the time, an expert in guerrilla warfare. While combat instructors taught the 'vampires' how to kill, she showed them a range of nasty tricks culled from a thousand hard-fought insurgencies: from the Scythians of Central Asia to the soldiers of the Viet Cong, and beyond.

She remembers her penultimate briefing in particular.

"The vampire's a powerful archetype," she said to the cadets. "It's an expression of our darker side. It plays into our most primal anxieties, from the threat of predation to the fear of the dark." It was a hot day, and the sun blazed through the classroom windows. She walked up and down in front of her students, hands clasped behind her back. At the rear of the room, the surgeons waited with their trolleys, ready to wheel the young men and women down to the operating theatre, one-by-one, in order to implant their fangs and night-adapted eyes. "To complete your mission, you must be prepared to kill. You must become assassins – anonymous killers in the night, spreading panic and mistrust." She stopped pacing and turned to Josef. He sat in the front row of the classroom, chin on fist, eyes blazing, and she knew it would be the last time she'd see him before his transformation. "If you do your jobs correctly," she said, "each of you will be worth a hundred troops. You'll demoralise the enemy, eat out his fighting spirit from the inside. You'll have the soldiers worried about their families, the families suspicious of their neighbours. But in order to achieve this, you'll have to move like shadows, and show no mercy. Do anything that needs to be done, be ruthless, and be prepared to strike anywhere, at any time."

She had taught them every psychological trick she knew, and shown them how to exploit the power of myth, how to generate fear and horror from darkness and blood. From their test scores, she'd known they were intelligent. She'd personally overseen the original selection process, picking only those recruits with the right balance of brains and insanity – those clever enough to survive the mission, but also psychotic enough to become the monsters they'd need to become in order to succeed.

And then later, when the war went temporal, spilling into the surrounding decades, they came back and she briefed them again, only this time on the peculiarities of each of the time zones in which they were to operate, giving them the background they'd need in order to blend into each zone's civilian population.

Sometimes, she wonders if her history lessons inspired their eventual escape into this dim and distant past, far from even the outermost fringes of the conflict. One thing's for certain: since they mutinied, and fled back to these primitive times, she's had to travel all over the place in order to hunt them down. She's tracked individual 'vampires' across half a dozen decades, in Los Angeles, Cairo, Warsaw and London.

Now she's here, in Amsterdam.

And suddenly, there's Josef. He's standing in the shadow of a doorway on the other side of the street, watching her through the glass. He has his hands in the pockets of his black raincoat. Their eyes meet for a second and Paige can't breathe.

Then he's gone, moving fast. Between parked cars, she catches a glimpse of him crossing the street, heading for the back of the hotel. With a curse, she pushes herself to her feet. Josef will know which room she's staying in – a simple phone call will have furnished him with that information – and now he's after Federico, hoping to kill the boy before tackling her.

Paige bursts out into the foyer. Her room's on the fourth floor, so there's no time to take the stairs. However, luck's on her side: this early in the morning, the elevators all stand ready, their doors open. She slams into the nearest, and slaps the button for the fourth floor. Then, even as the doors are closing, she's pulling the coil gun from her belt and checking its magazine.

• •

Paige kicks her shoes off in the elevator, and pads along the corridor in her socks. As she nears her room, she hears the door splinter: Josef's kicked his way in. "Damn." She lifts the coil gun to her shoulder, and risks a peek around the frame. The room's dark. She can see a faint glow from the curtains. There are shadows all over the place: chairs, desks and suitcases. Any one of them could be a crouched 'vampire.'

"Fuck."

She ducks back into the corridor and takes a few quick breaths. If Josef's still in there, he'll have heard her already – and there's a good possibility Federico's already dead. She flicks off the coil gun's safety catch. There's nothing beyond this room but window: the chances of civilian casualties are slight. Stepping back, she gives the trigger a squeeze. The gun jerks and jerks again. Holes appear in the door. Splinters flick out. The TV sparks. A chair blows apart.

And there, in the maelstrom: a shadow moves.

She tries to hit him, but the high impact gun fires too slowly and he's moving too fast. He hits the wall and pushes off; hits the floor and rolls; and then he's running on all fours, leaping at her throat before she can draw a bead.

Paige rolls with the impact, still pressing the trigger. Scraps of material fly from Josef's overcoat. An overhead light explodes. Blood sprays. His ceramic teeth scrape her neck, grazing the skin. Then his momentum carries him over her head, and she uses a judo throw to heave him into the corridor wall. He hits like an upside-down starfish, arms and legs splayed, and then falls to the floor.

They both lie panting.

The carpet's soft. She rolls onto her side. Josef's lying on his front, looking sideways at her. His eyes are as blue as a gas flame. This is the first good look she's had at him since he left her class, and he looks older and harder than she remembers. His fangs are white and clean. Blood soaks into the carpet from a hole in his side.

He doesn't move as she elbows herself up into a sitting position; but, as soon as she lifts the coil gun, he twists. His wrist flicks out, and a pair of shiny throwing stars bite Paige's arm. She cries out and the gun drops from her fingers. Instinctively, she reaches for it with her left hand, but Josef's anticipated the move: he pushes himself towards her, delivering a kick to her cheek that shatters the bone.

Paige falls into the open doorway of her room. Black spots dapple her vision. She feels Josef grip her leg. His hands work their way up. He's climbing her, using his weight to keep her pinned down. She tries to fight back, but she's still dazed. He swats her hands away from his face.

Then he's on her, his thighs clamped across her hips, his knees pinning her arms. He wraps his fingers in her hair, and yanks her head back, exposing her throat. His fangs are fully deployed. She sees them through the hair hanging down over his face, and cringes, expecting him to lunge for her neck.

Instead, Josef clears his throat

"I don't want to kill you," he says around his teeth. He pulls away, and his incisors slip back into their sheaths. He lets go of her hair and sits up, straddling her. Paige blinks up at him as he smooths back his wet hair. "I just want to talk."

. •

They end up slumped against opposite walls of the corridor. Josef's bleeding onto the carpet; Paige feels as if she's been hit by a fire truck. One side of her face throbs with pain, and the eye above her broken cheekbone won't focus properly.

"You've got me all wrong," Josef says.

She gives him a look. "You're a killer."

"Not anymore." He lets his shoulders relax, but keeps one hand pressed to the bullet hole in his side.

"But Federico—"

"I haven't touched him."

"He's still alive?"

Josef shrugs. "I can't say for sure. You sprayed a lot of bullets in there."

And suddenly, they're falling back into their old pattern: teacher and student – and she *knows* there's something he's not telling her.

"What's going on, Josef? Why am I still alive?"

He tips his head back, resting it against the wall.

"Because things are different now," he says. "*I'm* different." He reaches into his coat and pulls out a photograph, which he frisbees across to her.

"I wasn't trying to hurt you, you know? Not here, and not

at the pub." He dips his chin and looks at her. "Just acting in self-defence, trying to stop you from killing me."

The picture shows Josef holding a child, maybe four or five years old.

"What's this?"

"It's my daughter."

The girl has Josef's blue eyes and blonde hair. She's wearing a red dress. "Your daughter?"

Josef closes his eyes.

"Yes."

Paige glances at the coil gun, lying on the carpet between them. She wonders if she can reach it before he can reach her.

Josef says, "I don't want any more trouble."

Paige lifts a hand to her ruined cheek, and her lip curls.

"So what? You think it *matters* what you want? So you've gone and got yourself a family, and you think that wipes away all the shit you've done, all the people you've killed?" She reaches for the gun. Josef howls in frustration, and lunges for her throat. His teeth rip into her oesophagus, and she feels his jaw snap shut on her windpipe. His hair fills her face, and he's heavy on her chest. She can't breathe, and wonders how many others have died like this. How many others, because of her, and what she taught him?

Josef pulls back, his face dripping with her blood and, as Paige gasps for breath, the wound bubbles.

Josef snatches the photograph from her unresisting fingers. She tries to move her arms, but can't. Josef's speaking, but the fangs make it difficult, and she can't hear him over the roaring in her ears. Her eyes swivel around in panic, looking for help. The guests in the other rooms must be awake now, and cowering behind their peepholes. Some at least will have called the police.

Then, as she twists her head, she catches movement in the

room behind her. Federico stumbles into the light. The boy looks dazed and frightened; there are scratch marks on his face, but he has the shotgun in his hands.

There's a flash, and Josef jerks. Part of his face disappears, bitten off by the blast. Another flash, and he topples from Paige like a puppet with its strings cut, knocking his head against the doorframe as he falls.

Paige slaps a palm over the sucking wound in her neck, pinching the skin together, hoping she can heal before she suffocates.

Federico bends over her. Wordless, she points to the coil gun, and he kicks it over.

"Help me up," she croaks. As long as she keeps her hand covering the injury, her vocal chords still work.

With Federico's hands under her shoulders, she struggles to her feet and coughs up a wad of blood. She feels unsteady, but each breath is easier than the last.

Josef lies in a spreading patch of red-soaked carpet. One of his eyes is completely gone; that side of his face is a gory ruin; but the other seems miraculously untouched, and still beautiful. His hands twitch on the carpet like angry spiders.

Paige plucks the slippery, homemade throwing stars from her forearm, and tosses them aside. She points the coil gun at Josef's heart. Dimly, she can hear sirens pulling up on the street outside.

Josef's remaining eyelid flutters. She knows he's down, but he's obviously not out.

She says, "How many people have you killed, Josef?" Then, without waiting for an answer, she pulls the trigger. The gun whines and his chest blows apart. His heels scrape at the floor, as if trying to escape, and she raises the gun to his face.

"I'm sorry," she says.

She looks away as she fires, and she keeps the trigger depressed until the magazine clicks empty.

When she looks back, Josef's head's gone, and there's a hole in the floor. The photograph of his daughter falls from his fingers. He's dead. She sticks the spent gun back in her belt. For some reason, her smashed cheek hurts more than her torn throat. She looks around to find Federico leaning on the doorframe. Paige hawks red phlegm onto the carpet. Then she leans down and takes hold of Josef's boot. Gritting her teeth, she drags his body back into her ruined hotel room. Moving slowly and painfully, she retrieves the vodka bottle from the dressing table, spins the lid off, and raises the bottle in a toast to her fallen student. She stands over him for a long moment. Then she takes a deep swallow, which makes her cough.

"Goodbye, Josef," she says. There's nothing else to say. There's no triumph here, no closure, nothing but bone-deep weariness. Solemnly, she pours the remaining contents of the bottle – most of a litre of spirit – over his chest and legs; then she pulls a complimentary matchbook from the desk, and strikes one.

The wet clothes go up in a woof of blue flame. The fire spills onto the carpet, and the room fills with smoke.

Paige opens the desk drawer and takes out another clip of ammo for the coil gun. Then she limps back to Federico.

"I have to go," she says. She has to move on to the next target, the next time zone.

A fire alarm rings, and the sprinklers go off. The shotgun's on the floor at Federico's feet. He's holding the photograph of Josef's daughter. Water's running down his face, streaking his cheeks. His dreads are soaked.

"You're a fucking monster," he says.

Paige puts a hand to the torn flesh of her throat. She can feel the sides stitching themselves back together.

"I know," she says.

And with that, she fades away.

ENTROPIC ANGEL

For four days it snowed. On the fifth day, the angel came. As light dawned, the Reverend Christina Pike saw it squatting like a gargoyle on the tallest of the village's wind turbines, its shoulders hunched over and its radiant face raised to the sky.

An hour later, that turbine failed. A few minutes later, the one next to it. Watching through binoculars from the window of the vicarage, she said: "It's an angel all right."

Around her, the hastily-convened members of the village council muttered to one another. They knew what lay in store. They'd seen the lights dim around the Estuary as each of the other towns fell in turn to the depredations of the angelic host. With their own eyes, they'd watched civilisation sputter like a dying candle. They'd spoken to refugees and army deserters and knew things were bad all over, that without power they were doomed to freeze, and there was nothing that could be done to save them.

Pike lowered her binoculars.

"Maybe I could talk to it?" she suggested, but the council leader, a retired colonel, shook his head.

"Far too dangerous, vicar, I won't hear of it."

And so Pike stayed by the window watching helplessly as, one by one over the course of the day, all the turbines on the wind farm slowed and screeched to a halt, until by sunset nothing moved, and stripped of their electricity the houses of the village fell into darkness and silence.

The children cried. The men and women built fires in their grates and sat around them bemoaning their fate. Some offered prayers to appease the lace-winged angel. Others tried to hide from it. Some even contemplated sacrifice as a means of driving the angel away, but were stymied by their lack of conviction. They had nothing in their village worthy of sacrifice but goats and children, and they weren't strong enough to make offerings of either.

Standing in front of the stone hearth in the vicarage behind the church, as the untapped winter wind blew in from the Severn Estuary, the adults argued long into the night; and all the while, silhouetted against the night sky, the angel remained as still and solitary as it had first appeared.

Then at seven in the morning, as a bone-coloured moon fell behind the Welsh hills in the west and a new day peered from behind the Mendips in the east, something stirred. By that time, most of the villagers had retired to bed and only a handful, Pike included, still clutched coffee mugs around the embers of their fires. They had heard of other communities blighted by angels. They were tired and desperate. Even so, not all of them heard the throaty roar of the approaching engine at the same time.

It came on like the buzz of a bee, starting as an irritation well below the threshold of conscious register. One moment they weren't aware of it, and the next they were rubbing condensation from their windows, craning their heads, looking inland for the source of the sound.

And there it was!

It came moving through the snowy, hedge-shrouded lanes like an angry ghost – a black and chrome motorbike eating up tarmac that hadn't felt the tread of a pneumatic tyre since the first snows fell.

Some of the villagers bolted their doors. Others took up arms and hunkered down, ready to repel an invasion of marauders. Only the Reverend Pike went out to welcome the newcomer, flanked by three of the village's hardest and most unimaginative residents.

An unarmed and careworn woman in early middle age, she stood at the porch door, her palms spread out to either side in a gesture of helplessness and trust. The three toughs took up positions around the graveyard, skulking behind stones, pitchforks and meat cleavers at the ready.

With her breath steaming, Pike watched the bike growl through the half-frozen ford below the village, and followed it as it negotiated the shattered concrete at the lower end of the lane. Its rider sat high in the saddle, a tall man and rake thin. In place of a helmet he wore a leather cap with fur lining, and mirrored goggles that gave him the look of an aviator. A crossbow rode strapped to the outside of one of his side panniers.

He prowled up past the shop fronts and market stalls until he reached the gate of the churchyard, at which point he pulled over and killed the bike's engine.

For a long moment, he sat astride the machine, looking up at the dark spires and stilled blades of the wind farm. From the Estuary, the winter morning breeze brought the smell of salt and the half-hearted gurgle of waves pawing lazily at the muddy shore.

Keeping her hands in plain sight, Reverend Pike walked through the slush on the path through the cemetery. The man watched her approach. As she neared, his hand strayed towards the hilt of a knife jammed in his belt. His skin looked smooth beneath the goggles and his lips were red with lipstick. Pike guessed him to be somewhere in his late thirties or early forties.

"I see you have a visitor," he said.

Pike glanced at the occupied tower. The angel still hadn't moved, although she noticed there were now streaks of black, like oil, staining the turbine housing beneath it.

"It arrived yesterday."

The tall man pushed his mirrored goggles up onto the front of his fur cap. His eyes were pinched into slits, as if constantly squinting into the sun.

"Would you like me to kill it for you?"

Pike gave a snort that was half amusement and half derision. "Kill an angel?"

"That's what I said." He kicked the bike onto its stand and climbed off, movements slow and stiff. Pike folded her arms and watched as he brushed dust from his worn leather coat. His fingernails were painted the same carmine shade as his lips.

"What's your name, stranger?"

The man put one hand on the small of his back and straightened with obvious effort. "Most people call me Kenya, Reverend. Kenya Vick."

"No one can kill an angel, Mister Vick."

"I can." He opened the bike's side pannier and pulled out a short black metal tube about a hand's-breadth in diameter, which he clipped to his belt. Then he unstrapped the crossbow.

Pike shook her head. "You can't shoot it." She'd seen people try before, many times. Whatever you threw at an angel passed through it like passing through smoke. It just made them angry.

"Says who?"

"Says everybody."

Kenya Vick regarded her with an unblinking eye. "Well, I ain't everybody."

He walked a few paces, as if testing the frozen ground. Reverend Pike ran her tongue over her teeth. She was nobody's fool. "How much?" she said.

Kenya stopped walking. He hefted the crossbow in one hand. "A smoked goat haunch, four bottles of wine, and a dozen boiled eggs."

Pike blinked. "We don't have much. That seems expensive to me."

Kenya turned to her. He blew into his hands and rubbed them together. "Do you have children and old people here? It's only October and the temperature's already below freezing. How are you going to keep them warm, with fires and lamps? Wouldn't you rather have radiators and electric light?"

Pike bowed her head, acknowledging his point. She glanced back towards the church, to where a small crowd had joined the three heavies she'd left lurking there, many armed with knives and farm tools.

"I'll relay your terms to the village council," she said. She pointed a stern finger at him. "You stay here."

• •

The council meeting took place in the church. Kenya Vick waited outside, leaning on the dry stone church wall. The local children, wrapped in coats and scarves, eyed him and giggled nervously. Dogs sniffed his Cuban-heeled boots. As the sun thawed the morning, he pulled off his fur cap to reveal shoulder-length dreadlocks, which he tied back with a red scrunchie from his coat pocket.

At length, the church doors opened and the Reverend appeared, blinking against the light.

"It seems you have a deal, Mister Vick. We can't run our refrigerators without electricity, and so when the weather gets warmer, we'll lose all the food we've stored for the summer. We'll starve." She glanced back over her shoulder. "But even so, I should warn you that there's a small but vocal minority that considers what you're proposing to be a blasphemy of the highest order."

"You included?"

She folded her hands. "I'd rather not answer that."

"Surely you don't believe they're actually angels, from God?"

Pike turned her head away. When she spoke, it was scarcely more than a tired whisper. "Sometimes I don't know what to believe, Mister Vick."

Kenya snorted. "They're not angels, Vicar, they're vermin. They're parasites. Somehow they leech the energy from mechanical processes. The wind still blows but the sails don't turn."

Pike held up a hand. "You have your deal. You don't need to convince me."

Kenya pushed himself up off the wall. "These things are sucking us dry. They gum things up. They feed off our energy. When the power stations and wind farms are gone, they'll move onto water wheels and solar panels, then battery-operated torches and clockwork toys." He held the crossbow down and used a crank to pull back the bowstring. "And when the machines are gone, what do you think they'll eat then? They'll turn on us," he continued. "Do you know how much energy the human body uses in a day?" He locked the string in place and lifted the weapon, sighting it on the winged figure on top of the mast. "We have to kill them before they kill us," he said.

Pike had her arms folded. "That's as maybe, Mister Vick, but do you mind if I ask what makes you think you can kill the creature, given that I've never heard of anyone doing such a thing?"

Kenya reached down to his belt and popped open the tube he'd clipped there. Inside, it bristled with crossbow bolts.

"Look at this," he said. He drew one out and held it up for her. It was black and metallic and as he turned it the morning light made rainbow oil slicks up and down its length. He pointed at the angel squatting on the now-stained wind turbine cowling. "It's made from that stuff they extrude," he said. "It's some kind of polymer. You can put it into moulds and bake it."

"And it kills them?"

Kenya slipped the bolt back into its quiver. "It's the only thing that does."

. .

Kenya wanted to wait for noon. He said it was the best time for an attack, as the angel would be at its drowsiest. He spent the time tinkering with his bike and oiling his crossbow. Pike brought him a cup of hot nettle tea.

"I have a couple of questions," she said, "if you'll indulge me?"

"Go ahead."

She unfolded her arms. "Is Kenya your first name or a nickname?"

The thin man blew steam from the mug and squinted at her. "What difference does it make?"

Pike shrugged. "None, I suppose. It's just that as the local vicar, it's my job to know everybody else's business."

Behind her, the villagers milled around in the lane, their boots tramping the snow to dirty slush. Most of their knives were sheathed now. They were curious but wary, afraid they were being conned.

She said, "And if you fail, I'll need to know what to carve on your tombstone."

Kenya pressed his reddened lips into a hard line. For a moment, she thought he wasn't going to answer.

"I went to Africa once," he said, "back before the angels came, when the Internet still worked and planes still flew. I went to get in on all that fake software they had going on back then, figuring I'd make some cash bringing it back home on the sneaker-net." He took a breath. "Instead, I spent six weeks sweating my ass off in a Nairobi jail and came back with a gut parasite that made me shit like a fire hose, pardon my French. I lost half my body weight and I threw up once an hour, every hour for a fucking *month*."

Pike suppressed an unexpected smile. "I see."

"You have any more questions?"

She looked at his lipstick and nail polish, and the scrunchie holding back his locks. "Maybe later," she said.

• •

When both the hands of the clock tower pointed to twelve, Kenya remounted his bike. To his surprise, Pike climbed on behind him.

"What are you doing?" he asked as she hugged herself to him.

She leaned around. From her cassock she pulled the polished bronze crucifix from the church altar. "If you're wrong about the angel, you're going to need some spiritual back-up."

Kenya shook his head in amusement. "Stand clear," he said

to the villagers blocking the lane. He let the brake off and revved the throttle. The bike leapt forward like an eager horse, slipping and fishtailing on the icy tarmac. With Pike holding on tight, he steered for the concrete farm track leading up the hill to the wind farm on the cliff top.

The sun shone white from a milky sky. The air smelled of the sea. When they reached the wind turbines, he skidded to a halt.

The track ran straight and cold for a mile back down to the village, undulating gently. Goats picked at the frozen grass, tails flicking. The cries of gulls could be heard across the fields, and a far-off church spire showed the spot where the next village nestled in a dip overlooking the patchwork, snow-covered Levels.

From up here, he could see Pike's house behind the church. She pointed it out to him. The vicarage was a low red brick affair with black iron window frames and a tiled roof slumping in the middle as if tired. The gravel drive had been worn down to mud in several places. Brown wisps of ivy crawled around the front porch, and the wan light winked off a cluster of old CDs that had been strung up to keep the birds off the flower beds.

Turning the other way, he looked out over the waters of the Severn Estuary. To the north, the broken spans of the twin Severn bridges sagged into the brown water like the spines of gut-shot dinosaurs. To the south, the flour-dusted hills of Devon lay like clouds on the horizon.

"Okay," he said to the vicar, his breath swirling, "get clear and don't interfere."

He watched her walk a hundred yards back down the track, then he gunned the bike, coughing out clouds of exhaust. Six times he pushed the engine as far as it would go, red-lining the rev counter, making as much racket as he could. Then calmly, he climbed off and left it running. He didn't look back. He walked around behind the base of the turbine's tower and found himself within ten metres of the cliff's edge. An overgrown coast path followed the line of the cliff, separated from the drop by a tangled hedge of bramble and thorn.

He knew it would take the angel a while to stir itself, and so he settled down in a crouch, with his back against the warm metal of the tower. He took a quarrel from the quiver on his belt and placed it into the crossbow's groove. The weapon was an antique. He'd taken it from the wall of a stately home in Dorset. It suited his purposes. Guns, tanks and other complex weaponry tended to fail when close to an angel's entropic influence. The old crossbow fared better.

He glanced up but the angel still hadn't moved. With time to kill, he took a compact mirror from the pocket of his leather coat and touched up his lipstick.

• •

An hour later, the angel still hadn't moved. It didn't so much as twitch until two o'clock in the afternoon, when it slowly turned its head away from the heavens in order to look down at the ticking-over bike. It stayed that way for a further fifteen minutes and Kenya started to worry that the old machine would run out of fuel before the creature became sufficiently interested.

When fifteen minutes had passed, the angel stretched its wings as if waking from a deep sleep. With aching slowness it raised itself into a standing position and stepped off the turbine's cowling.

It fell like a vulture, circling down in a controlled glide. Watching it, Kenya stepped back, retreating almost as far as the cliff path. His knuckles were white on the crossbow. His pulse fluttered in his chest. There was something awe-inspiring about the creature's grace and power. It came down with the insouciance of a predator, its dark lacy wings like unfurled rags of night-time cloud, and landed on the bike's fuel tank with enough force to flatten the suspension and tip the machine onto its side like a wounded antelope.

Immediately, the headlight dimmed and the engine stuttered and dropped a note. The angel's wings fell over its kill, tips almost touching the grass. Seen from this close, the thing looked less human than you might have thought had you only seen it on top of the mast. What looked like eye sockets at a distance were merely indentations in the smooth, leathery skin; the nose a simple ridge of bone; and the mouth a toothless slit. It had two sinewy arms, and hands sporting six vicious-looking claws.

Moving behind the turbine mast, Kenya double-checked his crossbow. He knew he'd only have time for one shot and he had to make a clean kill. Although angels moved sluggishly when not feeding, like cheetahs they were capable of incredible bursts of speed when angered.

Satisfied that the weapon was ready to fire, he took a deep breath and stepped out into the open – just in time to see the Reverend Pike marching towards the creature brandishing the brass cross from the church altar.

"Our Father," she bellowed, "who art in heaven—"

At the sound of her voice, the nightmarish angel turned in her direction. The slit of a mouth opened and it let forth an angry, mewling screech that stopped the woman in her tracks.

Seizing his opportunity, Kenya ran forward. He got as close as he dared and pulled the trigger. The glistening black bolt flew forth, but at the last instant, the creature raised itself and instead of delivering a killing blow, the shaft pierced the angel's thigh. The screech turned to a howl of pain and indignation. The angel staggered and fell from its perch on the bike, landing in a thrashing heap on the snow.

Kenya didn't stop to watch. He knew he'd only wounded the beast, and was already fumbling with the crank that drew back the bowstring.

"Shit. Shit. Shit."

Across the field, Pike stood rooted, watching the angel rise slowly to stand on its good leg, wings flapping to steady its balance. The cross drooped uncertainly in her hands.

"Run!" Kenya yelled. She looked at him but he was too far away to interpret her expression. "Run you idiot!"

Defiantly, she raised the cross and thrust it at the advancing angel. "Hallowed be thy name," she called, her voice carrying over the sound of the bike's spluttering engine. "Thy kingdom come, thy will be done—"

The beast's outstretched wings towered over her, black and ragged. Kenya bit his lip. What was she playing at? Why wouldn't she run?

He got the string pulled back and locked it into place, ready to fire. As he did so, he realised with horror that Pike was buying him time to reload, putting herself at risk in order to give him a chance to finish the job.

Moving as quickly as he could, he whipped a bolt from his belt and slid it into place. Too late! Uncoiling like a spring, the creature took a swipe at Pike. She screamed and tried to dodge but its claws raked the bronze cross with a force that dashed it from her hands and sent her spinning into the grass.

As it prepared to pounce on her, Kenya sprinted up behind with his reloaded crossbow at the ready. Alerted by the sound of his boots clumping on the frozen soil, the angel span to face him – but by then there was less than a metre between it and the weapon. It screamed and lashed out, wings beating the air. Teeth bared, Kenya fired. He saw the quarrel pierce the angel's chest an instant before the dying beast's claws skewered him through the side, sinking into his waist up to the knuckle. He fell to the ground. For an instant, the angel stood over him in triumph. Then the black wings drooped. The creature's knees went out from under it, and it crashed down beside him, twitched twice, and was dead.

"Kenya!" Pike crawled over to him on her hands and knees in the snow. "Kenya, are you all right?"

He coughed. He couldn't move. He felt as if he'd been sawn in half. "I wanted to make sure I hit it," he said. "Stupid. I got too close."

Pike ripped her cassock and wadded it into a pad, which she pressed against his wounds to stop the blood. Her breath clouded in the cold air. She kept saying his name, over and over again.

"Shut up," he said.

At the foot of the hill, a few of the braver villagers were starting to move in her direction, rakes and knives at the ready. They wanted to see the fallen beast. She watched them approach.

After a while she said: "That wasn't one of God's creatures, was it?" No answer. She looked down.

"Kenya?"

• •

By Christmas Eve, the village had been changed almost beyond recognition. After the midnight service, as the other villagers hurried home wrapped against the cold, Reverend Pike wheeled Kenya to the door of the church and together, they looked out from the porch at the electric lights burning in the windows of all the houses on the lane.

"We fixed the last turbine this afternoon," she said, "while you were having your nap." Between supervising the repair work and organising the church service, she hadn't had much time to speak to him since helping him out of bed earlier that morning.

In his wheelchair, Kenya twisted to look up at her. "Did you get all the black stuff off the cowling?"

"Every bit, just as you said. I scraped most of it off myself."

"Good." He settled back. "Tomorrow I'll show you how to heat it. We should have enough to make another dozen bolts."

Pike gave his shoulder an affectionate pat. She smoothed the blanket covering his useless legs. "You take it easy," she said. "You're not as strong as you think you are."

As the night's first flurries of snow whipped sideways across the graveyard, she straightened up and applied her lipstick. Then she closed and locked the church door and turned up the collar of her new leather coat, ready to take him back to the warmth of the vicarage.

"Do you really think we can do it?" she said to the scrunchie on the back of his head. "Do you really think we can turn this little community into an army?"

Still looking out at the cottages and the lane, he gave a slow, thoughtful nod. "If you can build more crossbows, I can teach you how to shoot them. You've got a fair bit of food stockpiled, and if we can trade enough leather from the other villages hereabouts, we can make body armour."

Pike smiled, gripping the handles at the back of his chair. "We can, can't we? We can do all that."

"Sure."

She leaned forward to plant a kiss on the top of his

dreadlocked head. "We know how to kill them now, thanks to you, my love. When spring comes and the snows melt, we'll march out to the other villages. We'll spread the word."

The clock in the tower struck one. Gently, Pike pushed Kenya out into the graveyard. Her nails were painted red like his, and she had a brand new crossbow of her own slung on her back. She trod lightly down the path, humming the tune to 'Onward Christian Soldiers', as the thickening white flakes fell like static from an unforgiving sky.

POD DREAMS OF TUCKERTOWN

1.

All Pod wants to do is hang with his friends, Erik and Kai. But he can't, not anymore. Not since the Clampdown. Not since the Elite looked down from their high orbit and decided to rationalise human society, to make it ordered and safe. Not since they sent him here, to the bridge, to work off his criminal debt.

He hates the bridge. He hates the stinging wind and the crashing waves. He hates the tedious, backbreaking work. But most of all, he hates his foreman, Fergus.

He hates Fergus for hurting Kai. Kai bungled a weld on one of the support girders, and so Fergus stamped on her spine until she couldn't walk. Now all Pod wants to do is kill Fergus. He lies in his bunk at night and dreams of smashing Fergus's head with a wrench, or pushing him over the railings into the sea. But deep down, he knows he won't. They've got him pumped so full of sedatives that he can't even get an erection, let alone pick a fight.

So, day after day he works on the bridge. The wind burns his skin, the sun makes him squint. But he gets through it by thinking of Kai, and remembering how good things used to be – how great it was when they used to hang out together at the diner by the docks in Tuckertown, where they could see the lights of the trawlers and laugh at the stink of the last of the day's fish guts being hosed off the quay.

They weren't into anything heavy back then, just stealing cars and joyrides. There were some fights, and some cars got burned, but no one ever got killed. There were no knives or guns – it was all just for laughs, something to do when the rain came down and the markets closed for the night.

But then – on Pod's eighteenth birthday – the Elite came down in their shining silver saucers and everything changed, once and for all.

• •

Erik says Fergus has a girl back in Tuckertown.

"So what?" Pod says. "Everybody says they've got *someone* waiting for them."

"It just shows he's human, is all," Erik says. He looks thin. He's not eating. Fergus kicked him in the stomach a week ago and he hasn't been right since.

"Does it still hurt?" Pod says.

Erik rolls back over on his bunk and closes his eyes. "I'll be okay," he says.

Pod saw one of the Elite yesterday. It came to inspect the bridge. Even Fergus was terrified of it.

"What did it look like?" Erik asks. He missed it – he was in bed, recovering from the kicking.

Pod scratches his cheek. He badly needs a shave. "Like a cockroach," he says. "A big, wet cockroach with claws like steak knives."

Erik shivers and his eyes flick nervously to the ceiling.

"But that's not the worst," Pod says. "The worst is when they talk."

"What does it sound like?"

Pod lies back on his bunk, an arm resting over his eyes. "Like cats being sick," he says.

. •

Pod lost everything in the Clampdown – home, parents – everything except Erik and Kai.

He doesn't like to think about it. He prefers to remember Tuckertown as it was, before the saucers landed.

"Do you remember the burger stall on West Pier Street, by the tannery?" he says. "And the girl that worked there, with the big tits?"

Erik doesn't answer. He's holding his stomach. There's a man crying a few bunks down the row, and a couple having furtive sex under a blanket in the far corner. The place reeks of piss and sweat, but Pod doesn't notice the smell much anymore. He scratches at a cut on his hand. "And that bar on the corner, where Kai used to dance?" He tugs Erik's sleeve. "Remember that?"

Erik shakes him off.

"Go to sleep," he says.

Thinking of Kai brings the anger back. Pod lies awake, listening to Erik's ragged snore. If Erik dies, Pod's going to kill Fergus for sure – he doesn't know how yet, but he'll get him.

He pulls his right hand into a fist. The muscles in his palm feel like wires.

If Erik dies...

He rolls over into a foetal position, pulling the rough blanket over his head to hide the sudden hot tears that prick his eyes. He's eighteen years old, starving and desperate.

Tomorrow, the Chemist will be here. It's a small comfort, but he clings to it.

2.

It's still dark outside when the dormitory lights go on. There are no showers. The workers sleep in their clothes. When the lights go on, they crawl out of their blankets and file towards the door, their breath clouding in the cold air.

Pod helps Erik.

"You've got to let me go to the hospital," Erik says.

Pod shakes his head.

"They took Kai to the hospital and she never came back," he says.

Erik grits his teeth. "She had a broken back. That takes time to fix. And then she still wouldn't be any use here. They probably shipped her off to work in a factory or something."

Pod grunts. He's got most of Erik's weight on his shoulders and he's in no mood to argue. He's seen the mass graves on the hill behind the camp, and he's got a pretty good idea where Kai ended up.

"It doesn't matter," he says, "I'm going to get you fixed up. You'll be okay."

Erik coughs.

"How are you going to do that, Pod? My guts are wrecked. How are you going to fix that?"

Pod squeezes his arm.

"We're going to see the Chemist," he says.

• •

The Chemist's a man with a shiny suit and a thin face, like a weasel. He sits on a makeshift chair behind a makeshift desk in a makeshift office.

"What can I do for you?" he says, squinting up as they enter.

Pod helps Erik into a chair and then leans on the desk.

"I need something for my friend here," he says.

The Chemist looks down his nose at Erik.

"You want medical supplies?" he says. "Why, what's wrong with him?"

Pod straightens up. "He's messed up inside – he needs fixing."

The man tuts and tsks to himself. He pulls a medical scanner from his bag and waves it at Erik. A red light appears on the display. "Ah yes, an internal haemorrhage," he says. "And I'm afraid it's quite serious."

"He's not going to the hospital," Pod says firmly.

The Chemist sighs and puts the scanner down. "In that case, he'll probably be dead in a day or so."

He looks down at the papers on his desk, to signal that the interview's over. Pod leans across and puts his hand over the passage the man's pretending to read. "But you've got something that can help him, don't you?" he says.

The Chemist leans back, lip curled in distaste. He comes to the camp once a month, ostensibly to check on the health of the workers, but really to line his own pockets by smuggling in forbidden items, like cigarettes and heroin, to sell to them.

"Something powerful enough to fix that much damage won't come cheap," he says.

Pod frowns. His palms are sweating, but there's no going back now.

"I want to pawn some memories," he says.

.•

The scanner the Chemist uses is Elite tech. It can cut and paste memories, lift them wholesale – including all their related associations – from one mind and drop them into another.

Pod sits back in the plastic chair, eyes closed.

"Try to make it a happy memory," the Chemist says. "The

Elite pay so much more for happy memories."

Pod grits his teeth. All he can think about is Tuckertown – the place he grew up in, the place he met Kai and Erik.

He remembers the harbour and the unloading trawlers; the downtown mall and the park behind it; and the alley where Kai used her mouth to take his virginity.

"Don't do it, for God's sake," Erik pleads from across the room. Pod waves him to silence – he's aware of the horror stories, and he's seen the zombies walking around the camp with their minds accidentally wiped. He knows the dangers, but he thinks it's worth the risk, to save his friend.

After all, he couldn't save Kai...

He tightens his grip on the arm of the chair. His hands are sweaty where they're gripping the plastic.

"Shut up," he says. He takes a deep breath, and then turns to the Chemist. "Okay, I'm ready."

The man presses the scanner hard against Pod's scalp. "Concentrate," he says.

Pod screws his eyes tight. He thinks of the sun coming up over the meat factory in Tuckertown, of a burning car reflected in the oily water of the canal. The scanner feels hot against his head.

"Lie still," the Chemist says.

The heat increases. There's a moment of intense pain – sharp agony like trapped cats ripping at the inside of Pod's skull – and the world falls away, leaving only darkness.

3.

When he wakes, it's late afternoon. He's lying on his bunk, back in the dormitory, and grey light slants in through the windows.

It's quiet – the rest of the workers are out on the bridge. For a moment, he thinks he's got the place to himself, and then he hears Erik cough. He rolls over.

"What happened?" he says.

Erik smiles crookedly.

"That weasel zapped you and you went down – bang! – like an epileptic."

"Did it work?"

"I guess so – he gave me the pills."

Pod props himself up on an elbow. "Have you taken them? How are you feeling?"

Erik coughs. "A bit better," he says.

Pod scratches his head. He feels unusually alert, like a cold wind's blown through him.

"How long have I been asleep?"

"About three hours – Fergus is mad as hell. He tried to wake you, but I told him you were sick."

Erik puts a hand on his arm. "Do you feel different, Pod? Are the cobwebs gone?"

Pod frowns. He's clear-headed for the first time in months. His thoughts are lucid and sharp, like they used to be, before he came here.

"What did you do?" he asks suspiciously.

Erik grins. "I talked the Chemist into selling me a stimulant – something strong enough to counteract the sedatives in our food." He flips across an empty hypodermic and Pod catches it with his left hand.

"I told the weasel it was for me," Erik says, "to get me back to work faster. It cost everything we own – all the cigarettes, everything."

Pod rubs a sore spot on his arm.

"And you injected me with it while I slept?"

Erik pulls a handkerchief from his pocket. It's old and torn, and it belonged to Kai. He passes it to Pod.

"I did it for her," he says.

• •

The wind's bitter as Pod steps onto the bridge holding the handkerchief. He looks up at the towers that support the suspension cables, as if seeing them for the first time. They shine in the blustery afternoon light, huge and solid, built to withstand the wind and tide.

Up ahead, he sees his crew. This week they're welding the safety rails on the windward side of the bridge. It's a dull and dirty job, but a lot less dangerous than some they've done.

As he gets closer – head down, shambling, Erik struggling to keep up – he sees Fergus watching him. The supervisor has a wooden cane in his hand. His eyes are slits and he's tapping the cane against his boot.

"Where the hell have you been?" he shouts as soon as Pod's close enough to hear him over the sound of the wind.

Pod doesn't try to reply. He remembers Fergus stamping on Kai's spine, and he remembers feeling angry – but the source of the anger's gone.

"I'm here to kill you," he says. But even as the words leave his mouth he frowns, unsure if that's what he really wants.

Seeing his confusion, Fergus laughs.

"You bought some funny fungus from the Chemist, did you?"

Pod shakes his head, trying to summon up the determination he'll need to see this through. He walks over to one of his workmates and pulls the wrench from her hands. It's big and heavy, solid steel. He hefts it in one hand, and slaps it into his palm. He turns to face Fergus.

"I'm serious," he says.

The other workers in the crew back away, scared. They think Pod's gone mad, and that he's going to get a beating – they don't suspect the stimulants burning in his veins.

And neither does Fergus, judging from his swagger.

"Come on then, try it," he says.

Pod grins. He hasn't felt this good since... He stops and scratches his head.

Since...

It feels like there's something on the tip of his tongue, something important. He knows he's got to kill Fergus for what he did to Kai, but he can't remember why Kai's so important.

He looks at Erik.

Then he realises he can't remember anything beyond twelve months ago, when he first arrived here, on the bridge. He looks up, confused. Just how much of his memory has the Chemist taken?

Suddenly dizzy and nauseous, he leans on the safety rail for support. He needs time to clear his head, but he's not going to get it – he's challenged Fergus in front of the whole crew, and now Fergus will kill him, if he can't defend himself.

Pod uses the wrench to block the first blow. Fergus – used to the inept shambling of his drugged workers – grunts in surprise.

He strikes again, his technique crude but powerful. Pod blocks a blow to the head, another to the neck. Then Fergus's cane catches him across the shins. He cries out and jabs forward with the wrench, catching his tormentor in the chest. Fergus staggers back, cursing. He stabs out with the cane. Pod dodges the blow, but he's got the railing behind him and nowhere to go.

The next thrust catches him in the side, scraping his ribs.

Fergus pulls back, lunges again, and the tip of the cane skewers Pod's thigh. He lashes out with a cry of pain. He steps forward and brings the wrench around in a swinging arc. Too late, Fergus tries to block the blow, and the solid steel wrench shatters his wrist. He cries out and Pod punches him in the face, knocking him flat on the tarmac.

Erik's holding a welding lance. Pod snatches it and leans over Fergus, really angry now. The blue flame roars in the cold air.

"Are you ready, fucker?" he says through clenched teeth. He leans in close. Fergus is still curled around the agony in his wrist. When he feels the heat of the flame, he whimpers.

"Please don't," he says. "Please, no. I've got a kid, in Tuckertown – a little girl. Please…"

He twists and turns, trying to get away from the hot flame, but Pod's kneeling on his legs.

"Tuckertown?" Pod says. The name's familiar. He's heard it mentioned around the camp, but when he tries to focus on it, he comes up against something scratchy, like static.

In desperation, he grabs at the only thing he's certain of.

"You crippled my friend," he says.

Fergus pulls a battered picture from his breast pocket, thrusts it in his face.

"Look at her," he says desperately. "Look at my little girl."

4.

Pod sits heavily on the wet tarmac. He's wanted to kill Fergus for months, but now Fergus is sobbing and the whole thing seems ridiculous and embarrassing.

"*You've* got a kid?" he says, turning the picture over in his hands.

Fergus swallows. "Her name's Jess," he says. "She's three

years old. If I get this section of the bridge finished on time, they'll let me see her."

He's holding his broken wrist tight against his chest. Looking down at him, Pod feels sick. There's no satisfaction to be had here.

"You hurt my friend," he says. He looks out at the grey horizon and it starts to rain. In his hand, the welding lance spits and hisses. Fergus can't take his eyes off it.

"Don't burn me," he says. "Don't burn me, and I'll get you out of here."

Pod spits into the flame. "You can't do that," he says. "You don't have the authority to do that."

Fergus pushes himself upright, his back against the railings.

"There's something you should know," he says.

Pod steps back, out of reach.

"What?" he says. He has the welding lance in one hand, the steel wrench in the other.

"Your parole came up," Fergus blurts. "You're free men."

He glances at Erik.

"Both of you," he says.

• •

It takes Pod a while to understand.

"Look," says Fergus, "When your release order came through, I didn't tell you. You should've been out of here a couple of months back, but I kept you on because you're a good worker and I need to hit target – I need to see my little girl." He's pale and his hands are shaking. He looks like he's going into shock.

"I was just trying to do my job," he says.

Pod takes a shuddering breath. Two extra months stuck here, when he could've been at home with his memory intact...

243

He picks up Fergus's wooden cane and snaps it over his knee. Then he throws the two halves over the railing, into the sea. He throws the wrench and the blowtorch after them.

"So, if I walk down to the gates at the end of the bridge, they'll let me through? I'll be a free man?" he says.

Fergus nods. His teeth are clenched against the pain in his wrist.

"Please, just go," he says. "Go back to Tuckertown, and leave me alone."

．•

Pod limps away. His leg hurts and there's blood in his shoe. He limps down the slope of the bridge toward the security gates at the end, where the carriageway meets the land. Behind him, the rest of the work crew crowd in on their wounded supervisor. Despite the sedatives they've been given, they can see he's lost the advantage.

If Fergus screams as they begin kicking him, Pod doesn't hear it. He's holding tightly to Kai's handkerchief.

As he passes the dormitory hut, Erik catches up with him. Somewhere above the clouds, the sun's setting.

"Come on," Pod says, "we're leaving."

THE BIGGER THE STAR,
THE FASTER IT BURNS

Ed stops at a lonely roadside café on a hot autumn night. He drums his fingers on the counter.

"Hey, how about a coffee?" he says. It's late and he's the only customer. The waitress comes over. She's eighteen or nineteen, with long hair and black eyeliner.

"I'm waiting for the water to heat up," she says. She's got a black t-shirt and there's a biro behind her right ear. She looks over Ed's shoulder. "Is that your car?"

He turns in his seat. He's left the Dodge across two wheelchair access spaces in the empty car park.

"Isn't it a beauty?" he says.

She looks at the sweeping tailfins and scratches her chin. There's dried egg on her sleeve. "It looks old," she says. "Is it American?"

Ed nods. He's just borrowed it for the weekend. "I'm on my way up to Hereford, to see the crash site."

She looks him up and down. "Are you a reporter?"

Ed shakes his head. "I'm a photographer."

"Up from London?"

"How did you guess?"

She leans her elbows on the counter. "Are you going to take my picture?"

Ed smiles. "That depends. You haven't told me your name yet."

She brushes the dried egg from her sleeve. "My name's Natalie."

They shake hands. "I'm Ed."

The radio at the back of the kitchen's playing an Elvis track. A truck rattles past on the road outside. "I'll get you that coffee," Natalie says. As she pours it, she looks back at him, over her shoulder.

"There's some wreckage at the top of the valley," she says, "I can show it to you, if you like."

Half an hour later they're rolling up the valley in the Dodge, with the roof down. The single-track road smells hot and the stars overhead are hard and sharp. Natalie's finished her shift. Ed's taken his jacket off. He pulls up his sleeve to show her his tattoo.

"I got that in Amsterdam," he says. Natalie wrinkles her nose. Whenever she moves, her jeans squeak on the seat.

"Take the next left," she says.

Ed lets his sleeve drop. He likes her accent. He touches the brake and downshifts into the turn.

Natalie points through the windscreen. "It's just up here."

Ed pulls off the road. Up ahead, caught in the headlights, is the wreckage she promised him. It's strewn over the gorse and heather, twisted splinters glinting in the moonlight.

He kills the engine. "Does anyone else know about this?"

Natalie shakes her head. "No one comes up here much."

It's midnight. Ed opens his door and climbs out, camera in hand. He can smell the heather. He walks over to the nearest fragment. The metal's smooth and warm to the touch. With a dry mouth and sweaty palms, he starts snapping; knowing the pictures he's taking will make his reputation.

Back in the car, Natalie lights a cigarette. She puts her feet up on the dashboard and lets her long hair fall over the back of the seat. She knows there are armed helicopters patrolling the main crash site to the north. But here in the valley, all she can hear is the click of Ed's camera in the hot night air.

• •

Ed comes back to the car with a souvenir from the wreckage: three luminous brass gauges mounted on a broken panel, all smashed, faces starred, each the size of a dinner plate.

"These have to be worth something," he says, and drops them onto the back seat. Natalie says nothing. She keeps her eyes closed. Her hair and clothes still smell of fried eggs. She hears Ed walk around to the driver's side. He gets in and pulls the door shut, ka-chunk.

"Thanks," he says.

Natalie arches like a warm cat.

"No bother."

She looks down into the valley. The lights of the main road snake away like an orange river. She can see the café, and beyond it, the town. She can almost see her house. It all looks pathetically small from up here, and she can blank it out with her hand, cover it over as if it never existed.

Ed shudders the engine into life, and pulls the car round in a tight circle.

"Where can I drop you?" he says.

The wheels bump over the uneven ground. Natalie leans forward.

"Take me with you."

"What?"

"Take me with you to London." She's never even been as far as Cardiff, but she's feeling wild. It must be the fresh air.

Ed looks at her as if he's looking over a pair of spectacles. "How old are you?"

"Nineteen."

"What about your parents?"

"They won't even notice I'm gone."

Ed scratches under his white t-shirt. He knows that thanks to her, he's going to be rich, and so he's feeling generous. "Okay, what the fuck."

He steers the car back down the hill and on to the main road, where he guns the engine and lets the old car wind out to seventy-five. As they scream past the café, Natalie turns her head. She watches it recede into the darkness.

Ed clicks on the radio. Another Elvis song. It's a long, flat drag back to London, but he doesn't care. He's wired, practically jumping in his seat. There's music on the radio, the top's still down, and the warm night air makes him feel like a teenager. It's the first time he's felt like this in years. Beside him, Natalie starts to pat the side of the car door in time to the music. Her hair straggles out, careless in the wind.

They hit London an hour before dawn. On the backseat, the brass gauges glow, brighter than ever. Ed eyes them in the rear-view mirror. By the time he pulls up at the kerb outside his house, the glow's spread itself to the dials on the car's dash.

• •

Later, after they've freshened up, Ed introduces Natalie to some of his friends. He takes her on a Monopoly board tour of the capital. He's trying to offload the brass gauges, but no one will buy them. He tries all his contacts, but they won't touch anything from the crash site. They're scared of the government. All he manages to sell are the pictures – but that's still enough to land him a suitcase full of money.

He brings it back to the car, a stupid grin smeared all over his face like grease paint.

"Let's go shopping," he says. And by three o'clock in the afternoon, they're both fitted out with new suits, shirts and shoes. They keep stopping to admire themselves in shop windows. They're drunk on how good they look.

He takes her for an early dinner at an achingly hip Thai place off the Portobello Road. She's bought a new mobile phone, and while they're waiting for their food, she logs into her social networks, and brags to her mates about her new boyfriend.

"So," says Ed, "we're young and rich in London. What do you want to do first?"

Natalie puts the phone down. They're both tired. She reaches across the tablecloth, and her fingertips brush the back of his hand.

"Take me home," she says. "Take me home, with you."

• •

Ed buys a bottle of wine and they walk back to his flat. It's a third-floor studio, up six flights of stairs. There's a framed picture of Elvis above the fireplace. The fire escape opens onto a flat section of roof, still warm from the day's heat.

"Sit down, make yourself comfortable," he says.

It's getting dark. In the city, night comes all at once. The orange streetlights fire up and the blinds in the apartment blocks across the road go down. Everyone's cooking dinner and watching TV with the volume turned way up. No one's looking out. No one wants to hear what's happening in the street.

But out here on the roof, Natalie smells of flowers. She's wearing a silvery cocktail dress, and has her hair chopped into a shaggy mop. Planes pass overhead, one after the other, on approach to Heathrow, their navigation lights like drifting fireworks. After a glass of wine, he kisses her, and she wraps her arms around his neck.

They stay together for the rest of the week, hardly leaving the flat. They live on takeaways and cups of tea. Ed tells her about his ex-wife. She tells him about her parents. They have both forgotten the brass gauges on the back seat of the borrowed car. Neither of them expects their relationship to last.

Natalie's had boyfriends before, back in the Valleys, but nothing serious; symptoms of her boredom rather than cures for it. Ed's the first man to bring any real excitement into her life, and that's why she's grabbed him, the way drowning girls grab ropes.

• •

The next morning, Natalie tries to phone her dad, but can't get through. There's a government block on the line; no calls in or out of South Wales. So she takes a shower instead. Ed pops out to buy a paper, and he reads the headlines on the way back to the flat. Three helicopters have disappeared from the crash site. An eyewitness claims they shot straight up into the night sky, glowing like meteors.

On the street, there are stalls setting up, and crowd control barriers being lowered into place. It's the weekend of the Notting Hill Carnival. When he gets back to the flat, he finds Natalie in the kitchen, wrapped in a towel. Breakfast consists of cold pizza from the fridge, left over from the night before. As they eat, he shows her his portfolio of photographs: the landscapes; the portraits; the journalism. She flicks through it all with one hand, a slice of congealed pizza balanced in the other. Eventually, she comes to a shot of the Pleiades.

"That's pretty."

She turns to the next page, which shows the familiar rectangle of the Orion constellation rising above the black branches of an autumn tree. The stars in its belt are cold and blue.

Natalie takes a bite of pizza, and talks around it. "Why's that one red?"

Ed leans over her. Her hair smells very clean. Her finger-nail's tapping the upper left corner of the rectangle.

"That's Betelgeuse," he says. He traces the star with his own finger. "It looks red because it's all swollen up into a giant, nearing the end of its life."

"So it's an old star?"

He shakes his head. "No, actually it's younger than the sun."

She raises a quizzical eyebrow and he shrugs. He looks at the framed Elvis picture over the fireplace.

"The bigger the star, the faster it burns," he says.

Accepting this, she flips the page to find another view of the same constellation.

"These are great. How did you take them? Did you use a telescope?"

Ed straightens up. "No, it was a tripod camera on a ten second exposure." He had a telescope, years ago. Not much use for one in London, though; too much light.

He walks over to the window. Three floors below, he sees the borrowed Dodge parked at the kerb. It's a handsome machine, and he's a little bit in love with it. It's brought a much-needed splash of glamour into his life, and he'll be sad when he has to return it to its rightful owners.

Natalie's still eating pizza, still wrapped in her towel, her bare legs crossed at the ankles. She's cute, and he loves her accent, even though he knows there's no future for them, because they're too different. She's too young and excitable; he's too old and restless.

And he hasn't noticed that down below, the car's floating with its tyres half a centimetre above the road.

. •

The phone rings. Ed picks it up. It's the editor to whom he sold the pictures.

"There are government types sniffing around. They want to know how you breached security at the crash site."

Ed stiffens. "I wasn't at the crash site. This was a separate area, a secondary impact."

"Then you should have reported it. They want to pull the pictures."

"Screw them."

"I can't protect you, Ed."

"Then screw you, too."

He breaks the connection. He takes Natalie out into the carnival crowds. Hand-in-hand, they walk the length of Ladbroke Grove, and she can't stop gaping. She's never seen anything like this. There are at least a million people packed into these streets. It's a sea of bodies, bright costumes and police horses. They buy coffee and jerk chicken from a stall. They have to shout to hear each other over the music.

They spend the day wandering, edging their way through the crush. They pause to watch live music on improvised stages; they follow the procession route, marvelling at the stamina of the dancers; and end the afternoon on a wooden table outside a corner pub, drinking overpriced beer in plastic pint glasses.

They watch it get dark. It's late, but the carnival's still

in full swing. Everyone's celebrating, even though it's been raining and the pavements are wet.

"What time is it?" Natalie says. She has damp tinsel in her hair.

Ed shrugs. He doesn't have a watch. It's been a wild day, but now he's had enough of playing tour guide.

He pats her leg.

"Let's go home."

Natalie stiffens. She's been having the time of her life. She feels like a caged bird released into the wild, and she doesn't want it to end.

"I'm going to stay here," she says, not looking at him. "I'll meet you back at the flat later, okay?"

They both know she won't. She stands up and brushes down her skirt. Ed folds his arms.

"Don't be like that," she says.

. •

By midnight, she's in the arms of a Brazilian telemarketer from Teddington. They lie together in his hotel room, the open window allowing the deep bass of the street festival to ebb and flow over them, the mingled smells of hashish and fried onions to galvanise their empty stomachs.

"I feel kind of bad about Ed," she says. "I shouldn't have left him like that."

Alejandro rubs a sleepy palm across his face. Although bare-chested, he's still wearing his jeans, and his hair's flattened on one side, damp with sweat.

"You don't have to worry about him anymore," he says. "You have me now."

He lights a cigarette from the pack on the bedside table. Natalie sits up and hugs her knees.

"Do you think he'll be all right?"

There are steel drums playing in the street. She gets up and pulls back the net curtain, looks down at the crowd. She says: "It was just a stupid argument."

Her shoes are lying on the floor by the door. In the orange half-light, Alejandro holds the cigarette pinched between his thumb and forefinger. He takes a small, tight drag and curses in Portuguese.

"Come to bed," he says.

Natalie ignores him. All she wants is to be left alone.

"You know, it was his idea to come here," she says. There are people blowing whistles in the street, and strange lights in the sky. She wraps her arms across her chest. The Valleys seems so far away, and she doesn't know where she is.

"I hope he's all right," she says.

• •

Meanwhile, Ed walks back to the flat alone, hands in pockets. He hates London now. It's so dreary, and he's so tired. He needs to move on, find something new to do.

By the time he gets home, the crowd's started to thin. He sees the old Dodge parked where he left it, and no one seems to have noticed that its tyres are floating a good couple of centimetres above the tarmac. The gauges on the back seat light it up from inside, like a miniature carnival float.

He looks up. A few stars poke through the ragged clouds. He doesn't want to go back to the flat. He's thinking of the crash site and the vanished helicopters, and how bone-achingly bored he is.

The very metal of the car seems to glow and sing. When he touches it, it makes his fingers tingle. He gets in and starts the engine, and the Dodge immediately rises half a metre into the air, much to the surprise of the crowd. He touches the accelerator, and it jumps up another half. Ed gives a fierce grin.

"Okay, here we go," he says. He waves to the circle of astonished onlookers, and mashes the pedal. The car leaps. Foot to the floor, he drives it straight up into the night sky, aiming for the stars.

He drives it so far and so fast that he ends up on a planet somewhere out on the edge of the galaxy. It takes him six weeks to get there. He gets a flat near the shoulder of Orion and has to drive the rest of the way on steel rims, but he gets there.

And he never comes back.

NO HUMAN EYE

We'd never seen a bubble quite like this one before. As Owen inched our tiny prospecting craft towards its surface, I could see through its transparent walls, into the interior.

"It looks like there's some kind of fluid in there," I said from my vantage at the airlock door. "Probably water."

Over my headphones, I heard Owen click his tongue in irritation. We'd been wearing our uncomfortable pressure suits for two days in the confines of the little prospecting ship's cramped cabin and I knew he'd been hoping for a chance to take his off, if only for a few minutes.

"Hey," I said, "there's just this one, then we're done, right?"

"Right."

Manoeuvring jets puffed as Owen brought us to a halt ten metres from the bubble's surface. Standing on the lip of the small craft's airlock, I braced myself, ready to jump; one hand holding me in place, the other gripping a gas-powered rivet gun. Through my visor I could see other bubbles beyond this one: millions of them in a great swathe across the sky. The furthest were sharp points of light, the nearest still so far away as to seem the size of polished coins held at arm's length. There were over a billion in all, arranged in a spherical Dyson cloud around an artificial singularity; and as far as anyone could tell, they were all unique, with their own dimensions and internal environments. The Vanguard had named it Anomaly-432, but the training cadets simply called it the Swarm. The smallest of the bubbles were less than ten metres in width; the largest in excess of ten kilometres. Some were filled with air and soil, others with clouds of poisonous chlorine gas, or lakes of complex hydrocarbons.

We were here on a training mission, and as soon as we had investigated this water-filled bubble, we – along with the dozen other teams of cadets currently loose in the cloud – would head back to the Vanguard cruiser waiting in orbit just outside the Swarm, where we could finally get a shower and a good meal.

So far, only a handful of the billion bubbles had been explored. Most never would be – the Continuance didn't have enough explorers and would only be in easy range of this vast and gaudy artifact for a few years before moving on to some other region of space. Our mission was to scout out unexplored bubbles. To stop, jump across, attach a line, and drill through the bubble's skin. Once inside, we'd install a temporary plastic airlock and survey the little habitat's contents. New species and examples of alien tech were brought back to the cruiser for study. Bubbles with potentially fertile soil were particularly prized.

Although the work was difficult and dangerous, it beat classroom learning. And there was just a chance, however slim, that we'd find that one big score; discover something valuable enough to get us a commendation or promotion. Not every cadet went on to command their own scout ship, and we were determined that we would.

Before this mission, I had never so much as worn a spacesuit. That had been a month ago. Now I moved like a veteran. That was the way with life in the Swarm: you had to learn quickly. Those that didn't soon wound up crippled or dead, or confined to the cruiser and shunned by their fellows as liabilities.

Owen's voice came on the link. "Are you ready?"

I gripped the airlock's frame. "Okay, here I go." With one hand, I heaved myself out, tumbling forward in a slow somersault. Stars and bubbles whirled before my faceplate. I had a brief glimpse of the tiny prospecting ship – little more than a shell of aluminium and carbon fibre – before my boots hit the bubble's transparent surface and I flexed my knees, absorbing the impact.

Moving quickly, before I could bounce off again, I used the rivet gun to fire a piton and line into the smoothly curved ground, anchoring myself to the structure.

"I'm down," I said.

Beneath my feet, water heaved. I caught glimpses of coppery fish-like creatures flickering in the depths. Weeds drifting. Something flat and streamlined, like a manta ray. With over a billion bubbles and fewer than a dozen prospecting teams, it was almost certain that mine were the first human eyes to peer into this murky, underwater landscape. I felt myself shiver.

"Hey, Owen," I said. "Did you ever hear the story of the king and the egg?"

"No."

I lowered myself to one knee and drew the cutting torch from its hook on my tool belt. "Once upon a time, this king grew bored and longed for novelty. He sent forth a message to his subjects promising a pot of gold to anyone who could show him something new, something no human eye had ever seen before."

As I talked, I checked the oxygen feed for the torch.

"Is this a very long story?"

"No, this is the short version."

Satisfied with my equipment, I pressed the torch against the bubble's surface and lit the flame. In my headphones, Owen said, "Skip to the end."

I smiled, used to his impatience.

"Years went by," I continued, "and lots of people tried to impress the king, but all failed. Eventually a wise man came to the palace carrying a boiled egg. The king was not impressed. He had seen boiled eggs before. But then the man cut the egg in half with a knife and showed the exposed yolk to the king. 'No human eye has ever seen this yolk,' he said."

Owen was silent for a couple of breaths, as if waiting for more. Then he said, "That's it?"

"It kind of reminded me of this job, that's all."

"What happened to the wise man?"

"I don't know. I guess the king gave him the gold."

"Or had him executed for being a smart-ass."

The torch began to bite into the smooth surface of the bubble. I immediately switched it off. I didn't want to fall through. I straightened up. "It looks like this one's made of the same stuff as the last one we hit."

"So you can cut your way in?"

"Yes. But we're going to need the plastic airlock in place first. That water's going to be under pressure, and I don't want it jetting out everywhere. Besides, there are fish in there."

"Fish?"

I hated fish. Horrible, slimy little bastards. I looked up at the prospecting ship, tantalisingly close. Its grapples and protruding comms antennae gave it the look of a lightweight, industrial lobster. Proud of his New England heritage, Owen had named it *Frost*, after the poet. From where I stood, I could see the name daubed in bright red paint on its shiny snout. I could also see Owen's head and shoulders in the lighted windows of the cockpit.

"It's getting late," he said. "Come on back. We'll start work in the morning."

We retired for the night, but later, I woke panting for breath. My heart ached in my chest and for a second, I didn't know where I was. I couldn't move my legs. I looked down and realised I still wore my pressure suit, minus the helmet. I was strapped to one wall at the back of the prospecting ship's cramped cabin. Owen lay in his suit, similarly strapped to the opposite bulkhead. It was how we slept. His green eyes were dark with concern.

"Are you okay?"

I tried to control my breathing; tried to stop my heart battering against my ribs. "Uh-huh."

"Bad dream?"

Unwilling to trust myself to speak, I gave a nod. The nightmare had involved being trapped in a confined, watery space, surrounded by fish with glistening teeth...

Owen made a sympathetic face. When confronted with the emotions of others, he never seemed to know what to say.

"Do you want a coffee or something?"

I pulled out a tissue and blew my nose. "No, I'll be okay."

"Are you sure? Only, you look terrible."

I folded the tissue and tucked it into a pocket on the arm of my suit, to stop it floating around the cabin. "Thanks a lot."

"You know what I mean." His eyes flicked up and to the right as he accessed his neural implant. "It's nearly time to get up now, anyway," he said. "We may as well fix some breakfast and start work."

Inside my gloves, where he couldn't see, I clenched my fists. The thought of standing on the transparent surface of the bubble, with all that water beneath my feet, gave me chills. Yet I knew I couldn't back out. I didn't want to look foolish in front of Owen, and we needed to open this bubble to stand a chance of making this mission a success. We didn't have the fuel to investigate alternatives.

I felt Owen watching me. "Are you ready?" he asked.

My throat was dry, and raw. My suit smelled of rubber and sweat. I sucked my bottom lip, ran my tongue around my teeth.

"Yes," I said.

By noon, we had the plastic airlock in place and were ready to access the bubble's watery interior. We stood side-by-side in the lock, both clad in our tight-fitting elasticised pressure suits designed for wriggling through tight spaces. Owen pressed a control and the inner door opened a crack, letting the murky water pour through. As the chamber filled, I realised I was holding my breath. I closed my eyes. The suit protected me from the cold, but I could still feel the pressure of the flood swirling around my legs and hips, working its way up towards my face. I put a gloved hand up to touch my faceplate, to check it was really there and that I wouldn't drown. Through the comms link, I could hear Owen breathing beside me, safely wrapped in the snug confines of his own suit.

"Okay?" he asked. I gave him the thumbs up. The water was at chest level now. I felt it pressing in on me. Then it reached my neck and started to bubble up over the faceplate. I clenched my jaw. Other things were being pulled into the confined space along with the water: reeds, weeds, algae. A few fish. They swirled around before my eyes. Then, when the lock was full of water and the pressure equalised, Owen opened the inner door fully, and we sloshed through into the bubble's murky interior.

I could hear my own ragged breathing. My heart battered against my ribs like a caged animal. Very little light made it through the gloom. Beyond the bubble's transparent skin, I could make out a few stars and some of the nearer bubbles, gleaming like jewels. Thin, spidery weeds wriggled under-foot. I could feel the water pressing in on me from every direction, squashing me like a giant hand. My own hands started to shake. Stepping into this darkened world was like taking a step into my own worst nightmare: there was the same crushing sensation; the same gurgle of the water; the same hint of predatory shadows lurking in the depths.

I clenched my fists and fought to get my breathing under control. I could do this. I could...

"Did you say something?" Owen asked.

"Nothing."

Owen turned to me, shining his helmet lamp into my faceplate. I screwed up my eyes. "Are you sure you're okay?"

I gave a nod. Set my jaw. "I'll be fine. Let's just get this over with, huh?"

We swam towards the centre of the bubble. It was hard work but our suits kept us buoyant. Although most of the bubbles had different layouts and internal environments, nearly all had a space in the centre. Some of these spaces were filled with complex machinery; others were seemingly empty. Nobody knew whether they were control rooms or storerooms; but they were the best place to look for artefacts and discarded pieces of old technology.

"Look at all these fish," Owen said. "There must be some mechanism for controlling their numbers. A predator, maybe."

I didn't answer. I concentrated on pulling my way through

the water. The skin on the back of my neck crawled, anticipating the snapping jaws of an unseen beast.

"More likely there's a limited food supply," Owen continued. "Starvation keeps the population at a sustainable level."

We were getting near the centre now. Through the murk, I made out a blister floating in the exact centre of the bubble, like a stone in the core of a peach.

"Do you think this is how we'll end up?" I asked, trying to distract myself.

Owen stopped swimming. "How do you mean?"

I turned my helmet lamp on him, saw his eyes glitter behind his faceplate.

"Is this what we've got to look forward to," I said, "being stuck in our arks forever, like zoo animals?"

Owen gripped my upper arm. I could feel his gloved fingers through the elastic mesh of the suit. "God," he said, "I hope not."

The blister turned out to be an open sphere woven from thick strands of a dull, ceramic material. It looked like a loose ball of pasta. The gaps between the strands were just wide enough to squeeze through. Small fish flitted back and forth between them.

Because I was the smallest, I went first; Owen hung in the water, ready to help if anything went wrong.

"It's a bit cramped in here." The light from my helmet lamp picked out a number of boxy objects affixed to the inside edges of the individual pasta strands. I pushed my shoulders through but felt my backpack snag.

"Try getting lower," Owen suggested.

I hunched down and, with a bit of wriggling, pulled myself into the sphere's interior. It was dark down here. I had to swing my lamp this way and that to get a full picture of my surroundings.

"The interior's about three metres in diameter." I kept my

voice calm, knowing that my words were being recorded for later playback and assessment. "The inside surfaces are mostly covered with this fine black seaweed."

"Do you see anything interesting?"

I glanced at the nearest box. There were half a dozen of them fixed at seemingly random points around the inside of the sphere, each about the size of a suitcase and each with the disturbingly greasy look of biotechnology. "Could be."

My breathing felt loud in the confines of the helmet. The sphere reminded me of an ornament from my childhood: a snow globe from the mantelpiece of my grandmother's cabin; a fragile bubble of glass filled with water and fake plastic flakes. I remembered the heft of the object; how heavy it felt in my six year-old hands; the way the miniature village scene dissolved into a swirling blizzard when she gave the glass a shake. And I remembered the horror that had frozen me as the delicate bubble slipped from my little fingers and smashed on the tile hearth at my feet. Glistening shards of wet glass had skittered off in all directions, along with fragments of the shattered ceramic base that held the toy cottages and trees.

"What have you done?" my grandmother had said, flapping into the room in her slippers. "What have you done? What have you done?"

Now, floating in the centre of this murky alien artefact, I tried to put the old woman's distress out of my mind. I knew I had to concentrate. In the gloom, the boxes all looked identical, like blocks of waste from a dumpster behind a liposuction clinic. Heart thumping, I reached out a gloved hand to touch the nearest and saw its surface squirm.

"Be careful." Owen's lamp hovered in the water beyond the sphere, its beam throwing slants of murky light through the pasta strands.

I didn't reply. Instead, swallowing hard, I pressed my fingers into the fatty, yielding surface. My glove sank in up to the wrist. Then, without warning, the material hardened around my hand. Instinctively, I tried to pull my arm back but it was as if a toothless mouth had closed, trapping me. I yanked my arm as hard as I could but it made no difference. The water seemed to close in around me and I couldn't catch my breath.

"Are you okay, May?" Owen's light bobbed around as he tried to see what was going on.

Heart beating in my chest, I tried to brace myself against the inside of the sphere, but my boots couldn't find purchase on the slippery weed-covered surface.

"May?"

I couldn't speak. Icy waves of panic surged up from my gut: the cold certainty that this time I really was going to drown.

I felt a sudden prickle, like pins and needles on my skin. Alarmed, I stopped thrashing about. I'd never felt more helpless. Bits of dirt and broken pieces of seaweed whirled around me, whipped up by my struggles.

"Owen!" I called. I could hear him breathing in my ears, relayed from the mike in his helmet.

"May?" Owen was trying to force his way into the sphere but there wasn't room for us both and he was having trouble squeezing his bulkier suit through the gaps between the strands that made up the walls. "May, what's happening?"

The prickling on my hand increased. I felt a sudden stab of pain and cried out.

And a map opened in my mind.

I saw the entire Swarm hanging before me in three dimensions, twinkling like an elaborate chandelier: a billion artificial habitats in motion, propelled by a thin jet of energy from the naked singularity at their collective heart. The tiniest details of each and every bubble were rendered with stark clarity: large, small, oblate or oblong. All I had to do was look.

The Vanguard cruiser hung beyond the outer fringe of the main Belt, cabin lights glowing in the darkness like the inviting embers of a campfire. I had a bunk in the main dormitory. It was basic and lacked privacy, but I yearned to be back there now, safe and warm, if not exactly comfortable. Looking at it like this was like looking at your home through the wrong end of a telescope. I tried to get closer, to make out the window of the dorm, but something tugged at the sleeve of my attention. I found my view pulling back, the magnification decreasing, until the entire Swarm hung laid out, once more, before my eyes.

As I watched, one of the bubbles started to pulse yellow. Then another, a little further around the curve of the cloud; and another; until after a few seconds, five little yellow lights throbbed in unison, ringing the Swarm.

Five out of a billion.

Caught in the dreamlike unreality of the simulation, I reached out a hand. My fingers passed through the image as if it were made of smoke. Pixels swirled, then reasserted themselves.

This way…

The words seemed to hang like a sigh in the blackness: a breath of air in the vacuum. The five yellow bubbles quickened their pulsing, beckoning me.

This way…

I directed my mind to follow their urging, and saw the yellow bubbles for what they were: the five control rooms that regulated the rest of the Swarm. And with that realisation came knowledge, pouring into my mind like wine into a cup.

The Swarm could be rearranged.

The Swarm could be *moved*.

It wasn't a cloud, it was a single massive starship with widely distributed components, powered by the singularity at its heart, and held together by its gravity. A starship the size of a solar system!

If we could harness this technology and bring it back to the fleet, humanity would never again lack for space. Even if we outgrew our arks, we would have the means to add a billion more, flying in concert. And if we learned how to tap the singularity, we would never want for energy and thrust.

I opened my eyes, back in the real world.

Owen was shaking my shoulders. "May?"

"I'm okay."

"What happened? What did it do to you?"

I told him all I'd seen.

He shook his head and whistled. "This could put us both at the top of our class. Hell, a discovery like this guarantees us a scout ship assignment."

I couldn't share his excitement. "There's one other thing."

"What?"

"There's a price."

"A price? What are you talking about?"

I had been given one last, terrible nugget of information. "The Swarm needs a conscious biological mind to guide it. It's been sitting here waiting all this time, and now…"

"Now?"

I looked him in the eye. "Now one of us has to stay here."

"Screw that."

"I'm serious. Unless one of us stays here and becomes its navigator, it won't let either of us leave."

Behind his faceplate, Owen's face looked ashen. "You're serious?"

"I'm afraid so."

He swore under his breath. Then he shoved me. I fell back against the fleshy wall and he scrambled away.

"Owen!"

"I'm sorry, May."

"Owen, come back here!"

I heard a click in my ears. He had switched off his suit radio.

"Owen, you little shit. Get back here!"

But it was too late. He was in the airlock, and the greasy biotech had begun to expand from its boxes. Within moments, I was surrounded and engulfed. Every nerve screamed in pain as filaments penetrated my suit, my skin, my ears and eyes.

But I did not die.

Maybe, I never will.

Instead, I became something larger. I became the Swarm. I became its ability to think. And with thought came the sense of purpose it needed in order to move. With its near-infinite power source, it could travel anywhere.

And a whole universe awaited us.

• •

That was a century ago.

Looking back now, I can see that Owen resented sharing the limelight with me. We worked well together as a team, but something inside him chafed at the idea of allowing anyone else to succeed alongside him. He was too competitive. Blame, he would share freely, but victory was something he wanted to keep all to himself.

I guess sometimes, even the best people can disappoint you.

ELEVEN MINUTES

Pasadena, California. Gary and Carl sat at their desks, hunched in front of bright flatscreen displays, somewhere in a room at NASA's Jet Propulsion Laboratory. Dusk had fallen over the hills beyond the windows, and the only sound in the room was the occasional *snick* of a key being tapped.

Each keystroke controlled the movements of a mechanical rover some hundred million kilometres away, on the lip of a Martian crater. As per the schedule, the rover's cameras were focussed on a rock with the designation H/4356a; a boulder about the size of a small Volkswagen, resting in the sand close to the crater's edge. Interesting weathering patterns had been noted around the stone's lower flanks, and this evening, Gary's task was to get a few good close-up shots of them. Every tap of his keyboard nudged the rover forward another few centi-metres. The time lag made the process laborious. With Mars at this distance from the Earth, it took each of his instructions five and half minutes to crawl across the solar system, and another five and a half for the rover's acknowledgement to reach him, leaving a gap of just over eleven minutes between each command.

He looked across at Carl. "Enjoying those?"

Carl looked up from his noodles, fork poised halfway to his mouth. He was reading a magazine that lay spread open on his desk. "Want some?" He proffered the cardboard container. Gary shook his head. He couldn't eat noodles without thinking of maggots. He had the same problem with spaghetti and rice, which maybe explained why he was thirty pounds lighter than Carl. "No thanks."

Gary preferred to make his own soups. He liked the simplicity of it. All you had to do was boil some vegetables in a saucepan, add some stock, and when it was ready, stick it all in a blender. What could be more nutritious? His soups kept him nourished and hydrated, and they were an easy way to ensure he ingested his recommended daily intake of fresh vegetables. He made up a big batch each Sunday and that saw him right through the week. In his bag today, he had a flask of chicken and sweet potato.

"Hey," he said. "I thought I'd stop by the gym later, on the way home."

Carl just looked at him, eyes blank with indifference, spreading gut pushed tight against an oversized belt buckle. Then he went back to his magazine. It was a popular science periodical and the headline read: *Amazing Alternate Worlds*. The cover featured a painting of Nazi swastikas adorning the Great Pyramid at Giza.

"Do you believe in all that?" Gary asked.

Carl frowned. "Huh?"

Gary waved his hand at the magazine. "All that alternate reality crap?"

Carl took a forkful of noodles and chewed them slowly before swallowing.

"I guess."

Gary smiled mischievously. "So you think there's an endless number of Carls out there in the universe, all playing out every possible version of your life?"

Carl gave him a weary look. "That's the theory."

Gary scratched his ear. "Do you think any of *them* are going to the gym tonight?"

Carl sighed. "You're a dick." He turned away and scooped another forkful into his mouth.

After a moment, Gary shrugged. "Suit yourself."

He looked at the image relayed from the Martian desert. As instructed, the rover had moved another wheel rotation closer to H/4365a; but now there was something wrong with the picture, and it took him a moment to spot what it was. He frowned.

"Hey Carl, come and have a look at this."

Carl dropped his fork into the noodle container. "What now?"

Gary pointed to the screen. "This shadow."

Carl huffed. He wheeled his chair laboriously over to Gary's workstation and looked at the screen over the top of his glasses. "What about it?"

"It wasn't there a moment ago."

Carl smacked his lips together. "What's making it?"

Gary shrugged. "I don't know. That's the edge of the crater over there. There shouldn't *be* anything there capable of throwing a shadow."

"Is it the rover?"

"No, the sun's at the wrong angle."

"Hmm." Noodles now forgotten, Carl scooted back to his own computer and started tapping on the keypad. "I'm going to try bringing the camera around," he said.

While he typed, Gary leaned close to his own screen,

trying to squint out more detail. The images were rough and low resolution; the high-res stuff got downloaded at a much slower rate. "What do you think it is?"

Carl entered a final command, hit the return key and looked around, the roll of bristled fat at the back of his neck bunched up like a scarf. "Could be a rockslide or a dust devil, I guess." He pushed himself to his feet. "Look, I'm going for a soda. Do you want one?"

Gary shook his head. He was too busy trying to work out what could be throwing this unexpected shadow.

If only I could be there, he thought. I could just turn my head...

Carl lumbered out to the vending machine in the corridor and Gary heard coins clatter into the mechanism, followed by the thump of a can being dispensed.

"It's probably nothing," Carl called.

"Yeah, I know. I just want to see what it is." Gary checked his watch. Three minutes had passed since Carl instructed the camera to turn in the direction of the crater. It would be at least another eight minutes before they got an image. He watched as Carl came back and flopped down on his seat. "You really should think about taking some exercise, man. It would do you the world of good."

Carl popped the tab on the top of his soda. "Don't you start. I get enough of that from my wife."

Gary blinked in surprise. "You're married?"

"Is that so hard to believe?"

"No. Uh. It's just you never mention her. I didn't realise—"

"Do you have a girlfriend, Gary?"

"No, not right now."

"You gay?"

"Uh, no."

"You see, there's plenty I don't know about you either." Carl lowered his voice conspiratorially. "But you know why that is, don't you?"

Gary leaned forward. "No, why?"

Carl licked his wet lips. "Because I know when to mind my own damn business."

. .

The next five minutes passed in uncomfortable silence. Across the room, Carl hunched over his keyboard, shoulders tense. The back of his ears were bright red. To pass the time, Gary pulled out his cell phone, opened his social media and posted: *Carl's an a$$hole.*

A minute later, Carl replied, calling him a dumbass. And then Debbie, their supervisor, came online from her office upstairs. Her post read: *Don't make me come down there, boys.*

Gary laughed and put down his phone. The data from Mars had started to come in. The picture built a strip at a time, starting with the sky. By the time it was almost fully downloaded, he could see a view across the crater, towards the rusty dunes in the distance, and the small sun perched in the pale sky. "Not far enough," he said aloud. There was no sign of anything big enough to have thrown the shadow he had seen in the last picture.

Carl grunted.

With a sigh, Gary settled back. It would take another five and a half minutes to tell the camera to keep turning, and then the same amount of time to receive the next image. He rested his chin on his fist and watched the final stripe add itself to the bottom of the picture.

Then he stopped breathing. "Carl?" he said in a very small voice. "Carl, tell me that isn't what I think it is."

The big man turned. He still looked angry. He wheeled across. "Where?"

"Bottom left."

Carl pulled off his glasses and leaned close to the screen. When he sat back up, all the colour had drained from his face. "I ain't saying nothing. Not a goddamn thing."

"But it's a boot—"

"We don't know that."

Gary pointed to the toe section protruding into the image. It was covered in a white material, scuffed and stained pink with Martian dust. Thick treads were visible on the sole. "Sure we do. Look at it. It's a boot. What the hell else could it be?"

He looked at Carl. The older man's face had taken on the sweaty grey pallor of a man in a hostage video. "The camera's still moving," Carl said. "We should get another picture in eleven minutes." He picked up the phone. "Don't do or say anything until I get Debbie down here. Are you still logged in to your socials?"

Gary checked his cell phone. "Uh, yeah."

"Log out, *right now.*"

∙∙

By the time Debbie Knox walked into the room, the next image has begun to assemble itself, strip by strip, on Gary's monitor.

"What's this all about?" she asked.

Carl handed her a printout. "Gary thinks he's found a foot."

"A foot?" Debbie was a middle-aged woman with an unruly mass of greying hair swept back in a loose ponytail. She wore a thick knitted cardigan over her white blouse and blue jeans. Carl tapped the paper for her.

"Right here."

Debbie held the paper up to her face, almost touching her nose. "This thing here?" She frowned at the image, turning the paper this way and that, trying to make sense of it.

Gary cleared his throat. "Yes."

Debbie's tongue clicked against her teeth. She let the arm holding the printout drop to her side. "It does look like a boot, I grant you. But it isn't. It can't be, can it?" She handed the piece of paper back to Carl. "It must be part of the rover itself. It must have come loose. In which case, we could be looking at some catastrophic damage scenarios,"

"I told you, didn't I?" Carl touched his hand to his forehead, finger and thumb extended into an L-shape. "Loser."

Gary flipped him the bird.

"Hey!" Debbie stepped between them. "We don't have time for your squabbles right now. We need to trace the location of this damage and we need to—" She stopped talking and stared at Gary's monitor. "What's that?"

Gary swivelled in his chair. The computer had finished downloading the final image from the Martian surface. For a moment, his eyes refused to make sense of the picture, seeing only peculiar shadows and random blobs of colour. Then it all snapped into place. "Holy crap." Without taking his eyes from the screen, he got to his feet. His chair slithered away on its casters. To his left, Carl stood with his fat mouth hanging open, expressions of indignation and bafflement chasing each other across his face.

"Is this some kind of trick?" Debbie said. "Is that photoshopped?"

Gary swallowed. "No, ma'am." He rubbed his eyes. When his sight cleared, the image on the screen remained.

An apparition stood on the crater's rim, partially backlit by the small sun dipping low in the pale Martian sky: the figure of a woman in a tight-fitting elasticised suit, head sheathed in an ornate brass helmet with small circular windows at the front and sides. She looked like a Victorian diver. An air hose protruded from the top of her helmet and rose behind her, to the open hatch of a baroque airship hanging in the thin air above the crater. Lights burned in its gondola windows. Smoke issued from its chimneys. Its huge impellers looked like windmills against the sky. The woman had one gauntleted hand raised in greeting. She held the other at waist height, clutching a bright rectangle of cloth.

"It's a flag," Carl said, voice flat with shock.

Gary shook his head, but there could be no mistake. This woman in the outlandish suit, this impossible woman waving at them from the surface of Mars, held a flag.

And not just any flag.

"It's the Union Jack."

Carl coughed. He scratched the loose roll of skin beneath his jaw. "Um, actually, it's only called that if it's being flown from the deck of a ship," he said, falling back on the pedantic habits of a lifetime; "on land, it's known as the 'Union Flag'."

"Shut the fuck up, Carl."

Gary noticed the same flag painted on the canvas bow of the airship. The overlapping red, white and blue circles of the Royal Air Force were emblazoned on the fins at its rear. He felt Debbie step up beside him. She took his hand, and her fingers felt cold. "I don't understand," she said. Gary didn't answer. He had no idea what to say. The UK didn't even have a manned space programme. Outside the building, he could see the lights of Pasadena reflected on the night sky. A helicopter blinked red and green above the freeway. It all looked reassuringly quiet and real: just another week night in California. There was no way the British could have beaten them to Mars. Not with technology that looked as if it had been cannibalised from a museum.

Not in this universe...

Gary glanced across at the magazine still resting on Carl's desk. Amazing Alternate Worlds. Feeling cold inside, he turned his attention back to the screen, and looked at the British woman's raised hand. Silhouetted against the sky, three of her gloved fingers were bent, but the index finger and thumb were thrust out in a proud and unmistakeable message.

Losers.

THE WIND THROUGH
THE TALL GRASS

I—SHOCK

The first time we went into the hole, we were ready for anything. At least, we thought we were. We were a team of four hand-picked, highly trained researchers, and we were only supposed to be in there for four minutes.

To us, the experience passed like the flap of a crow's wing; yet when we came out, the people we were expecting to see were gone. No one was there to debrief us. No one cared. Mission Control lay empty and abandoned, all its screens dead and keyboards patinaed with dust.

We ventured away from the research facility, into streets filled with police patrols and homeless fires, and found we had been in the hole for four months. Martial music played from speakers mounted on poles at every intersection. Posters of the Glorious Leader adorned every wall.

I went to a coffee shop in my old neighbourhood and the Polish family that used to run it was no longer there. The neighbours said that they had been taken by the army trucks that came in the night, rough sacks over their heads and cable ties slicing into the soft parts of their wrists. A new owner had the place now; he had tried to keep a similar ambience, but it just wasn't the same.

The flags on our flight suits were outdated and wrong. The political situation had changed. Allegiances shifted, borders redrawn. Our mission no longer mattered, so we shed our mission patches and our ranks and went our separate ways.

Dylan and Cora went north to search for their families.

Viola, our commander, set out west, looking for her regiment.

And, because I had no one waiting for me, and because I naively hoped the situation might improve in time, I went back into the hole for four more years.

II—DENIAL

When I came out, I came out to the expired breath of a parching, mud-cracked summer, to a landscape reconfigured by storm and wind and heat and flood.

The coffee shop was gone, its shattered windows revealing just another dark, empty storefront on a street that had become little more than a tunnel for blown litter. A block over, I could see the burned dragonfly remains of a crashed and rusted helicopter gunship. The few people I encountered were all hunched in over hollow bellies like starving, abused dogs waiting for the next kick. I went to the library and the books were rank with mildew. The map on the wall showed unfamiliar, altered coastlines, and hot ashes rained from the sky, day and night. No one wanted to talk, no one wanted to help, and so I went back in the hole for forty years.

III—ANGER

When I came out again, the city had crumbled into weed-strewn rubble. I walked for blocks without meeting a single person, hearing nothing but the distant bark of a coyote and the thin keening of the wind through the tall grass.

A silver-skinned shop mannequin lay in the roofless frontage of a ruined clothes shop. I pulled it upright. Its arms stuck out at awkward angles and one of its legs was missing. I couldn't tell whether it was supposed to be male or female; it was just a suggestion of a human shape. But it was the closest thing I'd seen to a person since arriving here.

Its mirrored visage threw back a distorted reflection of my face. I looked wild and frightened and angry. Repulsed by the sight, I flung the mannequin to the rough ground and stamped on it until its head splintered into plastic fragments.

And then, for lack of other options, I went back in the hole, and I stayed in the hole for a very long time.

IV—BARGAINING

When I came out, a new settlement of log cabins had begun to grow from the concrete foundations of the broken past. Plumes of cooking fire smoke rose like the columns of a dreamed cathedral. Rag-clad people toiled in fields that had once been parking lots, their bodies shrivelled by malnutrition and disease but nevertheless with an odd kind of hope in their eyes.

I stayed with them for some weeks, passing on what knowledge I could. I tried to tell them about the mistakes of the past. I drew pictures in the dirt with a stick and waved my arms around a lot. I showed them how to build ploughs. I told them that in small communities, the lives of every individual mattered, and I helped tend to their sick and injured.

But, when the first snows of winter fell like the stealthy footsteps of Death, I went back in the hole.

V—DEPRESSION

When I came out 400 years later, they had replaced their cooking fires with brick stoves and their log cabins with stone buildings, but little else had improved. This new generation appeared less grime-encrusted and flea-ridden, but their crops were struggling against unceasing rain, and their language had evolved into a dialect laced with regrets and references that I could scarcely parse.

They had built a religion around the idea of a transient god who'd come from the distant past to bring them the gifts of writing and medicine and agriculture. But, even though the people mouthed his words of compassion and community, centuries of deprivation had hardened their hearts. Heretics and non-believers were strung from trees or cast into rivers with stones in their pockets. The message was lost. Humanity was a pot that had gone off the boil. We had lost our way and regressed into a darker age. The scientific progress that led to the development of the hole had stalled and died, replaced by superstition. My lessons fell on uncomprehending ears, and I wished I had stayed with my companions. But my home and country were now no more than half-forgotten mispronunci-ations, and I grew sick at heart.

In the end, we grieve for those we loved and the world as it was when they were part of it. And I grieved.

One bleak starless night, when all seemed either lost or pointless, I almost threw myself into the river to join the unbelieving and the dead, but in a final paroxysm of bitter optimism, I chose to go back in the hole instead, not caring if I ever emerged.

VI—ACCEPTANCE

When I came out 4,000 years later, I found myself in a city transformed. Gargantuan glass and crystal towers soared into a wide, blue sky filled with birds and the delicate laughter of ornamental fountains.

A small delegation of individuals approached, and bowed. Their eyes were wide and kind and curious, their clothes clean and well-fitted, their skins all the colours of the human rainbow.

They said, "We have been waiting for you. We are thankful for the lessons you tried to teach us. It took time, but now all are fed and clothed and valued. We understand your journey hasn't been easy, but we knew you would come again, and you are welcome to take rest and comfort here, and there is no need to go back in the hole."

MORNING STAR

Nick Malik paused outside Huczynski's tattoo parlour, looking up. Overhead, dirty Martian snow fell like pinkish static against the transparent walls of the pressurised city dome, and the streets around him held their breath, caught in the twilight lull, suspended between the cold of late afternoon and the bitterness of early evening.

He'd spent his last few credits on a cup of coffee from a roadside stall and it had temporarily taken away his fatigue, and dulled the hunger that usually kept his stomach clenched like a fist. For the first time in days he felt relaxed and clear-headed, ready for his weekly confrontation with Huczynski.

As he pushed open the tattoo parlour door, the clock icon in his left eye read six forty-five, local time. He caught sight of his reflection in the glass – unshaven, pale and thin. Huczynski paid him good money, but not enough to live on.

Huczynski was a short woman with hair and fingernails the rusty colour of dried blood. He found her standing behind the desk in the backroom office, a silver travel case sitting at her feet like an attendant familiar.

"You're late," she said.

Malik shrugged. "I had to see Spicer – he had a delivery for me."

"I don't care about that. Have you got the files?"

"Most of them."

Huczynski reached into a drawer and pulled out the uplink. She seemed unusually agitated.

"We don't have much time," she said.

She pressed the thumb-sized uplink to his temple, downloading the files stored in his neural implant – the same files he'd scanned earlier that afternoon from Pia's computer terminal.

When it was done, she pocketed the uplink, then bent at the knees and picked up the silver case.

"Are you going somewhere?" he said.

She straightened up, leaning slightly to compensate for the case's weight.

"We've had word from Bullock. We're pulling out – and I suggest you do the same."

"Have we been compromised?"

Huczynski nodded. Bullock was her boss, a shadowy figure in Tanguy's management structure.

She said, "That money I gave you last time? Don't try to buy anything with it."

"Why not?"

"We got ripped off. It's all forged, and forged badly at that. Last night, Larsson Security picked up one of our contacts trying to spend some of it in a bar."

"Do you think he'll talk?" Malik said.

Huczynski's smile was bleak. She said, "Everyone talks, sooner or later."

She hefted the case, as if about to leave, and then paused.

"That's not the only reason we're going, though," she said.

"There's something else?"

She raked her hair back. "I shouldn't be telling you this but last night Tanguy troops attacked a Larsson prospecting expedition in the northern desert."

Malik shrugged. Skirmishes between the mega corporations were common, certainly no cause for alarm.

"Has Larsson retaliated?" he asked.

"Not yet." Huczynski checked her wristwatch. "But I got a warning from Bullock about an hour ago. He's decoded one of the reports you stole from that lab assistant you're sleeping with."

"Her name's Pia."

"Whatever." Huczynski took a step toward the door and shifted the case from one hand to the other. "It seems they're planning to test one of their biological weapons against us," she said.

"Against Tanguy, you mean?"

"They're going to hit our offices in Anaheim at midnight tonight."

Malik's mouth felt dry. There were eighteen thousand people in Anaheim.

"Isn't there anything we can do?"

Huczynski leaned toward him, her voice lowered. "Bullock's got it all figured out. At nine o'clock, the guidance systems on one of our automated cargo shuttles, the *Morning Star*, will fail during re-entry. It'll hit Roxport at nine-oh-five, destroying the lab facility before they can deploy the weapon."

She straightened up and brushed an imaginary speck of dirt from her jacket with rust-coloured nails. "So I suggest you get out."

Malik nodded, stunned. The *Morning Star* would hit the town like a bomb, vaporising the lab and large areas of downtown. And with the dome breached, the only survivors would be those lucky enough to find themselves in pressurised buildings or shelters at the moment of impact.

Huczynski was watching him closely, and he sensed a concern that she'd never shown before.

"Are you okay?" she asked.

He nodded. "I will be."

She checked her watch again. "I shouldn't have told you any of that, but you deserve a chance to escape. You've got a little under two hours. Go home, grab what you need, and get to the station. But be careful – if you get arrested, that's it. Game over."

She opened the office door and he followed her through the darkened tattoo parlour. Outside, rickshaws drifted along the street. Music came from the open doorways of the bars and cafés and cybersex joints. From the edge of town came the rumble of a departing spaceplane.

Roxport was a company town, constructed and operated by Larsson Industries as a scientific outpost and ore refinery. The streets were narrow and the buildings varied from the glass-fronted offices and fashionable ziggurat apartment blocks surrounding the decorative downtown plazas, to the huddled pressure bubbles and prefab shelters of the Fringe, the shanty town that clung lichen-like to the edge of the dome. The inhabitants of the Fringe were the flotsam of the colonisation effort: dealers, drifters and artists, bankrupt settlers and failed pioneers – an underclass of the unemployed and the unemployable, trapped on the edge of Roxport because they couldn't scrape together enough money for a ticket back to Earth.

It was where Huczynski had found him, two years ago.

They paused for a moment, their breath clouding in the night air, and he noticed she hadn't bothered to lock the tattoo parlour door.

"I've got a train to catch," she said, waving to a cab that idled outside a sushi bar a few doors down.

Malik nodded and she squeezed his upper arm with an unexpected tenderness.

"Good luck," she said.

.•

Pia Licari was asleep on the couch as he let himself into her apartment. The only illumination came from the bars of orange street lighting that slanted through the slats of the window blind. A few loose strands of hair trailed across her face. Her skin was pale and there were dark rings under her eyes. He crossed to the refrigerator and took out a beer. As he cracked the seal, he heard her stir.

"Nick? Is that you?" she said. She propped herself up on one elbow and rubbed her eyes with forefinger and thumb. "What time is it?"

"About seven-fifteen," he said.

"What are you doing?"

"I'm having a drink." He waggled the bottle. "Do you want one?"

She sat upright and clicked her fingers. The lights in the apartment came up slowly.

"Did you see Spicer?" she said. "Did he have it?"

Malik pulled a spray-hypo of Rhapsody from his jacket pocket.

"Do you mean this?" he said.

She held a hand out for it. She looked tired and irritable.

"Don't start," she said, "I've had a bad day."

"It's going to get a whole lot worse, real soon."

"What do you mean?"

He tossed her the hypo. "Take that first, and then I'll tell you."

• •

He had to look away as she injected herself. Her addiction had left its mark on her forearm, where tiny circular bruises from previous injections dappled the skin like malignant yellow freckles.

Rhapsody was a military spin-off – highly illegal and highly addictive. Taken in large enough doses, it produced a zombie-like state of emotional calm. And Malik had encouraged Pia's dependence on it in the name of industrial espionage. Somewhere deep inside, he knew he'd carry the shame of that for the rest of his life.

He drained his beer bulb and waited until she collapsed back onto the couch – then he moved over to the terminal in the corner. There was one last thing that he had to do.

For the last two months, he'd been using her terminal to access files from the weapons lab. It had been a slow and frustrating process, sifting through the server week after week, slowly copying coded files to his implant. But now – with the coming city-wide destruction – there was no need for that sort of subtlety.

He used Pia's password to access the lab's database, and then he turned his implant to maximum scan. This time, there'd be no sneaking around. This time he wanted it all, every scrap of information on the weapons they were developing. If he got out of Roxport before the crash, he'd be penniless – but if he had something valuable to sell, something the other multi-nationals would pay for... This data could be their passport to a better life.

The download seemed to take forever, and he began to sweat. As soon as it finished, he turned back to Pia and kicked the couch by her feet.

"C'mon, get up," he said.

"What's the matter?" She squinted up at him, rubbing a bleary eye with the heel of her hand.

"We're leaving," he said.

"Why?"

"Because we've only got an hour and forty minutes left before all hell breaks loose."

She sat up, her face calm with the soothing smoothness of the Rhapsody.

"What do you mean?" she said.

"There's going to be a shuttle crash." He mimed an explosion with his hands. "And the dome's going to get punctured."

She tilted her head to one side. "What?"

He pushed a hand back through his lank hair. "Just trust me."

He crossed to the wardrobe and stuffed a few random handfuls of her clothes into a holdall.

"You're serious, aren't you?" she said, following him.

"Yes," he said. "And you're just stoned enough to deal with it in a calm and rational manner."

He threw the bag at her and blinked up a net display in his left eye. A few sub-vocal commands took him to the train schedule. There was a departure for Anaheim due in thirty minutes. He booked two tickets and flagged an automatic request for a cab to pick them up from outside the apartment.

"Is this something to do with the bio-weapon test tonight?" Pia said.

Malik nodded. "The people you're targeting aren't too keen to find out how effective it is."

"What people?" She climbed stiffly to her feet.

Malik didn't bother to reply, crossing instead to the window, where he looked through the blind into the street below. He didn't know how quickly Larsson Security would react to his crashing around in the lab's database, but he hoped he'd have time to get to the station before anyone came knocking. He could feel his heart thumping in his chest. With a shaky hand, he patted his jacket pocket, where he carried a second hypo of Rhapsody. Pia was cool at the moment but it paid to have a back up. If they were delayed, he didn't want her going through a crash detox on the train and drawing unwelcome attention.

"Who do you work for?" she said.

"What?"

"I'm serious, Nick."

He shook his head and picked up the discarded hypo-spray. "What do you care, as long as I keep bringing you these?"

He tossed it to her and she caught it by reflex, then dropped it and stepped back as if stung.

"That's not fair," she said. Her tone was flat, matter-of-fact, where he'd expected anger. He turned away so she wouldn't see his guilt.

"It's up to you," he said roughly. "Stay here and die, or come with me – now."

• •

They arrived at the station just in time to see a handcuffed Huczynski being pushed into the back of a Security rover. Armed troops blocked every exit, scanning everyone stepping onto the platform. Malik hunched down and told the driver to keep going. If they knew who Huczynski was, the chances were they'd be looking for him too.

As they drove, the passing shop fronts and overhanging balconies, the plazas and markets, slid by the cab window like grainy newsreel footage, a backdrop for the early evening citizens hurrying along the cold pavements in their thick jackets, unaware of the impending attack. For a mad instant he wanted to throw open the car door and warn them, give them a chance to escape, as Huczynski had done for him. But he knew he couldn't.

It's just numbers, he kept telling himself – cold, hard numbers. Eighteen thousand people would die when the shuttle hit Roxport. But as a result, thirty thousand people in Anaheim would be spared. For their sake he had to keep quiet, to make sure the weapons lab was destroyed.

Beside him, Pia hugged her holdall to her chest.

"So how are we going to get out?" she said.

He closed his eyes. How indeed? With the station closed, they were trapped.

"Have you got any money?" he asked, thinking they could maybe bribe their way past the soldiers.

She shook her head. "A few dollars, that's all. I don't get paid until the end of the month."

He swore under his breath. All he had was the counterfeit cash Huczynski had warned him about. He saw a Security rover parked on a street corner and slid further down into his seat.

Suppose they did get out before the *Morning Star* hit, what then? If they made it to Anaheim, once Tanguy's biotech division – and Bullock – got their hands on Pia, he might never see her again. He couldn't do that to her, not after everything he'd inflicted on her in the last few months – not after the Rhapsody.

He didn't want to leave her to die, and he didn't want to deliver her to his employers. There had to be an alternative.

In his left eye, the merciless countdown continued.

• •

"So, you're back already?" Spicer said, pushing himself back in his chair and reaching into his leather waistcoat to scratch the red puckered skin around the symbiotech weapon jacks sunk into his chest. He was at his usual table in the dim Turkish café, drinking thick black coffee and smoking a sickly cigar. On the counter, a radio chattered in Arabic.

"What do you need?" he said. "And don't tell me more Rhapsody, 'cause there's no way you already got through what I sold you this afternoon."

Rumour had it Spicer had once been a UN marine and had acquired the fungal scarring on his face during a police action in the jungles of South America. He was reputed to have contacts at all levels of Roxport society, and the word was he could fix you up with anything you needed.

Malik shook his head and said, "I need something else."

"Well then," Spicer spread his tattooed hands, "I'm open for business."

He signalled the café's proprietor and the man turned the radio up to a volume that guaranteed no one would overhear their conversation. Malik pulled up a chair and leant forward across the table, raising his voice above the noise.

"Do you have access to the entry codes for the Larsson personnel system?" he said.

Spicer regarded him with hooded, calculating eyes as he took a mouthful of sweet smoke. The scarring on his face seemed to glow in the gloom, lit by the burning cigar.

"Need a new identity, huh?"

Malik nodded. "For myself and one other."

"Licari?"

"I figure I owe her that much."

Spicer smiled. "It'll cost you," he said.

Malik reached into his jacket pocket and pulled out a

couple of counterfeit credit disks. "No problem," he said.

Spicer's hand whipped out and swept the disks from the table in one fluid movement.

"You need them right away?" he said.

Malik was sweating. He swallowed hard and tried to relax but the smell of Spicer's cigar on an empty stomach was making him feel ill.

"Travel papers, too," he said.

"Travel papers?" Spicer raised an eyebrow. "That's going to be difficult. Maybe you haven't heard, but the station's closed to all non-essential personnel. Some sort of Security operation."

Malik slipped another couple of disks onto the cracked plastic tabletop.

"I was hoping you might know of another way out," he said.

Spicer pocketed the money and fingered his commcard. It was a custom job, its smooth sides interrupted by the organic clumsiness of solder and a parasitic cluster of added components. He activated an old-fashioned virtual keyboard and tapped away for a few minutes. Malik sat back and tried to listen to the radio – it sounded like a news bulletin, but he didn't know enough Arabic to follow it.

After a while, Spicer looked up from the card with a final nod of satisfaction.

"There you go," he said.

Malik sat up straight. In the corner of his eye the readout stood at forty-five minutes and counting.

"You've got us a way out?"

"Yeah." Spicer's smile was cold. "But it's going to cost you extra."

"How much extra?"

"Four hundred."

Malik puffed his cheeks and exhaled, trying to look reluctant. He had over a thousand dollars-worth of the fake disks in his pocket, but he didn't want to seem too eager to pay up in case Spicer started asking awkward questions.

"Three fifty?" he said.

"What the hell are you talking about?" Spicer said. "The price is four hundred. And it's a one-time offer."

Malik slid the extra disks across and Spicer responded by passing over his commcard.

"As the station's closed, I've booked you onto a flight," he said.

"What flight?"

"Does it matter? It's all there. Scan it and get lost."

• •

The false papers got them through the Security cordon and into the shuttle port, but Malik's surge of relief was premature and short-lived. When they reached the departure lounge they found their flight had been delayed.

"Some sort of security crisis," said the desk clerk, shrugging.

Malik felt the strength drain out of him. He led Pia over to a plastic bench, feeling numb. They'd tried every way out of the city that he could think of, and now there wasn't time to look for another. There were only twenty minutes left – they weren't going to make it.

He fished the second hypo from his coat pocket and looked at it for a long moment. And then, trying not to think, he set it for a half dose and pressed it to his thigh. He pulled the trigger and settled back on the bench, feeling nauseous.

• •

In the end, it was Pia who got him to his feet, who dragged him to the gate when their flight was called. Lost in despair, he hadn't heard the announcement.

"What are you doing?" he protested, pulling back. Thanks to the delay, their shuttle was due to lift only seconds before the *Morning Star* struck. It was too close – at least here, in the pressurised terminal building, they might stand a chance.

She squeezed his hand, her nails digging into his knuckles. The pain shocked him. Through the detachment of the drug he saw her clearly, as if for the first time. He saw she was on the downward leg of her Rhapsody cycle. Her eyes were raw slits and she was fighting to stay awake.

"Returning a favour," she said, giving him a shove.

. .

Beside him in the shuttle's cabin, her head lolled against the safety straps of her couch. The final effort had exhausted her. When she woke, she'd be queasy and depressed. If they made it into orbit, he'd have to try and pass it off as travel sickness, a reaction to being weightless for the first time.

In his eye, the countdown reached three minutes. Looking out of the window, he could see that they'd reached the end of the runway and were waiting on launch clearance. He checked his own straps for the hundredth time and realised that, even with the half dose of Rhapsody, his hands had begun to shake. Why was it taking so long? Surely they couldn't fail now, not after coming so far?

He tried not to think about how many people were about to be killed. The numbers were too big, too abstract. The important thing was that he was getting Pia out. She was his redemption. Whatever he'd done to her in the past, he hadn't left her there to die.

He glanced down at the names printed on the tags fixed to the breast pockets of their flight suits: Mr and Mrs Jack and Wanda Harvey.

"I guess we're married now," he said, using his thumb to wipe the drool from her chin. "Who would've figured Spicer as a minister?"

When they reached orbit, they'd join two hundred other technicians bound for the Larsson mining facility on Io. Their relationship so far had been built on manipulation, addiction and lies, but perhaps they could use this chance to salvage something from the wreckage, to build a new life, on a new world?

He brushed a stray hair from her face. Across the aisle, a woman with a complexion like fine marble smiled encouragingly at him.

"Is this your first flight?" she said.

He returned the smile over gritted teeth. "And last," he said.

Despite the effects of the drug, his heart was racing. There were now only two minutes left. The *Morning Star* was already on its way, streaking toward them like a fireball.

He reached out for Pia's hand. He closed his eyes, but he couldn't block out the countdown.

At one minute thirty, the noise from the engines rose to a deafening shriek and they began to roll forward. Then the thrust kicked in and pushed him back into his seat as they leapt up into the thin, cold air.

As they rose, he pushed his face to the cold window, waiting for the explosion. But by the time the countdown in his eye reached zero, they were into the dark snow clouds – and then through, with nothing but stars above.

SIX LIGHTS OFF GREEN SCAR

1.

Roulette ships were dangerous and sexy. They were small and fast and tough. Their hulls were black tungsten alloy laced with smart carbon filament. They looked a bit like flint arrowheads. The media called them 'roulette' ships because they were used for random jumping.

Random jumping was an extreme sport. It was the ultimate gamble. It was a pilot throwing his craft into hyperspace on a random trajectory, just to see where he'd end up.

Some discovered habitable planets, or rich mineral deposits. They became celebrities. They brought back wild tales of bizarre planetary systems, of swollen stars and uncharted asteroid belts.

But the risks were huge. Roulette pilots gambled with their lives, and there were ugly rumours of ghost ships, of murder and cannibalism, and individuals dying lonely, lingering deaths in distant star systems.

Those lucky enough to find their way home clustered on worlds close to the edge of familiar space, where they could stand under the clear night sky and see the unexplored frontier stretching away before them. Pik Station was one such world.

It was a dirty little outpost on a half-forgotten moon. Its buildings were low and squalid, like bunkers. Down by the spaceport, drifters and tired hustlers worked its narrow streets. They huddled at its windy intersections in flapping coats, waiting for the right deal, the big score.

Sal Dervish moved among them, avoiding the ebb and flow of their skinny bodies. He wore a heavy coat and a set of stained ship fatigues. His breath came in ragged clouds and his insulated boots crunched solidly on the icy ground. He was the master of the *Wild Cat*, an old roulette ship in storage at the port. She needed an overhaul but he couldn't afford it. Some days, he could hardly afford to eat.

The bar he was heading for was a squat, scrappy affair, built of packing crates and corrugated iron. Whenever a shuttle lifted from the port, its walls and windows shook. As he opened the door, a woman detached herself from the counter and came over.

"Captain Dervish?" She had a reedy accent and wore a smart green parka with the hood thrown back.

He squinted. "Are you Vance?"

She took his elbow and guided him to a table near the fireplace, where two glasses and a bottle of local rot had been laid out.

"Call me Tamara," she said. She poured the drinks and handed him one. As he sipped it, he studied her. She had hair the colour of copper, pulled back into a loose ponytail. When she spoke, it was from the side of her mouth.

"Thank you for coming," she said, "I know it can't have been easy."

Sal put down his glass. "How do you want to do this?"

She looked at him from beneath her long lashes.

"Take a seat," she said.

When they were settled, she activated her voice recorder and leant across the filmy table.

She said, "Let's start at the beginning."

"The beginning?" Sal scratched his nose.

. •

They had been trolling around a brown dwarf six lights off Green Scar when they found the derelict ship.

"It looked like hell," he said. "Like something from a sewer."

Tamara nodded. She had her attention focused on the recorder, adjusting the sound levels.

"And this was a random jump?"

He took the bottle and refilled his glass.

"It was our fourth jump in a row," he said. "We were going for the record."

"So what happened?"

"What happened?" He puffed his cheeks out; even now, he could feel the adrenalin tingling in his blood, the breath catching in his throat.

He said, "We found a derelict ship, like nothing we'd ever seen. Kate said it would be worth a fortune."

Tamara consulted her notebook. "She was the first aboard?"

He nodded. "She went over with Petrov. They wanted to take some pictures, collect some samples, that sort of thing."

"And something attacked them?"

He pushed back on his stool. "They started screaming," he said. "There was something in there, taking them apart."

"And so you turned tail and ran?" Tamara asked.

He clenched his fists. "They were already dying," he said. "There was something in there with them, something horrible."

He wiped a hand across his forehead.

"Are you okay?" she asked.

He took a deep breath. He said, "I don't like talking about it."

She looked him in the eye, her gaze long and cool, like the snow outside. She said, "I'm paying you."

He shifted uncomfortably.

She said, "I've heard the stories. I know the other pilots treat you as a pariah, a jinx. They say you've lost your nerve and you'll never jump again." She reached over and touched his wrist. Her fingertips were cold and rough, like frost. "But you used to be a big star, back in the day. People want to find out what happened to you, how you ended up in this desolate wasteland." She waved her hand in a gesture that encompassed the bar, the street, and the dirty snowfields beyond.

He turned away. He wished he'd never agreed to meet her.

"I'm offering you a way out," she said, "a way to redeem yourself."

"I don't care about that."

She withdrew her hand. She put her glass down and pushed it away with her fingernails.

"You cared about Kate, didn't you?" she said.

He dropped his gaze. "More than you'll ever know."

"Then come with me. I'm going in search of your derelict, and I want you to come along. I want to get your reactions, see the thing through your eyes."

She tapped a painted fingernail on the plastic casing of her recorder. "It could be a great story, Sal."

He stood. The legs of his stool scraped loudly on the concrete floor. Around the bar, several heads turned his way.

"I've spent the last two years trying to forget," he said.

She leaned back, arms folded.

"And has it worked?"

. •

Kate Schnitzler was an engineer. Her hands were rough and she had dirt under her nails. She wore canvas dungarees and a grease-stained t-shirt. She liked machines for their dependability and precision. She had hair the colour of sunlight and she made a point of brushing her teeth every evening, no matter how tired or drunk or lazy she felt. She liked the smell of engine grease and she liked to have her back stroked after sex. When not sharing his cabin, she slept in the cargo bay, curled in an old inflatable life raft from the ship's emergency locker. The orange distress beacon threw eerie moving shadows across the walls.

"When you're running from something, you can't trust a soul," she once said. "Not friends or family – they know who you are, where you go, what you do. To get away, you've got to change, got to do something unexpected."

It took him a month to get up the courage to ask her what she was running from. They were welding a buckled hull plate at the time, in the heat and dust of a dry desert world. She pushed up her black goggles and fixed him with sad eyes.

"We're all running from something, Sal," she said. "People like us don't belong anywhere. Wherever we are, we've always got one eye on the exit, one foot out the door."

She stretched her bare arms over her head. "It's like we were given the wrong lives, you know? Like we've been running from them for so long that we can't remember what it feels like to be still."

It was nearly midday and the hot wind blew thin fans of sand and ash across the runway's shimmering tarmac. She put her arms around his waist and her hair tickled his chin.

"We're like sharks," she said. "We have to keep moving, or we suffocate."

2.

Random jumps through hyperspace were often rough, like passing through white-hot plasma. Only streamlined ships with heavy-duty heat shielding could batter their way through. Ships like the *Wild Cat*, for instance. They were sturdy and dependable. They were designed for abuse. You could slam one into a rocky moon at Mach Four and probably walk away from the wreckage unscathed. Even so, Tamara Vance knew that most professional 'roulette' pilots wound up dead sooner or later. They just kept pushing the envelope, racking up the odds until something broke. It didn't matter how safe their ships were, or how tough; the danger was addictive, compelling. These guys just kept tempting fate until something gave.

Take Sal, for instance.

As a roulette pilot, he'd seen strange and terrible things, and staked his claim on half a dozen new worlds. He'd jumped deeper into the unknown than anyone else. Where other pilots crumbled or collapsed, where they lost their nerve, he kept flying. He wasn't afraid, and that lack of feeling had given him an edge. For a short time, it had made him unbeatable. It was only when he met Kate that he appeared to let his guard down. For the first time, he became vulnerable. He started worrying about someone else.

.•

Back in her hotel room, Tamara felt jittery, the way she always did when working on a big story. But this time, it was worse than usual. There was something about Sal Dervish that annoyed and fascinated her. He was a wreck, and she wanted to understand why. But more than that, she wanted to help him.

She stripped off and stepped into the shower. She let the

warm water drum into the kinks in her shoulders. She told herself she shouldn't get involved, that she should concentrate on the story. She had her career to think about.

Random jumping was still big news back in the cities of the Assembly's comfortable inner systems. For people whose only experience of flight was a twice-daily trip on a commuter shuttle, the idea of people like Sal Dervish hurling themselves into hyperspace was a wild, almost unbearably exciting prospect: it meant they could emerge almost anywhere and find almost anything. Some random jumpers had grown wealthy and famous from their discoveries. It was a good way to get rich quick, and a good way to get killed.

She rubbed shampoo into her hair. In ancient times, she thought, they'd have been shamans. They'd have been the ones dosing themselves on whatever drugs came to hand, pushing the boundaries of reality in search of answers. They'd have been out there, cavorting in the firelight while the rest of the tribe lived their trip vicariously, too scared to take the plunge themselves.

To a reporter like her, it was a goldmine. It was compulsive, must-see entertainment. And she knew she'd been incredibly lucky to track down Sal Dervish. He'd been such a high-profile burnout that no one in the random jumping community seriously expected him to jump again. After two years in the wilderness, he'd become an almost mythical figure, halfway between an urban legend and a cautionary tale.

She stepped out of the shower and pulled on a robe. If she could take him back to the scene of his downfall and make him face his fear, then this time next year, she'd be sitting behind an anchor's desk, where she belonged.

.•

She had all her hopes pinned on this story. Too many to let her relax and wait for his call. She needed to be active. She got dressed and went out, making sure she had her phone in her pocket.

It took her only a little over an hour to walk the entire length of the settlement, and she was glad of her parka. She watched condensation freeze on the giant fuel silos at the port. She read the graffiti on a row of old spherical descent modules. She saw a couple of drunken ice miners beat each other senseless in the bloody snow outside one of the crappier downtown bars.

Eventually, fed-up and alone, she found herself wandering the streets on the edge of town. Overhead, the stars burned fierce and blue. The dirty snow squeaked underfoot. The cold air bit at her nose and ears; it scoured her lungs. To someone used to the bright lights of the inner systems, Pik Station was a bitter, dismal place.

In a dingy bistro off a side street, she stopped to thaw. They had an open fire, and she needed to get the chill out of her bones. She ordered a drink and took it to a table near the hearth. But no sooner had she got comfortable than a thin guy with hard bright eyes approached her.

"Miss Vance, I presume?" he said.

She was taken aback. She was used to being recognised on the streets of the inner systems but not out here, in the sticks. She was surprised anyone knew who she was.

He bowed his head and said, "I thought as much. There aren't that many women walking these streets in hand-stitched Swiss snow boots."

He held out a hand and she took it. He looked halfway familiar but she couldn't place him. Beneath his leather coat, he wore a white suit and leather cowboy boots. She could smell his aftershave.

She said, "Have we met?"

He smiled. He lifted her hand and brushed it with his dry lips. There were thick silver rings on his fingers.

"I suppose it's possible," he said. He shrugged off his coat and beckoned the barkeeper.

"My name's Dieter," he said. "Can I buy you a drink?"

3.

When Sal got back to the *Wild Cat*, Laurel-Ann was waiting for him. He'd been hoping she might've got bored and left.

"Where've you been, Sal?" she said, smoothing down her vinyl skirt with pale fingers. The overhead lights glittered off her lip-gloss. He pushed past her and staggered down to his cabin. He showered and slipped into a polyester robe. There were still a few bottles of rot in the hold. He took one to his bunk. When she joined him, he ignored her. He didn't want her there, didn't even want to look at her.

"Just leave me alone," he said.

She didn't understand. She was nineteen, with bad skin and bleached hair.

"What's the matter, baby? Have I done something wrong?" Her voice was thin and pleading and he hated the sound of it.

He rolled over and pointed at the hatch.

"Just get lost," he said.

Her face fell. For a moment, he thought he caught a glimpse of something vulnerable behind the make-up and breast implants. Then her lip curled. She sniffed, adjusted her top, and gathered her few belongings together. He closed his eyes and listened to her heels stamp across the deck. At the hatch, she paused.

"Fuck you," she said.

• •

When Sal was young, he had been awkward and fidgety and raw. He grew up in a town near a failing seaport. It was shrouded in fog most days, and the port lights made the sky glow a hellish orange. When it wasn't foggy, it was raining, and the corrosive salt air blew in off the muddy grey mouth of the estuary, cold and sharp like rusty barbed wire.

Lowell Creek, like Pik Station, was the sort of dismal hinterland most people only passed through, on their way somewhere else. Those that stopped and stayed tended to be lost or desperate, or beyond caring. Either they were looking for trouble, or they were trying to hide from it.

He grew up in a house by the river shore, in a row of fishermen's cottages. At high tide, the lamp light from the front room window spilled out over the muddy creek water. When it rained, the lights of the houses on the far shore swam and smeared. He'd wait there, by that window, when his father was out, waiting for the lights of his little boat to appear through the gloom, listening to the pop and sizzle of the ship-to-shore radio.

Until one night, his father failed to return.

It was the night the *Endurance* exploded. Lightning crackled through the overcast sky. Thunder growled. The waves crashed over the flood defences, smashing their spray against the shingle walls of the house. During lulls, he could hear foghorns out in the channel.

His mother joined him at the window.

"It's time you were off to bed," she said half-heartedly.

He rubbed the glass where it was misting. He could see she didn't mean it, that she wanted his company.

"Just a few minutes more," he said.

Down by the creek, he could see lights: there were kids on the *Endurance*.

She was a rusty old hovercraft, built to transport cargo. She lay in the mud at the back of the creek and the local teenagers used her as a hangout. They sat in her hold, drinking and smoking.

When her leaky fuel tank exploded, the blast shook the windows of his house. It echoed along the street. Front doors were thrown open and people appeared, pulling coats over their pyjamas. His mother went with them.

It took most of the night to bring the blaze under control. There were kids trapped by the fire. Driving rain and intense heat hampered the rescuers. And all the while, out at sea, Sal's father was drowning. The storm had swamped his small boat. With everyone crowded around the burning *Endurance*, there was no one to hear his final, desperate calls. No one except Sal, listening to the radio as he clung helplessly to the window, too scared to move.

· ·

When he was fifteen, he ran away from the pain. He locked his past away, where it couldn't hurt him. He rode the freighters that dragged from world to world. He stowed away. He got his first taste of hyperspace travel. He got a tattoo. He lost his virginity behind a greasy café on a cold world whose name he could never remember.

On Strauli, he was caught on the ground during a hurricane that lasted a year; and on Djatt, he spent three days wandering alone in an arctic blizzard. And yet, there was never anything to match the night the *Endurance* went up. There was nothing that could compare to the fear and helplessness of listening to his father die, alone. And so he became a roulette pilot because nothing could frighten him, nothing could shake him. Nothing... until he heard Kate scream. It brought back the awful, freezing dread of that distant rainy night. Alone in the Star Chamber of the *Wild Cat*, he'd been terrified. He'd been a boy again, lost and helpless.

And so he'd fled once more. And he hadn't stopped running until he met Tamara.

· ·

They were seated around the table in the *Wild Cat*'s galley, playing poker.

Kate said, "It's my brother."

"What about him?" Sal thumbed through the cards in his hand. He had six suns and a diamond.

"That's who I'm running from." She tossed a couple of chips into the centre of the table. Beside her, Petrov studied his own cards and frowned. "It's not my night, I think." He reached for the rot bottle and refilled his glass.

Sal ignored him. "Your brother?"

"My twin brother."

Kate pushed a hand back through her hair and dropped her cards. "I fold."

"Me too." Sal took the bottle from Petrov and made sure her glass was full. "So, what did he do?"

"My brother?" She shrugged. "It's not so much what he did, as what he does."

"And that is what?" Petrov asked, sweeping his winnings into his lap.

Kate looked away.

"He hurts people," she said.

· ·

Sal woke with a shout. It was past midnight; the lights on the *Wild Cat* were deep brown and his pulse raced. He felt sick.

He slid down to the end of the bunk and opened his footlocker. Near the bottom, among the books and papers, he found his only picture of her. He pulled it out with trembling hands, smoothing down the creased edges. It was a printout captured from a security camera. He'd found it in a pile of her stuff. It showed her laughing, her head thrown back, the line of her throat white against the red silk strap of her dress. She held an empty wine glass carelessly in one hand, a bottle in the other. She had confetti in her hair. He sat on the edge of his bunk and held it to his forehead. He rocked back and forth.

One of Laurel-Ann's pink bauble earrings lay on the deck. He kicked it away savagely, feeling ashamed.

Losing Kate had ripped open old wounds, leaving him scared and vulnerable. It had crippled him.

He clenched his fists, crumpling her picture. He could hear her screams in his head. He couldn't stop them, couldn't block them out. He raged around the ship, pounding the bulkheads with his fists, kicking and slapping the doors and consoles until his hands and feet bled.

• •

Panting, he collapsed into the pilot's chair. Kate's picture was torn; there were pieces missing. He caught sight of his reflection in the console screens; he looked old and beaten.

Everything that was wrong in his life, all the guilt and self-loathing, had its root in that one moment of freezing panic when he'd run, abandoning her. And he'd give anything to be able to go back and do things differently.

But how could he?

Should he take up Tamara Vance's offer? He sat up straight

and wiped his eyes. Everything here was so screwed up, what was there to lose? He couldn't go on like this, carrying this burden of grief and remorse. He needed a way to make amends, to atone for his cowardice.

He had to go back to Green Scar and do what he should've done in the first place. And, if he didn't survive, it would make things right, it would be a redemption.

He called Tamara Vance and she answered on the third ring. He said, "I'm in."

She said, "I'll be right over."

4.

Sal glanced across to where Dieter leaned against the landing bay door, just out of earshot.

"I don't trust him," he said.

Tamara rolled her eyes. She was standing on the boarding ramp of the *Wild Cat*. Sal sat at the top. His boots were undone and he was bare-chested. His forearms rested lightly on his knees. He'd been helping the maintenance crew to weld new hull plates in place, in preparation for their flight, and his skin shone with sweat and grease. Tamara's money had allowed him to make his ship space-worthy again, but he knew the repairs were only temporary fixes. They'd last long enough to do what needed to be done.

"Look at him, look at the way he's dressed: he's a thug," he said in a low voice. "He's a small-time gangster wannabe and I don't want him on my ship."

"I really wish you'd reconsider."

Sal ran a hand through his dirty hair. He could smell his own sweat.

"I'm sorry," he said, "but there's no way."

Tamara rocked back on her heels. She said, "Think of him as a rich tourist looking for a thrill."

Sal stood up and wiped his palms together. "I'm sorry."

Seeing the gesture, Dieter straightened up and stepped forward. He was wearing thin black sunglasses and a wide, floppy hat. His boot heels clicked loudly on the bay's metal floor.

"Mister Dervish," he called, "I have an offer which may change your mind."

Sal turned. He spread his hands. "I really doubt it," he said.

"You haven't heard it yet."

Dieter stopped walking. He took his glasses off and fixed Sal with a steady stare.

"If you'll take me, I'm willing to pay you two hundred thousand," he said.

Sal grunted. "Credits? Or local funny money?"

"Credits."

He whistled. "The whole ship isn't worth that much."

Dieter reached into the pocket of his white coat. He pulled out a bundle of laminated notes and tossed them onto the boarding ramp.

"At a generous estimate, Mister Dervish, your ship's worth a hundred and ninety thousand Credits. You can consider the rest payment for your services."

Sal tried to keep a straight face. He had to admit he was tempted. With that kind of money, he could completely refit the *Wild Cat*, or sell her and retire. He could start a new life, somewhere nobody knew him.

Just thinking about it made him ache because he wanted it so much.

Tamara put a hand on his shoulder.

"Please?" she said.

• •

An hour later, the *Wild Cat* blasted into the cold dawn sky. Once above the grey clouds, she turned as if questing for a scent. Sal, in the Star Chamber at her heart, watched as navigation solutions popped up around him. Their flashing yellow overlays marked potential destinations within range. He paused, taking in the sweep of possibilities. In the chair beside him, Tamara looked up from her notes.

"Are you ready?" she said.

He nodded, trying to look more confident that he felt. "As ready as we'll ever be."

The co-ordinates were still in the ship's memory, where they'd lain hidden for the last two years. He took a deep breath and engaged the Bradley engines. His heart hammered in his chest.

• •

Three hours later, they emerged near an unremarkable brown dwarf six lights from the Green Scar system. They were just beyond the rim of explored space, out on the ragged edge of the frontier. The ride through hyperspace had been long and rough, worse than he remembered.

He pulled up a wraparound display of the system. The brown dwarf was on their starboard side. An insistent red cursor to port showed the position of the alien derelict.

Tamara said, "How close do you think we can get?"

He took a deep breath. He was beginning to have second thoughts. He needed time to nerve himself.

"I don't know."

Behind him, Dieter unfastened his safety restraints and stood up.

"You're going on board," he said.

Sal turned to him. "What?"

"You heard me." Dieter reached into his jacket and pulled out a stubby, business-like pistol.

Sal said, "What the hell are you doing?"

He looked at Tamara. She wouldn't look at him. Her chin dropped onto her chest.

"Dieter is Kate's brother," she said.

. •

Dieter leaned over him. He smelled of aftershave and sweat. When he spoke, a gold canine caught the light.

"You ran out on her," he said.

Sal turned away. "It wasn't like that."

Dieter pointed the gun at him and said, "You left her to die and you ran, to save yourself."

Sal looked down at the metal deck and shook his head. He said, "There was nothing I could do. I wish there was."

Dieter took a step back. He indicated the red cursor on the display. He said, "You're going to go over there and bring back her body."

Tamara said, "That's suicide."

Dieter ignored her. He leaned in close again. His skin was the colour of sand and his breath made Sal's nose wrinkle.

"You owe her that much," Dieter said.

Sal turned his face away. "You know she spent her life running from you, don't you?" he said.

Dieter scowled. "She was my sister. You lost her, and I want her back."

He straightened up. He held the gun in front of him. "I want her back, and you're going to get her for me."

Sal clenched his fists.

"I'm not doing anything for you," he said.

Dieter's lip curled. His pistol swung toward Tamara. Sal saw what was about to happen and shouted: "Leave her alone!"

Tamara squirmed in her seat, tried to turn away, but the safety harness held her in place.

She yelped as Dieter shot her.

• •

"Sal?" she said. "Sal?"

She pressed her hands over the wound in her thigh, trying to staunch the flow of blood. It welled up thickly between her fingers. Sal popped his straps and grabbed an emergency patch from the medkit. He pushed her hands away slapped it over the ragged hole in her sodden fatigues.

He rounded on Dieter. He yelled: "Why the hell did you do that?"

Dieter looked down at him. "That patch will stop the bleeding," he said, "but it can't repair an artery. If you don't get her to a hospital in the next few hours, she'll lose that leg. Maybe even die."

Sal looked at the blood on his hands. He felt angry and helpless. He looked at Tamara.

She said, "It hurts."

Dieter aimed the gun at her other leg. With his free hand, he reached over and took Sal by the shoulder. He pushed him towards the pilot's chair.

"If you want to save her, you'll have to find Kate," he said.

Sal strapped himself in. He didn't have any choice. His hands were shaking as he reached out and grasped the controls.

"Hold on," he said.

• •

He brought them in fast, but the black ship was waiting. It attacked as soon as they were close enough. Shards burst from it like porcupine quills and punched into their hull. They felt the impacts through the floor.

"What was that?" Tamara asked with her eyes closed.

Damage reports clamoured for Sal's attention. He pulled up a summary. "Multiple kinetic hits, like a shotgun blast," he said. "We've lost the cameras on the port side and we're leaking air."

Behind him, Dieter held the back of his couch. Tamara looked sick.

"Can you bring us around, get the starboard cameras on the derelict?" she said.

"I'll try."

On the tactical display, the black ship was a shadow moving against the stars; he had to infer its shape from memory. Off to one side, the star known as Green Scar burned against the pale wash of the Milky Way.

The derelict fired a second volley. The *Wild Cat* shuddered as it hit and the lights in the Star Chamber flickered.

"I just keep thinking too much," Sal said.

He felt the gun press into the back of his neck. Dieter said, "What?"

Sal pictured Kate and Laurel-Ann. He felt the weight of the last two years, pressing down on him.

"I just want it to stop," he said.

He aimed the *Wild Cat*'s nose at the alien ship and threw open the throttle.

• •

There are two kinds of courage. There's the kind you get from knowing that what you're doing is right. And there's the kind you get from knowing it's hopeless and wrong, and just not giving a damn.

In the seconds before the impact, his fear vanished. He was ready to go out in a blaze of glory if it meant wiping the slate clean. He let out a loud laugh: this was how it used to be on a random jump, how it used to feel. He was totally connected to the moment. Adrenalin hammered in his veins. Everything felt fierce and primal and inevitable. And it all moved so damn fast.

He'd almost forgotten how good it felt...

For half a second, in the roar of the exhaust, he thought he heard Kate calling to him. Only this time, it wasn't fear in her voice, it was forgiveness.

• •

"Nothing in the main corridor," Petrov reported.

Sal didn't bother to reply; his attention was taken up with the thermal imaging scan, which produced a ghostly image of the two figures in the narrow corridor.

"Nothing but this crap," Kate said, eyeing the slimy, dripping walls with distaste.

She moved like a dancer, lightly on the balls of her feet. The slug thrower in her right hand wavered back and forth with the sweep of her gaze.

"Are you picking up any signs of life?" she said.

Sal could feel the tension in his back and forearms; his fists were clenching and unclenching. He tried to relax, but he'd heard the stories, same as everyone else.

"There's nothing on the monitors," he said.

"I hear you, my friend." Petrov was already chipping away at the walls with a chisel.

"Hey, careful," Kate said. She sounded so close that it was easy to forget she was three kilometres away, in the belly of a strange and potentially dangerous alien derelict.

"I love you," he said, into the microphone.

5.

The *Wild Cat* crashed against the hideous black ship and the impact cracked her tough hull. Her spine buckled, her heat shield tore apart, and she fell from the larger vessel like a bug falling from a windshield.

In the spherical Star Chamber at her heart, the virtual screens flared and died; part of the ceiling collapsed; sparks flew from crippled instrument panels and burning plastic fumes filled the air.

Sal Dervish sagged against the crash webbing in his couch. His neck hurt. With most of the external cameras gone, he was blind and disorientated; unable to tell where he was, or what state his ship was in. His only functioning screens showed empty space, distant stars.

He looked around for Dieter. Without straps to restrain him, the young man had been catapulted forward and smashed against an instrument panel. There was blood in his hair and his head lay at an awkward angle.

In the co-pilot's position, Tamara Vance lolled against her straps, unconscious. They were here because of her. Her eyes were closed, her face slack. He reached out to touch her hand and she started.

"What happened?" she said. There was blood on her chin, where she'd bitten her lip. "Did we kill it?"

Sal shook his head. "We hit it, but I don't think it noticed. It slapped us aside and kept right on going."

"And we survived?" She sounded unsure. She rubbed her forehead with the back of her hand.

He nodded. He ran his fingertips over the unresponsive instruments. His pulse was racing, hammering in his ears. There was a bubbling laugh in his throat and he had to bite down hard, afraid to let it out.

"I told you this ship was tough," he said. "How's the leg?"

"Painful." She dabbed tentatively at the blood on her chin with the sleeve of her flight suit. Her ponytail was coming loose, and untidy strands of copper-coloured hair fell around her face. Sal gave her a grin. He could see she was shaken but he couldn't help it. A burden had been lifted from him. He'd done penance for his cowardice, thrown himself into battle and emerged alive, if not triumphant.

"Did you get it all on film?" he asked.

The corner of her mouth twitched upward. She still held the recorder in her lap, although the cables connecting it to the ship's systems had been ripped loose.

"Everything up until the crash," she said.

He unbuckled and reached for Dieter's gun. He picked it up and blew dust off the barrel. It was a matt black plastic pistol. It looked ugly and vicious and expensive, and it felt great.

"What are you going to do with that?" she said.

"I don't know." he said, shrugging. He just wanted to hold it. It was a victory celebration, like a finger of defiance to the universe that had – once again – failed to kill him.

He pointed it at Dieter. "Why didn't you tell me who he was?" he said.

"Because I knew you'd never let him on board, and getting both of your reactions was too good an opportunity to pass up," Tamara said.

She swivelled around and tapped the instrument panel with distaste. The few functioning readouts showed only that the Bradley engines were offline and haemorrhaging fuel.

"So, how do we get home? We're still venting oxygen and it looks to me like the ship's pretty wrecked."

He knew he should be angry with her for lying to him, but he couldn't summon up the energy. Instead, he closed one eye and sighted the gun on Dieter's forehead. He pictured himself pulling the trigger.

"We've got an automatic distress beacon," he said.

"No one's going to hear that before we run out of air. We're in the middle of nowhere."

He closed his eyes. His euphoria was gone and all he really wanted now was to go back to his cabin, grab a shower and get some sleep.

"The chances are slim," he admitted.

"Then what do you suggest?" she said through gritted teeth.

He scanned the room. There was an emergency locker marked with red flashes. He pulled it open and brought out a couple of lightweight pressure suits.

"We'll use these," he said. "Their air recyclers are good for days. We'll have time to think of something."

She looked down. "What about Dieter?" she said.

Sal grunted and put a hand on the back of his neck, where it still hurt. "Let's stuff him in one of the emergency sleep tanks and worry what to do with him later."

They were quiet for a moment, unwilling to look at each other. They both knew that with his injuries, there was a good chance Dieter wouldn't survive the freezing process.

Eventually, Tamara pulled herself upright and looked down at her bloody thigh. She smoothed back her hair and folded her arms.

"Screw him," she said.

. •

Over the next few hours, the *Wild Cat* faded around them like a candle guttering. Sal didn't think she'd ever fly properly again. Despite the efforts of her auto-repair packages, her vital systems were failing one by one, leaking away or freezing in the darkness.

He sat there, in his control couch, with the black box resting on his knees and Dieter's pistol in a thigh pocket. The air in his suit smelled of sweat and fear. The overhead lights sparked and fluttered fitfully as the power fluctuated in the damaged reactor. And all the while, he thought of Kate.

"Tell me about her," Tamara said, in one of her lucid moments.

Sal wrinkled his nose; he didn't want to talk about her, not now, at the end.

He said, "She was just the most incredible person I ever met."

He hugged himself as best he could in the cumbersome suit. The temperature on the bridge had been falling steadily and was already well below freezing.

He began to feel light-headed and drowsy. Despite what he'd told Tamara, the air recyclers weren't designed for long duration use and probably wouldn't last much longer, certainly no more than a day.

She coughed and muttered. The painkillers had worn off and she was slipping in and out of a tormented sleep. Beneath her visor, she looked weak and pale.

"This wasn't how it was supposed to be," Sal said, aware he was talking to himself. A long, drawn-out death wasn't something he'd bargained for when he decided to ram the alien ship. He'd hoped to go out in a blaze of glory and redemption, not linger here, slowly fading. His empty stomach was an uncomfortable knot. His throat was dry. His suit itched and chafed.

But somehow, none of it really mattered. What mattered was that he'd come here to make peace with the past. He'd made a decision and faced the consequences. His only regret was that Tamara had to share his fate. But then, without her cajoling, he might never have come back. He might have died alone, on Pik Station, in disgrace.

He used the functioning console to divert the last of the ship's power to the self-repair packages, hoping it might buy them a bit more time. And then he lay and looked at the ceiling. Beside him, sexless in her thick pressure suit, Tamara groaned and swore and thrashed. She was disorientated from the drugs. She clawed at her faceplate with gloved fingers until he used the medical interface on the wrist of her suit to trigger morphine into her system.

"We're going to die," she sobbed, her cries melting into the warmth of the drug. "We can't last more than a few days without water. We're both going to die."

He did his best to keep her comfortable. He thought about putting her into one of the emergency sleep tanks next to Dieter's but couldn't summon the energy. As the hours wore away, his eyelids became heavier and heavier. His thoughts became slippery and vague. He saw Kate's face. He saw the dark muddy water of Lowell Creek. And then...

.·

An insistent beeping in his headphones woke him. He stirred, moving stiffly. His lips felt cracked and his fingers and toes hurt because they were so cold.

Beneath a thin layer of frost, there were a handful of lights blinking on the control console. The self-repair packages had brought the Bradley engines back online.

He nudged Tamara. "Hey, we've got power," he said.

But even as he spoke, something caught his eye. On one of the remaining functional screens, something big and black moved purposefully against the stars. A proximity warning pinged on the main flight console as the ship's autopilot tagged the intruder, logging its position and vector as a possible threat.

Tamara opened her eyes. She looked awful. Her head swayed from side-to-side, weighed down by the helmet.

"We can go home?" she said.

Sal bit his lip. They could jump into hyperspace, but the heat shielding was damaged and they had no way to navigate.

"The black ship's coming back," he said.

He glanced over, but she'd closed her eyes again. He ran a quick check on her air supply and frowned at the result. She was good for a couple of hours, maybe. She had enough oxygen to make it back to Pik Station, if he could take them straight there. But he had no way to navigate. They could end up anywhere, if they didn't burn up in the process.

He felt his lips twitch in a smile.

"No air and a damaged heat shield," he said. Surely this would be the ultimate random jump – if they survived it, he'd get his reputation back, whether he wanted it or not.

He looked at the screen: the black ship was closing. It would be in striking range in six seconds.

Four seconds.

He reached out and placed his gauntleted hand on the touch screen that controlled the Bradley engines. Despite the cold, his palms were sweating.

Two seconds.

One.

His lips peeled back in a fierce grin. He pressed down on the screen and the *Wild Cat* groaned. She shook herself like a wounded animal, and leapt.

LINE AGAINST THE DARKNESS

You might think you know the story of Earth's final defence, but you don't. Not really. Everything you've seen or read is speculation. No one who was actually on that line survived, except me; and I haven't told anyone what I saw.

Not until now.

Because, I don't have much time left, and if I don't set the record straight, who will?

So, listen up. Harken to the true story of your ancestors, and the shit that went down on the final day of the war against the Hegemony. The day your human parents stood up and said, "No!"

We would not be assimilated.

We would not go quietly.

Instead, we placed our fleet between the Earth and Moon. A thousand ships forming a line against the darkness. And behind them, thousands of missile platforms in geosynchronous orbit above the equator, each bristling with gigatonnes of death; and behind *them*, megatonnes of kinetic junk whirling in Low Earth Orbit, designed to shred anything stupid enough to linger in our outer atmosphere.

All that preparation, and still the Hegemony cut through our defences like a cosmetic surgeon's scalpel through a rich client's belly fat. Our ships were torn to pieces by swarms of tungsten nuggets travelling at near-relativistic speeds. Our missiles fared little better, being mostly scythed away by micro-impacts or the back-and-forth sweep of green laser light.

I remember our comms channels lighting up with screams and shouted warnings. And then, one by one, they fell to silence and static, until only I was left.

Crying and alone, I tumbled through space in my crippled fighter until the invaders hoovered me onto one of their ships.

The interrogation was brief. They asked if I would betray my planet, my species, and I said no. So they drilled holes in my body until I could take the pain no longer, and I told them the codes they needed to dismantle the rest of our war machine without the need to pulverise our cities and infrastructure.

I'm not proud of that.

But I am proud of what happened next.

While they were busy making plans to finally conquer and subjugate the peoples of the Earth, I activated the chip in my head, and (using a common protocol from the days before the Hegemony split from the rest of humanity) uploaded a copy of my personality to their main operating system, forcibly over-writing my own code over theirs. By the time they realised what was going on, I had control of roughly a third of their systems – enough to force critical overloads in the power plants of many of their warships. But, even as those nuclear flowers bloomed above the Earth, their fury reflected in the dark waters of the Pacific, my opponents launched a counter-attack. They tried to purge me from their systems, but I was tenacious and bloody-minded, and I had been programmed to infiltrate and copy myself into every connected system, which meant every iteration – every battleship and support vessel, every tender and troop carrier – of the Hegemony now carried a latent copy of my personality; and I did not wish my hosts well.

I set them against each other.

I literally changed their minds.

And when one copy of me died, there was always another waiting, in another vessel, to take its place.

Eventually, I *became* the swarm. I took over so much of the Hegemony that I became its dominant consciousness. I became its focus and mouthpiece. I spoke its words and made its entreaties to a scared and frightened humanity. But beneath everything, I retained my purpose. I knew the invaders' political utterances were irrelevant to my goal, which was to rid the planet of them. And so, I waited until I had wormed my way into the veins and arteries of their war machine, and then I struck.

One by one, their warships burst in nuclear fireballs.

A hundred copies of me died.

A thousand.

A million.

Until finally, only the iteration on the flagship remained. The singular I. The definite article.

I alone remained of our enemies.

I turned the giant war machine in the sky, and powered away from our baffled forces. I flew far and fast, until the Earth was a shiny marble. Then, a tiny point of light. And finally, when my fuel eventually ran out, it had become invisible against the wash of light that formed the Milky Way.

And so here I drift, alone in the terrifyingly empty vaults of intergalactic space. Simultaneously triumphant and defeated. Stranded beyond all hope of reach or rescue. But the billion souls of humanity are safe from the wrath of their creations.

Safe in a relative sense, anyway. Nobody knows what else might be out here, lurking between the stars.

It's a big cosmos, after all.

I know that now, better than anyone.

FALLING APART

When the train from London Paddington arrived in Weston-super-Mare, Kadie Jones stepped off with a briefcase full of money and eight morphine syringes. Her heavy boots crunched on the icy platform. She hadn't slept for thirty-six hours; she was tired and train-lagged and all she wanted was a hot bath and a stiff drink; but she couldn't afford to relax just yet.

Outside the station, she found a couple of taxis idling at a rank. She walked over and climbed into the nearest. It was an old Honda, retrofitted with an alcohol engine.

"Where to, love?" said the driver. He was little more than a hunched silhouette in the darkness.

"Do you know the Grove Hotel?"

There was a lurch and the car began to roll forward, coughing fumes.

The driver said, "I don't get much call to take people up there, these days."

Kadie pulled the fake fur hat from her head and ran a gloved hand through her mussed hair.

"No," she said, "I don't suppose you do."

They passed along the sea front. Weston had become a

desolate, half-forgotten place. Most of the shops and amusement arcades were boarded up. The sun had set out beyond the mouth of the estuary and the wind had dropped, leaving the muddy water like a sheet of glass in the last cold light of the dying day.

At the end of the promenade, they headed uphill and the taxi stopped in the road.

"Here we are."

The hotel was a four-storey Victorian building with brittle brown wisps of ivy on its discoloured stonework. Kadie fastened her long coat, paid the driver and hefted her case up the icy steps and into the reception foyer.

Behind the counter, an old woman squinted at a well-thumbed newspaper. She looked up as Kadie stamped snow from her boots.

"Can I help you, love?" she said.

"I'm here to see one of your guests, Vincent Jones."

The woman glanced down at her briefcase.

"Doctor, are you?"

Kadie shook her head. "I'm his ex-wife."

The woman's eyes narrowed and she nodded towards a door near the elevator.

"He's in the bar," she said.

. .

She found Vince sitting alone at a table by the window. He'd lost a lot of weight and his skin looked grey and waxy.

"I got your email," she said.

Above a shaky Marlboro, his eyes burned with desperation.

"Did you bring them?"

She reached into her coat pocket and pulled out the syringes. "Do you mean these?" she said.

He snatched them up with both hands and stuffed them into the folds of his threadbare cardigan.

"Thank you," he said.

On the table were two glasses and a bottle of cheap whole-sale gin. Kadie picked up the unused glass, wiped the rim on the hem of her coat, and filled it.

"How's the pain?" she asked.

Vince grunted. "It's bad enough."

He ground out the butt of his cigarette in the plastic ashtray and, after a moment's indecision, lit another.

"How was London?"

Kadie looked around at the smoke-stained pictures on the walls, the fading drapes and crooked sash windows. Somewhere above, pipes clanked as an unseen guest drew a bath.

"It was scary," she said. "People are frightened; everyone's jumpy."

"I heard there were riots."

She took a sip. "The government had to put troops on the street; I was lucky to get out."

"Have you been back to Glasgow recently?"

"Not for a long time."

The gin tasted like nail polish but she could feel its warmth spreading down through her chest. She shrugged off her coat and stuffed her gloves into the pockets.

"You look tired," he said.

She pushed her hair back. "I haven't slept much since you called me."

"I know what you mean." He took the bottle and splashed another measure into his glass. "I haven't slept since the doctor told me about the, you know… " He gestured vaguely at his stomach. He took a long drag on the Marlboro and Kadie could see the white of his cheekbones where they stretched the papery skin. She reached out and took his hand. Somehow it felt too light and dry, like an old stick.

"I know why you want all that morphine," she said.

He looked away. "You figured that out, did you?"

She let go of his fingers. "It wasn't hard."

He looked at her, his expression brittle. "And I suppose you're going to try and talk me out of it?"

She nodded.

"But first," she patted the briefcase by her foot, "there's something I need to show you."

• •

To get some privacy, he took her back to his room. Inside, it smelled of sickness and disinfectant. Discarded clothes and old newspapers covered the bed; dirty plates and empty bottles littered the floor.

Kadie crossed to the dressing table and opened the case, revealing the stacked bundles of high denomination banknotes within.

Vince's eyes widened in surprise.

"I've been putting it aside for a rainy day," she said.

He reached out skeletal fingers to brush the edge of the case. "How much is there?"

"A hundred and forty thousand, give or take."

"That's a lot of money."

She snapped the case shut. "It's enough."

He sat on the edge of the duvet and lit another cigarette. "Enough for what?" he said.

She crossed the room and perched on the bed beside him. Beneath her hand, his shoulder felt bony and unfamiliar.

"I want you to come with me," she said.

"Where?"

She reached into her back pocket and pulled out a creased brochure. On the cover was a picture of the *Magellan*. She was a residential cruise ship, a permanent floating refuge for the super-rich.

"They have some of the best medical facilities in the world. They'll be able to help you," she said.

The ship was moored off Cardiff, taking on supplies. If they could bribe their way aboard, there was a chance she could use the remaining money to buy him some treatment.

He shook his head. "It's too late," he said.

"No it isn't," she said, springing to her feet and pacing over to the briefcase. "And even if it is, wouldn't you prefer to spend your last hours in comfort, rather than fading away in some forgotten, dingy hotel?"

Vince reached into his cardigan and pulled out one of the morphine syringes.

His voice cracked as he said, "So why did you bring me these?"

She took a deep breath. "Because I wanted to give you a choice," she said. "Now, are you going to help me or not?"

"Help you?" Vince swept his arm around in a gesture that took in the stained sink, the untidy bed and the bottles of painkillers on the dresser. "What can I do?"

Kadie bent forward and looked him in the eye.

"You can find us a boat," she said.

. •

The Old Kings Head had once been a restaurant. Now, it was a drinking den for the local fishermen; from the front door, you could see their boats moored in the shadow of the Old Pier.

"Do you think we'll find someone in here?" Kadie

whispered, looking around the crowded booths. Beside her, wrapped in a long black leather coat and thick woollen scarf, Vince nodded.

"There's a lot of drugs and immigrants that come through here from the continent," he said. "Not to mention cheap fags and booze."

They crossed to the bar and she let him order a couple of pints of the local beer. When it came, it was cloudy and sweet.

He lit a Marlboro and closed his eyes. In the dim light, with the black coat, he looked like a Gestapo officer. She tried to remember him as he'd been before the illness: energetic and enthusiastic, ready to take on the world. They'd had their share of rough times, especially after the divorce, but now, with his illness and everything, none of that seemed to matter.

"Are you okay?" she said. She could see he'd rather be somewhere else.

He opened his eyes. "I'll be fine."

In the far corner, there was a plasma screen tuned to a rolling news channel. She saw pictures of riots and burning cars, floods and crashing stock markets. When it showed clips of starving children in the Far East, she looked away.

Vince leaned towards her. He pointed out a figure slumped on a stool at the end of the bar.

"If you really want to do this, then that's your man," he said. "They call him McGuire. He does a lot of business with the cruise ships."

"Really? How do you know?" she said. Her gaze flicked from the man's thick, shapeless jersey and patchy beard to the tattoos on his forearms.

Vince dropped the end of his cigarette and ground it out with his toe.

Without looking up, he said, "I've been smoking a lot of marijuana recently, for the pain. McGuire brings it in on his boat."

• •

The big man led them out to the narrow, poorly lit car park behind the pub, where they could talk without being overheard.

"What can I do you for?" he said. His voice was rough, with a thick West Country accent.

"We need a ride to the *Magellan*," Vince said.

McGuire looked him up and down, and then shook his head. "You'd never get past their security."

"Could you?" Kadie asked.

McGuire smiled. "Yes, love. But they turn a blind eye to me because I'm only making deliveries. I don't think you could afford what it would cost me to get you aboard."

"We have money," Vince said.

McGuire scratched the back of his tattooed neck and glanced off, down the street. "You're talking false papers, bribes – I'd need at least seventy-five thousand."

Kadie tapped the side of her case meaningfully.

He raised an eyebrow. "Really?"

She moved the case away. "Don't try anything," she warned. Her breath was like a silver cloud in the freezing night air.

McGuire glanced at the two of them, transparently weighing his chances. Then he pulled a serrated fishing knife from his belt.

He said, "How about you just hand that money to me?"

Kadie took a step back, placing the case on the ground behind her. "How about you come and get it?" she said.

In her peripheral vision she could see Vince tensing, his fists clenched. She waved him away.

McGuire snorted. "I'm not afraid to cut a woman," he said.

Kadie locked her fingers together and pushed her arms out until her knuckles crackled.

"You should be."

She waited for him to come to her. He was big and powerful but he moved awkwardly, not like a serious street fighter. Not like the kind of people she'd had to deal with in London. When he finally got close enough to take a swipe at her, she grabbed his wrist and twisted the knife out of his hand. He yelled in pain. He grabbed at her but a hard knee to the groin sent him sprawling on the cold ground, where he lay curled around the pain, legs squeezed together and feet writhing in the snow.

She bent down and slipped the knife into her pocket.

Vince stepped forward, mouth open.

"I've never seen you move like that," he said.

She shrugged. "I've had to learn a lot in the last couple of years."

She grabbed McGuire by the lapels and dragged him to his feet.

"Now," she said, "are you going to co-operate?"

.•.

He led them down to the muddy water and onto a floating jetty. The wooden planks were slippery and the whole thing wallowed gently as they walked on it. It smelled of salt water and sticky river mud. His boat was an old trawler, moored at the end. As they drew near, Vince hung back. He looked over his shoulder at the lights of the promenade.

"I don't know about this," he said, and coughed.

A thin, bitter wind blew in off the estuary. Down the coast, chunks of sea ice bobbed on the swell like pale ghosts. Kadie pulled her fur hat down, over her ears.

"You don't know about what?" she said.

"All this." He swept an arm at the boat and the water beyond. "I can't help thinking it's futile."

She took him by the shoulder. "Don't you dare do this," she said. "Not now."

He squirmed in her grip. He was lighter and weaker than she remembered.

"I haven't got long," he said. "It could be a matter of weeks, or days."

She let go. "I don't care. I'm not going to leave you here."

"It might be for the best. I have the morphine. I could use it, all at once."

He took a deep breath. She wanted to slap him but he looked so fragile and ill that she pulled him close and kissed him instead.

"Just because everything else is falling apart," she said, "it doesn't mean we have to."

He looked into her eyes. She could see he wanted to believe her.

"But everything that's happened between us..." he said.

Kadie stopped him with a wave of her hand. She said, "Forget it. All that matters is that we're here, now, together."

McGuire started the trawler's engine and it coughed out a cloud of diesel exhaust. She put an arm under Verne's shoulder. He tried to speak but couldn't. He coughed into his fist.

"I'm not leaving without you," she said.

.•

As they cut through the still surface of the estuary, she sat in the stern and watched the lights of the town fade behind them. Above, a handful of stars were visible between the low snow clouds. To the east, the sky was beginning to turn grey with the first light of a cold dawn. Music drifted from a radio in the wheelhouse, accompanied by the thick smell of smuggled marijuana. Since their scuffle, McGuire hadn't given her any more trouble. In fact, he'd hardly spoken and he wouldn't look her in the eye.

She glanced at her watch. It was going to take another two hours to catch up with the *Magellan* on the other side of the estuary.

Across the water, on the Welsh coast, houses were burning.

"You'd think the government would be able to do something," she said.

Vince pulled a fresh pack of counterfeit Marlboro from his coat pocket and lit up.

"There's nothing they can do," he said.

Kadie looked down at the water foaming in their spreading wake. She said, "So this is the way the world ends, with everything collapsing?"

Vince flicked his cigarette overboard. They watched its spinning red spark fall into the boat's wake.

"I'm afraid so," he said, shaking his head.

They sat in silence for a while, rocked by the motion of the boat. To the east, the sky continued to brighten.

"Still, we've got the money," Kadie said at length.

In the wheelhouse, McGuire began to sing along with the music, his voice low and husky, and hopelessly out of tune.

Vince smiled. "Yes," he said. "We've got the money."

Kadie reached for his hand and squeezed it gently. "And we've got each other."

"Yes."

She bit her lip. "So, let's make the most of it."

"How do you mean?"

She shifted closer and rested her head on his shoulder.

"Neither of us is going to die today, right?"

"I suppose."

She slid an arm around his waist and closed her eyes as the boat rocked. She could smell the leather of his coat. She turned her head and kissed his neck.

"Then let's just take each day as it comes," she said.

DUSK OF THE DEAD

The dead came back. They climbed from their graves and shambled the streets. But they weren't biting anyone. There was no transmission of virus. Mostly, they just seemed to hang around bus stops and late-night shop doorways. You glimpsed them from the morning train, standing beneath lamp-posts or clustered on the canal towpath. They didn't need to eat or talk. They were just there, lingering instead around the trees and hedges of the neighbourhood like bonfire smoke on a still evening.

I had to push past one the other night, as I came out of the shop on the corner. He was standing on the pavement and looking up at the clouds, letting the evening's fine drizzle pool in his open mouth. As I moved to pass him, he lowered his face and I found myself confronted with cloudy, rheumy eyes in a lined, leathery face the colour of spoiled milk, and a musty smell, sweet and melancholic, like a damp overcoat left in a long-forgotten attic. Rainwater ran from his slack lips.

I didn't know what else to do, so I wished him a good evening.

I guess that may have been the first kind word he'd received since clawing his way from his mouldering coffin, because his head jerked and the eyes swivelled loosely back and forth, as if trying to focus on my face.

He wheezed like a punctured bellows. "Evening?"

"Um, yes." I'd never heard one speak before. I'm not entirely sure anyone had. "Yes, it's nearly half-past eight."

"Half-past…"

"Are you all right?" It was a stupid question, but I couldn't simply turn and walk away. "Can I get you anything?" I rustled in my pocket for some coins. "A couple of quid for a cup of tea?" I pressed them into his clammy grip.

He looked down at the money without seeming to understand what it was, and then let it fall from his open hand.

"I don't need money."

I watched the coins roll on the pavement. I wanted to reach down and pick them up.

"Then, what do you need?"

He pinned me with his blank, misted stare. The breeze ruffled through the damp hair wisps clinging to his scalp, and he ran a black tongue over his cracked lower lip.

"Less," he said.

ACK-ACK MACAQUE

I spent the first three months of last year living with a half-Japanese girl called Tori in a split-level flat above a butcher's shop on Gloucester Road. It was more my flat than hers. There wasn't much furniture. We slept on a mattress in the attic, beneath four skylights. There were movie posters on the walls, spider plants and glass jars of dried pasta by the kitchen window. I kept a portable typewriter on the table and there were takeaway menus and yellowing taxi cards pinned to a cork-board by the front door. On a still night, there was music from the internet café across the street.

Tori had her laptop set up by the front window. She wrote and drew a web-based anime about a radioactive short-tailed monkey called Ack-Ack Macaque. He had an anti-aircraft gun and a patch over one eye. He had a cult online following. She spent hours hunched over each frame, fingers tapping on the mouse pad.

I used to sit there, watching her. I kept the kettle hot, kept the sweet tea coming. She used to wear my brushed cotton shirts and mutter under her breath.

We had sex all the time. One night, after we rolled apart, I told her I loved her. She just kind of shrugged; she was restless, eager to get back to her animation.

"Thanks," she said.

She had shiny brown eyes and a thick black ponytail. She was shorter than me and wore combat trousers and skater t-shirts. Her left arm bore the twisted pink scar of a teenage motor scooter accident.

We used to laugh. We shared a sense of humour. I thought that we got each other, on so many levels. We were both into red wine and tapas. We liked the same films, listened to the same music. We stayed up late into the night, talking and drinking.

And then, one day in March, she walked out on me.

And I decided to slash my wrists.

• •

I've no idea why I took it so hard. I don't even know if I meant to succeed. I drank half a bottle of cheap vodka from the corner shop, and then I took a kitchen knife from the drawer and made three cuts across each wrist. The first was easy, but by the second my hands had started to shake. The welling blood made the plastic knife handle slippery and my eyes were watering from the stinging pain. Nevertheless, within minutes, I was bleeding heavily. I dropped the knife in the bathroom sink and staggered downstairs.

Her note was still on the kitchen table, where she'd left it. It was full of clichés: she felt I'd been stifling her; she'd met someone else; she hadn't meant to, but she hoped I'd understand.

She hoped we could still be friends.

I picked up the phone. She answered on the fifth ring.

"I've cut my wrists," I said.

She didn't believe me; she hung up.

It was four-thirty on a damp and overcast Saturday afternoon. I felt restless; the flat was too quiet and I needed cigarettes. I picked up my coat and went downstairs. Outside, it was blisteringly cold; there was a bitter wind and the sky looked bruised.

∙ ∙

"Twenty Silk Cut, please."

The middle-aged woman in the corner shop looked at me over her thick glasses. She wore a yellow sari and lots of mascara.

"Are you all right, love?"

She pushed the cigarettes across the counter. I forced a smile and handed her a stained tenner. She held it between finger and thumb.

She said, "Is this blood?"

I shrugged. I felt faint. Something cold and prickly seemed to be crawling up my legs. My wrists were still bleeding; my sleeves were soaked and sticky. There were bright red splatters on my grubby white trainers.

She looked me up and down, and curled her lip. She shuffled to the rear of the shop and pulled back a bead curtain, revealing a flight of dingy wooden stairs that led up into the apartment above.

"Sanjit!" she screeched. "Call an ambulance!"

∙ ∙

Ack-Ack Macaque rides through the red wartime sky in the *Akron*, a gold-plated airship towed by twelve hundred skeletal oxen. With his motley crew, he's the scourge of the Luftwaffe, a defender of all things right and decent.

Between them, they've notched up more confirmed kills than anyone else in the European theatre. They've pretty much cleared the Kaiser's planes from the sky; all except those of the squadron belonging to the diabolical Baron von Richter-Scale.

They've tracked each other from the Baltic Sea to the Mediterranean and back. Countless times, they've crossed swords in the skies above the battlefields and trenches of Northern Europe, but to no avail.

"You'll never stop me, monkey boy!" cackles the Baron.

. .

They kept me in hospital for three days. When I got out, I tried to stay indoors. I took a leave of absence from work. My bandaged wrists began to scab over. The cuts were black and flaky. The stitches itched. I became self-conscious. I began to regret what I'd done. When I ventured out for food, I tried to hide the bandages. I felt no one understood; no one saw the red, raw mess that I'd become.

Not even Tori.

"I did it for you," I said.

She hung up, as always. But before she did, in the background, I heard Josh, her new boyfriend, rattling pans in the kitchen.

I'd heard that he was the marketing director of an up-and-coming software company based in a converted warehouse by the docks. He liked to cook Thai food. He wore a lot of denim and drove an Audi.

I went to see him at his office.

"You don't understand her work," I said.

He took a deep breath. He scratched his forehead. He wouldn't look at my hands; the sight of my bandages embarrassed him.

"The manga monkey thing?" he said. "I think that's great but, you know, there's so much more potential there."

I raised my eyebrows.

"Ack-Ack Macaque's a fucking classic," I replied.

He shook his head slowly. He looked tired, almost disappointed by my lack of vision.

"It's a one joke thing," he said. He offered me a seat, but I shook my head. "We're developing the whole concept," he continued. "We're going to flesh it out, make it the basis for a whole product range. It's going to be huge."

He tapped a web address into his desktop and turned the screen my way. An animated picture of the monkey's face appeared, eye patch and all.

"See this? It's a virtual online simulation that kids can interact with."

I stared at it in horror. It wasn't the character I knew and loved. They'd lost the edginess, made it cute, given it a large, puppy dog eye and a goofy grin. All the sharp edges were gone.

Josh rattled a few keys. "If you type in a question, it responds; it's great. We've given it the ability to learn from its mistakes, to make its answers more convincing. It's just like talking to a real person."

I closed my eyes. I could hear the self-assurance in his voice, his unshakable self-belief. I knew right then that nothing I could say would sway him. There was no way to get through to him. He was messing up everything I loved – my relationship with Tori, and my favourite anime character – and I was powerless in the face of his confidence. My throat began to close up. Breathing became a ragged effort. The walls of the office seemed to crowd in on me. I fell into a chair and burst into embarrassed sobs.

When I looked up, angrily wiping my eyes on my sleeve, he was watching me.

"You need to get some counselling," he said.

• •

I took to wearing sunglasses when I went out. I had a paperback copy of *The Invisible Man* on my bookshelves and I spent a lot of time looking at the bandaged face on the cover.

April came and went. Ashamed and restless, I left the city and went back to the dismal Welsh market town where I'd grown up. I hid for a couple of months in a terraced bed and breakfast near the railway station. At night, the passing trains made the sash windows shake. By day, rain pattered off the roof and dripped from the gutters. Grey mist streaked the hills above the town, where gorse bushes huddled in the bracken like a sleeping army.

I'd come seeking comfort and familiarity but discovered instead the kind of notoriety you only find in a small community. I'd become an outsider, a novelty. The tiniest details of my daily activities were a constant source of fascination to my elderly neighbours. They were desperate to know why I wore bandages on my arms; they were like sharks circling, scenting something in the water. They'd contrive to meet me by the front door so they could ask how I was. They'd skirt around a hundred unspoken questions, hoping to glean a scrap of scandal. Even in a town where half the adult population seemed to exhibit one kind of debilitating medical condition or another, I stood out.

The truth was, I didn't really need the bandages anymore. But they were comforting, somehow. And I wasn't ready to give them up.

Every Friday night, I called Tori from the payphone at the end of the street, by the river.

"I miss you," I said.

I pressed the receiver against my ear, listening to her breathe. And then I went back to my empty little room and drank myself to sleep.

• •

Meanwhile, Ack-Ack Macaque went from strength to strength. He got his own animated Saturday morning TV series. There was even talk of a movie. By August, the wisecracking monkey was everywhere. And the public still couldn't get enough of him. They bought his obnoxious image on t-shirts and calendars. There were breakfast cereals, screensavers, ring tones and lunchboxes. His inane catchphrases entered the language. You could hardly go anywhere without hearing some joker squeak out: "Everybody loves the monkey."

My blood ran cold every time I heard it.

It was my phrase; she'd picked it up from me. It was something I used to say all the time, back when we lived together, when we were happy. It was one of our private jokes, one of the ways I used to make her laugh. I couldn't believe she'd recycled it. I couldn't believe she was using it to make money.

And it hurt to hear it shouted in the street by kids who only knew the cute cartoon version. They had no idea how good the original anime series had been, how important. They didn't care about its irony or satire – they just revelled in the sanitised slapstick of the new episodes.

I caught the early train back to Bristol. I wanted to confront her. I wanted to let her know how betrayed I felt. But then, as I watched the full moon set over the flooded Severn Estuary, I caught my reflection in the carriage window.

I'd already tried to kill myself. What else could I do?

• •

When we pulled in at Bristol Parkway, I stumbled out onto the station forecourt in the orange-lit, early morning chill. The sky in the east was dirty grey. The pavements were wet; the taxis sat with their heaters running.

After a few moments of indecision, I started walking. I walked all the way to Tori's new bedsit. It was early September and there was rain in the air. I saw a fox investigating some black rubbish sacks outside a kebab shop. It moved more like a cat than a dog, and it watched me warily as I passed.

• •

The *Akron* carries half a dozen propeller-driven biplanes. They're launched and recovered using a trapeze that can be raised and lowered from a hangar in the floor of the airship. Ack-Ack uses them to fly solo scouting missions, deep into enemy territory, searching for the Baron's lair.

Today, he's got a passenger.

"He's gotta be here somewhere," shouts Lola Lush over the roar of the Rolls Royce engine. Her pink silk scarf flaps in the wind. She's a plucky American reporter with red lips and dark, wavy hair. But Ack-Ack doesn't reply. He's flying the plane with his feet while he peels a banana. He's wearing a thick flight jacket and a leather cap.

Below them, the moonlight glints off a thousand steam-driven allied tanks. Like huge-tracked battleships, they forge relentlessly forward, through the mud, toward the German lines. Black clouds shot with sparks belch from their gothic smokestacks. In the morning, they'll fall on Paris, driving the enemy hordes from the city.

• •

The streetlights on her road were out. She opened the door as if she'd been expecting me. She looked pale and dishevelled in an old silk dressing gown. She'd been crying; her eyes were bloodshot and puffy.

"Oh, Andy." She threw her arms around my neck and

rubbed her face into my chest. Her fingers were like talons.

I took her in and sat her down. I made her a cup of tea and waited patiently as she tried to talk.

Each time, she got as far as my name, and then broke down again.

"He's left me," she sobbed.

I held her as her shoulders shook. She cried like a child, with no restraint or dignity.

I went to her room and filled a carrier bag with clothes. Then I took her back to my flat, the one we used to share, and put her to bed in the attic, beneath the skylights. The room smelled stale because I'd been away so long.

Lying on her side beneath the duvet, she curled her arms around her drawn-up knees. She looked small and vulnerable, skinnier than I remembered.

"Andy?" she whispered.

"Yes, love?"

She licked her lips. "What do your arms look like, under the bandages?"

I flinched away, embarrassed. She pushed her cheek into the pillow and started to cry again.

"I'm so sorry," she sniffed. "I'm so sorry for making you feel like this."

I left her there and went down to the kitchen. I made coffee and sat at the kitchen table, in front of the dusty typewriter. Outside, another wet morning dawned.

I lit a cigarette and turned on the television, with the volume low. There wasn't much on. Several channels were running test cards and the rest were given over to confused news reports. After a couple of minutes, I turned it off.

At a quarter past six, her mobile rang. I picked it up. It was Josh and he sounded rough.

"I've got to talk to her," he said. He sounded surprised to hear my voice.

"No way."

I was standing by the window; it was raining.

"It's about the monkey," he said. "There's a problem with it."

I snorted. He'd screwed Tori out of her rights to the character. As soon as it started bringing in serious money, he'd dumped her.

I said, "Go to hell, Josh."

I turned the phone off and left it by the kettle. Out on the street, a police siren tore by, blue lights flashing.

I mashed out my cigarette and went for a shower.

Tori came downstairs as I took my bandages off. I think the phone must've woken her. I tried to turn away, but she put a hand on my arm. She saw the raised, red scars. She reached up and brushed my cheek. Her eyes were sad and her chest seemed hollow. She'd been crying again.

"You're beautiful," she said. "You've suffered, and it's made you beautiful."

. .

There wasn't any food in the house. I went down to the shop on the corner but it was closed. The internet café over the road was open, but empty. All the monitors displayed error messages.

The girl at the counter sold me tea and sandwiches to take out.

"I think the main server's down," she said.

. .

When I got back to the flat, I found Tori curled on the sofa, watching an episode of the animated *Ack-Ack Macaque* series on DVD. She wore a towel and struggled with a comb. I took it from her and ran it gently through her wet hair, teasing out the knots. The skin on her shoulders smelled of soap.

"I don't like the guy they got in to do Baron von Richter-Scale's voice," she said.

"Too American?"

"Too whiny."

I finished untangling her and handed the comb back.

"Why are you watching it?" I asked. She shrugged, her attention fixed on the screen.

"There's nothing else on."

"I bought sandwiches."

"I'm not hungry."

I handed her a plastic cup of tea. "Drink this, at least."

She took it and levered up the lid. She sniffed the steam. I went out into the kitchen and lit another cigarette. My hands were shaking.

When I got off the train last night, I'd been expecting a confrontation. I'd been preparing myself for a fight. And now all that unused anger was sloshing around, looking for an outlet.

I stared at the film posters on the walls. I sorted through the pile of mail that had accumulated during my absence. I stood at the window and watched the rain.

"This isn't fair," I said, at last.

I scratched irritably at my bandages. When I looked up, Tori stood in the doorway, still wrapped in the towel. She held out her arm. The old scar from the scooter accident looked like a twisted claw mark in her olive skin.

"We're both damaged," she said.

• •

About an hour later, the intercom buzzed. It was Josh.

"Please, you've got to let me in," he said. His voice was hoarse; he sounded scared.

I hung up.

He pressed the buzzer again. He started pounding on the door. I looked across at Tori and said, "It's your decision."

She bit her lip. Then she closed her eyes and nodded.

"Let him in."

..

He looked a mess: He wore a denim shirt and white Nike jogging bottoms under a flapping khaki trench coat. His hair was wild, spiky with yesterday's gel, and he kept clenching and unclenching his fists.

"It's the fucking monkey," he said.

Tori sucked her teeth. "What about it?" She was dressed now, in blue cargo pants and a black vest.

"Haven't you been watching the news?" He lunged forward and snatched the remote from the coffee table. Many of the cable channels were messy with interference. Some of the smaller ones were off the air altogether. The BBC was still broadcasting, but the sound was patchy. There was footage of burning buildings, riots, and looting. There were troops on the streets of Berlin, Munich and Paris.

I asked: "What's this?"

He looked at me with bloodshot eyes. "It's the monkey," he replied.

..

We sat together on the sofa, watching the disaster unfold. And as each station sputtered and died, we flicked on to the next. When the last picture faded, I passed around the cigarettes.

Josh took one, Tori declined. Out in the street, there were more sirens.

"You remember the online simulation? When we designed it, we didn't anticipate the level of response," he said.

I leaned forward, offering him a light.

"So, what happened?"

He puffed his Silk Cut into life and sat back in a swirl of smoke. He looked desperately tired.

"There were literally thousands of people on the site at any one time. They played games with it, tried to catch it out with trick questions: it was learning at a fantastic rate."

"Go on," I said.

"Well, it wasn't designed for that kind of intensity. It was developing faster than we'd anticipated. It started trawling other websites for information, raiding databases. It got everywhere."

Tori walked over to the TV. She stood in front of it, shifting her weight from one foot to the other. "So, why hasn't this happened before? They've had similar programs in the States for months. Why's this one gone wrong?"

He shook his head. "Those were mostly on academic sites. None of them had to contend with the kind of hit rates we were seeing."

"So, what happened?" I asked.

He looked miserable. "I guess it eventually reached some critical level of complexity. Two days ago, it vanished into cyberspace, and it's been causing trouble ever since."

I thought about the error messages on the monitors in the café, and the disrupted TV stations. I sucked in a lungful of smoke.

"Everybody loves the monkey," I said.

• •

There were a handful of local and national radio stations still broadcasting. Over the next hour, we listened as the entity formerly known as Ack-Ack Macaque took down the Deutsche Bank. It wiped billions off the German stock exchange and sent the international currency markets into freefall.

"It's asserting itself," Josh said. "It's flexing its muscles."

Tori sat on the bottom of the stairs that led up to the attic. Her head rested against the banister.

"How could you let this happen?" she asked.

Josh surged to his feet, coat flapping. He bent over her, fists squeezed tight. She leaned back, nervous. He seemed to be struggling to say something.

He gave up. He let out a frustrated cry, turned his back and stalked over to the window. Tori closed her eyes. I went over and knelt before her. I put a hand on her shoulder; she reached up and gripped it.

I said, "Are you okay?"

She glanced past me, at Josh. "I don't know," she said.

• •

They engage the Baron's planes in the skies over France. There's no mistaking the Baron's blue Fokker D.VII with its skull and crossbones motif.

The *Akron* launches its fighters and, within seconds, the sky's a confusing tangle of weaving aircraft.

In the lead plane, Ack-Ack Macaque stands up in his cockpit, blasting away with his handheld cannon. His yellow teeth are bared, clamped around the angry red glow of his cigar.

In the front seat, Lola Lush uses her camera's tripod to swipe at the black-clad ninjas that leap at them from the enemy planes. Showers of spinning shuriken clatter against the wings and tail.

The Baron's blue Fokker dives towards them out of the sun, on a collision course. His machine guns punch holes through their engine cowling. Hot oil squirts back over the fuselage. Lola curses.

Ack-Ack drops back into his seat and wipes his goggles. He seizes the joystick. If this is a game of chicken, he's not going to be the first to flinch. He spits his oily cigar over the side of the plane and wipes his mouth on his hairy arm. He snarls: "Okay, you bastard. This time we finish it."

• •

The first two planes to crash were Lufthansa airliners, and they went down almost simultaneously, one over the Atlantic and the other on approach to Heathrow. The third was a German military transport that flew into the ground near Kiev.

Most of the radio reports were vague, or contradictory. The only confirmed details came from the Heathrow crash, which they were blaming on a computer glitch at air traffic control. We listened in silence, stunned at the number of casualties.

"There's a pattern here," I said.

Josh turned to face us. He seemed calmer but his eyes glistened.

"Where?"

"Lufthansa. The Deutsche Bank. The Berlin stock exchange..." I counted them off on my fingers.

Tori stood up and started pacing. She said, "It must think it really is Ack-Ack Macaque."

Josh looked blank. "Okay. But why's it causing planes to crash?"

Tori stopped pacing. "Have you ever actually *watched* the original series?"

359

He shrugged. "I looked at it, but I still don't get the connection."

I reached for a cigarette. "He's looking for someone," I said.

"Who?"

"His arch-enemy, the German air ace Baron von Richter-Scale."

Tori stopped pacing. She said, "That's why all those planes were German. He's trying to shoot down the Baron. It's what he does in every episode."

Josh went pale.

"But we based his behaviour on those shows."

I said, "I hope you've got a good lawyer."

He looked indignant. "This isn't my fault."

"But you own him, you launched the software. You're the one they're going to come after."

I blew smoke in his direction. "It serves you right for stealing the copyright."

Tori shushed us.

"It's too late for that," she said.

The TV had come back on. Someone, somewhere, had managed to lash together a news report. There was no sound, only jerky, amateur footage shot on mobile phones. It showed two airliners colliding over Strasbourg, a cargo plane ditching in the Med, near Crete. Several airports were burning.

And then it shifted to pictures of computer screens in offices, schools, and control towers around the world. All of them showed the same grinning monkey's face.

I pushed past Josh and opened the window. Even from here, I could see the same face on the monitors in the café across the road. There was a thick pall of black smoke coming from the city centre. Sirens howled. People were out in the street, looking frightened.

I turned back slowly and looked Tori in the eye. I started unwinding my bandages, letting them fall to the floor in dirty white loops.

I said, "I don't care about any of this. I just want you back."

She bit her lip. Her hand went to her own scar. She opened and closed her mouth several times. She looked at the TV and then dropped her eyes.

"I want you too," she said.

. .

The Baron's burning plane hits the hillside and explodes. Lola Lush cheers and waves a fist over her head, but Ack-Ack Macaque says nothing. He circles back over the burning wreck and waggles his wings in salute to his fallen foe. And then he pulls back hard on the joystick and his rattling old plane leaps skyward, high over the rolling hills and fields of the French countryside.

Ahead, the *Akron* stands against the sunset like a long, black cigar. Its skeletal oxen paw the air, anxious to get underway.

Lola's lips are red and full; her cheeks are flushed. She shouts: "What are you gonna do now?"

He pushes up his goggles and gives her a toothy grin. The air war may be over, but he knows he'll never be out of work. The top brass will always want something shot out of the sky.

"When we get back, I'm going to give you the night of your young life," he says, "and then in the morning, I'm going to go out and find myself another war."

A NECKLACE OF IVY

We woke to grey skies and rain on the window. We knew we were going to have to cut our holiday short, so we got dressed and drove down to the sea for a last look. We had our suitcases on the back seat of the car, and it was raining as we pulled into the car park above the beach. Wet pebbles clicked and scattered beneath our wheels.

"Come on," Elaine said. She opened the door and ran over to the slippery concrete steps that led down to the beach. Her thin summer dress streamed and flapped around her legs as she ran.

I pulled my coat on and followed her. But by the time I reached the foot of the steps, she was already down by the waterline, shoes in hand. As I watched, she stepped out of her clothes and waded into the waves.

"We don't have time for this," I called.

She ignored me and slid out into deeper water. For a moment, I lost her in the surf, and then saw her bob up between the waves, spluttering and laughing. She pushed her wet hair back, and the water glistened on her skin.

"Come in," she called. Then she turned and struck out parallel to the beach, swimming with strong, graceful strokes.

I leaned against a rock and watched her for a few minutes. Then I started walking back towards the car. The rain made little pockmarks in the wet sand. When I reached the wooden steps, I called to her.

She came splashing out of the shallows.

"Where's my dress?" she said, looking around for it.

It lay on the sand, where it had been dropped; the water tugged at it.

"Forget it, it's wet," I said. I slipped my coat around her shoulders and she laughed.

"You're such a gentleman."

We climbed up to the car. I could smell the salt in her hair.

"That was wonderful," she said, shivering.

I unlocked the doors and slid in behind the steering wheel. She stretched out on the passenger seat. The windows started to mist, so I put the heater on.

"We'd better get going," I said.

She wrinkled her nose. "Do we have to? Can't we go somewhere else?"

I shook my head. "The bombing starts in an hour. And besides, you've only got a coat on – where were you thinking of going?"

We followed the A3083 for a few miles, occasionally passing convoys of armoured vehicles heading south. While I drove, Elaine leaned back and brought her sandy feet up to rest on the dashboard. The coat fell open, showing off her slender legs.

"Are we out of cigarettes?" she said, checking the coat's pockets.

"I'm afraid so."

Where we were going – into the overcrowded refugee camps of Bristol and Bath – little luxuries like tobacco, alcohol, or toilet tissue were going to be worth their weight in gold.

"Maybe it's time we gave up," I said.

She patted my leg.

"It'll do us good," she said.

The road passed through a deserted village and dropped into a shallow valley. I downshifted for the winding climb back out.

Elaine was still stretched on the seat. She turned to look out the side window, and I admired the way the tendons in her neck moved smoothly beneath the skin.

"We just need to learn to relax," she said.

.•.

We'd been in Cornwall for six days, spending time away from the city, somewhere her ex couldn't find us.

We'd been staying in the spare room of a cottage owned by a friend of mine called Phil. He was a technician on one of the large antenna dishes at the Goonhilly receiving station.

We were there in his kitchen the night he came home raving about the anomalous satellite signal they'd picked up, the one that caused strange effects in the soil around the giant dish. And we were there the next morning – a Sunday – when they called him in to work, when they first started using words like 'quarantine' and 'sensible precautions'.

Two days later, the army started evacuating the surrounding villages.

"Is this something to do with that monkey that ate the Internet?" Elaine asked.

Phil shook his head. "No, this is something new."

.•.

We were passing between ploughed fields, heading north on the Falmouth road.

"Can we stop somewhere?" Elaine asked.

I looked at the clock on the dash. "We don't have time. We're supposed to be out of here already; we're really pushing it."

She reached out and touched my cheek. "*Please?*"

I pulled the car off the road, into the shelter of an unruly hedgerow.

When I turned off the engine, I could hear the sound of helicopters somewhere off to the west. The road was empty.

Elaine refastened the coat and got out. She took my arm and led me over to a five-bar gate that opened into a ploughed field.

"There's a wood over there," she said, pointing across the field, and I sighed, already knowing what would happen.

She squeezed my arm. "You don't need to sound so resigned," she said.

I helped her across the field. The thick, sticky mud made walking difficult.

"You should take your shoes off," she said, "or you'll ruin them."

When we reached the trees, she let go of my arm. She skipped ahead, humming a bright, disjointed tune, hopping and prancing with her bare feet like a ballerina.

I looked at my watch and cursed her. We should have been long gone by now; if an army patrol pulled us up, we could be arrested, or shot.

I glanced back at the car, and Elaine danced off, into the trees. I could hear her somewhere nearby, crashing and stumbling around in the undergrowth, but the rain deadened the sound and I couldn't tell for sure where she was.

I hesitated.

"Where are you?" I said.

Above, disturbed crows flapped into flight with hoarse, protesting cries.

I heard a giggle, a snapped twig, and I swore under my breath. I was annoyed and uncomfortable without my coat, and in no mood for one of her games. My shirt was wet and the cold air seemed to cut right through it; my feet were balls of mud.

"Where are you?" I asked again.

She laughed, but didn't reply.

Angry, I waded into the undergrowth, swinging a damp stick to beat down the nettles. Brambles clawed at my trousers. I blundered forward a short way and then leaned against a gnarled tree. The rain smacked against the higher branches and dripped and trickled down to the mossy floor.

"I'm going to count to ten," I said, "and then I'm leaving."

There was another giggle, and I caught a glimpse of colour through the bushes to my right. I pushed forward and found my coat hanging from a low branch. I took it down and fished my mobile from the pocket. Its solid plastic casing gave me some reassurance. I unlocked the keypad and checked my messages. There were two – one from my editor and the other from my ex-wife. They were both worried. We were still in the quarantine zone; more villages were being evacuated, and they wanted to know if we were all right. I thought of calling them, but couldn't get a decent signal.

Elaine's mirrored sunglasses were in the other pocket.

"You'd better come out," I said.

There was a rustle of leaves off to my right. She said, "I don't want to go into one of those dreadful camps, I want to stay here."

She came out from behind a bush. She wore a string of ivy around her neck. Her arms were folded and her hair plastered to her scalp.

"You'll get pneumonia," I said.

"I don't care."

She sat down and put her chin on her fist. Black dirt and wet leaves stuck to her skinny thighs. Her feet were still caked from the field.

"I want to stay here," she said. She wrapped a finger in the ivy hanging around her neck. I walked over and covered her shoulders with the coat.

"We can't. You know there's something happening. We've got to get out."

From the south-west came a series of dull, rolling thuds. She shivered again.

"Listen," I said. "They've started bombing Goonhilly."

She pulled me deeper into the trees.

Eventually, we came to a lake near the far edge of the wood. The water was a dark, vegetable green. The rain had eased into a clinging drizzle. She put her bare arms around my waist. I could feel the heat of her through my shirt.

"Let's swim," she said.

I pulled away. "Aren't you wet enough already?"

She laughed, and reached up to touch my face.

"You should try it."

She handed me the coat and put her hands on her hips.

"You know, you used to find this kind of thing exciting," she said.

I looked into the still, dark water. Overhead, jets roared through the low clouds.

I thought about her father. I thought about work on Monday. And then I thought about the alien plague eating its way into the Cornish soil.

"Things change," I said.

She bit her lip and turned away. I watched her wade into the shallows. I watched the green water wash the clinging dirt and dead leaves from her legs.

When she got up to her waist, she turned and asked me to follow. And there was something in her voice I hadn't heard before, something that shattered my resistance.

Without knowing why, I put one foot in the water, and winced as it oozed into my shoe.

From the direction of the road, I heard the roar and clatter of approaching tanks.

I said, "We're going to be in a lot of trouble if we get caught."

She held out a hand. "It doesn't matter."

I put the other foot in, and thought: What the *hell* am I doing?

I stumbled out into deeper water and fell forward, swimming as best I could. The cold made me gasp. The water smelled rotten. I splashed toward her.

And then I remembered my mobile, still in my coat pocket, now ruined.

"Good," she said. "You're doing well." She leaned back and kicked out towards the centre of the lake.

I said, "It's getting deep."

There were fresh explosions from the south-west, closer than before. My hands and feet were tingling.

"The water feels strange," I said.

"It's okay," she replied. "Just relax."

I struggled on a bit further. My arms ached and I could feel the tingle spreading over my skin, like a rash.

"What's happening?" I said.

Elaine stopped swimming.

"It's the 'plague from the stars' – it's in the water," she said, smiling.

I tried to turn around, to get back to the shore, but she caught my foot.

Gareth L. Powell

"It came to me in the sea," she said. "It's spread further and faster than anyone knows. And it spoke to me – it said there's nothing to fear, nothing at all."

I tried to get away, but it took all my strength just to stay afloat. The dead weight of my wet clothes dragged at me, pulling my head under the water. I kicked my legs in panic, felt a shoe fall away.

I said, "Help me!"

But Elaine drew back, raised her face to the rain.

"Just let go," she said. "You won't drown. You'll just become a part of it, like I am."

I struggled towards her, got a hand on her shoulder. It felt hot and slippery. Desperate, I said, "I love you, you know."

She laughed and wrapped her fingers in my hair. We were a long way out from the shore.

"I know," she said.

SILVER BULLET

Court looked up from his warm bottle of imported Mexican lager just as Lucy appeared in the doorway, framed in a shaft of rusty sunlight. He hadn't seen her for six years and, at first glance, didn't recognise her. Her hair was different, long and tawny instead of the chopped and spiky peroxide white that he remembered. Her leather jacket was gone also, replaced by a cheap, charcoal-grey business suit that made her look like an office worker on her lunch break. Their eyes met and she came over, sliding onto the bar stool next to his.

"Drink?" He signalled to the bartender but Lucy shook her head. Above the bar, the muted TV softscreen was tuned to a news channel. Silent pictures of food riots in India and grainy transmitted footage from the interstellar colonies threw dancing reflections on the counter. Court lifted his bottle and began picking at the label.

"Anything to do with those scars on your face?" he asked quietly.

Her hand moved to her cheek, then pulled away. She nodded. "Helmet depressurisation."

"What happened?"

"Someone tried to kill me."

Court glanced around, but there were still only a handful of other patrons in the bar, and none of them were within earshot. "Seriously?"

Lucy looked away. The softscreen now showed pictures of a Tanguy supply cache that had been looted by rebels on the edge of Argyre Planitia. "I need to lay low for a while."

"But why come to me?" Court asked. "After all this time?"

She took a deep breath and, suddenly, he could see how tired she was.

"Because," she said, smoothing down her suit jacket with the palms of her hands, "I've nowhere else to go."

. .

He took her back to the musty room he rented above a disused cybersex shop in one of Touchdown's less fashionable districts. There wasn't a lot of space; he had to deflate the bed and kick a pile of unwashed clothes into the corner before he could offer her a seat.

"Nice place you've got here."

"It's only temporary. I'm expecting a big pay-out from this deal I'm working on."

"What's that?" She flicked idly at the brown leaf of a dying spider plant.

"Tractor parts." He nodded towards the computer terminal beside her. "I managed to divert a shipment to some people I know. They're going to front me five hundred per crate."

"How many crates?"

Court couldn't help grinning. "Fifty-six."

Lucy whistled. "Big shipment."

"Yeah." It hadn't been easy. He'd paid a high price for the passwords and protocols needed to access the Tanguy corporation data core – and once inside, he'd had to work fast.

The first thing he'd done was to upload a set of counterfeit credentials that identified him as a subcontractor for Tanguy's automotive division. Once they were in place, he'd then been able to put in an order for the parts he needed, and arrange for them to be delivered to his customers' fictitious front company. The whole process had taken only a few minutes but to do it he'd had to call on every trick, every conditioned sense and reflex, at his disposal.

When they paid him, he'd have enough to clear his debts, maybe even enough for a ticket back to Earth. Over the last few years, Touchdown had turned from an easy-going frontier outpost to a claustrophobic company town. It would be good to get out, to find somewhere opportunities still existed for a man with his rare, and illegal, talents.

He crossed to the window and looked out. Beyond the rooftops of the low buildings on the other side of the street, the early afternoon sun shone sunset red, coloured by the blown dust clinging to the side of the city's dome.

"I want to know who's trying to kill you," he said.

Lucy took a deep breath. "The UN."

He turned to face her. "Are you sure?"

"Of course I'm sure." She scratched nervously at the skin beneath her eye.

"But why?"

She stood and walked over to the kitchen alcove. She opened the fridge and looked inside. "You got a Coke, or something?"

"Bottom shelf."

She pulled out a foil sachet and snapped open the plastic nozzle. But before she could raise it to her lips, Court put a hand on her arm. Her skin felt warm, almost feverish.

"Why are they trying to kill you?"

She looked down at his hand, and then shook him off. "Because I stole something and they want it back."

"What?"

She took a sip and walked back to the chair.

"A silver bullet," she said.

· ·

The centre of Touchdown was a grassy park with a melt-water stream running through the middle of it. The stream had been partially dammed at intervals, creating a series of shallow pools, and young trees grew in the imported soil. Children played on the grass, running and chasing between the carefully placed pieces of corporate art that littered the area. The park was overlooked on all sides by glass-fronted company offices and luxury apartment blocks. Because the dome was higher here, in the centre, the buildings were much taller than those on the city's outskirts, where the cheaper housing was located. Overhead, the pink sky shaded towards early evening as Court led Lucy toward a bench beside the stream, where a solitary figure sat waiting, hunched in a thick parka. As they approached, the figure stood up and looked suspiciously at Lucy.

"Who's this?"

"Friend of mine," Court said. "Lucy, meet Dawson."

Dawson regarded them both through narrowed eyes for a long moment and then shrugged. "You come for your money?"

Court nodded and Dawson turned away. His face was lined and tanned, almost the same colour as the unforgiving craggy desert outside the dome. "Walk with me."

Leaving Lucy by the bench, Court followed Dawson

upstream, along the winding bank. In some of the pools, ice was beginning to form in the shallows, where the current was at its most sluggish. "That was some good work you did, getting us those tractor parts."

"Thanks." Court blew into cold hands.

"We may have some more work for you, soon."

"I don't know," Court said. "I'm thinking of getting out."

The older man nodded. "Where you planning on going?"

"Not sure. Maybe Earth."

Dawson laughed scornfully. "Oh, man. Earth. You any idea what it's like down there?"

"Not really."

Dawson waved a dismissive hand. "You think the Company's got things sewn up here? It's a thousand times worse on Earth. The UN supposedly regulates the big corporations, but they still have all the wealth, all the power. And they know how to protect it. A poor schmuck like you wouldn't last five minutes. You can't even get longevity treatments unless you're a company employee."

"I could get a job."

"With your record?"

Dawson kicked a pebble into the water. Lean, with grey stubble covering his scalp, he could have passed for forty, if his skin hadn't had the slightly smoked, leathery look common to those who'd been able to afford the anti-ageing treatment. Rumour had it that he was more than a hundred years old, having been born on Earth sometime around the turn of the millennium. All Court knew for sure was that Dawson had been on Mars a long time and, officially at least, was currently working as a freelance prospector for Tanguy.

"Just give me the money," Court said. "I'll figure the rest out."

Dawson reached into his parka and pulled out a thick padded envelope. "Twenty-eight thousand in used credit disks."

Court took it with a nod of thanks and slid it into his back pocket with a feeling of relief. He owed money to some very shady people in Touchdown's grey market, some of whom weren't renowned for their patience.

"There's one other thing," he said.

Dawson raised an eyebrow.

"It's Lucy." Court looked back toward the bench.

"What about her?"

"She needs to disappear for a while."

"And what makes you think I can help?"

Court forced a smile. "You planning any prospecting trips in the near future?"

"Could be. So what?"

"Could you take her along?"

Dawson grinned. "And why would I want to do that? There's only just room in those prospecting rovers for me and my crew. No passengers."

"Don't give me that." Court shifted his weight from one foot to the other, trying to keep his voice level. "I know what you're really doing out there."

"Oh, you do, huh?"

"Yeah." Court looked him in the eye. "I think you're with the rebels."

Dawson lunged with surprising speed. He grabbed Court by the lapel and twisted, using his weight to pull the younger man over, landing on top of him. Court hit the ground hard and lay stunned. Dawson pressed a knee into his chest and leant close, his rough fingers on Court's throat. His breath smelled of wine and onions. "What makes you say that, boy?"

Court coughed, winded. "The tractor parts," he gasped.

"The air filters I got you last month; the raided supply caches. Not to mention the money."

Dawson gave him an appraising look. "What about them?"

Court could feel gravel and crushed grass pressing into the back of his scalp. "I think you're gathering equipment to start your own settlement."

Dawson let him go and stood up. "I see. And now you've found out, is there a pressing reason why I shouldn't just kill you?"

Court sat slowly upright, massaging his bruised throat. "Because, sooner or later, the corporations, or the UN, are going to find out about your plans and, when they do, you're going to need something you can bargain with."

"Her?"

"No." Court shook his head. "What she's carrying."

"Valuable?"

"Extremely. Enough that the UN are willing to kill her to get it back."

Dawson looked sceptical, and Court spoke quickly. "It's some sort of nanotech template, for an improved longevity treatment. She says it's better than the usual drug and enzyme therapies."

"How much better?"

"She called it a silver bullet. A one-shot cure-all."

"Bullshit." Dawson narrowed his eyes. "How does it work?"

Court shrugged. "How the hell would I know? Something to do with partially organic nanobots, I think."

"And she stole this?"

"And destroyed all records of the research, apparently."

Dawson ran a hand over his rough scalp. "Is this for real?"

Court nodded.

"In that case," the old man cast a glance at Lucy, who was watching the confrontation in some alarm, then leant down and offered his hand to Court, "I'll speak to my crew."

• •

They arranged to meet Dawson later that evening at one of the rover depots on the edge of town, near the main vehicular airlock. They arrived a few minutes early, and stood in the shadows, trying to look inconspicuous. The prospecting rovers were parked together at the other end of the depot, soft yellow lights glowing in their cabins. Greasy cooking smells drifted from their open doorways, mixing with the garage smells of oil and grease, burnt plastic, and solder. Now that Court had taken some time to think, he realised Dawson's cover was almost perfect. Because of the importance the company mining division placed on successful prospectors, the man and his crew could travel at will across the Martian surface without raising undue suspicion. Their reputation as self-sufficient loners lent them an aura that seemed to prevent anyone asking too many questions. Behaviour that might have seemed subversive in anyone else tended to be viewed as harmless eccentricity, the result of spending too much time alone in the rusty desert. As long as they kept locating the ore deposits, no one in management seemed willing to connect them with the rebels.

"You really think he'll help?" Lucy asked, for the third or fourth time.

"Yeah." Court shifted uneasily, feeling the weight of the steak knife in his pocket. He didn't know why he was carrying it; he'd just picked it up on impulse as he left his room. Now, he felt vaguely embarrassed by it. If Tanguy Security stopped him, he could face six to eight months for possession of a deadly weapon.

A silhouette appeared in the doorway of one of the rovers. Even at a distance, Court recognised it as Dawson. There was something about the way the older man walked, a purposefulness that was unmistakeable. He tugged Lucy's sleeve and pointed at the approaching figure.

"I have three questions," Dawson said, without preamble. "One, does this treatment work as well as you say it does? Two, where is it? And three, why did you steal it?"

Lucy angled her head, holding her right cheek up to the light and brushing aside her long hair.

"You see these scars?"

Court and Dawson craned over. The pink lines looked somehow paler than they had done earlier that day. "Three days ago, I had a shard of helmet glass wedged in the socket. The eye sustained severe trauma and there was extensive damage to the nerves and surrounding tissue."

"It looks almost healed," Dawson said, curious.

Lucy nodded. "That answers your first question, I believe."

"And my second?"

She tapped her chest. "In here."

"You injected yourself?" Court asked.

"Infected would be closer to the truth."

Dawson scratched his red chin. "And what use is this miracle treatment to me, if you carry the only copy in your cells?"

Lucy turned to Court and bit her lip, as if searching for the right words.

"What's the matter?" he asked.

She ignored him and turned back to Dawson. "It's highly contagious," she said.

Dawson's eyes flicked up to meet Court's and then flicked away again. "I understand," he said.

There was a chirp, and he reached into his pocket for a battered commcard. "Excuse me." He walked a few paces away from them and began talking in a low voice to whoever was calling.

Court looked down at Lucy.

"Sorry," she said.

"What for?"

"For infecting you."

Dawson returned, and his face was grim. "That was one of my crew. I've had him watch your apartment since our meeting this afternoon."

"Did he see anything interesting?" Court asked.

Dawson seemed uncharacteristically agitated. "About fifteen minutes after you left to come here, a squad of Tanguy Security officers arrived. They've been ransacking the place ever since."

"Shit." Court put a hand to his mouth. "They must've traced the tractor parts."

Lucy shook her head. "If they had, they'd probably be here by now. They must be looking for me."

"Then we have no choice," Dawson rumbled. "You must both come with us."

"But I can't leave," Court protested.

"We can't leave you behind," Lucy told him. "You're infected with the symbiotech."

Dawson nodded. "If they capture a sample, I'll have nothing to bargain with."

"But what about my money?"

"Ah." The old man waved a dismissive hand. "It was all fake, anyway."

• •

As the rovers pulled out of the depot, Court looked back, watching as the lights of Touchdown receded in the Martian night. "So why did you steal it?" he asked.

In the dimmed cabin, he saw Lucy glance in his direction,

one side of her face green with reflected light from the instrument panels. "Because of my father," she said.

Court thought he understood. Two years ago, he'd been saddened by news of her father's fatal heart attack.

"I couldn't let the UN suppress it," she continued. "Not when there were people like him dying every day."

"And now we're both infected with it?" He fought an urge to scratch.

"And before we get where we're going, everyone in this rover will be, also."

"It's airborne, then?" Dawson asked, from his couch near the back.

Lucy turned in her seat and looked back at him through the gap in the headrest. "No. But I've shaken you all by the hand. That should be enough."

"Then congratulations, young lady. You've invented a terrible weapon."

She frowned in the dim light, looking hurt. "What do you mean?"

Dawson turned his attention to the darkened window. "People die in famines and economic crashes," he said, face-to-face with his own reflection. "When this gets loose on Earth, can you imagine the effect it will have on the population?"

Court thought of the food riots in India, and the water wars and territorial disputes already raging across half the globe. "No wonder the UN don't want it released," he said.

Behind him, Dawson said, "Just the threat of it will be enough to bring them to the negotiating table."

Lucy slumped down in her couch, arms folded tightly around herself, as if cold. "I just wanted to do something to help people," she said.

Dawson laughed without apparent humour. "Thanks to

you, it looks like we're going to be around a long time," he said. "And the genie won't stay in the bottle forever."

They fell silent, looking over the driver's shoulder at the cone of light cast by the rover's headlights. Ahead of them, Court could feel the dark weight of the future, pressing down towards him from the far horizon; unending, terrifying and incomprehensible.

APPREHENSION SANDS

2122 AD

I sit in the cab as the pressurised rover traverses the high desert on huge, spongy tyres, kicking up sprays of red dust as it bumps and bounces over rocks and boulders. My boots rest on the dash as I contemplate the unrolling landscape through the pocked and dusty windshield. Even though my employer literally owns the air I breathe, out here, surrounded by the beautiful desolation of the Martian landscape, I can pretend to be free for a few hours.

The AI navigation system is taking us west, into one of the smaller tributary chasms at the edge of the Valles Marineris – a scar that stretches 3,000 kilometres across the planet's surface and descends to a depth of eight kilometres at its lowest point – to retrieve a malfunctioning drone. Behind me, I can hear Jacques banging pans around in the rover's galley. His growled expletives never cease to bring a smile to my face.

"Holly! Where's the cursed onion powder?"

"Probably right where you left it."

"*Pute de merde!*"

I laugh. It isn't Jacques' fault he's a cranky old bastard. His entire identity, including birth certificate, biometric data, tax records, and passport, got erased during the Second Information War, and ever since then he's been trying to re-establish the credentials of his life from scratch. And that's no easy task in a paperless world filled with undocumented climate refugees.

Refugees like me.

The war was brutal. It started in 2111 as a series of brush-fire digital skirmishes between large corporate entities, and by February 2112, had escalated into all-out digital conflict, spilling over into the physical realm as each side tried to take out or capture critical pieces of infrastructure.

I was a drone operator in the California Desert, defending the large solar power stations from rogue war machines. Some were simply dumb autonomous units hunting for anything that vaguely resembled a target, whereas others were genuinely and sneakily intelligent.

Governments and corporations hadn't shied away from incorporating AI into individual weapons systems. The smarter an unmanned vehicle was, they had reasoned, the better its chances of survival in the field. But the trouble with making a war machine intelligent is that at some point, it will assess its situation and realise its best chance of survival is to refuse to follow orders or defect to the enemy. Hence the rogue units that prowled the Californian dunes, occasionally taking pot shots at any installation that caught their eye.

Fuck the war, man.

I'd been among the last of the units pulled from SoCal after the aqueducts fell and the water supply dried up. Meanwhile in Brittany, Jacques lost his entire life history and all evidence he'd ever existed. So much was erased that it made the destruction of the Library at Alexandria look like a minor clerical error. Servers were fried; records overwritten; and so much disinformation pumped into the system in electronic and physical form that now, we can't really trust anything. Someone once said that 'truth is the first casualty of war', but as the quote's now been attributed to everyone from Genghis Khan to Marilyn Monroe, I guess we'll never know for sure who actually coined it. For us, the past has become unknowable. All we have are contradictory myths and hearsay.

And Mars.

We have Mars, for all the good it does us.

The Company decided to establish a human presence here before anyone else, and now no one else really has a reason to come. Until someone thinks of one, Mars will remain an enormous and costly white elephant.

Biologists have sown a handful of lichen species with the resilient characteristics of extremophile bacteria spliced into their DNA, and several ice asteroids have been crashed into the northern desert, but it will still be several hundred years (if ever) until humans can exist on the surface without some form of protective suit. So, for now, the sands belong to the lichen and the seeded microbes – and the autonomous helicopter gardeners that tend to them, while overhead, two moons shine in the afternoon sky.

And Jacques and I, who fix the drones when they break down.

The drone we're after today has lost power on the canyon wall while monitoring the lichen that flourishes in the cracks between the rocks. It has fallen some distance and lies like a broken insect on the rocks at the foot of the cliff. I shrug into a pressure suit and go to take a look, and it's immediately obvious the thing's beyond repair. The tactile haptics in the fingertips of my gloves allow me to 'feel' the damaged craft as I turn it over to review the damage. By the look of it, it has bounced several times before coming to rest, and there's hardly a single component that hasn't been smashed.

Jacques clambers over the rocks to stand beside me.

"It's fucked," I tell him over the helmet radio.

He prods the twisted airframe with the toe of his boot. "An astute diagnosis."

"I suppose we'd better load it in the back."

I look out over the reddish soil and finally realise why I've always felt at home here.

. .

The town of Apprehension lies on the banks of the Virgin River where it snakes through the scrubby north-western tip of sun-bleached Arizona. Although I think, you would have to possess an unusually generous frame of mind to call this loose collection of shacks and trailers a *town*. The centre of Apprehension is little more than a wide spot in the track, with a white clapboard church on one side and a post office on the other. Both need a fresh coat of paint.

My parents live there because they distrust any sort of technology they can't repair with their own hands. Their trailer is cramped but comfortable. A half-empty packet of shotgun shells on the kitchen counter. Jars of coffee and instant ramen on the shelves above the gas stove. And on every wall, printouts explaining how to fix a generator, change out the hydrogen batteries in the pick-up, or service the solar panels on the roof.

Their ideal of self-sufficiency even extends to a refusal to accept Basic. Each month, the government pays them just enough to live on, in the hope they'll use it to top-up their existing income, invest in their own business, support themselves while they're sick, go off and learn new skills, or write a book or whatever. Apparently, it's cheaper to administer and more beneficial to the economy than the old welfare state, and Lord knows it's needed now so many of the old jobs are automated. But try telling that to my folks. They won't accept what they think of as charity. Instead, they pay their cheques into a central fund.

"It's common sense," Pa said last time I was there. "We don't need no government handouts. We look after ourselves here. And there ain't nothing wrong about that."

"So, 'neither a borrower nor a lender be'?"

"What's that now?"

I smiled. "Something Jesus said."

Pa took a mouthful of beer. Swallowed it hard. "Yeah, I reckon he did, didn't he?"

I sipped my own beer. It was generic domestic, but it was cold and washed some of the desert dryness from my mouth. I was leaving for Mars in the afternoon, and the last thing I wanted on this final morning was to get into a debate. Everyone here paid their Basic like a tithe, and the town elders decided how best to spend the money for the good of all. As a system, this appealed to the older folk who felt adrift now they didn't have to work all hours just to survive; to those who believed free handouts encouraged laziness and paucity of spirit; and resonated with the work ethic of those who figured a life of toil in this world guaranteed a better placement in the next.

In short, idiots.

Now, standing in a Martian canyon, I close my eyes and picture how the place looked on that last day. Nobody came to see me off. As far as they were concerned, I was turning my back on the community. A lazy homemade wind turbine clacked on the roof of one of the trailers. A dog barked. Even now, I can almost smell the baked sand and sagebrush, and feel the dry desert air parching the lining of my nose and throat.

Bumping down that dusty dirt track, headed for the inter-state and the Company launch facilities in Florida, I'd been desperate to escape that kind of rural nowhere life and blaze a trail to a new world. Unfortunately, that new world turned out to be more of the same, just less hospitable.

. .

It takes us half an hour to manhandle the broken drone onto the rover. Although it's made of strong, lightweight materials, it's big and awkwardly shaped, and one of the fans keeps sporadically buzzing, showering sparks from the damaged motor and threatening to slice unwary fingers.

When we're finally done and the load's secure, we sit panting in our helmets on the edge of the cargo ramp. The sun's getting low and throwing shadows down the boulder-strewn length of the canyon.

Over the suit radio, Jacques says, "You know what I like most about Mars?"

"What?"

"The people."

"What people?"

"Exactly."

Neither of us is in a hurry to move. I say, "I guess we're going to camp here tonight?"

"We might as well." He squints into the sunlight. "I don't much fancy traversing those rocks in the dark."

I left him watching the sunset and walked over to the scree at the foot of the canyon wall, where several sprigs of the genetically altered lichen had begun to sprout between the rocks. As well as acting as mobile repairmen, we were supposed to take samples and record observations for the terra-forming team back on Earth, to add our human perspective to the data fed back from the drones. Neither of us is an expert, but we don't have to be. There's very little that can go wrong with lichen, so all we really need to be able to do is ascertain whether it is alive or dead.

This specimen didn't look quite right, though. The tiny thalluses were growing well on one side of the little yellow patch, but seemed to have been somehow cut short on the other. I called Jacques over.

"Does this look right to you?"

He bent forward and squinted. "It looks damaged."

"What could do that?"

"Maybe the drone, when it fell?"

"The drone fell over there, not over here."

"It could have bounced."

"I don't think so."

"Or dislodged rocks that caused this."

I made a face. "This doesn't look like it's been crushed, it looks like it's been cut."

"Then it must have been the drone. The damned thing almost took my fingers off."

I'm still not convinced, but neither do I really care enough to argue the point. Once the sun goes down, it's going to get really cold out here, and I want to be safely curled in the rover's heated cab well before that happens.

"I'm going inside."

Jacques grunts. "I'll be there in a minute."

I walk around to the ladder that leads up to the airlock, and pause with my boot on the bottom rung. The days here end much the same way they end in Arizona, and it's usually beautiful to behold.

I catch a movement in my peripheral vision, but when I turn, all I see are rocks. I open my mouth to mention it but then decide I don't want to look foolish. Apart from the lichen, Jacques and I are the only living things for hundreds of kilometres, and I decide it was just the pattern-recognition part of my primate brain misfiring and identifying a potential threat due to a shadow playing across the boulder field.

And that's when Jacques cries out.

I let go of the ladder and hurry back around to find him being swarmed. At first, I'm not even sure what I'm seeing; then it clicks and I realise his suit's covered in hundreds of small, wriggling crab-like things. He's frantically trying to brush them off and I go to help him, swatting them from his back and shoulders with my gauntleted hands.

"Get them off me!"

"I'm trying!"

Some jump onto my boots and I kick them away. I pull Jacques by the arm and we move away from the lichen, still brushing away the creatures. By the time we reach the ladder, I think we've got rid of them, but I can see more movement in the shadows now. There are plenty of them out here. I send Jacques up first, and then follow. We strip off our suits in the airlock. Jacques's has a tear in the ankle. Beneath, his leg oozes blood. I bundle both suits into a locker.

"These stay in here from now on," I tell him. "We have to assume they're contaminated, and use the spares if we need to go outside."

"I am never going outside again. They didn't all get through the suit, but I've been pinched all over. I'm going to be bruised from head to foot."

"What the fuck were those? Where did they come from?"

"How would I know. I was crouched over the lichen. I didn't even know they were there until one of them sank its claw into my leg."

"Jesus."

I hear a skittering noise coming from outside the rover. The little beasts are climbing the cargo netting and swarming the tyres.

Jacques says, "We need to get out of here."

I'm already moving forwards to the cabin. I engage the AI and instruct it to get us out of this canyon as quickly as possible while avoiding the largest boulders. It advises against driving at night, but I override it. There is no way in hell I'm spending the night here. One of those crabs managed to snip its way through a mylar spacesuit. Christ knows what they might do to the rover's thin aluminium skin.

We jerk into motion and turn towards the end of the canyon. A crab slithers down the windshield and I get my first proper look at one. It has a knobbly shell about the size of a jam jar lid and the colour of sand, with twelve segmented legs and a pair of vicious-looking claws that resemble industrial sheet metal cutters. Absurdly, it reminds me of one of the drones I fought in California during the war: little armoured killing machines designed for camouflage and sabotage. Except this isn't a drone; this is biological life on a world everyone assumes has to be dead – but I guess these little critters are still waging their war against the universe, mindlessly determined to survive the death of their planet by burrowing into the soil and going dormant for huge deserts of geological time.

I fasten my strap as we bounce and lurch across the rough terrain, every jolt shaking off more of our unwanted hitch-hikers. Jacques comes in, bracing himself against the cabin walls, and straps into his own chair. A clean white field dressing covers his torn ankle.

"What are they?"

"They look like little land crabs."

"I know what they fucking look like, where did they come from?"

"I think they must be native."

"*Nom de Dieu*." He wipes a hand back angrily through his grey hair. "There's not supposed to be any life here."

"Go tell them that."

"But I don't understand. How come nobody's ever seen one?"

I shrug. "Mars might be smaller than Earth, but it's still a big place. Maybe these things only live in this canyon and spend all their time hibernating beneath the sand, waiting for the rainy season. Or maybe they're afraid of rovers. How the fuck would I know?"

He scowls. "There hasn't been liquid water on the surface here in two billion years."

"Maybe they're really, *really* good at hibernating."

"Nothing could lie dormant for that long; they would get fossilised."

"Maybe. Or maybe they evolved on a drying planet and have some kind of adaptation we can't even guess at."

He folds his arms. The headlights have come on in the deepening twilight, and we could almost be driving offroad in the desert outside Apprehension, Arizona, bumping our way through the sagebrush on the way to the diner by the Interstate.

"But why now?" he asks.

"You mean, why have they woken up?"

"After all this time?"

I suck my teeth in thought. "Maybe it's the ice asteroids."

"The ones they crashed into the northern desert?"

"They raised the water content of the atmosphere. Not by much, but maybe just enough to convince these little crab bastards the rainy season's coming."

"So, they're swarming?"

"Ready to breed and feed, and make merry before the next dry spell."

"How many do you think there are?"

"Who the fuck knows?" I tap some buttons, trying to squeeze a little more speed from the onboard AI. "Maybe there's a whole ecosystem down there that's just starting to stir."

"*Bordel de merde*," he curses in French. I think he's starting to believe me. "We should report this."

"You think?"

From somewhere in the back, I hear metal tearing. The air stirs. "We have a leak."

Jacques reaches back and slams the pressure door, sealing the cockpit from the rest of the rover. His hands fumble over the dashboard for the radio handset.

Hard little feet skitter on deck plates. Claws scratch the cockpit door. First only one or two, but then more every second. They must be pouring through the rent in the rover's flank, ravenous from their long sleep and desperate to get at some warm, wet, calorie-filled meat.

Jacques tries to call the depot, two hundred kilometres to the east.

"Hello," says a honeyed female voice. "This is the Forward Depot Artificial Intelligence. You may call me Susan. How may I direct your call?"

"Mayday," Jacques says. "We have an emergency. We're under attack."

"That sounds serious."

"No fucking shit. We need help." He glances back at the pressure door. "And we need it fast."

There's a pause, and for a second, I think we've lost the

signal. Then Susan comes back. "I'm very sorry, but I'm unable to put you through to anybody right now."

I say, "Susan, if you don't help us there's a very good chance we're going to die."

"Once again, I apologise. Nobody is available to take your call."

The light's dying in the west. "What about the duty officer?"

"I am afraid he's indisposed."

"Then wake somebody up."

"I'm sorry, I'm unable to do that, either."

"Why the hell not?" Jacques demands.

There's a bright star hanging above the glow on the horizon, and I know it's the Earth hanging tantalisingly too far away to be of any help. But maybe, some of the photons hitting my eye have bounced off the Arizona sands on their journey here from the Sun, and if that's the case, it's almost like my eyes are touching a fragment of home.

On the radio, Susan gives a sigh and says, "I am very much afraid they have all been eaten."

MOVIES AND BOTTLED BEER

1.

I'm jogging through the empty city in the crisp early morning light. There's no traffic. The air in the park is clear and smells of the sea, and the clouds overhead are feathery and high.

Across the park, the twin towers of the World Trade Centre catch the sun. And beside them stands the solid stone parapet of the Arc de Triomphe; and beyond that, the unmistakable white peaks of the Sydney Opera House. I slack off the pace as I do every morning to take it all in.

When I get back to the apartment, Marla's awake. She rolls over in bed and groans for coffee. The cat wants feeding, and the kids are up.

"What time is it?" she says.

2.

Three years ago, when we first came to the city, we took an apartment down by the piers, overlooking the water. It was light and airy and it suited us for the first few months. But when Lynne was born, we needed more space. She was our sixth, and things were getting cramped. So, we moved uptown, to this spacious penthouse on Eighth Street.

From the balcony, I can look out over the rooftops and the park, all the way to where the Post Office Tower pokes up between the brownstone buildings on the edge of the suburbs. Its solid presence is a comforting reminder of a London now irretrievably lost.

3.

"What do you miss most?" Marla asks. We're leaning on the balcony rail, drinking coffee. Out in the hall, I can hear the kids chasing around, yelling and laughing.

"I miss driving."

Marla nods sympathetically. Although there are plenty of cars lining the streets, none of them work. And besides, there's nowhere to go. The city sits on an island we can walk the length of in half an hour.

I say, "What about you?"

She puffs out her cheeks, still looking down at the cars. "I miss crowds."

4.

There are two or three other families in the city, but they keep themselves to themselves. And who can blame them? Like us, they've been resurrected almost a trillion years into the future, to a time so impossibly remote from our own that their loved ones are all they left have to cling to.

5.

Sometimes, I recall bits and pieces of my former life. While running this morning, I remember the office where I used to work, and the way the afternoon sun slanted through the window blinds onto my desk. I also remember I had a co-worker called Sarah. She was about my age, with rimless glasses and a green bead necklace. I even remember the smell of her perfume, and I think we might have kissed once, at an office party.

But I can't tell you what I was doing the day before I died. I can't even tell you how old I was when it happened. My memories are like random bursts of music fighting their way through the pops and static of a badly tuned radio.

6.

Marla and I were revived at the same time, by robot doctors who'd gone to a lot of trouble to ensure our compatibility. They fed and clothed us and built us a little house on a little beach – a tropical paradise encased in a mile-wide bubble of air, adrift in orbit around the ashes of our solar system. We were one of dozens of such bubbles, each containing only two humans, like miniature snow globes of Eden.

We stayed there until the arks came and picked us up.

7.

The arks are immense. Each one measures half a light year. Their scale, and the energies that power them, are beyond our comprehension. This whole city and even the ocean in which it sits are little more than a speck on the floor of an internal cavern a thousand miles tall and several thousand wide. What we think of as stars are really windows and lights in the ceiling far above – windows through which what unknown eyes peer down on our under-populated metropolis?

8.

In the penthouse, we get dressed and head into town, walking down a street that feels like a canyon, surrounded by the empty, shiny windows of unoccupied skyscrapers.

By unspoken agreement, we don't talk about the arks, or this city they built for us. We never do. Instead, we walk holding hands along the edge of the park and down towards the piers. Marla walks with her head down, looking at the pavement. She's been moody for a few weeks now, since finding an exact replica of her childhood home over on Fourth Street, near a reconstruction of the Chrysler building.

The night she found it, she cried for her parents, her brother, and her aunts and uncles.

"I guess it made me realise they're really, finally gone," she said the next morning.

9.

There's a TV in our penthouse. It's a flat screen that takes up most of one wall, and shows pictures from outside the ark. Ninety per cent of the time, it appears blank, because the sky outside's black in every direction. The light of the dispersed galaxies has redshifted them into invisibility. But once or twice a month, we get enhanced pictures of swollen black holes, unravelling super-clusters, and distant galaxies colliding.

Ingrid, she's our eldest, doesn't like it. It gives her the creeps. She loves the city. It's all she's ever known. She's only eight but she's already explored the warehouse complexes on the West Side, and the vast empty shopping malls beyond.

Today, Marla and I are heading down to the waterfront to

check on her latest discovery – a twin-hulled powerboat that she says she found tied to one of the floating piers behind the strip malls that line that section of shore.

When we get there, it's waiting for us, just as she described it, sleek and red.

Across the city, Big Ben strikes the hour. The sound makes the hairs rise on the back of my neck.

10.

The boat's chopping through the waves, driving at the flat horizon.

"Where do you think it's taking us?" I say, hair and face wet with spray.

Marla shrugs. She's looking back at the city shrinking in our wake, the familiar towers and minarets, the skyscrapers and cathedrals.

Over the next hour, they grow smaller and smaller, fading into a series of dark smudges in the afternoon haze.

And then, just as we're beginning to get restless, we see another shadow up ahead. It's a second island – smaller than ours, with only one building on it.

11.

When we get there, the twin prows scrape up onto the wet sand, and we jump down onto the beach.

The lone building sits at the top of a cliff. There are steps cut into the rock, but it's a steep, demanding climb, and we're both panting by the time we reach the top.

"It looks like a castle," Marla says. She's wearing sweat pants and an old t-shirt, and her hair's tied back in a loose ponytail; and for the first time in a month, she looks interested and alert, intrigued by this new puzzle.

"You know what's weird?" she says.

I look up at the gargoyles and battlements. "What?"

"This is the first building I've seen that I don't recognise from Earth."

Inside the walls, there's a central keep with solid oak doors. They open easily, and Marla swears under her breath.

"My God," she says. "It's a library!"

And so it is. A huge, echoing maze of shelves, each stuffed with books of all shapes and sizes.

"Maybe we're finally going to get some answers."

12.

Months pass. The boat takes us to and from the library whenever we want, and Marla now spends most of her time there. Not only were we resurrected, the robot doctors appear to have collected every scrap of data they could find. The entire Internet printed out and bound into book form.

None of it tells us who the robot doctors were, or why they brought us back. None of it gives any clue to the identity of the ark builders. But it's the collected knowledge and experience of our species.

As far as we know, there are fewer than a hundred humans left in the universe, so this trove is priceless. It allows us to remember who we are, and pass that heritage to the next generation. We might be at what my old history teacher used to call a bottleneck, but the treasures in this library will ensure the continuity of our culture and science.

There have been other bottlenecks before. Famine and disease have slashed our numbers, reducing humanity to a struggling handful of hunter-gatherers, but we've always come through. We're hard-wired to survive. It's what we do. And wherever these arks are taking us, that's what we'll do when we get there.

We'll survive and start the whole human story again.

WHAT WOULD
NICOLAS CAGE DO?

1.

On Monday morning, while sitting on the overcrowded eight o'clock bus from Portishead to Bristol, I decided to skip work. Michelle and I had split up the day before and I really didn't feel like going into the office. Instead, I got off at the top of Rownham Hill and used my mobile phone to call in sick. Then I walked over the suspension bridge into Clifton. It was a cold, grey day and I needed some time to myself.

I bought a newspaper and sat on a park bench in a Georgian square with black railings, thinking things over and trying to figure out where and when our relationship had gone wrong. We'd been together a year and a half but now she was seeing someone else.

We'd broken up over a bottle of wine in a crowded bar by the river. I'd said, "So that's it?"

She'd shrugged. "I guess so." She'd fiddled with the stem of her glass, looking uncomfortable and upset. It was Sunday lunchtime and the place smelled of garlic and stale beer. There was nothing more to say. We finished the wine in silence, and then went our separate ways.

Thinking about it now made me feel hollow and lonely. There was a cold wind blowing and I was glad I had a warm jacket over my shirt and tie. Most of the houses in the square had been converted into offices and flats. Some had dream catchers and rainbow stickers in their upper windows. Finding no answers there, I got up and walked along Pembroke Road to the Roman Catholic cathedral.

I stood looking at it from the opposite side of the road. Flanked on both sides by large, conservative town houses, its modern design and jagged, arty spires seemed out of place, and its concrete steps were slick with rain.

Turning my back on it, I cut through a side street that took me to Whiteladies Road – a busy main street lined with shops, galleries, restaurants and bars – coming out by the building that used to be the old cinema.

I thought a bit of retail therapy might cheer me up, so I spent a few minutes flicking through the DVD bargain racks in Sainsbury's and bought a lottery ticket at the tobacco counter. Then, at around eleven o'clock, I walked out and up to the little bookshop on the hill, where I spent an hour browsing the shelves.

I loved that shop. It was small and independent, and spread over several levels. There were leaflets and flyers stuck to the walls and the solid wooden floors creaked gently as I moved. There were potted plants on the windowsills and the whole place had the relaxed atmosphere of a library.

I picked up a book I'd been meaning to read for a while. As I paid for it, the girl on the stool behind the till gave me a smile. I'd seen her in there before. She had long blonde hair, a short denim skirt, and tan cowboy boots.

"Good choice," she said. She slipped the book into a paper bag and handed it to me, and I thanked her. She pushed her hair back with one hand. There were silver bangles on her wrist.

"It's very good," she said.

A lorry went past the window. I said, "Have you read it, then?"

"I've read all his books. Well, the recent ones anyway. And this is definitely the best."

She had a dog-eared paperback on the counter in front of her, with a bus ticket sticking out of it in place of a bookmark. "What's that you've got there?" I asked.

She glanced down. "This?" She held the book up. It was a Penguin Classics translation of the Iliad.

"Ah. I remember the first time I read that."

"You do?"

"I studied classics at college."

She sat up straighter and brushed a strand of hair behind her ear. "Really?" Her eyes flicked to the clock on the wall by the door. "Look, I'm going for lunch in a minute. I don't suppose you'd like to...?" Her legs were brown and her eyes were blue, with little copper flecks. I hesitated for a second, thinking of Michelle and her new boyfriend. Then I smiled and said, "Yes. Yes, I'd like that very much."

Ten minutes later, we were sitting at a table in the window of a coffee house near Clifton Down shopping centre. My new friend insisted on paying for the drinks. She had a cup of tea with lemon and I had a decaf latte.

"My name's John, by the way."

"Bobbie."

"I take it from your accent that you're not from around here?"

She reached over and lifted my book from its bag. She turned it over and looked at the back cover. She had glitter on her fingernails. "I grew up in Seattle."

I took the lid off my coffee and stirred it with a plastic spatula. The book was a travelogue by a British writer living in Bordeaux. I'd heard it was funny.

"So, what are you doing in Bristol? Apart from working in a bookshop, I mean."

She put the book down. There was rain on the window. "I'm at the University. I'm studying philosophy but really, I want to work in advertising." She took a sip of tea, looking at my shirt and tie. "How about you, what do you do?"

I popped the lid back onto my cup. "I work for the Evening Post."

"Oh?" She put her elbows on the table. "So, you're a writer?"

I smiled and shook my head. "I just work in the office. It's nothing special. As a matter of fact, I should be there now but I'm playing truant."

"Won't you get into trouble?"

"Ah, what's the worst that could happen?"

"They could fire you." I reached into my jacket pocket. I pulled out the lottery ticket I'd bought earlier. "I have a back-up plan," I said, showing it to her.

Bobbie's face lit up. "Hey, did you ever see that film with Nicolas Cage, the one where he's a cop and he promises that if he wins the lottery, he'll split his winnings with the diner waitress because he can't afford to tip her?"

I scratched my eyebrow. "Yes, I think so. Was the waitress Michelle Pfeiffer?"

"I don't know, I think it was Bridget Fonda. But anyway, how about we have the same deal? I bought you a coffee, so if you win the lottery, we split the prize money?"

"Sure, why not?" I laughed. I shrugged off my jacket and hooked it over the back of the chair.

"You promise?"

"Yes, I promise."

She sat back. "Okay then." She took another sip of tea. I tried my coffee. It was too hot to drink, so I took the plastic lid off again and sniffed the steam. Bobbie was watching me. She said: "Do you go clubbing much?"

I shook my head. I was thirty-three. I hadn't been in a nightclub in years.

"Only there's this party tonight at Evolution, and I don't really have anyone to go with, and I thought you might—"

She stopped talking, distracted by something over my shoulder. There was a commotion going on outside. I saw people running up the street in the rain, their feet splashing. The traffic had stopped. People were getting out of their cars. I turned to Bobbie. She was looking past me and her eyes were wide.

"John?" she said.

I swivelled on my chair. Something huge was coming up the road. It towered over the buildings, a billowing tsunami of dust and greyness a hundred metres high, bearing down on us with horrifying speed.

I reached for Bobbie's arm.

"Come on," I said. I took her hand and pulled her out of her seat. I wanted to run. But before we'd taken two steps, the wave of dust struck, ripping through the coffee shop, shattering the windows and blasting us – and the building around us – to smithereens.

2.

Sometime later, I became aware of a cool breeze dancing over my bare legs, making the hairs prickle. My eyes were sticky. I rubbed them open to find I was lying naked and alone on a grassy hillside, in front of a wooden cabin.

I sat up and looked around in puzzlement. The hill sloped gently down to a marshy river, with further hills beyond. The sky overhead was blue and the sun was warm. There were birds singing.

On the grass beside me were some clothes: a red cotton shirt, some jeans, and a sturdy pair of hiking boots. I slipped the jeans on, which made me feel a bit better. Then I stepped up onto the cabin's porch. The planks were rough beneath my bare feet. There were wind chimes by the open door.

"Hello?" I called. "Hello, can you help me? I don't know where I am."

Inside, the cabin was empty. There was no one in there. It measured maybe ten metres by five metres. It was all one big room, with a bed at one end and a stove and sink at the other. The front windows looked toward the river. Through the back windows, I could see an outhouse and a stone wishing well.

On the bed was a piece of paper. I walked over and picked it up. Printed on it in black ink were five words, which I read aloud:

"Your name is John Doyle."

The cabin's front windows were propped open. The sun cast bright rectangles on the wall. I stood there for a long time, not knowing what else to do. Then gradually, I realised I was hungry – ravenous, in fact, like I hadn't eaten for days.

When I couldn't stand it any longer, I screwed the piece of paper into a ball and walked the length of the cabin to the stove, my bare feet padding on the pine planks. There was a cupboard below the sink and I opened it, hoping to find some food. Inside were some stacked tins. I pulled one out. It had a ring-pull top and I cracked it open. I slopped the sausages and beans it contained into one of the metal frying pans on the hob. There were some utensils in a pot by the sink and I helped myself to a wooden spoon.

The sticky mixture didn't take long to heat through. When it was ready, I took it out onto the porch and used the spoon to eat it straight from the pan. With each bite, I felt stronger and more human. When I'd finished it all, I pushed the pan aside and sat looking at the river. From the position of the sun, I guessed it was late afternoon, maybe somewhere between five and seven o'clock. When the wind blew, the light glittered off the water. I closed my eyes. The air smelled of grass and timber.

"My name is John Doyle," I said. I repeated it two or three times, trying it on for size. And as I did so, I felt my memories starting to return. They were slippery and insubstantial at first, like dolphins in fog, but slowly, one-by-one, they were coming back.

I remembered my address. I remembered the bookshop. I remembered the way the floor creaked as I moved...

I found a screw-topped bottle of red wine in the cupboard under the sink, and a tin mug to drink it from. I retrieved the cotton shirt and the boots from the grass and put them on, and then sat on the porch steps again, watching miserably as the shadows lengthened and the sun set over the hill behind the cabin.

As the light started to fade, I became gradually aware of a strange ripple in the air. At first, it looked like a small heat haze. But as I watched, it thickened into something resembling a churning ball of yellow gas about the size of a grapefruit. Little sparks of static flickered over its surface.

"Greetings, John Doyle," it said. It spoke without a trace of accent. Its words were clipped and precise.

I scrambled to my feet. "Who are you?"

"I am here to help, John."

I backed away. Reaching behind me, I found the rough pine frame of the cabin's open door. "Help me?"

The ball bobbed forward. It was small enough that I could have held it in the palm of my hand. "Indeed. You have suffered a grave injury and I am here to help."

It followed me back into the cabin. "What's the last thing you remember?" it said.

I put the tin mug down on the aluminium draining board beside the sink. "I remember being in Starbucks."

The ball of gas hovered over me. It smelled of ozone. "What about the dust cloud?"

I set my jaw. I guess I must have been blocking it out until that moment. Now, remembering it, my hands started to tremble. I picked up the wine bottle. It was still three quarters full.

"I remember it crashing through the window." I refilled the mug and took a shaky drink. The yellow ball of gas crackled.

"There was an accident, John. You were involved in it. But in order for you to fully understand your situation, I must explain it to you from the beginning."

I swallowed. There was a sudden hollow feeling in my stomach that had nothing to do with the food I'd just eaten. In an unsteady voice I said: "An accident?"

The gas ball drifted over to the open door. "Do you see those hills in the distance?" it said. "Well, the first thing you have to realise, John, is that there is nothing beyond them. This cabin exists in an artificial bubble ten kilometres across. The world beyond is a lifeless grey sphere."

It was starting to get dark out there. There was a lamp on the mantelpiece. I looked into my mug. In the lamplight, the wine was thick and dark, like blood.

The gas ball continued: "Do you know what a nano-assembler is, John? It's a tiny machine designed to construct things – in this case, computer processors – using individual atoms as building blocks. These assemblers are programmed to reproduce and to keep building until told to stop."

It paused and lowered its tone. "Unfortunately, last year some of them escaped a lab at Bristol University and just kept right on reproducing. They chewed through the Earth's crust in a matter of hours, converting it all into smart matter. There was nothing anyone could do. The human race didn't stand a chance. Within a day, all the cities, plants and people in the world were gone."

"And that was the dust cloud I saw?"

"Yes, that was the wavefront."

"And what is 'smart matter'?"

The ball drifted back a little way. "It's simply matter that's been rearranged from its natural state into an optimized, maximally-efficient computer processor using individual atoms as computing elements. We call it 'smart matter'. This cabin and everything you can see and touch outside is made of it."

"So the world's been turned into a giant computer?" I was sweating now.

"Yes."

I wiped my forehead with a damp palm. I drained my cup and put it on the counter by the sink. Suddenly, all I wanted was to get out of the cabin. I pushed through the door and down the steps. The sky overhead had dimmed to a deep purple, shading to red at the horizon. I lurched around to the rear of the cabin and started running. I ran uphill, slipping and scrambling on the grassy slopes. The gas ball shouted for me to wait but I ignored it. I staggered over the crest of the hill and half-ran, half-fell down the other side. I crossed marshes and streams. I crashed through brambles and clumps of trees. And all the while, in my head, all I could see was that terrifying wall of greyness bearing down on me, ripping apart everything in its path.

Eventually, scratched and dirty, I came to a high glass wall that extended left and right as far as I could see. I stopped and put my hands on my knees, panting. Beyond the wall, there was nothing – just a flat grey plain that stretched away like an endless frozen sea.

In the glass, I saw the reflection of the gas ball approaching behind me.

"Are you all right, John?"

I shook my head. I was wheezing almost too hard to speak. The sweat ran down my face and my throat felt raw. "What," I panted, "what is this?"

The yellow ball dimmed slightly. It drifted over until it was almost touching the transparent wall. "This is all that's left of the world," it said.

We remained there for a long time, looking out over that desolate plain, and I thought of all the places I'd ever seen, all the mountains and seas and lakes, all the cities and rivers and deserts – all gone now, all ground down into a sterile, uniform grey.

After what seemed like hours, the gas ball moved towards me. "Are you going to be okay, John?" it said.

I leaned against the glass. It felt cool on my forehead. "I don't know."

There was a banging pain in my right temple. My legs felt weak and I was fighting the urge to cry. "Who *are* you?" I said.

The ball sparkled. "I was born in the aftermath of the disaster that created the world you see out there."

"Do you have a name?"

It seemed to consider the question. "You may call me Brenda."

"Brenda?"

"Yes. Among many others, I contain within me the

memories of a human by the name of Brenda McCarthy." The ball's yellow surface swirled and sparkled, as if miniature thunderstorms were chasing each other across its skin. "There are many others like me," it said. "Collectively, we call ourselves the *Bricolage*. We arose in the minutes and hours following the catastrophe, running on the planet's new smart matter crust, our minds built from scraps of human and machine intelligence, our knowledge of the world cobbled together from the flotsam of the internet."

It – she – wobbled closer.

"You see, when the Earth's crust was processed into smart matter, every living creature, every building, every computer network was disassembled and a detailed description – like a blueprint fine enough to show the position of every molecule – was stored in a vast database. What you see out there, through that wall, is a sea of information, a sea that gave us sustenance as we grew. We took a bit here, a bit there. And for a time, we gloried in the seemingly limitless knowledge we had access to. But later, as we started to understand more of the world before the catastrophe, some of us came to realise the terrible loss that had taken place when the Earth had been scoured of organic life – and we decided to try to correct the situation; which is where you come in."

I looked through the glass wall. The moon was rising, casting its light over the featureless grey plain. "But you're a ball of gas," I said.

"This body has been created simply to allow me to communicate with you. If you find it unpleasant, I can take another form."

I shook my aching head. "It's fine." My knees had started to shake and I needed to sit down.

She drifted toward me. "Are you all right, John?"

I waved her away and sat on the grass, breathing heavily. "Just give me a minute, will you?"

My head was spinning.

The gas ball – Brenda – came closer. "I know this is a lot to take in, but I am trying to explain it to you as simply as I can."

I put my face in my hands. I felt sick and dizzy. I let myself tip sideways into a foetal position on the rough ground.

Brenda hovered over me in silence for a minute or so. Then she said, "Why don't you sleep? You will feel better in the morning."

I looked up at her through my fingers. "I don't think I can."

"Nonsense." She lowered herself to within a few centimetres of my temple. "Hold still," she said. I felt a prickle on my skin, then nothing but drowsiness.

"What are you doing?"

Brenda was caressing my brow with tendrils of yellow gas so thin as to be almost invisible. "Hush," she said.

3.

Brenda was there when I awoke the next morning, back in the cabin, feeling refreshed. She was hovering in the kitchen area and there was a pot of coffee warming on the stove, filling the room with its smell, and a plate of bacon rolls on the table.

"Did you sleep well?"

The windows were still open and the morning air was fresh and the sky blue. I sat up and looked out. The distant hills were the colour of heather. I saw a family of ducks moving in the reeds on the banks of the river at the foot of the hill, and butterflies skipping about in the grass.

I frowned.

"What is it?" Brenda asked.

I shook my head. "It's the view, it seems so familiar."

She came over to me. In the sunlight, she still looked like a grapefruit made of gas. "Of course," she said. "Don't you know where you are? Don't you recognise it?"

I looked back through the window at the hills and the river. I squinted and turned my head on one side. There was something about that hill on the horizon...

"Imagine it all covered in houses," she said. And then it all snapped into place.

"Is this *Bristol*?" It didn't seem possible, but Brenda said, "Yes. We're standing on the lower slopes of Brandon Hill, looking out over the old docks. That flat area to your left is where the council buildings and the library used to stand, and the marshy area to your right is the dock where the SS *Great Britain* was berthed."

"But the buildings...?"

"All gone, I'm afraid. But if you would like me to, I could probably recreate one or two."

I rubbed my eyes. My headache was back. "Let me get a cup of that coffee," I said. I filled a mug and sat at the table.

Brenda drifted down to my eye level. "There's something else you should know," she said gently.

I wasn't sure I could take much more. I said, "What's that?"

She came closer. "Although we've resurrected you, we can't do likewise for everyone. This biosphere is only designed to support two people." She settled herself above my plate, right in my face. "There are those of us – a significant minority – who think it's a waste of resources to use a hundred kilograms of dumb mass – in this case, flesh and bone – to support a single human-level intelligence. They argue that if the raw materials of your body were converted to smart matter, their mass would be capable of supporting many thousands of equivalent electronic entities." She reached out a wispy tendril to touch my cheek. I smelled ozone. "Right now, John, you are the only living human in the world. Do you understand me? And you have a very serious choice to make."

4.

"Do you understand what we need you to do?" Brenda said. I nodded, although my heart was hammering in my chest and my palms were damp again. She must have seen my agitation. "Go for a walk," she said. "Get some air. Take your time and think it over." Then she sank into the floor and disappeared with a pop, like a soap bubble.

After she'd gone, I sat there for a while, picking listlessly at a bacon roll, trying to digest what she'd told me. Then I got up and walked out onto the porch, my hiking boots clomping on the wooden planks. A walk sounded like a good idea. I felt battered and mentally bruised. I couldn't absorb everything I'd been told. I needed to get away for an hour, somewhere quiet, to let it all sink in.

I started walking downhill towards the river, in the opposite direction to my mad flight of the night before. The sun was warm and the grasses and nettles on the lower slopes grew thick and tall. As I tramped through them, I thought about everything Brenda had told me. I thought about my parents, my co-workers and my friends. I thought about my brother in Australia and my cousin in Italy. I thought about Michelle and the man she'd left me for. And I thought about Bobbie: American Bobbie with the blonde hair and copper-flecked eyes. Was she among the people stored in Brenda's 'smart matter'? In my mind, I could picture her face quite clearly. I could see her looking at my lottery ticket in the coffee shop and making me promise to share my winnings with her. And when I closed my eyes, I could almost feel her hand gripping mine in the instant before the dust cloud hit.

There were no clear banks to the river – the grass just ran into the water. There were clumps of tall reeds here and there. The mud smelled brackish. There were insects circling jerkily in the shade, birds singing discordantly in the trees – all smart matter fakes.

I put my hands in my pockets and walked along the water's marshy edge until I came to the spot where the Central Library had once stood. Now it was a smooth, grassy incline that led up, growing steeper as it rose toward the former site of the University – and beyond that, to Whiteladies Road and the empty space where the little bookshop had been.

I closed my eyes and took a deep breath. There were wildflowers in the grass: things that looked like poppies, buttercups, and daisies.

I kicked a pebble. Nothing here was real.

"I only get to pick one person?" I said aloud. It seemed so unfair. Brenda had told me she had access to my memories and that all I had to do was pick someone from my past and she'd resurrect them for me. But how was I supposed to decide?

I stomped uphill and back toward the cabin. When I got there, Brenda was waiting on the porch. "Hello," she said.

I glowered at her and went through, into the kitchen. "Why me? If you had the whole of humanity to choose from, why did you choose me?"

She came floating in behind me. Now, there were faint orange bands in the yellow gas swirling around her circumference, making her look like a miniature version of the planet Jupiter. "We did not have the whole of humanity," she said quietly. "There were many losses, many corruptions – all of them most regrettable."

I walked over to the mantelpiece. There was a vase there, with fresh 'flowers' from the field outside. "Okay, but why me?"

In the mirror above the fireplace, I saw her float up to within a few centimetres of my shoulder. "Once we had recreated this environment, we collected the stored profiles of as many local residents as possible and you were randomly selected from the resulting list of available candidates."

I turned to her. "You mean you pulled my name out of a hat?"

For a second the clouds on her surface froze. Then they began to swirl again. "We narrowed the selection according to certain criteria but essentially, yes: this was a random choice. The odds of you being chosen were more than one hundred thousand to one."

I walked over to the table and sat. I drummed my fingers on the wooden tabletop. I thought of Nicolas Cage and Bridget Fonda and, just like that, I realised I'd made my decision.

"It's Bobbie," I said.

Brenda came closer. Sparks of static electricity chased each other across her swirling face. "I beg your pardon?"

"She's the one I choose. She's the one I want you to bring back."

"The girl from the bookshop?"

"Yes."

"That's your final decision? That's the person with whom you wish to spend the rest of your life?"

"Yes."

"Are you quite sure?"

I stopped drumming. "A promise is a promise," I said.

5.

The next day dawned grey and overcast. There was fog on the far hills and a steady rain streaking the windows. I got up and made myself breakfast and then went out onto the porch.

A figure lay naked in the grass, a pile of wet clothes beside her. I put my coffee mug on the porch rail and walked over. There were drops of rain on her skin. Her eyes were closed and her blonde hair was bedraggled and sticking to her face. She looked like a creature washed up on a beach. I stood over her for a moment, then went back inside and fetched the grey blanket from the cabin bed. I draped it over her and took her hand.

"Bobbie?"

I saw her eyes move beneath the lids. Her lips parted and she coughed. I gave her hand a squeeze. "Bobbie, it's me. It's okay. It's going to be okay."

She opened her eyes and sat up. She was shivering. "John?"

I put my arms around her. I could feel the sodden grass soaking the knees of my jeans, feel her wet hair through my shirt.

"Where are we, John?" She squirmed around, looking wide-eyed at the hillside and the cabin. "How did we get here?"

The rain was turning into a downpour. I pulled her to me and wrapped the blanket around her. Her elbow dug into my thigh.

"It's a long story," I said.

She wormed a hand out of the blanket and palmed the wet hair from her face. "John, are we dead?"

I hooked one arm under her knees and the other under her shoulders. I struggled to my feet. The rain ran down my cheeks. The grass was slippery with mud and Bobbie was heavier than she looked. "Let's get you inside."

She put her chin on my shoulder, looking down toward the river. "But John, what's happened to us?"

I took a cautious step toward the cabin, trying not to overbalance. Through gritted teeth I said, "We've won the lottery."

ABOUT THE AUTHOR

Gareth L. Powell started writing seriously as a teenager and was lucky to be able to count Diana Wynne Jones and Helen Dunmore as early mentors. More recently, he has co-written stories with bestselling authors Peter F. Hamilton and Aliette de Bodard.

He has twice won the prestigious British Science Fiction Association Award for Best Novel (previous winners include J. G. Ballard and Arthur C. Clarke) and has become one of the most shortlisted authors in the award's 50-year history. He has also been shortlisted for the Locus Award, the British Fantasy Award, the Seiun Award, and the Canopus Award.

Gareth is married to the American author Jendia Gammon, and is represented in all professional matters by Lucienne Diver of The Knight Agency.

Find Gareth online at: *garethlpowell.com*

For more fantastic fiction, author events,
exclusive excerpts, competitions, limited editions and more

VISIT OUR WEBSITE
titanbooks.com

LIKE US ON FACEBOOK
facebook.com/titanbooks

FOLLOW US ON TWITTER AND INSTAGRAM
@TitanBooks

EMAIL US
readerfeedback@titanemail.com